Thomas-Simon Gueullette, Leonard C. Smithers

The Thousand and One Quarters of an Hour

(Tartarian Tales)

Thomas-Simon Gueullette, Leonard C. Smithers

The Thousand and One Quarters of an Hour
(Tartarian Tales)

ISBN/EAN: 9783337074166

Printed in Europe, USA, Canada, Australia, Japan

Cover: Foto ©Andreas Hilbeck / pixelio.de

More available books at **www.hansebooks.com**

THE

THOUSAND AND ONE

QUARTERS OF AN HOUR

(TARTARIAN TALES)

EDITED BY

LEONARD C. SMITHERS

LONDON

H. S. NICHOLS AND CO.

3 SOHO SQUARE W

MDCCCXCIII

PREFACE

These very lively, ingenious, and entertaining imitations of the "Arabian Nights" are confessedly the work of Thomas Simon Gueulette. He was born at Paris in 1683, and held the office of substitute of the royal procurator at the Châtelet. Possessed of a very fertile imagination, he produced a great number of works of amusement. In the style of the fairy tales, he made his *debut* with *Les Soirées Bretonnes*, or the Evenings of Brittany, which appeared in 1712, and on which Voltaire founded his celebrated *Zadig*. In the year 1723 he produced the Thousand and One Quarters of an Hour, or the Tartarian Tales: which were followed in the same year by the Chinese Tales, or the Marvellous Adventures of the Mandarin Fum-Hoam, and by the Sultanas of Guzarat, or the Dreams of Men Awake, generally known under the name of the Mogul Tales. He imitated the tales of Count Hamilton, and, though his style is less brilliant, and his incidents have less of what the French call *bizarrerie*, the numerous stories which he has produced abound in interesting situations, and are, in general, true pictures of what they are intended to represent.

The collection of Tales here given is generally the work of Gueulette's own imagination : but he has often introduced allusions to, and incidents from, real Oriental fictions, and, in some instances from the works of European novelists.

The tale of the Three Crump-Brothers he acknowledges to have borrowed from the novels of Straparola: but asserts that it cost him great trouble to vary and adapt it to his own purposes. Several other novels, however, furnished subjects for these tales, amongst which Le Grand notices several fabliaux, viz., the Judgment of Solomon, the Lay of Hippocrates, and Le Chevalier de la Trappe.

Besides these works, he was author of a novel, entitled *Les Mémoires de Mademoiselle Bontems*, and of several short pieces for the *Théâtre Italien*, the profits of which he always resigned to the actors. He edited Rabelais, and the ancient French romances of Petit-Jean de Saintré, and Gerard comte de Nevers. His character is described as gentle and lively, and his company was generally sought after. He was of a beneficent disposition : and on the death of his wife resigned the whole of his right to her fortune in favour of her relations. Hospitality he practised to a great extent : and in his country house at Choisy-le-Roi, he instituted a private theatre, where some of the most distinguished of his friends performed. He is said to have had a wonderful talent for puppet-shows, and to have acted the part of Punch to perfection. His vivacity is reported to have often embroiled him with the clergy. He died at *Doyen de la Compagnie,* in the year 1768.

CONTENTS

INTRODUCTION

TALE OF KING SHAMS AL-DIN

Near Astrakhan lived a solitary darwaysh, who, returning one evening from angling upon the banks of the river Volga, was surprised to find on the threshold of his cell a new-born child, and stark naked. He took it in his arms, and ran to tell this accident to a tailor of Astrakhan, called Kurban, from whom he was often used to receive alms.

The tailor's wife happily was brought to-bed the very night before of a daughter, which died the moment it came into the world. She offered the breast to the child the darwaysh had brought her, and forgetting as it were her own daughter, turned her affection entirely to the little boy, whom she named Shams al-Din. The tailor and his wife having had no children for near fifteen years, loved little Shams al-Din with extreme tenderness; and the boy, believing himself their son, returned it with a respect and submission which augmented the affection they had for him. When he was grown up, notwithstanding the inclination he found in himself for arms, the sole will of Kurban engaged him to learn the trade of a tailor; and in less than two years he made

I

such extraordinary progress in that profession, that only by looking at a person, without taking any measure, he could make a suit of clothes as exactly fit as the best tailor in Astrakhan could make with ever so much measuring. Shams al-Din's skill quickly made a noise all over the town: nobody was thought to have a tolerable good taste, if he was not dressed in a suit of his making ; and most of the ladies employed him without giving umbrage to their husbands, because by seeing them only at a distance, he could in four days' time bring them such a habit as they desired.

One day as this young tailor was in his shop, an old slave accosting him, desired to speak with him in private. Sir, said she, be so kind as to come along with me immediately; two of the handsomest ladies in all Astrakhan have occasion for your service. Shams al-Din readily promised to go with her. But this is not all, replied the woman, you must consent to have your eyes muffled, otherwise I must not carry you along with me. Shams al-Din was surprised at such a proposal ; but resolving to venture any thing rather than miss seeing a couple of beautiful ladies, he immediately went with the old woman. She conducted him to a little house in the suburbs of Astrakhan ; carried him into a parlour, and pulling out a silk handkerchief embroidered with gold, presented him to two black slaves, who had their sabres in their hands ; ordered them to bind his eyes with that handkerchief, and to conduct him to the place where he was expected : but that if he shewed the least curiosity to discover the way they led him, they should that moment cut off his head. This order frightened the young tailor. Fear nothing, said the old woman to him; provided you are wise and discreet, your life is safe. He resumed his courage on these promises, suffered them to bind his eyes, and walked thus blindfold for the space of an hour; when the slaves taking off his muffler, he found himself in a hall magnificently lighted by above a hundred wax tapers.

At the upper end of the hall was a throne of massy silver, upon which sat three ladies, each covered with a veil, through which it was nevertheless easy to perceive, that one of them, though perfectly handsome, was about forty years old, and that nature had formed nothing so charming and so complete as the other two, who seemed to be hardly eighteen. A great number of female slaves, veiled in the same manner, and ranged on each side of the throne, kept a profound silence, and seemed respectfully to await the command of the three ladies. After they had given the tailor time to look about him and admire so much magnificence, the lady that appeared the eldest of the three rose from the throne. Shams-al-Din, says she, your reputation has excited our curiosity. We have heard wonders concerning your skill, and are willing to be judges of it ourselves; look well upon these two young ladies; view their shapes with attention: Dare you engage, without taking any other measure, to make each of them a genteel suit of clothes ?—Madam, replied the young tailor, I shall do my endeavours to keep up the reputation I have with some justice acquired: I have viewed these ladies enough; order me the silks, and in eight days' time you shall be satisfied.

The black slaves upon this led Shams al-Din into another room, and opened twenty coffers, which were all full of the finest silks of the East: he chose what was necessary to make the two habits complete. His eyes were again muffled, and he was led to the house of the old woman, who re-conducted him home. If you would have your good fortune continue, said she to him at parting, do not seek to know from whence you come, or for whom you are to work: The least step you take towards such a discovery will cost you your life : Think of nothing but how to execute as soon as possible the orders you have received. I shall fetch you again eight days hence, and carry you to the same ladies, upon the former conditions.

The old woman having taken leave of Shams-al-Din, he went to bed, after he had neatly laid up the silks, resolving to begin the suits at break of day: but he could not close his eyes all the night; the charms of one of the young ladies returned to his mind a thousand times. Two large blue eyes, whose brightness shot through the obscurity of her veil, had made such an impression upon his mind, that he was no longer master of himself. He got up, lighted his lamp, and after having studied some time in what manner he should cut out his silks, he hit upon a method so uncommon, and withal so advantageous to the beauty of the two young ladies, especially of her he admired, that he had very good reason to believe they would be pleased with his performance. He then set to work with abundance of care and diligence; and the clothes being finished at the day appointed, the old woman who came to fetch him, committed him with his eyes muffled into the hands of the two blacks, who, after having led him through the same passages as before, presented him to the three ladies, whom he found seated upon the throne of silver.

Shams al-Din had no sooner opened his bundle and spread out the habits, than they began to extol his wonderful fancy. The two ladies, for whom they were made, retired into a sort of wardrobe with four slaves. They returned into the hall a few minutes afterwards without veils, and in their new habits, but a thousand times more brilliant than the full moon. As soon as they appeared, the hall resounded with the applauses of the slaves, and the young tailor was so struck with the charms of her to whom he had consecrated his heart, that he fell backwards upon a sofa, and was ready to die with the extreme pleasure he felt in that moment. Indeed the beauty of those ladies was so great, that it could be compared to nothing but to that of the houris.

They extolled Shams al-Din to the skies, praised the invention and neatness of his work, gave him each of them a purse of a hundred pieces of gold, and begged him to make them two more suits, different from those which he had now brought them. The young man went into the silk-room, chose five pieces of a very pretty fancy, made two other suits more singular than had yet been seen; returned at the eight days' end with the same ceremonies, received greater applauses than before, two hundred pieces of gold, and orders for choosing silks to make up more. In short, this trade continued for seven weeks together, in which time, Shams al-Din had made up fourteen suits of clothes, and received as many purses of gold; when the passion he had conceived for one of the two ladies grew so violent, that notwithstanding the distance there appeared to be between him and her, he resolved to declare his love. After having considered a great while how he should go about it, he could think of no other expedient but to put a letter for her in the pocket of the next suit of clothes he should carry her. He executed this design; and expressed what he felt for her in terms so moving and so submissive, that he hoped, if she did not accept of his heart, at least she would forgive his rashness in offering it.

The letter had all the effect Shams al-Din could wish for : The next time he appeared before his lady, instead of anger, he read in her eyes something so sweet, that he had much ado to refrain from throwing himself at her feet. He presented her with her clothes, she went out to try them, and sent them back to him a moment afterwards, with word that they were something too little. The young tailor who well knew that the clothes were as they should be, soon imagined that this was only a feint to convey him an answer. He pulled out his scissors and his needle, and pretending to alter what was amiss, searched the pockets, and in one of them found a letter, which he dexterously put up; and then returned the habit, without having made the least alteration in it: the lady was very well satisfied with it, and came again into the hall. New orders were given to the young tailor, he was re-conducted as usual, and the moment he was got home he broke open the letter, in which he read what follows: " I could not, amiable Shams al-Din, be insensible to your passion: You describe it in colours so lively, and so natural, that I should be afraid of offending our great Prophet if I repaid it with ingratitude. I love you, and do not blush to confess it. Every thing in you pleases me; and you should quickly be happy if it depended upon me alone to crown your love, which I believe is sincere and honourable; but, dear light of my life, what tears must this confession cost you, when you know that I am for ever shut up in a place where all things are designed for the pleasure of the king of Astrakhan, and the unfortunate Zabd al-Katon must never hope to be united with the tender Shams al-Din."

If the young tailor felt an infinite deal of joy at reading of this letter, that joy was not unmixed with grief. Zabd al-Katon was the finest woman in all Tartary, but it was impossible not to know that she was the favourite of Al-Salah, king of Astrakhan. Shams al-Din was too conversant among the principal persons in the city not to have heard talk of the charms of that young lady, and her cruelty towards the king. As that prince was above sixty years old, and Zabd al-Katon hardly seventeen, she did not know how to reconcile herself to sexagenary sighs; and the king of Astrakhan, who loved her with unparalleled ardour and delicacy, being unwilling to make use of the authority he had over his slave, waited with patience, till his unbounded complaisance should gain him the fair one's heart.

Shams al-Din too plainly saw how impossible it was to carry off Zabd al-Katon from his king; this reflection threw him into such a violent despair, that when the old slave came to fetch him to the seraglio, she found him sick a-bed of a violent fever. She ran and told this news to the three ladies. They were very much alarmed at it; and without considering the danger to which they exposed themselves, they gained over the eunuchs, who had suffered the young tailor to visit them so often, and by this means had liberty to go out of the palace. Shams al-Din, who was resolved to use no remedies whereby he might be cured, was in the greatest surprise to see those ladies at his bed's head. He did his utmost to shew his acknowledgment of this favour; when the eldest of the three, having lifted up her veil for the first time, spoke to him in these words: Your health, charming Shams al-Din, is so dear to us, that we venture our own lives for an opportunity of trying if there is no way to save yours; we beg you to tell us the cause of your illness, and perhaps we may find out some remedy for it. The young tailor, seized with respect, and touched with the beauty of that lady, who felt a certain emotion she could not account for, raised himself up: Ah! madam, replied he in a languishing voice, however incurable I thought my distemper, your presence, and that of these ladies, has poured a salutory balm into my wounds. Grief alone was the illness which would have given me my death; but since you have the goodness to interest yourself in the preservation of a miserable wretch, I abandon the cruel resolution I had taken, and hope in less than six days' time I shall be able to deliver these two ladies the clothes they have commanded me to make for them. Zabd al-Katon, affected with the young tailor's extraordinary passion, pressed his hand; If that is possible, says she, without endangering your health, pray endeavour, my dear Shams al-Din, to keep your word with us; you cannot imagine the joy it will be to me in particular. The ladies after this, got up, and attended by the eunuchs, who had conducted them quite to the tailor's house, returned to the palace.

Shams al-Din passed a night in so great an excess of pleasure, that by the next morning he was in a condition to begin the clothes. They were finished at the six days' end as he promised, and the old woman, who often came to inquire after his health, having put him into the hands of the two blacks, they carried him to the hall, which at sight of him resounded with a thousand shouts of joy. Shams al-Din presented the habits to the ladies. They viewed them over and over, and found them of a fancy so superior to those which he had made before, that they were perfectly charmed with them. To add to their magnificence, they sent for a casket full of jewels, and ordered him to choose some out to fix upon those clothes. The young tailor obeyed their commands, and was fastening the sleeve of the charming Zabd al-Katon with a clasp of diamonds, when on a sudden the door of the hall burst open, and a man in whose face was painted the height of fury, came directly towards him with his sabre in his hand. Shams al-Din soon perceived him to be the king of Astrakhan, and now looked upon his death to be inevitable; but not thinking it proper to wait for the effect of that prince's revenge, nor to abandon to his fury the three ladies to whom he was so much obliged, he immediately seized a poinard set with diamonds, which was in the casket, and without giving the king time to come up, darted at him with so good an aim, that he gave him a deep wound, which felled him to the earth.

Al-Salah in this condition had not strength enough to get up. He called for help, and twelve black eunuchs running in at his voice, he commanded them to seize Shams al-Din, as likewise the three ladies and the two black slaves; to strip them to the waist, and to cut them to pieces with their sabres. While the king was laid upon a sofa, and his surgeon sent for, the cruel orders he had given were in part executed. They had now stripped all the criminals, who were just ready to undergo that cruel sentence, when the eldest of the three ladies, having by chance cast her eyes upon the young Shams al-Din, and spied the mark of a pomegranate which he had beneath the right pap: Ah, my lord, says she, throwing herself at Al-Salah's feet, suspend, I beseech you, for a moment, your just anger! I alone am guilty. The unfortunate Sutchumi your daughter, Zabd al-Katon, and the young man, are innocent; but destiny is not to be avoided; and notwithstanding all the precaution you have taken to escape the prediction of the astrologer, behold that prediction at length accomplished by the unavoidable dispensation of providence.

The king, surprised at this discourse, caused his eunuchs to retire; and after having ordered the ladies and tailor to cover themselves, he commanded her who had just now spoken to explain that enigma, which he was at a loss to understand. This lady obeyed the king's commands, and delivered herself in these terms:

HISTORY OF THE SULTANA DUGMI

You may, my lord, remember that at the time when I had the happiness to please you, upon your consulting the famous Abd al-Malik upon my pregnancy, that astrologer told you, I should bring forth a son who should give you your death, and be the cause of his too, if the child were not killed as soon as born. As Abd al-Malik's predictions always came true, this gave you abundance of uneasiness; and to prevent the misfortune you were threatened with, you had me watched with the utmost strictness. In vain I represented to you the little credit

that is to be given to a science so uncertain as astrology;
you resolved to be present at my labour, to hinder any
deceit on my side. My tears had no effect upon you;
you were inexorable: I could not dissuade you from the
cruel resolution you had taken to shed your own blood,
and I almost died away with grief and terror, at seeing
you enter my chamber with Abd al-Malik, at the moment
when you were assured I was just ready to be brought
to-bed. But, my lord, you cannot have forgot that I
passed from the most violent uneasiness to the most excessive joy, when, instead of a boy, I brought into the
world the unfortunate Sutchumi: Then you looked
upon Abd al-Malik with indignation: Ignorant or wicked
astrologer, said you to him, your eyes inflamed with
anger, I shall teach thee to mock thy king in this manner.
Thy malice had like to have cost my dear Dugmi her
life: but I will soon punish an insolent subject for his
temerity. Upon this, Abd al-Malik, continued the sultana, threw himself at your feet. My lord, said he, do
not begin with me to fulfil a prediction which will prove
but too true: Have but a moment's patience, and you
shall find that my science is not ill grounded. You did
not give the astrologer time to finish what he had to say;
you severed his head from his body at one blow of your
sabre, and went out of the room, after having sent away
the daughter I had brought forth.

You could scarce, my lord, be got into your own
apartment, when I felt new pains. The woman, who
had assisted me in my first, came to me. She found I
was going to bring forth another child: she sent every
body out of my chamber upon different pretences, and a
moment afterwards I brought forth a son, beauteous as
the light. Nature, which had formed nothing so complete, would not give me leave to sacrifice him to you.
My bowels rebelled against the cruelty which I accused
you of in my soul; I put my son, with jewels to a con-

siderable value, into the hands of the midwife, and begged her to go immediately to seek a nurse for it somewhere out of Astrakhan. Being now no longer watched, it was easy for that woman to carry out my son, and I impatiently expected her return, that I might hear what was become of him; when four days being past without seeing anything of her, I was at last told, to my unspeakable grief, that she was murdered a few leagues from Astrakhan. There was no mention made of any child being found with her, and that gave me some comfort; but notwithstanding all the secret search I have made ever since that time to find out what was become of my son, I have never been able to learn any news of him; and I looked upon him as irrecoverably lost, when at this moment, my lord, I know him in that young man, by the pomegranate upon his breast. as upon that of Sutchumi, his twin-sister. It was undoubtedly natural sympathy, continued Dugmi, that acted in me, when passing with your Majesty by Kurban's shop, about two months ago, I of a sudden felt for that young tailor an extreme tenderness, which had nothing in it that was criminal, and of which I knew not the secret cause. It is I alone, my lord, that under the pretence of employing him to make clothes for my daughter, and the beautiful Zabd al-Katon, corrupted your eunuchs to convey him into the palace; punish, therefore, in me, the only instrument of all your misfortunes.

TALE OF KING SHAMS AL-DIN (Continued)

THE king of Astrakhan was strangely surprised at this story; and though the melancholy state he was in should have made him think of nothing but revenge, he gave orders to send immediately for the tailor and his wife, who passed for the father and mother of Shams al-Din. While they were gone for, the surgeon dressed the king's wound; and it was not without inconceivable anguish, that Shams al-Din read in the surgeon's eyes, that his life was in danger. The tailor and his wife came at last. They confessed that the young man was none of their son; that he was brought to them about eighteen years before by a solitary darwaysh, who told them he found him stark naked in his little hut at his return from angling in the river Volga, and that the good old man died suddenly three months afterwards, without having been able to give them any further information.

The day on which Shams al-Din had been carried to Kurban agreeing exactly with that of Sutchumi's birth, and the pomegranate upon his breast which was in the same place as upon his twin sister, entirely convincing the king he was his son, he caused him to come near, embraced him affectionately, and ordered him to be covered with a sumptuous robe. If on one side Shams al-Din rejoiced at the nobleness of his birth, on the other his soul was full of the sharpest affliction. He threw himself at Al-Salah's feet: My lord, he said, melting into tears, I wait impatiently for death; I cannot look upon myself without horror, after what my hand has done: Purge the world of such a monster as I am. This is the greatest and only favour you can shew to a son so guilty as I am.— No, no, my dear Shams al-Din, replied the king, embracing him afresh, my death is not owing to any guilt of yours; what is written upon the table of light can never be avoided. Live, I command you, and assemble this moment my wazirs and all the emirs of Astrakhan: I will in their presence acknowledge you for my son and for my successor. Shams al-Din having a thorough sense of the goodness of the king his father, embraced his knees with respect, and made but very little haste to execute his orders: but the Sultana Dugmi having immediately sent out his commands by the twelve black slaves, the king's chamber was soon filled with the principal persons of the court.

That prince was laid upon his sofa ; The angel of death is not far from me, says he to them, and I find I shall quickly sleep under the wing of the mercy of the Almighty. Behold, wazirs, continued he with a feeble voice ; behold your master, shewing them the young Shams al-Din, this is my son by the Sultana Dugmi ; I command you to look upon him as your king.

The wazirs and emirs were mightily astonished at the approaching death of Al-Salah ; they were likewise ignorant that the king had ever had a son ; but the sultana having in a few words related to them the history of the young tailor, they all prostrated themselves with their faces to the ground, and swore by their heads to obey him till death. This ceremony was hardly over, when the king made the sultana, Sutchumi, and Zabd al-Katon draw near to his sofa : my dear Dugmi, said he to the first, I am too sensible of the injustice I did your charms in loving the beauteous Zabd al-Katon, who never rewarded my passion with any thing but ingratitude ; you did not deserve this infidelity from me : I die with extreme regret for having broken the oaths I so often made to be always yours.—Ah, my lord, replied Dugmi, shedding plenteous tears, whatever tenderness I felt for your Majesty I never wished to control you in your pleasures. I loved you, my lord, for yourself ; and you never knew me behold with an eye of envy your new affection for Zabd al-Katon. Whatever grief the loss of your heart was to me, your being contented was enough to keep me from murmuring at your sovereign will. The king's love for the sultana redoubled at this moment. He embraced her tenderly : I will give you a proof, my dear Dugmi, said he, of the truth of what I say ; the charming Zabd al-Katon no longer touches me: And to give an undoubted mark of it, I conjure her in your presence to give her hand to the prince, my son. As for Sutchumi, the wazir Ibn-Bukr — The king of Astrakhan could not any further explain his pleasure with regard to his daughter. He died in the arms of the sultana with these last words in his mouth.

It is impossible to paint the despair of Shams al-Din. They had much ado to keep him from attempting his own life. His mother, his sister, and Zabd al-Katon did not leave him a moment; the last particularly, being delivered from a king whose troublesome, though respectful love had more than once made her tremble, used all her endeavours to dispel Shams al-Din's sorrow. But insensible to all the honours that were done to him, he fell into so profound a melancholy, that his life was feared. Public prayers were ordered in the Mosques of Astrakhan. They in some measure appeased the wrath of the great Prophet against the new king. He found his mind more at peace in a few months : and after having nobly rewarded the tailor and his wife for the kindness they had always shewn him, he married Sutchumi to the wazir Ibn-Bukr, which was what he thought the king his father meant by his last words, and publicly espoused Zabd al-Katon himself. The prince spent nearly five months with his wife in the most perfect felicity. The days in her company seemed no more than moments; but this happiness was all of a sudden interrupted by frightful dreams, which continually represented to his thoughts his bleeding father. Zabd al-Katon to no purpose endeavoured by the most endearing behaviour to efface from her husband's mind the dark ideas with which it was filled. He was incessantly torn with remorse for the murder he had committed, and could think of no other way to put an end to it, than by taking a journey to Meccah. Zabd al-Katon, unwilling to part with the king, begged that he would permit her to go with him;

Shams al-Din being unable to refuse her that satisfaction, left his brother-in-law, the wazir Ibn-Bukr, regent in his absence, recommended his mother and sister to his care in the strongest terms, and set out from Astrakhan.

After a tedious journey, in which the king and his wife underwent a thousand fatigues, they at length arrived at Meccah. There Shams al-Din walked seven times round the temple; and after having purified himself with the water of the well called Zemzem, he went in the evening to Mount Arafat, where he caused two hundred sheep to be slain, which he distributed among the poor. From thence he took the road to Al-Madinah, and performed his devotion in the most holy Mosque: and afterwards, having offered a present of forty thousand pieces of gold as he had done at Meccah, he joined the Caravan, and travelled towards Grand Cairo, where they arrived without meeting with any accident. Shams al-Din no longer felt the cruel agitations which so often interrupted his slumbers. He began to enjoy an undisturbed happiness, and prepared to begin his journey towards his own kingdom, when the beauteous Zabd al-Katon was attacked with a violent fever. This unlucky accident hindered him from setting out with the Caravan, which could not defer its journey: but he soon had just reason to be alarmed, when the distemper of his beloved wife increased to such a degree, that her life was despaired of. The princess was almost two days insensible, and recovered for some moments the use of her speech only to pierce Shams al-Din's heart with the most cruel affliction. I must leave you, my dear husband, said she to him, embracing him with extreme tenderness, and I conceive before-hand all the horror of such a separation; but you must be patient under the loss of me. You are decreed for still greater misfortunes. This warning I give you from the great Prophet, who appeared to me some hours ago. It is good, said he to me, that princes should suffer some trials. Adversity purifies their virtue, and they govern the better for it. Shams al-Din shall quickly be convinced of this truth : Bid him from me begin to prepare for it. This, continued Zabd al-Katon, pouring forth tears in abundance, this is the message I have to deliver to you : Summon up all your reason, that you may not murmur at the orders of Providence—Adieu, my dear Shams——The princess had not time to conclude; the angel which waited for her soul cut short her speech.

Never was despair equal to that of the king of Astrakhan. He could not be removed from the body of his spouse. He was inconsolable for the loss of her, and knew no other remedy than immediately to have a large box made, of cinnamon wood, open only at the top towards the head; in this he put the body of Zabd al-Katon, and adorned it with a great number of jewels; then with his guard, which was about five hundred men, he endeavoured to overtake the Caravan, which was gone but some days' journey before him, intending, as soon as he should come up with it, to have the corpse of his dear wife embalmed. The prince had not been two days upon his march, when he was surrounded by almost two thousand Badawin. He made an incredible resistance ; but all his followers being cut in pieces, without excepting one, he himself fell among the number of the dead. The Badawin, after their victory, fell to stripping their enemies. They took every thing they could find, and did not forget the bier adorned with jewels, in which was the body of Zabd al-Katon. Shams al-Din, who defended himself like a lion, had however received never a wound that was mortal; and it was not so much the quantity of blood he had lost, as his being quite tired out, that was the occasion of his falling among the dead. When he had recovered his senses, he was surprised to find himself alone, and in the midst of his men, among whom there was not one that had the least sign of life. What a sad spectacle was this for the king! He got up as well as he was able, and not forgetting his dear spouse, he ran all over the field of battle, to see if the robbers, after having taken away the jewels, might not have left the box in which was the corpse of Zabd al-Katon. His search was all in vain; he almost died with grief at this new loss. But at length, leaving a place which had been so fatal to him, after having travelled an hour, without knowing whither he went, he came near to a little village, entering into which he met an Imam, who at first was frightened to see a man quite naked, and all covered with blood; but Shams al-Din having, without making himself known to him, informed him that he was the only one of his company that had escaped the cruelty of the Badawin, the Imam took pity on him, carried him home to his house, and cured his wounds; and having afterwards given him some pieces of money, the prince with them betook the way to his own kingdom.

After a long and painful journey, in which Shams al-Din travelled sometimes alone, and sometimes with little Caravans, which assisted him in his necessities, he at length reached a vast champaign country which was about half a league from Astrakhan. There he spied a nephew of the wazir his brother-in-law, with a pretty numerous train; and running to him with open arms, Receive, said he, my dear Zamin, receive the unhappy Shams al-Din, oppressed with the most cruel misfortunes and who for almost three years has been exposed to such miseries as would strike you with horror but to hear them. Zamin was surprised at the sight of his king; though the fatigues of the journey, the hardships he had undergone, and the meanness of his habit had altered him extremely, yet he could not help knowing him again. He prostrated himself before him with all the appearances of the sincerest respect; and taking off his own

robe, he covered the prince with it, and conducted him
to the palace through the most private streets; but what
was the amazement of Shams al-Din at his entrance
there, to see himself loaded with chains by the same
Zamin, who had but now been loading him with compliments! Then he learnt to his inexpressible grief, that his
cruel brother-in-law Ibn Bukr, after having himself
strangled his wife and the sultana Dugmi, had seized
the kingdom, massacred all his faithful subjects, and
those who opposed his usurpation; and that he himself
must shortly expect the same fate. Shams al-Din grew
motionless at this news. At first he gave himself up to
fury and rage; but presently calling to mind the last
words of Zabd al-Katon, he resigned himself that moment
to the Will of the Almighty. God, said he, is great, He is
just: I am not yet sufficiently punished for my crimes;
but what had my mother and sister done to come
to so tragical an end? Their death I hope will not be
long unpunished. The prince had not ended these
words, when the usurper, followed by four ruffians,
entered the room. His presence startled Shams al-Din.
Ah, barbarous wazir, cried he, the moment he saw him,
art thou come to fill up the measure of thy guilt? Cannot
the blood of thy wife and of my mother, which already
rises up against thee, assuage thy fury? Behold my
head; strike! But remember the day will come when
I shall accuse thee of these enormous crimes before the
tribunal of the Great God; and that when the angels shall
give testimony of the truth, all this mighty power of thine,
beneath which my subjects groan and tremble, shall not
then preserve thee from being condemned, and severely
punished for thy execrable parricide.

These sharp reproaches quite confounded the usurper; he had not strength enough now to command the
death of his lawful king; his menaces terrified him; he
thought he already saw the hand of God lifted over his

head: he contented himself with putting Shams al-Din out of a condition ever to re-ascend the throne; he caused a red-hot iron to be rubbed over his eyes, which deprived him of sight, and he afterwards sent him into a deep dungeon. There was not a day passed wherein the king of Astrakhan, though oppressed with miseries, and delivered up to the most bitter affliction, did not pay respect to the decrees of Providence, and return thanks to God, for having punished him so gently for his crimes: but one night, when grief had for some moments given way to sleep, he thought he saw in a dream the great Prophet, with Zabd al-Katon in his hand, assuring him of the change in his condition, and promising he should one day enjoy a perfect happiness with his spouse. Shams al-Din started up and waked; but this dream seemed to him so extraordinary, and to have so little foundation, that he gave very little heed to it. It even added to his sorrow; but yet it was not long before he felt the effects of one part of this prediction.

One morning as the prince was performing his devotions prostrate upon the earth, he heard the doors of his prison open with a great noise. Imagining that some body was going to dispatch him he did not alter his posture but waited the blow with intrepidity, when two of his former wazirs, whose zeal and virtue were sufficiently known to him, threw themselves at his feet. My lord, said one of them, embracing his knees, do you not remember the voices of Mutamhid and Kubirgh, your faithful slaves? The ungrateful wazir, on whom you heaped so many favours, together with the traitor Zamin, have just now met with their deaths by our hands. The people, tired out with his cruelties, rejoice exceedingly at his death. They knew nothing of your return, which we took care to inform them of; having pretended to be of Ibn Bukr's party, only that we might in time be able to push him from the throne he had so basely and cruelly usurped. Come then, my lord, and once more fill it ; since all your subjects call for their lawful sovereign with the utmost impatience. Shams al-Din praised God, and thanked the wazirs for their zeal. But how, my wise friends, said he, would you have me remount my throne ? Is such an unhappy prince as I in a condition to govern you ? No, no, wazirs, choose from among you a man that may be more capable of such a charge, and leave me to mourn in secret for all my misfortunes.—Ah ! my lord, replied Mutamhid, your contempt of greatness is a sure sign that none is more worthy to govern than yourself. We conjure you not to reject our entreaties; we are ready to sacrifice our lives and fortunes to defend you upon a throne which you have already so worthily filled. The king of Astrakhan, moved by these words, which shewed so much affection and loyalty, put himself into the hands of his two wazirs : they conducted him to the baths of the palace ; and after having clothed him in a robe of state, presented him to the people, who testified by a thousand shouts of joy how impatient they had been to see him again upon the throne of his ancestors.

Whatever satisfaction Shams al-Din took in hearing the love his subjects had for him, he continually wept in secret for the loss of his dear Zabd al-Katan, and for the privation of his sight. In vain the most skilful physicians and surgeons in Astrakhan tried all their art upon him. They agreed, at last, that there were not the least hopes that he would ever see again the light of the sun. There was one of them only, who told the king he remembered he had formerly read in an old Arabian manuscript that there was in the island of Sarandib a bird which might restore him to sight; but that besides the difficulties there were in finding and coming near it, he would not warrant the manuscript to be infallible. The bird, continued the physician, is upon the top of a very high tree, all the leaves of which are as hard as iron, and as sharp as razors. Some woman must, in order to restore to sight her blind husband, undertake to climb up this tree from branch to branch; if her affection for her husband has never suffered any alteration, the leaves will soften to her touch, and she will easily climb to the top, and draw in a golden vessel which hangs at the bird's neck, a liquor as white as milk, which distils perpetually from its bill. This liquor the Arabian manuscript affirms to be sovereign for restoring sight to those who have been deprived of it by any accident whatsoever, nay, even to those who have been born blind. After having received this divine liquor, she shall come down from the tree as easily as she climbed up; but if the woman, who ventures to fetch this marvellous juice, has ever had the least thought contrary to the purity of marriage, or has ceased one moment to have an entire love for her husband, she must expect nothing from her rash enterprise but certain death. The leaves indeed will grow soft to let her climb to the top of the tree; but when she is to come down they will resume their edge, and the woman falling from bough to bough shall be hacked into a thousand pieces. I believe, my lord, continued Abu Bakr, that this tree, if it is certainly in being, is still a virgin and untouched; and that no woman hitherto has offered herself to fetch a liquor, which is to be acquired with so much trouble and danger.

Shams al-Din listened to this story with admiration. It is not impossible, said he, that such a woman may be found in this city, though such women are but very rare; we must try if we cannot find out so great a treasure. The wives of all the blind men in Astrakhan were brought before the king: Abu Bakr in his presence declared to them what was to be done, and Shams al-Din promised an unbounded reward to her who could by this means restore him to sight : but there was not one of them durst venture to climb the tree; the conditions were a little too delicate, and death too certain: they all in general refused to undergo so dreadful a probation. The other physicians of Astrakhan made a wonderful jest of the king's credulity. This new kind of remedy, said they, is an invention of Abu Bakr's, who would fain set up for a man of prodigious learning; he is mightily set upon miracles, and always distinguishes himself by some new and particular opinion. These words came to Abu Bakr's ears; they touched him to the quick. Shall my zeal for the king, said he to his wife and son, be turned into ridicule? Well, I myself will undertake a journey to Sarandib, to see if what the manuscript report be true; if, notwithstanding all my wishes, I do not succeed in my enterprise, at least I shall have the consolation of having done more for my prince than all the other physicians of Astrakhan put together. Nothing could divert Abu Bakr from his resolution; the length and difficulties of the voyage did not at all dishearten him. He presented himself the next day before the king, and informed him of his design. That prince highly commended so noble an undertaking. He gave him every thing that was necessary for so tedious a voyage; and promised him, in case he died by the way, to take particular care of his wife, and of his only son, whom he loved entirely. My lord, said the physician, taking leave of Shams al-Din, if I do not return in three years, you may believe that death, or some strange accident which I cannot foresee, has obstructed the ardent desire I have to restore you to sight; but a certain confidence which I have in the Arabian manuscript, makes me hope my voyage will not be fruitless. At length Abu Bakr set out for Sarandib; and it was not without very great envy that the other physicians saw the king so biassed in his favour.

Shams al-Din, in the flower of his age, and blind as

he was, governed his subjects with admirable prudence. Shut up in the recesses of his palace, he was incessantly thinking of the means to make them happy ; and laid it down to himself as an unalterable law till the return of the physician Abu Bakr, to appear in public but one hour every day, which hour he divided into four parts. During the first he went to the great Mosque of Astrakhan to pray ; the second, third, and sometimes part of the fourth, were destined for doing acts of charity, and receiving the complaints of private persons against the public officers, either by word of mouth or in writing. Afterwards he commanded Mutamhid and Kubirgh, the two wazirs, upon whom he relied in most of his affairs, to punish or to turn out those officers if they deserved it ; and he distributed justice with so much equity and discretion, that his sentences were looked upon as so many oracles. As for what remained of the last quarter of an hour, he spent it in the conversation of learned men. This was the only diversion that prince enjoyed all the day, and as he liked their company, he gave them marks of his liberality. The honour of diverting the king who generally seemed sunk in melancholy, more than the view of interest, animated his subjects to find out persons who might dissipate his sorrows, by telling him some extraordinary story. If a famous traveller arrived at Astrakhan, he was immediately carried to Shams al-Din : and when the inhabitants themselves knew any singular adventure, they presented themselves before their prince, that they might have the pleasure of contributing to his entertainment.

It was now two years since Abu Bakr had been gone to the island of Sarandib, and since the king, exactly observing the rule he had prescribed to himself, had never failed to allot some moments every day to those amusements, when the two favourite wazirs discussing together

about the motive of Abu Bakr's voyage : If that physician
prove a cheat, said one of them, or should not return to
Astrakhan, we shall be very much at a loss to procure
the king fit persons to talk to him. He has committed that
charge to our care; and though a quarter of an hour is
quickly past, yet as it is to be renewed daily, I am afraid
that at last we shall not be able to find any thing new.—
That would be a pity indeed, replied the other wazir; the
king has now contracted a pleasing habit of hearing some
story or other every day ; it is almost the only satisfaction
of his life; for in the manner this wise prince conducts
himself, he enjoys no delight of royalty, but that of labouring incessantly for the good of his subjects. One of the
physicians of Astrakhan was present at the conversation ;
he thought this a fair opportunity of gratifying the envy
which he and all his brethren had conceived against
Abu Bakr: My lords, said he to the wazirs, all men of
sense are of your opinion ; and you will infallibly fall into
the inconvenience you already apprehend. I know but
one remedy against it : Abu Bakr's son, deriding the
perplexity he foresees you will soon be in, boasted yesterday in my hearing, that he himself was able, if he had a
mind to it, to find diversion for the king till his father's
return. It is true this young man has a good deal of
learning, and ever since he was ten years old has applied
himself with great eagerness to read all manner of books ;
but notwithstanding the prodigious memory he is said to
be endowed with, I very much doubt whether he could
succeed in so difficult an undertaking.

Kubirgh only laughed at the presumption of Abu
Bakr's son ; but Mutamhid falling into a violent passion,
Indeed, said he, it well becomes this insolent young man
to jest so unseasonably ! Well, since he talks at this rate,
he shall keep his word ; and his head shall be answerable
for the success of an enterprise he is so vain as to pretend
to. He that moment ordered somebody to fetch Ibn

Aridun, which was the name of Abu Bakr's son. This physician, said he to him when he had come, assures me that you have the boldness to make a jest of the perplexity Kubirgh and I may one day be in to provide his Majesty new subjects for recreation, and that you boast that you yourself could find him diversion till your father's return. Since you are so rash as to talk thus, I command you to look that you do so, continued Mutamhid, with a voice that might make Ibn Aridun tremble: I will be present at all your conversations; and I forewarn you, that if the prince grow weary of your discourse, and bid me bring him another, thou shalt that moment lose thy head. Ibn Aridun was strangely surprised at this order. He perceived so much anger in the wazir's eyes that he durst not deny his having been guilty of that vanity; he confided in his reading, and in the happy memory nature had given him, and throwing himself at Mutamhid's feet, My lord, said he, waiving whatever I might urge for my justification, the honour of diverting the king is so coveted by me, that I will not refuse to obey your sovereign commands; though it cost me my life, I am ready to appear before the throne of Shams al-Din. The perfidious physician, who had stayed by the wazir to be witness of what passed, was a little astonished at Ibn Aridun's answer, yet he made not the least doubt of his destruction. A young man, at most but five and twenty years old, said he to himself, can never have gathered stock enough to succeed in such an undertaking. He presently ran to inform his companions, who all felt a malicious joy at it, and tasted before-hand the pleasure of seeing themselves revenged upon Abu Bakr in the person of his son.

The wazir Mutamhid, pleased with the submission and modesty of Ibn Aridun, dropped all his anger: As your death is unavoidable, says he, if you do not fulfil your promise, so your reward, on the other hand, is no less certain, if you succeed in your design. Every time you leave the king, I will give you an hundred pieces of gold; I will have you eat at my table; you shall be served like me, and there shall be no other difference between us, but that you shall be narrowly watched.—My lord, replied Ibn Aridun, it is not the hopes of recompense, or your noble promises, that will prompt me to do my duty : the philosophy I make profession of has taught me to despise riches. Honour and glory are the only motives by which I am actuated; and if what you now require of me were contrary to their dictates, you should see me embrace the most cruel death, rather than obey you : but as there is nothing that is not extremely honourable in the command you impose upon me, you may put me to the trial when you please; I shall endeavour to confound the artifices of my enemies, and I hope my prince will be satisfied with me. Mutamhid was charmed with the prudent behaviour of Ibn Aridun; he then perceived the malice of the old physician, and that the young man was innocent of what was laid to his charge; but since he offered himself as it were voluntarily to try to divert his prince, he presented him to him the next day.

As soon as Ibn Aridun came within sight of the throne of Shams al-Din, he prostrated himself with his face to the earth. He afterwards arose, and addressing his speech to the king : May the Mercy of the Almighty be displayed upon your Majesty, said he; may the Angel that is one day to present you before his throne, forget no one good action of your life; and may you for ever enjoy the perfect felicity which our great Prophet has promised to those who exactly follow his laws! My name is Ibn Aridun, the son of Abu Bakr, who has been gone two years or thereabouts to the island of Sarandib : may heaven quickly send him back with the divine remedy which he travels in quest of to restore you to sight! Till that time comes, I have undertaken, my lord, to entertain your Majesty every day for that little while which you set apart to unbend your mind.—Do you consider what you have engaged to do? answered the king, somewhat surprised at these promises. Do you not know that such an enterprise is beyond your ability, and that your father may not return perhaps this twelvemonth?— My lord, replied the young Ibn Aridun, though great is the difficulty of entertaining my king as I ought to do, yet I know such a number of stories, each more curious than the other, that even though my father should lengthen out his voyage as long again as he intended, I do not despair of being able to fulfil the promise I have made to the wazir Mutamhid; and if your Majesty will do me the honour to hear me, I will begin with a very singular story.

Shams al-Din was yet more surprised than before. Thou must be a wonder in thy kind, said he, if thou keepest thy word. Difficulties do not at all discourage thee.—On the contrary, my lord, replied Ibn Aridun, they animate me with more vigour. I have so happy a memory, that I never forget anything I have read or heard; and as I always delighted in keeping company with the oldest and wisest men in Astrakhan, great part of whom are dead, I am possessed of such a number of different histories of every kind, that, without boasting, I may assure your Majesty there are few men like me in this city.—I shall quickly be a judge of that, replied the king: Sit down by Mutamhid on this sofa, and let me hear the story you offered to tell me.

Ibn Aridun obeyed the orders of Shams al-Din: He sat down upon the sofa, and began in this manner:

HISTORY OF SHARIF AL-DIN, SON OF THE KING OF ORMUZ, AND OF GUL-HINDI, PRINCESS OF TULUPHAN

THERE were formerly, my lord, in the Greater Tartary, two different sorts of jinnis; the one, disposed to do good to mankind, acknowledged the great Geoncha for their king; and the other, never pleased but when they were exercising their malicious inclinations, had no other master than the revengeful Zalulu. These two captains of the jinnis had for almost three hundred years been at continual war with each other. Geoncha protected nobody that Zalulu did not immediately endeavour to persecute; and Zalulu could do no ill action upon the earth, but Geoncha presently set about to redress it.

One day as these two jinnis were upon the banks of the river Salgora, endeavouring to decide their differences by conference, Mochzadin, king of Tuluphan, and the beauteous Riza, his wife, who were returning together from hunting the kid, passed by the place where the two jinnis were contending. Zalulu, always watchful to do ill, would not let slip so fair an opportunity of indulging his propensity that way; notwithstanding Geoncha's entreaties, that malicious jinni, going up to Riza, who rode side by side with Mochzadin, made so great a noise in her horse's ear, that the frightened beast ran away with the princess, notwithstanding all her efforts to restrain him, and was just going to precipitate her in the river, which was very deep in that part, if with one blow of a sabre, struck by a powerful hand, Geoncha, running to her assistance, had not cut off the horse's head, and caught the princess in his arms, who had swooned away with fear. The kind jinni, having afterwards made her smell at a nosegay of musk-roses which he had in his hand, she not only returned to her senses, but her clothes which were green before, were now changed into a rose-colour; and though her features were not in the least altered, her beauty was increased to such a degree, that the king himself, who justly alarmed at the danger of his spouse, had followed her with extreme swiftness, could scarcely know her again. He and all his train were in a surprise not to be imagined. The extraordinary death of Riza's horse, her rose-coloured habit, and her additional beauty, all these brought about in a moment, the author of so many wonders not appearing, for the jinnis had not made themselves visible; all these I say, happened so unaccountably, that the king and queen were almost ready to doubt of a truth, which their eyes could not but testify. After having returned to Tuluphan, and retired into their chamber by themselves, they were still, with admiration, discoursing of the prodigy they had seen, when they were seized with fear and respect at the sight of a venerable old man who of a sudden appeared before them, without their perceiving how he got in. Be not afraid, my children, said he to them kindly; I am Geoncha, king of the jinnis. It is I, that after having preserved the charming Riza from the danger into which Zalulu, who has made himself famous upon earth by a thousand malicious actions, had thrown her by frightening her horse; it is I, continued he, who had resolved that none of her sex should surpass her in beauty. But I do not stint my favours in so narrow a compass, I intend likewise to put an end to her barrenness; in nine months from this day she shall bring forth a daughter as beautiful as herself.

The king of the jinnis, continued Ibn Aridun, had no sooner spoken these words, than he disappeared, leaving the king and queen of Tuluphan, in an ecstacy of joy at so pleasing an expectation. However incredulous they had been till then, they soon ceased to be so; Riza, who during seven years' marriage had never had the pleasing

satisfaction of being a mother, quickly felt the effects of
Geoncha's promises.   At the end of nine months exactly,
she was brought to bed of a daughter, completely beautiful, whom she named Gul-hindi.   This little princess no
sooner enjoyed the light, that the same jinni appeared
again in the chamber where Riza and Mochzadin were
together.   I come with inexpressible pleasure, said he,
to put the last hand to so charming a work, and to inform
you of the destiny that is prepared for her.   I assisted
yesterday at the birth of a son of the king of Ormuz,
whom I named Sharif al-Din: I find so much resemblance
and sympathy between him and this lovely princess, that
I have resolved to unite them one day by the most holy
ties; but I foresee that the happiness they are to enjoy
will be crossed by such misfortunes, as will drive Gul-hindi
to the very brink of death, if they know one another before
they have attained the age of seventeen years.   It must be
your care, my lord, continued the jinni, addressing his
speech to Mochzadin, to keep the princess from seeing
any stranger, till she is past the fatal moment which the
stars have discovered will be so dangerous to her.   This
is the only remedy I can think of, unless you will put her
into my hands; for then I will warrant her free from
all the caprices of fortune.   Mochzadin and Riza were
surprised at Geoncha's words: but though they gave
entire credit to his prediction, they were not able to consent to part with a child they had so many years longed
for.   They begged the jinni very earnestly, not to be
offended if they kept the little Gul-hindi with themselves;
and assured him they would take so much care of her
that she would be in no manner of danger from the prince
Sharif al-Din.—So be it then, replied the jinni; only remember, when the princess is ten years old to keep her
from the sight of all the world.   The nearer she approaches
her sixteenth year, the greater danger she will be in.
Then having taken her in his arms, he enriched her with

all the fine qualities that could make a person of her sex accomplished ; and after having received a thousand thanks from the king and queen, he departed like a flash of lightning.

Scarce, my lord, continued Ibn Aridun, did the malignant Zalulu, who could not come to an agreement with Geoncha in their last conference, know what he had done for Gul-hindi and Sharif al-Din, than he resolved to gratify his malicious temper by crossing the felicity of these two lovely infants. He repaired in the night to the palace of the king of Ormuz, stole away the little prince, carried him to Tuluphan, drest him in Gul-hindi's clothes, and covering that little princess with those of Sharif al-Din, placed her a moment after in the cradle from which he had taken the prince of Ormuz. We may easily conceive the surprise the two nurses were in.

❋ ❋

Ibn Aridun was interrupted here by a black slave, who came every day to tell the king of Astrakhan that his hour was out. As soon as this slave appeared, Shams al-Din arose to return to his palace. He who had the honour to entertain him, gave over speaking, and resumed his discourse the next day, if he had not finished his story; if he had, there was brought to the king another, who told him some adventure he had not yet heard. Thus 𝕿𝖍𝖊 𝕿𝖍𝖔𝖚𝖘𝖆𝖓𝖉 𝖆𝖓𝖉 𝕺𝖓𝖊 𝕼𝖚𝖆𝖗𝖙𝖊𝖗𝖘 𝖔𝖋 𝖆𝖓 𝕳𝖔𝖚𝖗 are divided in the original Arabic ; but it is thought best to leave out all that follows and precedes Ibn Aridun's narration, being persuaded that the reader will read these stories with more pleasure than if they were interrupted by continual repetitions, which it would be almost impossible not to be guilty of.

❋ ❋ ❋ ❋

The two nurses were strangely surprised in the morning to find each her child so different from what it was the night before. They looked upon them with unparalleled amazement, when Zalulu appearing to each of them in the shape of a frightful dwarf, threatened to wring their necks if ever they divulged the metamorphosis that had happened; and departed, after having assured them, that if before those children had attained the age of seventeen years the secret was found out in any manner whatsoever, they would fall into his power, without any possibility of ever getting out of it. The poor women were so terrified, that they resolved to keep the strictest silence. Their lives depended upon it; and the jinni had so intimidated them, that they would have suffered any torment rather than have revealed the secret. Sharif al-Din then was brought up at the court of king Mochzadin by the name of Gul-hindi; and that princess, under the habit of the prince of Persia, rendered herself in a little time so perfect at the exercises of the body, that when she was fifteen years old she surpassed all the subjects of the king of Ormuz in those accomplishments.

The education of the young prince was not very agreeable to his sex; that which he seemed to be of, engaged him in quite different occupations. He generally amused himself by embroidery; and being, according to Geoncha's order, shut up from the age of ten years in Mochzadin's palace, which was grown inaccessible to every body but the king of Tuluphan, he never left off work but to hunt in the park, accompanied by his women and some of his eunuchs. His nurse, Marou, who never quitted him, seeing him approach to his sixteenth year, often recommended it to him to conceal his sex with the greatest care, since the repose of his whole life depended upon his so doing. But, said Sharif al-Din to her with tears, why am I educated like a girl, and deprived of the learning and sciences which ought to be communicated to a prince of my rank? And what unjust motive can oblige the king and queen to let me languish thus in an idle inactive state of life?—These are things I am ignorant of, replied Marou; but, my dear prince, or rather my dear princess, for it is dangerous to call you by the first name, all I can assure you of is, that Mochzadin and Riza are more deceived in you than any body. They believe you are a girl; they have been convinced of it by their own eyes; but things have had a strange alteration since that time. This is all I can tell you at present; you will know more hereafter: but I beg you not to expose yourself to the cruel miseries I have so often threatened you with, if you discover your sex till you are full seventeen years old.

The prince was surprised at this advice: the more he reflected with himself, the more he was confounded; he resolved therefore to follow the prudent counsels of his nurse; but in order to dissipate the uneasiness which preyed upon him, he went a-hunting as often as possible.

One evening as Mochzadin and Riza were conversing with their supposed daughter, the queen related to her, as she had often done before, the story of her birth, and the promises the king of the jinnis had made to unite her destiny with that of the son of the king of Ormuz. This story so often repeated perplexed the prince to the highest degree; he knew not what to fix upon, but at last resolved, let what would happen, to fly for ever from a place where he spent a life so unworthy of himself. It was no easy thing to compass this design; all the gates of the palace were guarded by eunuchs not to be corrupted; but to execute the project he had formed, he chose the time of his hunting; and after having taken with him two purses full of gold and a good many jewels, being very well mounted he easily rode away from his company, and spurring directly to a door of the park which led into the wide country, he commanded the eunuch that guarded it to open it to him. The slave refused to obey him; but the prince having despatched

him into the other world with one blow of his sabre,
which he always wore when he went a-hunting, took the
keys, and flying with incredible swiftness, chose the road
which was least beaten, and travelled all that day and
the following night without taking the least repose. The
ladies and eunuchs belonging to the false princess, made
the strictest search for her all over the park. After
having in vain traversed every corner of it, they came at
last to the door, which they found open; the dead body
of the eunuch increased their surprise. They concluded
that some unfortunate accident had happened to Gul-
hindi. Nobody cared to inform the king and queen of
this mournful news; yet it was not to be avoided but
they should know it. They almost died with grief when
they heard it. Oh Heaven! cried the queen, tearing her
hair and face, why did not we take the advice of the
wise Geoncha? We should not now have been thus
oppressed with the bitterest affliction : Gul-hindi is undoubtedly stolen away; the jinni too rightly predicted
this mischance. Pray Heaven my dear daughter don ot
feel the consequences of it !

While the king and queen wasted their time in vain
complaints and fruitless reflections, the prince continued
his flight. All the pursuit that was made after him was
to no purpose; he rode as hard as his horse could carry
him and did not stop till he fell dead under him. He was
now forced to travel a-foot in very great perplexity, when
there passed by him a young Tartarian. The prince
accosted him ; Do you know anybody, said he, that
could sell me a horse?—You could not have addressed
yourself more luckily, madam, replied the young man,
deceived by Sharif al-Din's female habit; my father who
lives but a little way off, has no inconsiderable dealings
that way. The prince followed him, furnished himself
with a good horse, and after having taken a few hours' rest,
renewed his journey, travelled several days almost with-

out stopping a moment, and at last arrived at a sea-port, where he found a vessel just ready to set sail for Surat. The master of the ship was a man of a good aspect, about forty years old. He received the prince with abundance of respect, as a young lady of quality going to the Indies to take possession of a very considerable estate left her by her father, and whose mother died suddenly at hearing the news of her husband's death : he made her an offer of his own table, which Sharif al-Din accepted the more willingly, because having embarked very hastily he had not had time to make any provision. The repast was served up with great delicacy ; but at the conclusion of it, he was very much surprised to see a lady of extreme beauty enter the cabin, and address these words to the master of the ship : Remember, Sinadab, that God has given us a father and a mother, that we should obey them ; it is God that speaks to us through their mouth : Woe to him that despises them and does not submit to their commands with respect and duty. Sinadab at these words rose from table ; the tears ran down his eyes ; he afterwards prostrated himself on the ground, remained some time in that posture, and then rising with the marks of the deepest sorrow engraved upon his face : Beauteous Rukia, said he to the lady, I shall never forget these wholesome counsels. My past misfortunes have sufficiently imprinted them in my memory ; but do you continue nevertheless to put me in mind of them daily, as you have been used to do.

The prince Sharif al-Din looked upon Sinadab with wonder : he perceived it. You will no longer be surprised, madam, said he, when I have told you the occasion of this ceremony, and why this lady at all my meals repeats to me the words you have just now heard. Sharif al-Din having testified a great desire to know the story ; thus, my lord, continued Ibn Aridun, Sinadab related it to him :

STORY OF SINADAB, THE SON OF SAZAN THE PHYSICIAN

My father, whose name was Sazan, was a physician at Suez. He exercised that profession with a good deal of honour for a considerable time. He had no child but me, and therefore spared no cost in my education. I was almost twenty years old, when he would fain have persuaded me to embrace his profession; but besides that I found myself extremely averse to it, as he was esteemed a very rich man I thought I had no occasion to qualify myself to get a livelihood. I imagined that the estate he was to leave me would be more than enough to maintain me in luxury and pleasure, without my giving myself the least pain or trouble. My father's remonstrances could not dissuade me from my resolution. This disturbed him so much that he fell sick; and after having kept his bed five or six months, died. Before his last groan, he called me to him; My son, said he, since in my lifetime I never received any comfort from you, give me at least so much satisfaction at my death as to promise me, that you will punctually follow three articles of advice, which I foresee will be extremely useful to you. Swear to me upon the Koran that they shall never be out of your memory. I melted into tears, continued Sinadab; I took an oath to my father to execute his will; and this, madam, is what the good old man said to me, embracing me: I leave you wealth enough, and perhaps too much, to live like a man of honesty and honour: endeavour, my dear Sinadab, to keep it; but if by any accident, which I cannot foresee, you should happen to lose it, never attach yourself to a prince whose good character you are not thoroughly assured of. Be sure, whatever love you bear your wife, never to trust her with a secret wherein your life may be concerned; and, lastly, never adopt for your son a child that is none of your own.

Scarce had my father made me swear a second time upon the Koran to obey him religiously in these three points, than he closed his eyes, and resigned his soul into the hands of the angel of death. I redoubled my tears at this mournful sight, and rendered him the last duties with all imaginable tenderness. Under his bed's-head I found the copy of a will which he had deposited with the Kadi. He gave me leave to dispose how I would of all his estate, excepting only a little garden which was without the gates of Suez, at the end whereof was a pretty neat summer-house, which he ordered me not to sell upon any account whatsoever. I paid little regard to this article, which seemed to me of no great consequence. I minded nothing but examining carefully what wealth he had left me. I found almost an hundred thousand dinars of gold, several diamonds perfectly rich, considerable inheritances, and very magnificent furniture. So soon as I could appear in public with decency, I called together my companions in my own house, to the number of eight. I presented each of them with a slave completely beautiful, and entertained them sumptuously for ten days together. In short, madam, continued Sinadab, not to weary you with a particular relation of all my follies and debaucheries, in which I plunged deeper and deeper every day, I shall only tell you that after having led this sort of life for almost two years, I found myself of a sudden without money. My comrades, who had never quitted me during my pleasures, advised me to dispose of my jewels and furniture; I sold them piece by piece, for half their value. I afterwards did the same by the houses my father had left me, reserving only the garden which it was not in my power to sell; and at length I was so reduced that I had nothing left but the

clothes I had on, and one single hawk which I had
trained up to flying.

When my friends saw me in these straits, they immediately deserted me. It was to no purpose my reproaching them for their ingratitude; they did but laugh
at me: there was only one of them, who, taking pity of
the condition I was in, gave me ten dinars. I had not
eaten anything for two days together; so that I received
this money as a present from heaven. Being now perfectly ashamed of myself, I went to the port of Suez, de-
signing to embark in the first ship I could meet with. I
found one that was just ready to depart for Adal; I had
scarce time enough to make some slight provision for my
voyage with the little money I was master of. I set
forwards with nothing but my hawk; and we arrived at
Adal without meeting with any accident. I had now remaining in my purse but three dinars of the ten which
had been given me; I resolved to be a good husband of
them, and to live upon the industry of my hawk. I had
a very particular talent for training up those sorts of
birds. Mine was very excellent at the sport: I had accustomed him not to kill his quarry; he only pecked out
their eyes with two strokes of his bill, and I took them
alive; so that I did not want for game to maintain
myself and a poor old widow-woman that had taken me
into her house. I had so much that I carried some every
day to the king's purveyor, who paid me for it nobly;
and who was so surprised at what I told him of my
bird, that he informed the king of it. The prince, who
was a great lover of sporting, sent for me; he told me
he would see my hawk take a flight, and bade me be ready
next day very early. I gladly obeyed, and the king was
so charmed at the swiftness, dexterity, and obedience of
my bird, that he asked me what I would take for it.—
Sir, replied I, it is all that I have left of above two
hundred thousand dinars which my father bequeathed

me when he died: this poor hawk has maintained me ever since I have been in want; but since he has been so happy as to please your Majesty, I shall be overpaid for him by the honour I hope you will do me in accepting him.

The king of Adal, continued Sinadab, immediately ordered me twenty thousand dinars, lodged me in his palace, and conferred on me the place of his chief huntsman. In a word, madam, that prince had so much kindness for me, that in a little time I became his prime wazir and sole confidant. I went with him every day a-hunting, in which diversion he delighted exceedingly; and I seldom was from him but when he retired among his women. How unhappy should I be, my dear Sinadab, said he to me one day, if I should lose you! You share the sweetest moments of my life.—My lord, replied I, the favour of the great is too uncertain a bottom for a wise man to build upon. I am loaded to-day with your goodness; perhaps to-morrow I shall be loaded with chains by your command.—No, no, wazir, said he, fear nothing; I shall always love you. And to bind you more strictly to me, and that you may entirely forget your own country, you shall marry one of my sisters: I have three that are tolerably handsome; you shall see them this moment, but without their knowledge; and if your heart is not already engaged, she you like the best shall to-morrow be your wife. I threw myself at the king's feet, confounded with the honour he did me; he raised me up, and embracing me tenderly, made me go into his closet, placed me behind a great curtain of black gauze, and commanded the captain of his eunuchs to fetch the three princesses. The king's orders were executed in an instant: immediately afterwards there entered the closet three ladies of unparalleled beauty, brilliant as full moons. The king talked with them some time upon different matters; then having sent them back to their own apartments, he called me from behind the curtain where I stood : Well, my dear wazir, said he, which of my three sisters gave your heart the most emotion ?—Ah ! my lord, replied I transported, those ladies are of such ravishing beauty that I could not decide in so little time.—Come, come, interrupted the king, one of the three did certainly please you more than the other two ; own which it was ; I give her to you freely, and I command you to discover your sentiments to me frankly.—My lord, replied I, since you absolutely lay your commands upon me, the youngest of the three princesses pierced my heart with the most irresistible charms ; but notwithstanding your Majesty's unbounded goodness to your slave, my happiness would be incomplete if I did not obtain the princess by her own consent.—These sentiments are extremely delicate, replied the king, but I will give you this satisfaction too. Then he ordered the captain of the eunuchs to fetch Buzamghar; this, madam, was the princess's name; she immediately came. My dear Buzamghar, said the king, embracing her, I intend to marry you, but will not force your inclinations; the wazir Sinadab, to whom I just now purposed you for a wife, will owe your hand to nothing but your love : I leave you with him; examine your heart before you give me a positive answer, and assure yourself that, let your resolution be what it will, I shall not be in the least displeased at it.

The king of Adal upon this retired, and left the captain of the eunuchs at the door without. It would be to no purpose, madam, continued Sinadab, to repeat to you the conversation Buzamghar and I had together; she gave me to understand, by the tenderest expressions, that she would esteem it her greatest felicity to have me for her husband ; and assured me more than once, that the obedience she owed to the king her brother had no share in the sentiments she so ingenuously discovered to me.

Upon this I espoused her with all imaginable magnificence ; and the city of Adal took part in my joy, for the
king upon that occasion discharged the inhabitants from
one-fourth of all their taxes.   At the end of some months
Buzamghar found herself with child.   As I loved her
tenderly, I was inexpressibly rejoiced at it : but my joy
was of very short duration.   She happened to fall, hurt
herself very dangerously, and had like to die of a mis-
carriage.   By the extraordinary care that was taken of
her, she soon recovered a perfect state of health ; but
five years being passed without having any children, we
consulted the skilfullest physicians in all Adal, who unanimously assured us the princess could never be a mother.
This gave great uneasiness to Buzamghar, whom I
adored, and who loved me with inconceivable tenderness.
My lord, said she to me, one night when we were alone
together, since I am for ever deprived of the sweet pleasure
of giving you an heir, let us least try to soften the rigour
of our fortune by adopting little Rumi.   This, madam,
continued Sinadab, was the son of one of my slaves, and
at four years old gave a prospect of all that could be
hoped for in a child of that age.   As I never knew how to
contradict Buzamghar in anything, I willingly consented
to this proposal, with the good liking of the king of Adal.
I brought up Rumi like my own son, and neglected
nothing that might make him accomplished.   Rumi had
now for ten years looked upon me as his father, and I had
received all possible satisfaction from him ; when one
night as I was in bed with Buzamghar, and not able
to sleep, my father's last words and the oath he had
made me take upon the Koran, came into my mind ; but
I only laughed at it.   How these old folks dote ! said I
to myself.   I have wasted all my substance ; I have
given myself to a prince whom I know nothing of; and am
I any the worse for it ? On the contrary, could I ever
wish for a fortune more considerable, more solid, and

more conspicuous, than that of being wazir and brother-in-law to a potent king, who places his whole delight in having me near him! I have adopted Rumi in spite of my father's command. What satisfaction do I receive from that child, who at fifteen years of age, gives marks of so excellent a temper, and from whom I may one day expect all the acknowledgment and gratitude in the world! No, no, we should not be too servilely strict in obeying the wills of our fathers; when they have attained a certain age, they are so far from being able to direct others, that they are hardly in a condition to conduct themselves.

I went to sleep, madam, after having made these wise reflections: they came into my head again next morning. Here are two articles of my father's advice already neglected, said I to myself, and not the least misfortune has ensued: let us see if it will be the same with the third. After having studied some time, I hit upon the stratagem which I am going to tell you. Buzamghar had often murmured at the king of Adal, when he tore me from her arms to carry me a-hunting, from which I generally returned very much fatigued. Her complaints put me upon trying if my wife were capable of keeping a secret. I went to the perch where the king's hawks stood, I took down that which he most loved, unseen by anybody; I carried it to a pleasure-house at the end of a garden which I had out of the city, and gave it to a mute who was the keeper of it, with orders not to stir from thence till some body came to him from me and shewed him my ring. I then took the key of the garden, and double-locked the door, and carried the key to a friend, whose probity I was perfectly well assured of. If you hear that my life is in danger, said I to him, which I foresee may quickly happen, oblige me so far as to go to my garden, of which here is the key, shew this ring to the mute that is keeper of it, and bring him to me with the depositum I just now entrusted him with; he will be serviceable in my justification. Then I returned home; and as I had always a pretty many hawks to teach, I took one that exactly resembled the king's, wrung off its neck, and carried it to my wife. Charming Buzamghar, said I, embracing her, behold a token of my tenderness; you have so often complained of the king of Adal, that I was resolved to cut away the root of the uneasiness he gives you. This hawk is the only cause, he it is that by being the sole delight of the king, deprives you of yours; I have killed him; but be sure you take heed not to reveal this secret. I am a dead man if the king should know of this my ingratitude to him; he would have but little regard to the motive that prevailed upon me to do it. Buzamghar at first seemed frightened at the danger I had brought upon myself: but presently afterwards tenderly pressing my hand, My dear lord, said she, light of my life, if only you and I are acquainted with this secret, you may be sure you are safe, and that the most cruel torments shall never extort it from me.—So far then we are well, replied I; do you take and conceal the hawk with the utmost caution, while I go and make my court to the king. I left Buzamghar, to wait upon the king of Adal. He had already been informed that his hawk was not to be found. He appeared extremely uneasy at it. My lord, said I, I know but one way to recover your bird: have it published all over Adal how much you are disturbed at the loss, and promise a reward for finding it, worthy the generosity of so great a monarch as you are.

The king took my advice; he had it cried at every street's end, that whoever should bring him tidings of his hawk, dead or alive, if it was a man, besides the confiscation of half the estate of him who committed the theft, he should make the informant one of the greatest men in the kingdom; and that if it was a woman, he would marry her to the wazir Giami, who was the handsomest man in all Adal, and who shared his favour with me. This proclamation was soon spread over the city. I thought it all in vain, relying upon the extraordinary love of Buzamghar, who for fifteen years had not let a day pass without giving me some fresh marks of it: but before sun-set I was in the utmost surprise to see myself arrested on the part of the king, and thrown into a dark dungeon, where I spent the night.

Day-light had scarce begun to appear when I was carried before the king of Adal, whose fury was visible in his countenance. Perfidious wazir! said he to me, hast thou so soon forgotten the favours I have showered upon thee? What! without the least gratitude for the station which I have raised thee to, hast thou the cruelty to stab me in the tenderest part?—My lord, replied I, from the dust in which I grovelled, you took me, and placed me upon the throne of greatness; it is in your power to tumble me from it with a single blast of your breath: but give me leave to represent to you that I am entirely ignorant of the cause of your anger, and that the persons who accuse me to you are much less innocent than I am. —Ungrateful traitor! said the king, hast thou not killed my hawk?—I! my lord, replied I in a seeming amazement; is it possible that I should rob my master of that only instrument of his delight, by which I had the happiness to please him? No, no, my lord, if this is all the reason of your anger, I am certain it will quickly fall upon another head.—Ah, villain! cried the king with fury, pulling out the dead hawk from under his robe, dost thou add this audaciousness to thy former crime? There, behold thy handywork.—I was very much confounded at this sight. My lord, said I upon this, appearances are often false; but though I have nothing to upbraid myself with as to the death of your hawk, I beg you would tell me the name of my accuser.—Well, answered the king of Adal, I will grant thee this satisfaction too; it is Buzamghar, thy wife; darest thou object to such a witness?—A thunder-bolt could not have fallen more heavy than this news did upon me; at that moment I called to mind my father's last words, and the remembrance almost sunk me to the earth. Just Heaven! cried I, Buzamghar my accuser! does she betray me! Was ever anything so black, so odious? Ah! my lord, continued I, I could, if I pleased, retort the whole guilt upon her; but though I am innocent towards you, I will not defend myself; I respect your blood; I deserve death, if you have not the goodness to bethink you of the promises your Majesty has made me in the warmest moments of your friendship.—No, no, replied the king of Adal, the more I have loved you, the more unpardonable is your crime. Do not hope for any mercy, but prepare yourself to lose your head.—In short, madam, continued Sinadab, notwithstanding all I could say to move that prince's heart, he turned his back upon me, and left me in the hands of his guards to be delivered to the executioner.

For fifteen years that I had been wazir, having never done anybody the least wrong or injustice, all men of probity were grieved to see me condemned to die for so small a matter; they endeavoured in vain to obtain my pardon; the king was inexorable. My guards, who could not without tears behold my approaching death, offered to let me escape. No, said I to them, I thank you for your good will, but will not expose you to the king's displeasure for my safety. I am not guilty; I am able to justify myself when I see a fit time to do it.—The king commanded me to be beheaded, but to no purpose; the executioner absented himself from Adal that he might not do his office, and all those whom the king commissioned to do it refused; so that he was obliged to publish throughout the city, that whoever would accept the employment should have the other half of my estate, which he had not yet disposed of. Though this offer was very advantageous, nobody yet appeared to give me my

death, when Rumi, my adopted son, went to Buzamghar. Madam, said he, without concerning myself
whether Sinadab is guilty or no, his head is devoted to
death, and I am in pain for him while he languishes in
this manner by everybody's refusing to despatch him.
Of his immense riches the one half is your's, as revealer
of his crime; so that I am the only sufferer, since the
king promises the other half to the man that shall execute
Sinadab. I will offer myself to the king to do this service.
I believe he, and Sinabad himself, will take it kindly at
my hands; and I shall put an end to the course of a life
which is certainly hateful to him, and get for myself the
wealth which ought not by right to fall in the possession
of strangers.

Buzamghar, who it is likely had conceived a violent
passion for the wazir Giami, from the description which
I myself perhaps had given her of him, namely, that he
was the handsomest man in all Adal, knew she could not
marry him while I was alive; this was what made her
so basely betray me. She approved the infamous resolution that Rumi had taken, carried him to the king, and
coloured over the action so artfully, that the prince,
who thirsted for my blood, brought himself into my
prison, and took a barbarous delight in shewing me my
executioner. I remained motionless at the sight of
Rumi. In vain with tears in my eyes, I upbraided him
with his ingratitude; he had the hardness of heart to tie
my hands, and would fain have persuaded me that I was
obliged to him for his offering himself to despatch me.
The king was present all the while at so mournful a sight,
without being in the least concerned at it: my tears
were not able to move him, and finding him inflexible:
O Sazan, Sazan! cried I, why did not I follow your
advice? These words which he imagined had no sense
im them, made him believe that the fear of death had put
me beside my wits. What do you mean by these words,

O Sazan, Sazan? said he, unfold this riddle to me.—My lord, replied I, they reproach me for disobeying my father, whose name was Sazan, in the only three things he recommended to me upon his death-bed; I must endure the punishment without murmuring. I have devoted myself to your Majesty's service without thoroughly knowing you; I have revealed a secret to my wife; and I have fostered in my breast a viper, which is now about to sting me to death. Notwithstanding all your promises, you deliver me up to punishment for the death of an hawk, which I am innocent of; Buzamghar, forgetting the inexpressible tenderness I have had for her these fifteen years, betrays me in the most perfidious manner; and Rumi, this boy, whom I have looked upon as my own son, seduced by sordid interest, offers himself to be my executioner. O Sazan, Sazan! once more why did I not take your advice? The king and all his spectators grew stiff with horror at this relation, when I turned my-self to Rumi. Strike, unworthy Rumi, strike, cried I; do not lengthen out the pain of the unhappy but innocent Sinadab, every moment of whose life ought to cover thee with shame and confusion.

Rumi, without being at all concerned at anything I could say to him, drew his sword, and prepared to cut off my head. Rumi, like an unnatural child, was just going to give the fatal blow, continued Sinadab, when the friend whom I had entrusted with the key of my garden, entered the prison with the king's hawk on his fist. My lord, said he, catching hold of Rumi's arm, which was not above two fingers'-breadth from my neck, behold the falsity of the accusation formed against Sinadab, and be convinced that this is your own hawk, by the mark you yourself placed upon one of its feet. The king of Adal was strangely surprised at the sight of the bird. The greatest confusion imaginable presently covered his face; he bent his eyes upon the earth, and fell into the pro-

foundest thoughtfulness at what had happened. For my
part, added Sinabad, however lucky my friend's arrival
was for me, I was almost sorry for it. Life was become
odious to me by reason of my wife's treachery, and the
ingratitude of my adopted son. However, I threw myself at the king's feet: My lord, said I, lo! this miserable
favourite, whom you had so often assured of eternal protection, was upon the point of losing his life unjustly.
Upon this he raised me from the ground, and ordered me
to explain the whole mystery to him; I did it in few
words: he examined all the circumstances of what I
told him, and perceiving his own fault and Buzamghar's
baseness of soul, he immediately sent to seize her, had
her brought before him, and having caused her to be tied
back to back with Rumi, he commanded me to cut off
their heads with the same sabre that had been designed
to cut off mine. I refused to dip my hand in the blood
that had been so dear to me: I even begged mercy for
those two vile wretches; but I could not obtain it; one
of the king's guards severed their heads from their
shoulders.

The king, contented with this execution, which I
could not see without shedding tears in abundance,
embraced me tenderly, and carried me back with him to
the palace. My lord, said I to him again, was I deceived
when formerly I represented to you, that they who rely
upon the favour of the great, build upon the sand; since the
death of a vile creature, which you thought me the author
of, could make you forget in a moment a friendship of
fifteen years ?—Forget this fault, wazir, said the king of
Adal; I am ashamed of myself, and will make you ample
amends; I will raise you to such a pitch of glory, that
there shall for the future be no danger of your falling.—
No, my lord, answered I respectfully, give me leave to
return to Suez, there to enjoy a quiet and peaceful life:
this is the only favour that Sinadab now desires from you.

The king strongly opposed this resolution, but I remained unshaken : nothing could persuade me to stay with him, and I set sail eight days afterwards in a ship which he gave me, and which I loaded with all my riches and furniture, and a great many jewels with which he presented me at my departure. This separation occasioned me some regret ; but at length I steered towards Egypt, and we were almost in sight of port, when a dreadful tempest, after having tossed us about for three days and three nights together, swallowed up my ship at some leagues' distance from Suez. All the mariners perished : I was the only man that by help of a plank was saved from the shipwreck, and got safe to shore; but I had lost all my effects, and saw myself in a moment reduced to the lowest degree of misery and want.

Not knowing where to lay my head, I called to mind my father's will : I remembered that I was still master of a little garden and summer-house without the gates of Suez. I was curious to know if any body had taken possession of it in my absence : I had been gone away above sixteen years. I found it in the same condition wherein I had left it, only that it seemed very much out of repair; I opened the door by means of a secret which my father had often shewn me, and which nobody else was acquainted with : I found the walls all overgrown with moss, and the room very much in disorder ; and as it was pretty late, and I extremely fatigued, I lay down upon an old rotten mat, where I slept till hunger waked me. I was master of no trade to get a livelihood by. Being unwilling to make myself known, I resolved to ask alms from door to door ; for this purpose I went out of the garden ; but I implored in vain the charity of the inhabitants of Suez ; nobody assisted me in the present want I was reduced to; so that at night I returned to my little house, very hungry and weary with walking about all day. I sat down upon an old joint-stool that stood in a corner of the summer-house, and revolved in my mind all that my father had commanded me at his death, and which I had given so little heed to, when I cast my eyes upon a small coffer, almost rotten, which I had not yet seen: it was fast locked; I very hastily broke it open, thinking to find in it some money that my father might have put there; but I was very much surprised when I saw nothing in it but a rope about the bigness of one's little finger, and a note in my father's own hand-writing, in these words: "You have not kept your word with me, Sinadab, though you swore upon the Koran to do so. Your ill management and disobedience have brought you to this condition; but if you have resolution to follow this last counsel, you will find an end of your misfortunes in this coffer." Yes, cried I with fury, yes, father, I will for this one time obey you; neither indeed have I now any thing further to hope for, but to finish my unhappy days by this rope. Then, taking a desperate resolution, I got upon a joint-stool, and after having tied the rope into a slip knot, I fastened it to a sort of hook, which stuck in the ceiling of the summer-house, and which seemed to have been placed there for that very purpose; I put the noose about my neck, and kicking away the stool, abandoned myself without reluctance to the rigour of my destiny.

By this means, madam, I expected to have found a certain death, when the weight of my body pulling down the hook, brought along with it a sort of trap-door, through which fell so great a number of pieces of gold, that I was covered with them. This happy discovery soon made me forget what little hurt I had received from my fall: I presently raised myself, climbed up through the trap-door, and was in an inexpressible amazement at finding there an immense quantity of riches, as well in gold as in diamonds. I thought I should have died with joy at this sight, which at once put an end to all my misfortunes. I took one of the pieces of gold, and having fast locked the garden door, went and provided myself with a good meal. Next day I distributed among the poor darwayshes a thousand pieces of gold, and having put myself in a condition to appear with honour in the city, I repurchased almost all my father's possessions; and that I may never forget the misfortunes into which I fell by my disobedience, I caused to be repeated to me at all meals the words you have just now heard, concerning the submission and respect due from children to their parents. It is almost five years, madam, continued Sinadab, since I returned to Suez; during all that time I have done my utmost endeavours to live like a man of virtue and of honour; my misfortunes have made me wise and frugal, and I spend my life agreeably with the beautiful Rukia, whom you saw immediately after dinner: of all my women she is the one in whom I have found most merit. She is of Surat; and having two sisters there whom she loves tenderly, and who are in narrow circumstances, I am going at her request to look them out, that I may carry them with me to Suez, where I mean to settle them.

When Sinadab, my lord, continued Ibn Aridun, had done speaking, prince Sharif al-Din let him know how glad he was to see him thus happy after the multitude of crosses he had gone through; and as the winds were very favourable, the ship was not long before it arrived at Surat. The prince, still in his woman's dress, there took his leave of Sinadab and of the charming Rukia, returning them a million of thanks for the civilities he had received from them, and after having rested himself for some time he took the way to China.

*   *   *   *

This story has afforded me extraordinary delight, interrupted the king of Astrakhan, addressing himself to Ibn Aridun; I am wonderfully pleased with you, and I order Mutamhid to give you an hundred pieces of gold for

every day that you contribute to relax my mind; but I am
no less impatient now to know the fate of Gul-hindi and
Sharif al-Din, than I have been these few days past to hear
the sequel of Sinadab's adventures; since we have still
some little time remaining, continue your history. Ibn
Aridun, charmed with being so happy as to please his
prince, went on thus:

CONTINUATION OF THE HISTORY OF SHARIF AL-DIN AND OF GUL-HINDI

SHARIF AL-DIN, my lord, still in a woman's habit, had
travelled but a few days before he came to a delightful
meadow.   Arabia the Blest does not produce such
variety of riches and grateful odours as nature displayed
in this place.   The earth was covered with a soft grass
which seemed as if it never withered: neither the heats
of summer, nor the nipping blasts of winter ever faded
the roses, jasmines, and violets, with which the country
was adorned; and those flowers which charmed the eye
by the diversity of their colours, did at the same time
gratify the senses by the exquisite odour with which they
embalmed the air.   At the bottom of this meadow rose a
kind of rock, in the form of a grotto, from the middle
of which there ran a spring into a great basin of
rustic marble. This water was so clear and beautiful,
that by its enticing murmur it invited the beholders to
rest themselves on its sides, which were decked with a
green turf; and a large tree, which grew close by it,
stretched out its boughs, so thick of leaves that its shade
was impenetrable to the rays of the hottest sun.
Here the prince endeavoured to enjoy for some moments
the sweets of sleep, which the solitude and freshness of
the place seemed to offer him. He tied his horse to a

shrub, and extended himself upon the grass; but he was scarce fallen into a gentle slumber, when a frightful giant who had but one eye, and who lived near that charming place, whither he was sometimes used to resort to refresh himself, came thither. He was deceived by the dress of the young prince, whom he mistook for a woman of the most ravishing beauty; he became passionately enamoured of him, and prepared to carry him off; he had already untied his sabre and thrown it at some distance from him, and was just about to execute his design, when an arrow, which seemed to be shot by an invisible hand, flew directly into his eye, and put it out, by this means disabling him from satisfying his brutish passion. The prince was soon wakened by the bellowing the giant made at his wound; and looking about for his deliverer, he spied a young man so like himself, that he was at first in doubt if it were not his own shadow.

The stranger and the fictitious princess of Tuluphan admired one another for some time without speaking; but at length the last, breaking silence: I am indebted to you, sir, for the preservation of my honour and of my life, said he to him; I beg you would tell me to whom it is I owe an obligation which will be eternally present to my memory. The stranger for some time hesitated answering the prince, whom he thought a woman: but prevailed upon by a secret motive which he could not resist: To any other but you, madam, said he, I call myself Mobarak, son of a merchant at Ispahan, and I have left Persia out of a curiosity to travel; but a certain impulse, the cause of which I am ignorant, forces me not to dissemble with you, and to confess that I am the prince of Ormuz. I was flying from my father's court to avoid a match I am extremely averse to, when passing by this place, I saw you come to the side of this spring. The parity of features there is between us, made me desirous to learn whom you are; and I was just going to accost you with that design, when I saw you, very much fatigued, endeavour to take some little repose, which I was unwilling to disturb, and which you might still have enjoyed, had it not been for the insolence of that monster whom I have deprived of light. But, madam, continued he, permit me to tell you, that though the duty of a prince obliges me to give assistance to persons of your sex, yet there was something more which animated me when I undertook your defence. Forgive this rash confession, madam, nor let this declaration offend your modesty. An invisible obstacle opposes the felicity I might hope for in obtaining your love. I therefore only beg your friendship; but, madam, I beg it with all the earnestness imaginable, and shall love you with so much purity, that your virtue shall not have the least cause to be uneasy at it.

The feigned princess of Tuluphan was so surprised when the stranger informed him that he was the son of the king of Ormuz that a flush diffused itself all over his face. In this moment he made a thousand dreadful reflections upon what Riza had told him of that prince, and upon the impossibility there was in the execution of the will of the king of the jinnis; but these reflections being all destroyed at the sight of so charming a prince, for whom, in spite of himself, he already felt the most perfect esteem, he was just upon the point of discovering himself to him, when calling to mind the misfortunes which Marou had threatened him with, he resolved to be silent only upon the subject of his sex, but to have in every thing else the same confidence for the prince of Persia, as he had had for him. My lord, said he to him, your actions are so respectful, and I am so much obliged to you, that I cannot be offended at the declaration you have made to me. You desire only my friendship, which is due to you without the least reserve. As for me, hunting was my only diversion, till some particular reasons, which I cannot reveal without exposing myself to the greatest miseries, made me leave my father's court. But though I had resolved to conceal my name from the whole world, by disguising myself under that of an Amir of Samarcand, I cannot help thinking it almost my duty to let you know, my lord, that I am the only daughter of the king of Tuluphan, and that my name is Gul-hindi. —Just heaven! cried the feigned prince, interrupting her, are you then that lovely Gul-hindi, whose beauty fame has published throughout the whole East? It is upon your account, madam, that I quit my father's court and betake myself to flight, for reasons which incessantly torment me; and it is you whom I now have met with! Ah! my princess, continued he, his eyes drowned in tears, and despair painted upon his face, why are we not born for one another? O ye sovereign arbiters of all things! You who see the bottom of my heart, what have I done to be thus tortured? And thou, perfidious love, why dost thou kindle in me so sharp a flame, when thou knowest how impossible it is that it should ever be quenched? Yes, my princess, I adore you, but I shall be obliged to fly from you. My father has lately sent ambassadors to king Mochzadin to demand you in marriage for me. The ancient friendship there is between these two monarchs inclines me to believe that the king of Tuluphan will not give a denial to the king of Ormuz. But, adorable Gul-hindi, I repeat it once more, let what will happen, and though the whole universe and our great Prophet himself should favour us, I can never be united to you, though I would spend the last drop of my blood to be in a condition to enjoy that happiness.

Prince, replied the pretended Gul-hindi, whom these words threw into an extreme amazement, I cannot penetrate the reasons that make you talk thus; but what perhaps would offend any other than myself, is the very thing that gives me a greater esteem for you.

Be informed that I have no less cause than you to avoid
the marriage that is preparing for me; and that what I
have just now heard will detain me for ever from my
father's court.—Well then, fair princess, cried the disguised prince, let us fly together, and conceal under
borrowed names from all the earth a prince and princess,
whose loss I am sure will cost the kings of Tuluphan and
of Ormuz abundance of tears. But, madam, continued he,
since fate has been so cruel as to order it so that I can
never be your's, I attest our great Prophet that I will
never be another's. I will love you with all the purity
imaginable, without the least hope, and I will never
have any other object of my desires and of my glory,
than the charming Gul-hindi. How happy should I be
if your sentiments were so conformable with mine, as
that nothing but death should ever dissolve so complete
an union! But I know not what I say : Pardon,
madam, these indiscreet transports. What! because I
cannot possess you, must I rob a prince, more happy than
myself, of the masterpiece of nature ?—Yes, my lord, replied the pretended Gul-hindi blushing, I permit you to
believe that what you propose is agreeable to me. Since
the stars oppose our union, I will never engage my heart
to any but the Prince of Ormuz. Let us at least be
joined by an inviolable friendship, though love has
undertaken, through a barbarous caprice, to keep us
asunder.

In short, my lord, proceeded Ibn Aridun, these two
lovers, miserable at not being acquainted with each other's
condition, but happy in the sympathy there was between
them and in the reciprocal tenderness with which Geoncha
had inspired them ; these two lovers, I say, after a conversation extremely passionate, vowed to each other a
friendship which should be proof against any thing that
could happen ; and after having remounted their steeds,
they left that charming meadow in company together.

They had travelled several days without meeting with any thing particular, when they perceived at the entrance of a forest of palm-trees a palace of an antique structure, but which seemed nevertheless magnificent in its simplicity. At the gate of the palace stood a venerable old man, who accosted them. My children, said he to them, with the greatest kindness, night draws on, there is neither town nor village in above six leagues hereabouts, nor any house where you can pass the night; if you will come into this palace you may repose yourselves in tranquility, and pursue your journey to-morrow. The prince and princess, charmed with the humanity of their host, accepted his offer. They entered into the palace, where they found a woman about threescore years old, and of a simplicity equal to that of her husband. She strove to receive them in the best manner she was able, and soon afterwards there was brought in a very handsome repast, but without prodigality, though there was far from being a want of any thing. Towards the conclusion of the supper, the old man sent the slaves that waited at table out of the room, and having desired his guests to tell him the motive of their journey, and for what reason they travelled in a track that was so far from the common road, Sharif al-Din took upon him to answer. Alas! sir, said he to the old man, I can give you that satisfaction in a few words. We are brother and sister, and are flying from Samarcand to avoid the persecution of a wazir, who, not satisfied with having cruelly put our father to death, and possessed himself of all his substance, pursues our lives with the same barbarity.—Ill men are very much to be dreaded, replied the old man, for sooner or later they perish miserably. I have had a melancholy experience of this truth in my own family; and it is but a few years since I have recovered the quiet of which two of my sons had robbed me by their crimes.—Gul-hindi was very much moved at the sight of the tears which a tender remembrance drew from the eyes of the good old man. Our grief is sometimes alleviated by telling the cause of it, said she to him; and if it is not too great a favour, we should be willing, sir, to hear the relation of your misfortunes.—With all my heart, my dear children, replied the old man. The tears you saw me shed were not altogether tears of sorrow; they rather express the joy I now feel in seeing all those misfortunes at an end. Listen to me therefore with attention:

TALE OF BADUR THE PEACEFUL, KING OF CAOR

I was born the sovereign of Caor, a kingdom not very extensive, and my ambition never prompted me to enlarge it, being more desirous to live in unity with my neighbours, than to run the hazard of destruction, by undertaking unjust wars; for which reason I was called Badur the Peaceful. In my youth, I wedded the Princess of Zarad, whom you here behold. She brought me several children, and among the rest a son and daughter, both born the same day. I named my son Abu Zaid, and my daughter Dijara: I mention these two first, though they were not my eldest, nay, were born to me even at the time when Zarad had no further hopes of being any more a mother; but because these have happily made amends for all the bitterness with which their brothers had dashed the tranquility of my life. Of my other two sons, one was called Salak the Violent, because of the excesses he daily ran into. I cannot imagine from whom he derived that humour. In all probability Allah sent him to us, together with his brother, to make a trial of our virtue. The other was named Azim; his manners were

not very different from those of Salak; and their joint
inclination for evil united them so to each other, that
they were never asunder. I every day received some
fresh complaint of their ill behaviour; and if they had
been private persons, I should a thousand times have
made them an example to my people, to whom they
were become odious by their crimes. But the tenderness
of a father stayed my hand. At length they grew so
weary of my continual remonstrances, that they both
resolved to be gone from my court; and I blessed the
hour wherein they executed that design.

They had been gone above four months, and I
began to think myself happy in being freed from their
presence, when I was struck by the most cruel blow
that it is possible for a father to feel. Guhullaru, the
princess of Nangan, was lately married to Rusang-jahun.
That prince was not young; but his agreeable com-
plaisant temper made amends for the merit which age
had deprived him of; and he lived with his wife in so
perfect an union, that he was an example to all his subjects. Salak and his brother passed through the
dominions of this monarch; they were received with a
great deal of distinction. Rusang-jahun even lodged
them in his own palace for several days; but his imprudence, in suffering them too often to see the beautiful
Guhullaru, cost him his life. Salak became excessively
enamoured of that princess. He was too well acquainted with her virtue to hope that she would ever
reward his unlawful ardour : but being very little accustomed to overcome his passions, he resolved to gratify
them at any cost; and to effect this, he hatched the
blackest design that can be imagined, and prevailed
upon his brother Azim to lend him a helping hand in
the execution of it.

One evening as they were walking with the king of
Nangan and his spouse in a wood which was at the end

of the gardens of the palace, they suddenly fell upon that
prince, who had only a little sabre by his side: and
their fury not giving him time to put himself in a posture
of defence, they stabbed him twenty times with their
daggers; and either out of contempt or cruelty, left the
odious instruments of their guilt sticking in the bloody
corpse of that unfortunate king.

Guhullaru uttered such cries as reached even to
heaven; but those barbarians seized her, and having got
out into the open fields by a door which they had secured,
by means of the eunuch who guarded it, and whom they
had corrupted, they used all their endeavours to set her
upon one of their horses, which they had before prepared, when about twenty soldiers of the king's guard,
alarmed by Guhullaru's outcries, came to the place.
This unexpected assistance struck terror into Salak and
Azim; they were forced to abandon the queen, and to betake themselves to flight. They were pursued, but in
vain; they were well mounted, and made their escape,
carrying with them the eunuch who had favoured them
in the execution of their infamous design.

It is impossible to express the affliction of Guhullaru; her complaints pierced the very skies. She
caused the bloody corpse of her husband to be carried
away, and instead of observing all the funeral ceremonies, she only embalmed it with her own hands, and
had it put into a coffin of gold, which she adorned with
the most precious of her jewels. She likewise deposited
in the coffin his bloody shirt, and the daggers with which
he was assassinated; and afterwards took a solemn
oath to revenge her husband's death, not only upon
the murderers, but upon all their families. She afterwards set out incognita, with prince Kiahia, her brother,
and twelve slaves, all resolved to sacrifice themselves for
her service.

My sons did not expect a fury like this; without

the least remorse for what they had done, they minded
nothing but flying away from a country which they knew
was filled with aversion against them; but they did not
carry their crime very far. At some days' journey from the
place where they had committed it, Salak's horse fell, and
broke his rider's leg; and his brother Azim, being gone to
the next town to get some speedy succour for him, that
wretch was carried into a neighouring house. Guhullaru, who, without losing a moment's time, pursued
the murderers as it were by the scent, came by chance
to that very house. She knew nothing of Salak being so
near her: but after having made a slight repast, looking
into the coffin of gold according to her custom, to renew
her cruel vow, she was in the utmost surprise to see
several drops of blood issue from her husband's body.
Just heaven! cried the princess, the murderers must be
somewhere in this place. Then rising from the table
like a mad woman, she took in each hand one of the
daggers, with which Ruzang-jahun had been stabbed;
and having searched most part of the house with her
brother and the twelve slaves, she came at last into the
chamber where Salak was reposing himself. The sight
of him transported her with rage. Traitor! cried she,
it is full time thou wert punished for the execrable crime
thou hast committed upon my husband; the slowest and
most violent torments were too little for such a villain as
thou art; but my revenge could not be entirely satisfied
if I deferred it a moment, or committed the care of it to
any other but myself. Then, without giving him time
to make any answer to these reproaches, which were but
too just, she plunged her dagger into his heart a thousand times; and after having caused his head to be cut
off, and exposed his body to the vultures, she went out
of the house, leaving the master of it terrified at her
cruelty. As she was informed by him that my other son
had gone to the next town, and that upon his not coming

so soon as was expected, the impatient Salak had sent a slave whom he had to fetch him; she took the road by which they were to come, and having met with them in a little wood, where they must necessarily be obliged to pass, she gave the unfortunate Azim the same treatment as she had given his brother, and put to death the traitorous eunuch, accomplice of their crime, by the most exquisite torments. I was as much surprised as disturbed at hearing these sorrowful news; whatever tenderness I had for my children, I could not blame Guhullaru's revenge; but I almost died with grief at the sight of their bloody heads, which she sent me in a box, with a letter full of threats to destroy me in the same manner, with the rest of my family.

Abu Zaid, the only son that was left me, was as much concerned as myself at the death of his brothers. My lord, said he to me, the enemy we have to deal with is an irritated woman, who will attack us by craft and subtlety; give me leave to take care of your life and that of the queen, and let me endeavour to defend you from a danger which makes me tremble both for you and for her. My grief was so excessive, continued Badur, that it deprived me of the use of my senses. Do whatever you think proper, said I, my dear Abu Zaid; for my part I will retire into the recesses of my palace, there to bemoan incessantly the ill actions of your brothers, and to pray Allah to forget them. I afterwards doubled my guard, and shut myself up in the innermost parts of my palace with the queen my spouse, accompanied only by three or four of the principal men of my court, who would not leave me in my affliction.

My son, after having prepared every thing that was necessary for the journey he meditated, accosted the princess Dijara: My dear sister, said he to her, you are not ignorant to what a pitch the fury of Guhullaru is raised. Our life is not in safety here; let us go together to seek for the means of preserving the king and queen from her cruel menaces. The famous jinni Geoncha, protector of the unfortunate, dwells in a magnificent palace which is at the foot of the famous mountain, Jabal-Assumum[1]: I have taken a resolution, while my father is shut up in his palace, to go and implore the succour of that king of the jinnis. Let us set forward, therefore, my dear Dijara, and under habits that may disguise our quality, let us try to obtain a remedy for the evils which our unhappy brothers have brought upon our heads.

Abu Zaid and Dijara, before they departed, embraced us tenderly. After above a month's travelling, they arrived in a vast champaign country, interspersed with a great number of little streams: as the heat was very excessive, and as they perceived, at some distance, a wood of a pretty large extent, they made to it, and reposed themselves there in the cool shade, with two slaves, who were all the train they had with them; when they heard a frightful noise, as of a great rock tumbling from the top of a high hill. They looked all round them to see what it was which occasioned this noise; but when they had advanced further into the wood, they found that it proceeded from a sort of cistern, covered with a small stone, and sealed at each corner with a seal, whereon was stamped the name of the great Sulayman. Immediately the horrible noise, which at first amazed them, began to to diminish; and was succeeded by the following complaints: Perfidious Zalulu! Traitorous jinni! Dost thou thus abuse the seal of Sulayman to detain me a prisoner in this place? and must the unfortunate Geoncha be for ever enclosed in the bowels of the earth, without having deserved so hard a fate?

At the name of Geoncha my children leapt for joy.

---

1 That is, the poisonous mountain, because the earth of it inspires melancholy into those who smell it.

King of the jinnis, cried out Abu Zaid, here is a prince who would succour you at the expense of his life, let me but know how it is to be done.—All thou hast to do, said the imprisoned jinni, is to get up this stone, by taking away with as much care as possible, the print of the seal of the great Sulayman. Abu Zaid, transported with joy, took off the seal without breaking it, as the jinni had expressly ordered him. A thick smoke in a moment rose up to the clouds, and extending itself over the cistern, made so dark a fog, that the prince and princess could not see one another. The darkness, which all of a sudden covered the wood, very much frightened the prince and princess; but the fog soon afterwards re-united into a solid body, out of which was formed the jinni.

Abu Zaid and Dijara immediately threw themselves at Geoncha's feet. We were going even to seek you in your palace, said the prince my son; I hoped, O powerful king of the jinnis! that without being subject to the fatal effects of the mountain Jabal-Assumum, the gate would have been open to me by virtue of the secret words, which I formerly learnt of the Yogi Kachokao,[1] and without which all who have the boldness to come near it are sure to fall into a distemper more terrible than death itself.—I praise God, interrupted the jinni, for having brought you to this place, to restore me the liberty which the perfidious Zalulu had for these twelve years past deprived me of, by the blackest piece of malice that ever was known : but I will not be un-grateful for the inestimable service you have done me.

That wicked jinni, continued Geoncha, to be re-venged upon me for destroying, as I have so often done, the

---

1 The Yogis, or Jogis, among the Hindus, are like pilgrims or vagrant monks, who generally frequent the desert and solitude. They live upon alms, and are in great reputation for sanctity, because they spend several days together in very austere abstinence; some-times without eating and drinking.

unjust projects he forms against young princes and princesses, whom he persecutes for nothing but his cruel
diversion, carried on his design in this manner. As he
knows that his power is very much inferior to mine, he,
by some subtle trick or other, stole from the good king
Zif the ring of the mighty Sulayman, which that prince
used for the benefit of mankind ; and, being master of
this treasure, he came to me, asked my pardon for all the
uneasiness he had given to the persons I protected, and
begged me to grant him my friendship, with protestations
so sincere in appearance, that I could not tell how to refuse it him.

After our reconciliation, we took a walk together in
this wood; when, having insensibly drawn me towards
this place, he sat him down upon the side of this cistern ;
then the traitor, who designed nothing but to circumvent
me, having desired to see a carcanet of diamonds which I
wore round my neck, let it fall into the cistern, as he
was pretending to return it to me. I immediately threw
myself into the cistern to fetch out my carcanet : this
was what the wretch wanted. He took advantage of this
moment, covered the cistern with that stone, and fastened
it with the seal of the great Sulayman. I leave you to
judge how much I was astonished at this stratagem, continued Geoncha ; the useless efforts I made to get out of
my prison convinced me that there was but one power so
superior as to be strong enough to detain me ; and this
place is so much out of the way, that I supposed I
should have stayed here for several ages. But since I am
obliged to you for so unlooked-for a freedom, you may
assure yourself, prince, that my gratitude shall have no
bounds.

The jinni, continued Badur, having given my son
to understand that he was not ignorant of the cause of
his journey, offered him the assistance he wished for.
The death of your brothers was just, said he, and

Guhullaru ought indeed to have sacrificed no less than those murderers to the manes of her husband; but I will moderate the sharp resentment she is actuated by, and from this moment you need no longer be apprehensive of that princess's fury. Then, having replaced the stone upon the mouth of the cistern, he again fixed upon it the print of Sulayman's seal, that Zalulu might not be sensible of his being at liberty: and having by his power formed in it a noise like that which he made there in the time of his restraint, he embraced the prince and princess, and conveying them through the air with extreme rapidity, set them down in a charming meadow which was on the frontiers of my dominions. I will not leave you, said he to them, until I have made you happy; but as I must hide myself from the traitor Zalulu, in order to get from him the ring of Sulayman, I will not appear to you in my proper shape. I will contract myself into so small a bulk that the beautiful Dijara shall be able to carry me easily by her side, and you need only wish that I should resume my former shape, and obey your orders, and it will be done that moment. Then the jinni having dissipated himself into smoke, the princess, my daughter, found at her feet a golden box, which hung from a chain of the same metal. She immediately opened it, and was in the utmost surprise to see in it, through a crystal, several springs, which performed all the internal functions of the human body: she tied it to her side.

The jinni, continued Badur, had given my children magnificent clothes, and had ordered them to conceal their quality no longer. They had already passed through some towns in my kingdom, when one evening being come to a sort of village, where the approaching night obliged them to stop, they knocked at the door of the house which had the best appearance there. They were very well received by the master of it: but just as they were entering into the chamber that was prepared for them, three Chinese travellers would have taken possession of it for a lady, who was at the gate in a palanquin. My son had no sooner discovered himself to be the prince of Caor, than the three men yielded him the place, went out of the house, and carried the lady to another lodging. My children, after a slight supper, went to bed; and sleep reigned profoundly in their chamber, when the very same Chinese travellers, the princess Guhullaru, who was the lady in the palanquin, her brother, and all her servants, came to the door of the house, where Abu Zaid and Dijara were buried in repose. She had been transported with joy when she heard they were so near her; but being willing to stay till they were asleep, it was not till she judged they were so that she knocked at the door of the house where they were. The master of the house had no sooner opened the door to them, than he found a dagger at his throat, with menaces of stabbing him that moment if he made the least noise. We have no design, said Guhullaru to him, upon any but two perfidious wretches who are lodged in your house, and who give themselves out to be the children of the king of Caor; deliver them up to our revenge, or thou diest this instant. The host, terribly frightened, was forced to shew them the chamber of Abu Zaid and Dijara, deploring in his heart the miserable fate he saw they were going to endure.

The queen of Nangan, pursued Badur, as she has since confessed to me, made terrible reflections at that moment. She was filled with remorse against the injustice of the action she was committing. But forget that thou art a woman, said she to herself: or at least, remember thou art an offended women. Then, having given one of her daggers to Kiahia, and armed herself with the other, they entered into my children's apartment; and, though with a trembling hand, they were just going to execute their cruel resolution, yet, when each of them cast their eyes upon the persons they were to destroy, they found their arms held back by a superior power. Never was Guhullaru so struck, as when she considered the regularity of Abu Zaid's features; and the charms of the princess of Caor so dazzled the eyes of Kiahia, who was going to pierce her heart, that the dagger fell out of his hand. Guhullaru was somewhat longer before she yielded, but the jinni Geoncha, who was watchful for the preservation of my children, having entirely touched the heart of the queen of Nangan, she waked the prince my son. Return thanks, said she, to the secret power that disarms me; the desire of revenge has quite vanished away from me; and I find my heart relent in the very moment when I least looked for such a change. Then turning to her brother: As for you, said she, my dear Kiahia, I am sensible that the extreme beauty of the princess has made a strong impression upon your soul. How glad I am to find this happy sympathy between us! I should have died with grief if you had executed one part of our unjust resolve; and I begin to feel that I was pushing my cruelty too far. The real criminals are punished; the death of my husband is sufficiently revenged.

Dijara awaked at this moment; she was frightened at seeing so many people in her chamber. Powerful king of the jinnis, cried she, come speedily to our assistance! She had no sooner pronounced these words than the gold box opened of itself; the chamber was filled with obscurity, which dissipating by degrees, exposed to sight the formidable Geoncha. This sudden aid struck terror into Guhullaru and Kiahia; they began to be afraid for their own lives, when the jinni encouraged them with extraordinary kindness. Forget, madam, said Geoncha to Guhullaru, forget the death of a husband whom you have sufficiently revenged. Let Abu Zaid and Dijara be the bonds of an eternal peace between your families, and let the field of battle be turned into the nuptial bed.

Guhullaru was at first so surprised at the sight of the redoubtable jinni that she scarce heard what he said to her; but Abu Zaid, who was that instant struck with the splendour of her charms, throwing himself at her feet: Suffer your heart to be touched, madam, said he to her, with a submissive air: I shall esteem myself the happiest of mortals, if my cares, my respect, and the most tender love, can one day prevail upon you to give me the place of a prince, whom you have indeed the greatest reason to bewail.

Guhullaru now began to be moved, continued Badur; she lifted up Abu Zaid; and Dijara, persuaded by the passionate expressions of Kiahia, gave him to understand that she would not oppose me, if I consented to this marriage. The jinni having then commanded the four new lovers and all their attendants to take hold of his mantle, he transported them in a moment into my palace, where, at length, after the Queen of Nangan had set apart some time for the decency of her widowhood, she married Abu Zaid, and the same day, Kiahia became the husband of the princess my daughter. This double marriage restored my heart to its former tranquility; and it gave me so much joy to see my family again settled in peace, that for fear my repose should again be disturbed by some new accident, I resolved with the queen my spouse to retire into this rural palace, built by the potent Geoncha. And here, free from the troubles of grandeur, and under the protection of that king of the jinnis, who has gone to an invisible island to wait for a fair opportunity of revenging himself upon the traitor Zalulu, the queen and I enjoy a quiet and peaceable state of life.

SEQUEL OF THE HISTORY OF SHARIF AL-DIN AND OF GUL-HINDI

THE night was pretty far advanced, continued Ibn Aridun: Therefore, Badur, after having concluded his history, perceiving that his guests stood in need of repose, conducted each of them to a separate apartment. That which he assigned to the real Gul-hindi was furnished with the utmost politeness, and adorned with pictures drawn by a Hindu, equal in skill to the famous Mani. That Hindu was so excellent in his art, and in the disposing of his colours and shades, that he could have expressed with his pencil the breath itself, and the respiration of animated creatures. There was described, in one of these pictures, a triumphal car all in flames, upon which stood a child supporting a sphere on his head, and his face surrounded with rays, which reflected a great deal of majesty upon him; his hands were filled with fiery darts; he had a quiver on his shoulder, a sabre by his side: and he dragged along in a chain behind his car an infinite number of persons of all ages, sexes, and conditions; one might read in their faces and attitudes the expressions of the most lively passions. This celebrated painter had outdone himself in this work; and by some nice touches peculiar to himself, the winds that he had painted at the corners of the picture seemed to keep in their breath, for fear of increasing the flames which glowed throughout this master-piece.

Gul-hindi looked attentively upon this picture: she sighed and blushed at the same time. She cast her eyes upon another, at the bottom whereof she read these verses:

A lawless passion Koka's bosom warms,
And her incestuous heart her brother charms:
Her flame with virtuous horror Kyni views;
The more he flies, the swifter she pursues.

> No ray of hope to cheer her suit appears,
> And sorrow melts her into floods of tears.
> Vishnu with pity saw her ceaseless grief,
> And, kind to the unhappy, brought relief;
> Into a fountain he transformed the dame,
> Where guilty love extinguishes his flame.

Never was anything more beautiful or more striking than this painting : but notwithstanding all the masterstrokes with which it abounded, the princess turned away her eyes from it. She met with another which seemed more apposite to the condition she herself was in. It represented the history of Fork and Onam : she read their adventures with great attention, and oppressed with a thousand cruel reflections : Just heaven ! cried she, must everything that offers itself to my view conduce to nourish a passion whose consequences must inevitably prove fatal to me ? I love, but whom do I love ? A woman like myself ; and this very obstacle, as invincible as it is, redoubles my affections. Ah ! miserable princess, do not form such unlawful wishes ; love nothing but what a woman may love without a crime, since nature opposes thy unreasonable ardour. But, said she again immediately, may not the example of Fork, which is now before my eyes, alleviate the uneasiness I am in ? Why should I be inspired with so extravagant a passion, if it is not designed that a miracle shall be wrought in my favour ? Fork was a beautiful woman : the god Vishnu, whose assistance she implored, in a moment changed her to the most amiable of all mankind. Ah ! I rave, continued Gul-hindi, let me fly from this adorable object : that is the only remedy for my misfortunes. But wherefore fly ? interrupted she presently afterwards : what harm is there in loving the princess of Tuluphan ? No, no, let me not find out a crime where there can be none ; but let me maintain with honour the character I am at present forced to act. Gul-hindi spent almost the whole night in these reflections : and rising at daybreak, she

descended into the garden to walk off her inquietude.
She found a little door that opened into the forest: she
went into it, and her thoughtfulness insensibly drew her
into a place where the wood was very thick: she sat
herself down there, and, fatigued with having spent the
night in so restless a manner, fell into a gentle and re-
freshing slumber.

Sharif al-Din was agitated with the like thoughts;
the night seemed very tedious to him. Aurora had hardly
begun to appear, when jumping from off the bed, upon
which he had only lain him down, he took his bow and
his arrows, and passing out of the garden into the wood,
he followed, without knowing it, the same track which
Gul-hindi had taken before him; he was walking pretty
fast, when he heard a little noise in a private place. He
went nearer to it, and seeing the leaves stir, he imagined
it was some beast moving out of its hold, and thereupon
shot one of his arrows at random. What was the surprise of Sharif al-Din, continued Ibn Aridun, when he
heard a doleful cry, which proceeded from somebody
whose voice he was acquainted with! His heart was
seized with the sharpest grief; he ran with all his speed
to the place, and found that he had wounded the very
man who had rescued him from the giant. What horror
and despair was the prince seized with at the sight of his
deliverer all in blood! His eyes were covered with an
obscurity which hindered him from seeing what he had
done. Unhappy bow! cried he, unhappy dart! but
rather, unhappy Prince! die, and bear the punishment
of thy indiscretion! In pronouncing these last words,
my lord, Sharif al-Din was just going to stab himself
with one of his arrows, when he heard his friend groan.
He immediately quitted his design of dying, to try to
save a life which was so dear to him: he ran to embrace
him, melting into tears; and going to staunch the blood
which trickled from the wound he had given him in the

breast, he remained without motion, when he perceived that he had wounded a woman. He was ready to expire with sorrow at this discovery. O heavens! said he, his eyes overflowing with tears, must I obtain the knowledge of the most charming person in the world by so tragical an accident? But let me, if possible, repair my error. Then tearing the muslin of Gul-hindi's turband, he stopped the blood as well as he was able. He afterwards in vain endeavoured to find the soul of that princess upon those lips where the paleness of death was painted. She gave no sign of life: but as there was a stream which glided along at some distance from thence, he ran to it, and brought some water in the princess's turband, when he beheld her in the arms of a frightful man.

Sharif al-Din, at this sight, immediately drew his sabre and prepared to fight the monster, who grew larger and larger every moment; when he cried out to him in a terrible voice: Stop, young madman, unless thou thyself wouldst be the murderer of this princess, whose neck I will wring at the least motion thou makest.—Ah, barbarian! cried the prince, you know too well how to take advantage of my tender concern. Were it not for that, I would let out thy life, or perish gloriously in attempting to succour the divine person, whom thou deprivest me of with so much baseness.—I am above your threats, replied the ravisher; know that I am called Zalulu, and that I am one of the most powerful jinnis upon earth: I took delight at the moment of thy birth, and of that of this princess, to traverse your lives. I made an exchange of you two; I laid thee in the cradle of the princess of Tuluphan, and her in thine: you were to have been happy in each other's love, if you had attained the age of seventeen years without knowing one another for such as you really are. You have, unhappily for yourself, discovered this princess's sex before the time prescribed: this is what puts her into my power: and you must never hope to see her more.

while I am what I am.—Zalulu then carried away Gul-hindi, leaving the prince in a despair so violent, that he resolved not to survive his misfortune. He fiercely set the point of his sabre against his breast, and was just going to pierce his heart, when he found his arm suddenly stayed by an invisible hand.

Geoncha, who incessantly watched over the malignant actions of Zalulu, and hindered the consequences of them as much as lay in his power, thought it high time to assist the prince of Ormuz. He disarmed him, therefore, in the very moment that he was making an attempt upon his life, and offering himself to his sight in the shape of a majestic old man: Sharif al-Din, said he, moderate a little the violence of your passions, and follow the wholesome advice of a jinni who loves you. It was I who presided at your's and Gul-hindi's birth: it was I who in the resolution to unite you together. formed between you such charming ties, and inspired you with that sudden reciprocal tenderness. But as neither of you was able to avoid what is written upon the table of light, you must wait with patience for the moment that may restore you to your princess, and by a perfect submission to the Will of Heaven deserve the happy destiny which is perhaps prepared for you. The prince was very much consoled by these words. Powerful jinni, said he, throwing himself at Geoncha's feet, since I am obliged to submit without murmuring, at least inform me what will be done with me till the arrival of that happy moment.—Do you find in yourself. prince, replied the jinni, so much courage as to face death in rescue of your princess? That is the only way to abridge your misfortunes, or to perish gloriously for her sake.—Can it be doubted? answered Sharif al-Din; I am ready to sacrifice a thousand lives to obtain the adorable Gul-hindi, and the most cruel death is not sufficient to turn me from so noble a design.

-I admire your intrepidity, replied Geoncha : give me

your hand; you shall quickly be satisfied. The prince gave his hand to Geoncha: he struck the ground, and the earth opened. They both of them plunged into its most dreadful abysses: and at last found themselves in a cavern, the mouth of which looked into a champaign country, adorned with a thousand various flowers, which led, by a walk of palms, to a magnificent palace, into which they entered.

To effect the deliverance of your princess, said the jinni then to the prince Sharif al-Din, I must begin by re-covering the superiority which naturally I have over the malicious Zalulu. I can never bring that about but by artfully getting from him the seal of Sulayman, which that traitor has undoubtedly stolen from the good king Zif: and to do this, I have occasion for a prince like yourself, who will fearlessly expose himself to almost unavoidable death. What you are to do is this. There is in the island of Jilolo a spring, called the Fountain of Oblivion, unknown to all mortals. There are very few even of the sages and jinnis who can tell precisely where this Fountain is: and though some do know it, they are ignorant of the proper dose, which is the chief point, because the remedy is to be found in the very distemper, and according to the quantity that is drunk of it, it takes away, and restores memory. This water is guarded by a jinni named Nihorah, who without mercy strangles all those who come near it: but as he holds all his authority from me, he has not refused me some water from this Fountain. Here is a bottle of it, enough to answer my necessity for it. The difficulty lies in presenting it to the perfidious Zalulu: and not one of all the jinnis who depend upon me would accept the commission, so much do they dread the power of Sulayman's ring. Have you, prince, firmness enough to undertake so perilous an action? It may endanger your life and even that of your princess, if Zalulu should mistrust the deceit you intend to put upon him; but if you can by your cunning bring him to drink of the water of the Fountain of Oblivion, you will that very moment become possessor of the princess of Tuluphan.

Sharif al-Din, continued Ibn Aridun, accepted Geoncha's proposal without the least hesitation; and that jinni, having conducted him into a spacious hall, made him enter into a bath. The prince had not been half an hour in the water, before he perceived a change in his person which frightened him. He jumped immediately out of it, and covering himself precipitately with a very fine cloth: Ah! jinni, cried he, what is the meaning of this new metamorphosis? Geoncha fell a-laughing. What, said he to the prince, who was then changed into the most beautiful woman that was ever seen, and whose features were quite different from those he appeared in when he was a man, are you already sorry for the promises you have made; and does the sex I have given you, for some time only, incline you to renounce the charming Gul-hindi? Go, prince, execute punctually what I am about to prescribe to you, and I can soon restore you to your former condition. The jinni, my lord, having then instructed the prince what he was to do when he should be with Zalulu, gave him the water of oblivion, and transported him, in less than four minutes, to the ordinary habitation of that perfidious jinni.

Zalulu, whose power was limited with regard to Gul-hindi, after having cured her wound with one single blast of his breath, had confined her to a dark tower, and had gone out in quest of some new subject for his malignant recreation, when he met with Sharif al-Din, who was stretched out upon the grass and who feigned a profound sleep. The jinni, after having viewed him with abundance of attention, owned to himself that he had never beheld so charming a creature. He fell passionately in love with him; and forming to himself a flattering idea of the happiness he should enjoy in being beloved by him, he assumed the form of a young man of about twenty, and beautiful even to a degree almost equal to his; he carried him away, conveyed him to his palace, and waited till he should waken to declare to him the extreme passion he felt for him.

Sharif al-Din, who was prepared for what might happen, acted his part to perfection. At first he pretended to be hugely afflicted, and shed abundance of tears; and afterwards, by a seeming resistance, so inflamed Zalulu, that the jinni, whose passion increased every moment for the prince, whom he mistook for a woman, declared to him who he was, and offered to make him a partner in his power, if he would make a kind return to his tenderness. The disguised prince feigned to be shaken by the greatness of his promises and by the personal merit of the jinni; he asked some days to consider it, promising to spend all the time in his company; and Zalulu, blinded by his passion, and without in the least suspecting that he designed to put a trick upon him, resolved to wait with patience for that happy moment, and in the meanwhile to procure him a thousand diversions that might prevail upon him to be grateful. To begin, he caused to be served a magnificent collation, and presented him with a very excellent wine; he excused himself from touching it, and told the jinni he drank only of a certain water he always carried about with him; but that this water was of so excellent a taste that it far excelled the finest wines. The jinni seemed surprised at it. Give me leave, madam, answered he, to doubt of so improbable a story, till I have myself experienced the truth of it.—You yourself shall be the judge, replied the prince of Ormuz. Then having poured into the cup just so much water as was requisite to take away the memory, Zalulu had no sooner drunk it off than he was perfectly besotted.

Sharif al-Din, seeing the operation of his liquor, was in a joy hardly to be expressed; he gave the jinni such tender caresses, that, moved with the charms of so beautiful a woman, he had much ado to contain himself, and wished to absolutely embrace him, when, pushing him fondly back, he told him he would not consent to his desires, unless, as a pledge of his eternal tenderness, he made him a present of the ring he wore on his finger. Zalulu, at this moment, by means of the water he had drunk, forgetting of what consequence it was to him to preserve Sulayman's ring, which all the powers of the earth could never have forced from him, took the ring from his finger and presented it to his new mistress. He had no sooner got it into his possession, than pouring him out a second glass of the same water, but which dose was so much as would restore him his memory, he earnestly begged him for his sake to drink that too, and assured him that he should no sooner have given him that last mark of his complaisance, than he would consent to gratify his desires. However insipid the jinni' thought the liquor he had already drunk, as he was so transported at the sight of this charming lady that he was no longer the master of his will, he presently swallowed the water offered him; but what a fury he was in the moment afterwards, when Sharif al-Din vanished from his sight, to perceive that he was no longer the possessor of Sulayman's ring, and to remember that he himself had foolishly given it away to the woman whose false charms had so grossly deceived him! He then abandoned himself to the most violent despair, and blasphemed against all the Supreme Beings.

When Sharif al-Din had given to Geoncha the ring he had so subtlely acquired, that king of the jinnis transported himself in the very moment to the place where the perfidious Zalulu was still making most dismal reflections upon the loss he had sustained. But though the seal of Sulayman, which with the utmost surprise he saw in Geoncha's hand, ought to have humbled him, and induced him to have recourse to his clemency, yet he had still the temerity to rebel against him; and forgetting that he was his king, he was so rash as to defy him to mortal combat. But Geoncha making use of all his superiority and immense power which that divine ring gave him, soon put an end to the fight. He annihilated the traitorous Zalulu; and after having carried to his palace the prince of Ormuz, while he washed in another bath which restored him to his primitive form, the jinni went and fetched the beauteous Gul-hindi out of her prison, and embracing them both, he conveyed them in a instant to the palace of the king of Tuluphan.

Mochzadin and Riza, who bemoaned the loss of their dear daughter, and according to Geoncha's prediction never expected to behold her again, almost died with joy at so unexpected a sight. The jinni told them, to their great amazement, of the error they had always been in by the malice of Zalulu; the dangers to which their real daughter had been exposed, as he had foretold them the moment she was born, and the annihilation of the malignant jinni; and commanded them to immediately unite in the most holy ties, Sharif al-Din and Gul-hindi; since the king of Ormuz, too, had already formed the same design. The king and queen of Tuluphan, continued Ibn Aridun, would not defer a moment the happiness of the prince and princess; and that illustrious couple under the protection of the great Geoncha spent the rest of their days in the most perfect union, and enjoyed a felicity which to their lives' end, was never interrupted by the least unlucky accident.

*   *   *

Ibn Aridun having thus concluded the adventures of Sharif al-Din and of Gul-hindi, the king of Astrakhan let him know the great pleasure he had taken in hearing them.

I could yet have wished, added that monarch, that there had been something in the catastrophe of your story a little more wonderful: I cannot help thinking that Zalulu runs too blindfold into the trap that is laid for him, and that Sharif al-Din too easily gets the ring of Sulayman.—My Lord, replied Ibn Aridun, I did not invent this history myself, but had the honour to tell it your Majesty, just as I had read it in one of our Arabian authors. And after all, love is so violent a passion, and deprives the wisest men of the use of their reason to such a degree, as to set them upon an equal footing with the weakest of mankind. I confess it, replied the king; and now that I reflect upon it more seriously, I perceive that it would have been very hard to rescue Gul-hindi out of Zalulu's power, by any other means than the blind passion he felt for Sharif al-Din, who seemed so beautiful a woman. That jinni, with the assistance of Sulayman's ring, might have defended himself against all surprises; nothing but so passionate a love could have torn it from him; and this thought convinces me that it very easy to criticise anything, but hard to mend it.—It is true, my Lord, replied Ibn Aridun; but since your Majesty was not at first entirely satisfied with the conclusion of that history, I will relate one which I am sure will please you, both for the wonderful and comical strokes that there are in it.—Nobody hitherto has succeeded so well as thou in diverting me, replied the king of Astrakhan; begin this history, therefore, since I have still some moments left. Ibn Aridun, in obedience to his prince, spake in these terms:

TALE OF THE THREE CRUMP TWIN-BROTHERS OF DAMASCUS

UNDER the Caliphate of Al-Mutawakhil 'alà 'lláh, grandson of Hárún al-Rashíd, there dwelt at Damascus an old man called Bahamrillah, who did but just get a poor livelihood by making steel-bows, swords, sabres, and knife-blades. Of thirteen children which he had by one wife, ten died all in one year; but the three that remained were such odd figures, that it was impossible to look at them without laughing. They were crooked both behind and before, blind of the left eye, lame of the right foot, and so perfectly like one another in face, shape and clothes, which they always wore the same with one another, that even their father and mother sometimes mistook one for the other.

Of the three sons of Bahamrillah, said Ibn Aridun the next day, the eldest was named Ibad, the second, Syahuk, and the third Babakan; and these three little hump-backed brothers never worked in their shop, but they served for laughing-stocks to all the boys and girls in the town. One day, as the only son of a rich merchant, named Murad, returned from walking with some of his play-fellows, finding himself more merry than usual, he leaned upon the bulk of the three crumps, and insulted them with so much keenness, that Babakan, who was then at work upon a knife-blade, lost all patience; he ran after those children, and, singling out his principal enemy, gave him a cut in the belly; but finding that he was pursued by the mob, he ran into his shop and pulled the door after him. As Murad was dangerously wounded, all the avenues of Bahamrillah's house were immediately secured, till the Kadi, who was sent for, should come.

He repaired thither immediately with his attendants, and having broken down the doors upon their refusal to open them, he entered into the shop, and demanded of those who had been witnesses of the action that was committed, which of the three crumps was the murderer. Nobody could affirm that it was one of them rather than another; they were so exactly alike that they were all at a loss. The Kadi examined Ibad, who assured him that it was not he that had wounded the boy, and that he could not tell whether it was Syahuk or Babakan; Syahuk averred the same thing; and Babakan, seeing himself out of danger, had the impudence to deny likewise that he had any hand in the crime.

The Kadi was, therefore, much perplexed what to do. There could be but one criminal, and here seemed to be three; and never a one of them would own himself to be the man. He thought he could not do better than inform the king of Damascus of so singular an affair. He carried the three crumps before his throne; and that prince having examined them himself, without being able to find out the truth, gave command, in order to discover it, that each of them should have an hundred bastinadoes upon the soles of his feet. They began with Syahuk, and afterwards proceeded to Ibad; but both of them being ignorant whether Babakan was the criminal or not, so much resemblance there was between them, they endured the bastinado without giving the king any clearer information than he had before. Babakan afterwards received his quota of stripes; but being judge in his own cause, he did not think fit to betray himself; he made the most earnest protestations of his innocence, and the king not knowing which was the murderer, and unwilling to put to death two innocents with one criminal, was contented with banishing them all three from Damascus for ever.

Ibad, Syahuk, and Babakan were obliged to comply

with this sentence immediately. They departed from the city, and having considered what they should do, Ibad and Syahuk were entirely for keeping together; but Babakan having represented to them that, let them go where they would, so long as they were together they would always be the jest of the public, but that if they were single they would each be infinitely less observed; this reason prevailed over the opinion of the other two. They parted from each other, and taking every one of them a different road, Babakan, having travelled through several towns of Syria, came at length to Baghdad, where I have already told your Majesty, Al-Mutawakhil 'alà 'lláh, the 'grandson of Hárún al-Rashíd, held the supreme power. This little crooked wretch understanding that there was in that city a cutler of tolerably good repute, went to him for employment; he told him he was from Damascus, and that he had a particular art in tempering steel. The cutler was willing to try if Babakan was as great a master of his trade as he boasted himself to be; he took him iont his shop, and finding, indeed, that not only was the steel he tempered as hard and as sharp again as what was commonly used at Baghdad, but also that his work was much more neat and perfect, he retained him in his service, and entertained him with great kindness, that he might keep him to himself. From that time his shop was always crowded with customers. The little crump could not work fast enough; the cutler sold his bows and sabres at his own price, and if he had not been a drunken extravagant sot, he might have made a very considerable fortune.

Babakan had scarce been two years at Baghdad, when his master fell very ill of a great debauch he had made; his body was so worn and wasted by wine, brandy, and women, that all the care of his wife and of Babakan could not save his life; he died in their arms. Though Nohud, which was the name of the cutler's wife, was very far from being handsome, Babakan had, nevertheless, been in love with her for some time; and his master's death proving a fair opportunity to declare his passion, he, without any hesitation, made the widow acquainted with his sentiments. She was not much alarmed at them; for, besides that his out-of-the-way figure began to grow familiar to her, she further considered that if Babakan left her, the shop would presently lose its reputation, and that the little money she had saved during her husband's life would soon be spent. These reasons induced her, like a sensible woman as she was, to make Babakan a promise of marriage so soon as she could do it with decency. She kept her word with him some months afterwards; and Babakan, not satisfied with his cutling trade alone, whereby in a little time he got a great deal of money, fell likewise in the way of selling brandy of dates, which he had a very considerable demand for.

The correspondence that Babakan had in several towns in the East, came to the ears of his two brothers, who after having lived for almost five years in abject poverty, were at last met together at Darbant. Here they learnt to their great joy the prosperity of Babakan, and not doubting but that he would assist them in their want, they resolved to go together to Baghdad; they had no sooner arrived there, than they sent for him by a poor woman, who had taken them into her house out of charity. Babakan was prodigiously surprised at the sight of his brothers: Have you forgotten, said he to them, in a violent passion, what happened to us at Damascus? Have you a mind to make me the jest of this city too? I swear by my head that you shall die beneath the cudgel, if you dare to come near my house, or to stay in Baghdad another hour. Ibad and his brother were amazed at a reception so little expected; it was in vain they represented their misery to Babakan, and shewed him the most abject submission: he continued unmoved; and all they could obtain from him were ten or twelve pieces of gold to help them to settle in some other town.

Babakan being returned home, his wife perceived an alteration in his countenance. She asked him the cause of it, and was answered that it proceeded from the arrival of his two brothers; but that apprehending at Baghdad the same railleries he had borne at Damascus, he had forbidden them his house, and had obliged them to leave the town. Nohud to no purpose remonstrated with him on the cruelty of what he had done; her husband's fury was but increased by her persuasions. I find, said he, you will be tempted to entertain them here, during the journey I am about to make to Bassorah; but take notice, I advise you, that if you do, it shall cost you your life. I say no more: look to it that you do not disobey me. Babakan's wife was too well acquainted with her husband's violent humour to contradict him; she had often enough felt the weight of his arm. She promised most punctually to execute his orders; but those promises did not make Babakan easy; he passed the whole night without taking a wink of sleep, and returning next morning at break of day to the woman's house where his brothers had lodged, he heard to his great satisfaction that they had gone from Baghdad, with the intention never to seek it again.

Ibad and Syahuk had indeed departed, with a resolution to go and seek their fortunes elsewhere; but the latter falling sick about two days' journey from Baghdad, and they finding themselves obliged to stay there almost three weeks, their money was soon gone, and they were reduced to their former want. Not knowing how to live, in spite of the severe prohibition they had received from Babakan, they resolved to go back to Baghdad. They went to their former landlady, and begged her to go once more to their brother, in order to persuade him, if she could, to take them into his house, or at least to give them a little money to defray the charge of their journey. The poor woman could not refuse to do them that service; she went to Babakan's house, and being informed at his shop that he had been gone twelve days to Bassorah, to fetch several bales of merchandise, she returned immediately to tell this news to her guests, who were so hard pressed by their necessity, that they went themselves to implore the assistance of their brother's wife. Nohud could not help knowing them: they resembled Babakan so exactly, that there was nobody but would have mistaken each of them apart for him. But though he had so strictly commanded her not to let them into her house, she was touched with their poverty and tears; she entertained them and set some victuals before them. It was now dark night; and Ibad and Syahuk had scarce satisfied their first hunger, when somebody rattled at the door; the voice of Babakan, who was not to have returned for three days longer, was a thunderbolt to his wife and brothers; they turned as pale as death; and Nohud, who did not know where to put them, to conceal them from her husband's fury, thought at last of hiding them in a little cellar, behind five or six tubs of brandy.

Babakan grew impatient at the door; he knocked louder and louder every moment; at last it was opened, and suspecting his wife of having some gallant hid in a corner, he took a stick and beat her soundly; afterwards his jealousy induced him to search all the house; he visited every hole with the greatest care, but never thought of looking behind the brandy tubs, though he went into the cellar. At last, my lord, continued Ibn Aridun, the hump-backed churl, having made no discovery, grew a little calmer; he locked all the doors, taking the keys according to his custom, went to bed with Nohud, and did not go out all next day till towards the evening, telling his wife he would sup with a friend. His back was hardly turned, when Nohud ran immediately to the cellar; but she was in the utmost surprise at finding Ibad and Syahuk without the least sign of life. Her perplexity increased when she considered she had no way of getting rid of the two bodies; but taking her resolution at once, she shut up the shop, ran to look towards the bridge of Baghdad for a foolish porter of Siwrihissar, and having told him that a little hump-backed man, who came to her house to buy some knives, having died there suddenly, she feared she should be brought to trouble about it; she proffered him four golden dinars, if he would put him into a sack, and throw him into the Tigris. The porter accepted her offer; and Nohud having taken him home with her, gave him two dinars by way of earnest, treated him with drink till it was night, put only one of the crumps into his sack, helped him up with it, and promised to give him the other two dinars, when she was sure he had performed his commission.

The porter, with the crump upon his shoulders, being come to the bridge of Baghdad, opened his sack, shot his load into the river, and running back to Nohud: It is done, said he laughing; your man is fish-meat by this time; give me the two dinars you promised me. Nohud then went behind her counter, under pretence of fetching him the money; but starting back with a loud cry, she pretended to fall into a swoon. The porter, strangely surprised, took her into his arms; and after having fetched her to herself, he enquired the cause of her fright. Ah! said the cunning hussy, acting her part to a miracle, go in there, and you will soon know the cause. The porter went in, and was struck as mute as a fish, when, by the glimmering of a lamp, he perceived the same body which he thought he had thrown into the Tigris. The more narrowly he viewed it, the greater was his surprise. I am sure, said he to Nohud, I did throw that plaguey crooked rascal over the bridge: how, then, could he come hither? There must be witchcraft in it. However, continued he, let us try if he will get out again; then having put the second crump into the same sack, he carried him to the bridge, and choosing out the deepest part of the Tigris, opened his sack, and threw in poor Syahuk. He was again returning merrily to Nohud, not doubting that his burden was gone to the bottom, when turning the corner of a street, he saw coming towards him a man with a lanthorn in his hand. He was ready to drop down dead with fear at the sight of Babakan, who was going home a little overtaken with wine. He dogged him, however, a little while, and finding that he took the ready way to the house from which he had fetched the two crumps, he seized him furiously by the collar. Ah, rogue! cried he, you think to make a fool of me all night, do you? You have served me this trick twice already; but if you escape the third time, I will be hanged. Then, being a lusty fellow, he threw his sack over his shoulders, and forcing him into it in spite of his teeth, tied the mouth of it with a strong rope, and running directly to the bridge, flung in poor Babakan, sack and all. He walked a pretty while thereabouts, for fear the crump should get out again to cheat him of his reward: but hearing no noise, returned to the cutleress to demand the other two dinars, which she had promised him. Do not fear his coming any more, said he, the moment he set his foot into the house. The wag had a mind to make me his sport for ever, I think; he only pretended to be dead, that he might make me trot my legs off; but I have done his business for him now so thoroughly, that he will never come to your house any more; I will engage for him.

Nohud, surprised at this discourse, desired him to tell her what he meant by it. Why, replied he, I had again thrown this damned crump into the Tigris, when as I was returning to you for my money, I met him about

five or six streets off with a lanthorn in his hand, singing
and roaring, under pretence of being drunk. I was so
horribly enraged with him, that laying hold of him I forced
him into my sack, in spite of all his resistance, tied it
with a cord, and so threw him into the Tigris, from
whence I believe he can never return, unless he be
Iblis himself. Babakan's wife was in an unparalleled
surprise at this news. Ah! sirrah, said she, what have
you done? You have now drowned my husband; and
have you the impudence to think I will reward you for
his murder? No, no; I will revenge his death, and go this
moment to make my complaint to the Kadi. The porter
gave very little heed to all her threats; he thought she
did this only to avoid paying him the money she had
promised him. Without jesting, said he, give me the
two dinars I have so lawfully earned; you have made a
fool of me 'long enough; I must begone home. Nohud
refused to pay him. I swear by my head, replied he, in
a violent rage, if you do not give me the two dinars this
moment, I will send you to keep company with that
crooked monster I have thrown into the river. Now,
added he, dispute my payment if you dare: I am not such
a fool as you take me for; I will have my money at once,
or I will make the house too hot to hold you. The more
the porter insisted upon his money, the more noise Nohud
made. He grew weary of so much resistance, and taking
her by the hair, he pulled her into the street, and was really
going to throw her into the Tigris, when the neighbours
ran to her assistance. The porter upon this, took to his
heels, very much in dudgeon at having, as he thought, been
so grossly put upon, and was going towards the bridge on
his way home, when he met three men, each with a load
upon his shoulder, as far as he could discern in the dark.
He that went first took him by the arm. Where are you
going at this time of night? said he.—What is that to
you, said the porter very snappishly; I am going where

I please.—You are greatly deceived, answered the stranger, for you shall go where I please: take this bundle off my head and walk before me. The porter, surprised at this command, would have resisted ; but the man having shaken at him a sabre four fingers broad, and threatened to cut off his head if he did not obey that moment, he was forced to take up the load and go in company with the other two, whereof one seemed a slave and the other a fisherman. They had not walked ten streets when they came to a little door, which was presently opened by an old woman. They passed through a long passage very dark, and arrived at last in a magnificent hall. But what was the porter's amazement, when, by the light of about forty tapers with which it was illuminated, he saw the crooked brothers he had thrown into the Tigris, two of whom were upon the shoulders of the slave and the fisherman, and the third upon his own head ! He was seized with such terror that he began to shake all over his body. He was more thoroughly convinced than ever that so extraordinary a thing could be imputed to nothing but conjuration. But recovering a little from his fright : The devil take this cursed crump-backed, one-eyed son of a whore, cried he, in a very comical tone; I believe I shall do nothing all night but throw him into the river, and not get rid of him at last. The rascal was so malicious as to come back again twice, to hinder me from having the dinars the cutler-woman promised me ; and here I find him again, with two others besides, not a farthing better than himself. But, sir, continued he, addressing himself to him who seemed the master of the house, lend me, I beseech you, that sabre of your's but for a moment, I will only cut off their heads, and then go and throw them all three into the Tigris, to see if they will follow me again. I am so horribly unlucky to-day, that I am sure the devil will carry them back, either to the cutler's house or to mine, do what I will.

The porter having finished this speech of his, the Caliph Al-Mutawakhil 'ala 'llah, for it was he himself, my lord, who, following the example of Harun al-Rashad, his grandfather, walked out very often in the night-time in the streets of Baghdad, to see what passed, and to be capable of making a judgment himself of how the people liked his government : this Caliph I say who was disguised like a merchant, was in the utmost surprise at these words of the porter. He had been out that night with his wazir, and having met a fisherman, he asked him whither he went ?—I am going, answered he, to draw up my net, which I have left ever since yesterday morning in the Tigris.—And what will you do with the fish you catch ? replied the Caliph.—To-morrow, said he, I will go and sell them in the market of Baghdad, to help to maintain my wife and three children.—Will you bargain with me for your whole draught ? replied Al-Mutawakhil 'ala 'llah.—With all my heart, answered the fisherman.— Well, said the Caliph, there are ten dinars of gold for it: will that satisfy you ? The fisherman was so amazed at such a piece of generosity that he almost imagined he was in a dream. But, putting the dinars in his pocket : My lord, replied he, transported, if I were to have as much for every draught, I should soon be richer and more powerful than the sovereign Commander of the Faithful. The Caliph smiled at this comparison : he went to the shore of the Tigris, entered the fisherman's boat, and, with his wazir, having helped him to draw up his nets, he was very much amazed at finding in them the two little crumps of Damascus, and a sack in which was the third.

An adventure so surprising struck him with admiration. Since this draught belongs to me, said he to the fisherman, who was as much surprised as himself, I am resolved to carry it home with me; but you must lend us a hand. The man had received too great marks of the Caliph's liberality to make the least scruple at obeying him; the wazir and he took, the one Ibad, and the other, Syahuk by the feet, and threw them on their shoulders; and the Caliph himself having shouldered the sack in which was Babakan, they turned back to go to the palace, when they met the porter, who had a few moments before thrown the three brothers into the Tigris. As Al-Mutawakhil 'ala 'llah was dripping wet with the water that ran out of the sack, he stopped the porter, and having forced him to ease him of his burden, he conducted him to a house which adjoined his palace. There it was, my lord, that the porter of Baghdad, having by the words he spoke, relating to the three crumps, excited the Caliph's curiosity, he desired him to explain himself more clearly upon so whimsical an adventure. Sir, replied the porter, this explanation you require is not so easily made as you imagine. The more I think of it, the less I understand it; however, you shall have it just as I think it happened to me.

Do you know, sir, said the porter, the cutler's wife who lives at the end of the street of the jewellers?—No, replied the Caliph.—You are no great loser by the bargain, replied the porter; she is the mischievousest jade in all Baghdad: I would willingly give the two dinars I am master of to have but five or six slaps at her foul chops, for the trick the witch put upon me this night: though I am but poor I should sleep the better for it. This cutler woman then——But stay, since you do not know her, I will draw you her picture. Imagine, sir, you have before your eyes a great withered old woman, with a skin as black as a dried neat's tongue, with a little forehead, and eyes so far sunk into her head that it is impossible without a telescope to see she has any. Her nose has so great a kindness for her chin, that they are always kissing one another; and her mouth, which exhales a charming odour like that of brimstone, is so wide that it is not unlike a crocodile's. Must not all this form a complete beauty?—Without doubt, said the Caliph, who, though impatient to hear the story of the three crumps, almost died with laughing at the porter's comical description. You are so excellent a painter that I fancy I see this cutler-woman, and would lay a wager I could find her out amongst a thousand.—Well, then, said the porter, since you know her now as well as if you had seen her, imagine that you see this lovely creature, covered with a great veil that hides all her perfections, come to choose me towards night, at the foot of the bridge, from amongst five or six of my comrades, and to promise me in my ear four dinars if I would follow her. The desire of gain entices me; I fly towards her house, and go in with her. She throws off the veil: I am frightened at the sight almost out of my wits; she certainly perceives it, and to encourage me, pops into my hand a great flagon of wine. I own, sir, it was so excellent that without enquiring what country it came from, I emptied the flagon. Yet I could not help trembling all the while I drank it; I was afraid she had a mind to make me drunk, that she might afterwards debauch me, and get me to spend the night with her. And it was not without good grounds that I feared this; for she caressed me enough to make me believe it. After the wine, she brought me a great bottle of date brandy; she amorously pours me out a large glass full, which I tipped off without any more a-do; then she proposed to me——But stay, stay, I think I drank two glasses of brandy upon further consideration.—Drink six if you will, answered the Caliph, so you do but make an end of your story.—Hold you me there, sir, cried the porter, one cannot swallow down brandy at that rate neither; it will fly into the head: I am half drunk with those two only, and you would have me here, after all that wine, tope down a bottle of brandy to boot. No, no, sir, I will do no such thing, though the sovereign Commander of the Faithful himself should beg me upon his knees to do it. So then it was that the cutler-woman, seeing me grow a little merry, as one may say, gave me to understand that a little crooked man, who came to her house to buy some cutler's ware, had died suddenly in her shop, and that fearing she should be accused of having killed him, she would give the four dinars she had promised me if I would throw him into the Tigris. I had not drunk so much neither, but that I was resolved to make sure of the cash. I demanded two of the dinars as earnest ; she gave them me : I puts little crump into my sack, does as I was bid, and comes back to take the rest of my money, when she shews me again the very same man. I leave you to imagine, sir, how much I was surprised. I put him once more into my sack, carried him again to the bridge, and choosing the most rapid part of the stream, tossed him in ; and I was returning to the cutler's when I again met the crooked toad with a lanthorn in his hand, and making as if he was drunk. I grew weary of so much jesting, took hold of him roughly, and pushing him into my sack in spite of his teeth, tied up the mouth of it, and flung him a third time into the Tigris with my sack and all, imagining that it would keep him from getting out again. I went back to the cutler-woman, and told her how I met the crump alive, and in what manner I got rid of him. But instead of paying me the two dinars I expected, she pretended to tear her hair in grief, and threatened to carry me before the Kadi for having drowned her husband. I never minded her tears, but swore I would have my money. I made a bloody noise about it ; the neighbours ran in at her cries ; I took to my heels. I was going home, grumbling in the gizzard very much, when you, sir, forced me to take up this sack upon my head, and bring it hither. Now, sir, continued the porter, you may easily guess the cause of my fright, when at my arrival here I found myself laden with the same man that I had three times flung into the Tigris, and beheld also two others so like him that it is impossible to distinguish between them but by their clothes.

Though the Caliph could not see into the bottom of this adventure, he took abundance of pleasure in hearing the porter's story. Then having viewed the three brothers a little more narrowly, he thought he perceived in them some signs of life, and sent immediately for a physician. He came soon afterwards, and finding that Ibad and Syahuk threw up, with the water they had swallowed, a great deal of brandy, he did not doubt, as indeed was the fact, that their drunkenness was the occasion of their being thought dead. As for Babakan, nothing but want of air had almost suffocated him ; but as soon as his head was out of the sack he recovered by degrees; so that in half an hour's time his brothers and he were entirely out of danger. Never was anybody so amazed as Babakan was at the sight of his brothers, who were laid upon sofas. He almost cracked his eye-strings with staring at them, and could not possibly conceive how he came into that strange place with them. He suffered himself to be undressed without uttering a single word, while the same was done to Ibad and Syahuk.

The Caliph having caused the three crumps to be carried into different chambers, had them put to bed and locked up. Then he sent away the fisherman, and having ordered the wazir to keep the porter, and to use him with great kindness, he prepared to divert himself at the expense of the crooked brothers and the cutler-woman, whom he arrested next morning at break of day. To heighten his diversion the Caliph caused to be made that night two suits of clothes exactly like that which Babakan wore, when he was thrown into the Tigris. He ordered them to be put upon Ibad and Syahuk, whose drunken fit was quite over, and being all dressed exactly alike, he placed them behind three different pieces of hanging, in a magnificent hall of the palace, and gave orders that they should be discovered upon his making a certain sign.

The wazir, who, with the porter and several guards, had been early in the morning to arrest the cutler's wife, brought her into the hall, where the Caliph was already placed upon his throne. He examined her with relation to what passed between her and the porter. She told him all that had happened, without concealing a tittle of the truth, and seemed very much concerned at the loss of her husband. But, said the Caliph, is this not a made-up story that you tell me? How is it possible these three crooked brothers should be so exactly alike that the porter should be deceived by them? Ah! my lord, replied Nohud, he was half drunk when I employed him; and besides my husband and his brothers resemble one another so perfectly, that if they were dressed in the same clothes, I hardly think I myself could be able to distinguish one from the other.—That would be pleasant indeed, said the Caliph, clapping his hands; I should like to be a spectator of such an interview.—This was the signal Al-Mutawakhil 'ala 'llah was to give for the crumps to appear. The pieces of hanging were immediately pulled up, and the cutleress was ready to die with fear at the sight. O heaven! cried she, what a prodigy is this! Do the dead come again to life? Is this an illusion, my lord, and are my eyes faithful testimonies of what I see?—You see right, replied Al-Mutawakhil 'ala 'llah; one of these three is your husband, and the other two are his brothers; you must choose out your own from among them. View them well; but I forbid them upon pain of death to speak or to make the least sign.

Nohud, in the utmost perplexity, examined them one after another; she could not distinguish her husband. And the Caliph, who was as much at a loss to know them as she was, ordering him of the three that was Babakan, to come and embrace his wife, was very much surprised to

see the three crumps all at once throw their arms round
her neck, and each of them affirm himself to be her
husband. Ibad and Syahuk were not ignorant that
they were in the presence of the Commander of the Faithful; but whatever respect they owed him, they thought
they could not be revenged on Babakan better than by
trying to pass for him; and this latter got nothing by his
rage and passion, for his two brothers obstinately persisted
in robbing him of his name. The Caliph could not help
laughing at this comical contest of the three crumps; but
having at length resumed his gravity: There would be no
such dispute among you, said he, which should be Babakan, if you knew that I want to distinguish him, only
to give him a thousand bastinadoes for his cruelty to his
brothers, and for his forbidding his wife to entertain them
in his absence.

Al-Mutawakhil 'ala 'llah, my lord, continued the son
of Abu Bakr, pronounced these words in so severe a tone
that Ibad and Syahuk thought it high time to give over
the jest. If it be so, my lord, said each of them separately,
we are no longer what we pretended to be, with a design
to punish our brother for his ill usage of us; if there are
any blows to be received, let him receive them, for they are
no more than he deserves. As for us, my lord, we implore
your generosity, and we are in hopes that your august
Majesty, who never suffers anyone to depart unsatisfied,
will have the goodness to alleviate our misery and want.
The Caliph then threw his eyes on Babakan, whom he saw
in the greatest confusion. Well, said he to him, what hast
thou to say for thyself?— Potent king, replied Babakan,
with his face prostrated to the earth, whatever punishment I am to look for from your justice, I am nevertheless
the husband of this woman. My crime is still the greater
in that, being the only cause of the banishment of my
brothers from the city of Damascus, for a murder of
which our resemblance hindered me from being known

the author, I ought to have let them participate in my good fortune, as they had shared in my bad. But if a sincere repentance can obtain my pardon, I offer from the bottom of my heart to give them equal parts of all the money I have by my labour gained since my arrival here at Baghdad; and I hope your Majesty will pardon my ingratitude, upon account of the sorrow it gives me to have committed it.

The Caliph, who never intended to inflict any punishment upon Babakan, was very well pleased to see him in this disposition; he therefore pardoned him. And being willing that Ibad and Syahuk, for the pleasure they had given him, should feel the effects of his liberality, he caused it to be published all over Baghdad, that if there were any women who would marry the two crump-brothers he would give them each two thousand pieces of gold. There were above twenty who were ready to embrace so considerable a fortune; but Ibad and Syahuk, having chosen out of that number those that they thought would fit them best, received of the Caliph twenty thousand dinars more, with which they traded in friendship with Babakan. And these three brothers spent the rest of their days in abundance of tranquility, under the protection of the sovereign Commander of the Faithful, who was moreover so liberal to the porter that he lived at his ease ever after without having any occasion for continuing his trade.

*

When Ibn Aridun had finished the adventures of the three crumps of Damascus: I swear by Ali, quoth Shams al-Din to him, that if I have been sensible of any pleasure since the loss of my dear Zabd al-Katon, it has been that of hearing thee. Nothing, I think, can be more comical than the unravelling of this story. You had good reason to promise me something wonderful; it is full of it throughout; and as I cannot reward too munificently----Ah! my lord, replied Ibn Aridun, without giving the king time to make an end of what he was going to say, it is not interest which I am actuated by. Rewards too great would only stir up more and more the hatred of the physicians of this city against my father, and against me your faithful slave. I have felt the effects of it too much already since his departure, and my being still alive is owing to nothing but the happiness I have had in pleasing your Majesty.—What dost thou mean? replied Shams al-Din, surprised at this discourse. Is there anybody in Astrakhan so bold as to try to do thee mischief? —My lord, replied the wazir Mutamhid, Ibn Aridun ought, I think, to have been entirely satisfied with the conduct I have used towards him. One of your physicians informed me that he made a mockery of the perplexity Kubirgh and I were in to find you new entertainment every day, and assured me he boasted that he himself could do it, if he pleased, till his father's return. This at first put me in a terrible passion against Ibn Aridun: I tried to frighten him with the punishment his rashness deserved; but I found him so unmoved at all my menaces, and so docile to execute what afterwards I perceived the physician accused him of falsely, that I have done him all the justice which is due to his merit, and ever since have looked upon him as my own son.—It is true, my lord, answered the son of Abu Bakr, addressing the king of Astrakhan; I am far from having any cause to complain of Mutamhid; I have received all the kindness imaginable from him; but in the meanwhile I am narrowly guarded, and the perfidious physician who sought my destruction walks at liberty. —That is by no means just, interrupted Shams al-Din; he shall be shut up in a dark prison till Abu Bakr's return: and to put thee out of all danger from the malice of the other physicians, I make you wazir, and set you upon an equality with Mutamhid and Kubirgh, upon condition that you have no resentment against the former; his intentions were good, and I know him to be too merciful to have ever punished thee with death, even though I had not been satisfied with thee.

Ibn Aridun, confounded at the goodness of his king, threw himself at his feet. He at first refused the honour which was bestowed upon him, but was obliged to obey. My lord, said he, since your Majesty forces me to accept a dignity I find myself incapable of, I submit to your supreme will, and do for a beginning assure Mutamhid of an eternal and inviolable friendship; but as the oblivion of injuries is the surest token of a noble soul, I beseech you to pardon, at my request, the physician that contrived against me. Let him only know that I had it in my power to punish his treachery, and would not make use of the opportunity.—No, no, replied Shams al-Din, in this I will be obeyed. He shall never see the light again till Abu Bakr returns from Sarandib, and he shall now wish for that return as much as before he feared it. But till then, my dear Ibn Aridun, continued that prince, do not abandon me to the cruel afflictions wherein I am involved, but contribute by the charms of thy conversation to dispel the gloomy melancholy into which the sad remembrance of my losses incessantly plunges me.—My lord, replied Ibn Aridun, prostrating himself on the ground, since your Majesty has been pleased to condescend so far as to hear with some complacency the humblest of your slaves, I swear I will never leave you so long as I have the happiness to please you. All the moments of my life shall be devoted to your service.— Continue then, said Shams al-Din, to give me marks of your affection by telling me some new story that may afford me as much diversion as these I have already heard.—I know one, my lord, answered Ibn Aridun, that is very particular; but I have already hesitated more than once to tell it you. I was afraid of reviving in your mind the image of your misfortunes, by the conformity it bears, in the beginning, to the fatal accidents which you have felt. It is true the sequel is very different, and will soon make you forget the melancholy part of it : but I dare not tell it without your Majesty's express command. Shams al-Din studied some moments, and then : My misfortunes, said he, are always so present to my mind that your relation cannot possibly make them more so ; therefore, my dear Ibn Aridun, you may safely begin your story. Let the nature of it be what it will, I will hear you with attention. Ibn Aridun obeyed so positive a command, and spake as follows to the king of Astrakhan :

TALE OF UTZIM-OCHANTI, PRINCE OF CHINA

FANFUR, Emperor of China, had espoused Katif, one of the most charming princesses upon earth; nothing in nature was ever more complete; and the moment one cast his eyes upon the globe of her face, he lost the idea of all the beauties he had ever seen before, to think of nothing but the perfections of that princess, whose qualities of the mind were superior even to those of the body. Such women ought to be immortal: but, my lord, the incomparable Katif seemed to appear in China, only to leave in that kingdom an internal regret for the loss of her. She died in the first year of her marriage, bringing into the world a prince, who was called Utzim-Ochanti. Fanfur was so afflicted at the death of his spouse, that he quitted the care of his dominions to give himself up wholly to despair. He built in his palace a magnificent tomb, upon which was in white marble the statue of Katif, and never failed to go to it twice a day to visit it with his tears.

That prince had now lived almost five years in this manner, when his chief wazir, who was a man of the greatest probity, presented himself before him; he prostrated his face to the earth, and getting up: My lord, said he, may your humble slave presume to remonstrate to you, that your grief is of too long duration, and prejudices you in the minds of your people. Though the worth of Katif was inexpressibly great, yet they are ashamed to see you for so tedious a space of time shed tears, which would better become a woman than a king so potent as your Majesty. Katif's beauty was really excellent: but are

there no other women in the world who may be equalled
to her ? If you are insensible to any beauty but her's, at
least consider that you are answerable to your son for a
throne, which I see your subjects almost ready to deprive
you of, if you continue to live in this retirement. Fanfur,
surprised at the wazir's discourse, awaked as it were from
a deep sleep; no less a reproof was necessary to rouse
him from the lethargy he was in. I am inconceivably
obliged to you, wazir, said he, for the sincerity with
which you talk to me. The interests of my son recall me
to life: I should be greatly to blame, if my despair should
bring him to misery. Inform my subjects, therefore,
that I will now appear to them, and will live for the future
in a different manner from what I have done since the
death of my dear Katif. The wazir had no sooner told
this news than the air resounded with nothing but shouts
of joy. Fanfur was very much beloved, and his subjects,
although they were very well satisfied with the wazir's
administration, testified by a thousand feasts and rejoicings the pleasure it gave them to see their prince himself rule over them.

As in all Fanfur's actions there still remained an
air of sorrow, the wazir, to dissipate it, brought him the
most beautiful women in the world : their charms could
not efface from his heart the image of the lovely Katif,
whose memory was so dear to him. He looked
upon them all with an insensibility which surprised the
mandarins ; and turning all his affections upon Utzim-
Ochanti, he declared that so long as he was alive, he
would never have commerce with any woman. This
only heir to the kingdom of China, my lord, had scarce
attained his sixteenth year, when he found in himself a
violent inclination for travelling. He one day asked leave
of Fanfur for that purpose; but that monarch, very much
surprised at such a request, after having represented to
him with wonderful tenderness all the danger he would

expose himself to, and the uneasiness it would be to him, conjured him to have no further thoughts of that design. These remonstrances were so far from persuading Utzim-Ochanti to desist from that purpose, that they did but inflame his desires: and he resolved with the first opportunity to depart without Fanfur's consent or knowledge. He provided himself with a great number of jewels, as much gold as he thought he should have occasion for, and having engaged in his interests six of his friends, they were the only persons with whom he embarked in a little ship which one of them had secretly bought.

Of these persons, one who had been his governor in vain dissuaded him from his design; the prince threatened him with all his indignation, if he ever opened his mouth about it to the king his father; and as Bakmas, which was his name, loved his pupil tenderly, rather than abandon him to the violence of the passions which the heat of his youth was subject to, he resolved to expose himself to the same dangers with him. The second companion of the prince's travels was called Ahmadi; he was a mandarin of sciences; he possessed almost all the living languages, and no man in the world ever equalled him in eloquence. The third was the son of the prince's nurse, and of a rich merchant. The fourth excelled in music, and touched an instrument with so masterly a hand, that he ravished all the senses. The fifth was a painter, equal to the celebrated Mani, and the last was so swift of foot, that he could overtake the nimblest beast in the course.

The winds being favourable, and the vessel an admirable sailor, the prince went almost eight hundred leagues in fewer than ten days. He arrived at a seaport, where, after having landed, he made a present of the ship and of all the equipage to the pilot, with express commands not to return to China for six years.

Bakmas and Ahmadi, finding that Utzim-Ochanti

was very lavish of his wealth in all the towns through
which they passed, soon represented to him that since
he intended to travel as a private man he should
not live at so expensive a rate : and that, if he managed
with as little economy as he had begun to do, his riches,
be they never so great, would soon be exhausted. The
prince gave very little heed to this advice : he was so
profuse that he was forced to have recourse to his jewels,
the value of which amounted to so vast a sum that he
thought it was impossible he should ever want money.
Yet, after having travelled about twelve thousand leagues
in different countries, he began too late to perceive that
he had better have followed the prudent counsel of the
mandarin and of his governor. He then grew sensible of
his fault with great affliction, and found himself in the
most melancholy condition in which a prince could be. To
add to his uneasiness, he had made his six companions as
miserable as himself; but he had the consolation to see
that none of them upbraided him with his want of conduct ; on the contrary, all offered to assist him in his
necessities, by practising everyone the art he was master
of. And, indeed, they had no sooner come to the next
great town, than the runner, having heard there was
pressing occasion for a man that could despatch some
very important affairs with expedition, offered his services.
He undertook to perform, in fewer than four-and-twenty
hours, a journey of above threescore leagues. His offer
was accepted, and the prince and his companions were
his sureties. He was paid the money, the greatest part
of which he left with them ; and having executed what he
had promised, to the great content of those who had employed him, the prince had the advantage of his diligence ; and, living with great economy, they came to
another town, having now but four pieces of silver left
them.

The moment they had arrived there, the merchant's

son, who was a perfect master of arithmetic, went to a
famous trader and offered to balance all the accounts he
had with his correspondents in fewer than three days.
Though this seemed almost impossible, the trader set
him about it, was wonderfully well satisfied with him,
and paid him liberally. This sum maintained the prince
and his train a fortnight; at the end of which time they
again found themselves reduced to the same necessity.
The musician then took his lute, and sang with so much
melody, that the chief men of the city had him to their
houses. They rewarded him nobly for the pleasure he
gave them; and with this money they lived for some
weeks. The painter then perceiving that they were
again falling into the same straits, went to the king of
the country where they then were; he offered to draw
his picture, which he did with so much art, and so
exactly like, that the king, amazed at such a novelty,
looked upon him as something divine. He could not
conceive it was possible to draw lines so just and so
natural that nobody could miss knowing him by the picture. He gave the painter a diamond of great value and
three thousand dinars besides. All the great men of
that court, after the example of their prince, were drawn
by him likewise. He succeeded perfectly well, and received such considerable presents, that he carried out of
that city above ten thousand pieces of gold. This was a
great sum, considering the condition the prince was in;
but very little compared to the immense riches he had
indiscreetly squandered away.

They all put themselves with this into better habits,
were very saving of their money, and resolved to return
directly to China. They had travelled about five
hundred leagues on their way thither, and had almost
come to Zoffala, when they were surrounded by more
than two hundred robbers. Though Utzim-Ochanti
was accompanied only by his six comrades, the number

did not frighten him. He resolved to put himself into a
posture of defence: but Ahmadi having represented to him
the rashness of such an enterprise, the prince laid down
his arms. A man of a tolerably good mien, who seemed
the captain of those rogues, accosted him with civility
enough for a person of his trade. We have no design
upon your lives, said he; since you do not resist, we
content ourselves with what you have. But if a man of
you had been so bold as to defend himself, you had all
been dead before this.—Utzim-Ochanti looked upon
him with indignation: If you were but fifty to our seven,
said he, I should not fear you; but there is no contending
against numbers; you are the master of our fortune. This
bold answer pleased the captain of the thieves. I see
thou hast courage, said he, and I like thee for it; upon
that consideration I will use thee well. Then having
examined what the booty amounted to, he returned the
prince an hundred dinars of gold, and fifty a-piece to each
of his companions, gave them their horses, and suffered
them to continue their journey.

At length they arrived at Zoffala, where the prince
of China falling dangerously sick, they spent most of their
money, and found themselves reduced to their former
want. It was now Bakmas's turn to employ his talent to
enable them to pursue their journey; but the city was
inhabited only by merchants, whose heads ran upon nothing but their commerce, and who had very little notion
of the politeness he had studied at the court of China,
and pretended to teach; it was to no purpose that he
boasted his nobility all over the city; he lost his labour,
and met with nobody that so much as offered him a glass
of water. He bit his lips with indignation.

Bakmas, my lord, continued Ibn Aridun, was returning home, in the deepest affliction, at not having been
able to do his prince the same service as his companions
had done, when he was met by a venerable old man,

whose foreign air sufficiently shewed he was not of Zoffala.
He judged by Bakmas's looks that he was stung with
vexation, and being informed of the cause of it, he
desired him, with his company, to come and refresh themselves at his house. The prince went thither with his train,
and during the repast, the good old man saw that Bakmas
boasted mightily of the prerogatives which an illustrious
birth gives a man. My friends, said he to his guests, the
poor man is always despised, let his quality be what it
will. If your circumstances are narrow, it will be much
the best way not to talk too much of your nobility; if on
the contrary, you are rich, were you descended from the
dregs of the people, you would be universally revered as
the greatest men upon earth. Having said this, he put
twenty pieces of gold into Bakmas's hand, and rising from
table to go about his affairs, the prince and his companions
took their leave of him.

What melancholy reflections did this advice bring
into the prince's thoughts! He wept for very shame.
What! said he to himself, am I reduced by my own fault
alone to subsist upon the talents of my followers?
Without their help I should be brought to the utmost
poverty. Ahmadi, seeing the prince overwhelmed with
sorrow, made use of all his eloquence to comfort him;
he even upbraided him with want of courage in
adversity; and having departed from Zoffala, they came
in a few days to a small but very pretty town. Ahmadi
had no sooner entered into it, than he made proclamation
that he would dispute for eight days successively upon
any subject whatsoever against the most learned men
there. At first people only laughed at his presumption;
but when they came to the trial, he so ravished the
hearers, and shewed so universal a knowledge, that he
confounded all who disputed against him. But in the
end, his learning only provoked the envy of the men of
letters; he gained by this dispute nothing but a vain and

fruitless glory, and his adversaries formed such cabals against him, under pretence that his doctrine was contrary to the interests of the state, that he was forced to betake himself to flight to save his life; and if our seven travellers had not still been masters of a little cash, they would have been very much at a loss. The learned Ahmadi was in a strange confusion. He declaimed a long time against the ingratitude and ignorance of the age; but at last, after eleven days' journey, they came to the gates of Zab.

The prince of China was oppressed with the cruel thoughts his misfortunes gave him. O Heaven! cried he, every one of you but Ahmadi has earned wherewithal to maintain us, and I alone have left my fortune untried. No, no, it shall never be writ in heaven, that I was always a burden to you. Then having told them he would leave them for an hour only, he ordered them to come to him in the principal place of Zab; and resolving to be obeyed, notwithstanding all their opposition he parted from them. After having traversed great part of the city, he sat himself down upon a stone seat which he found in his way, and was ruminating upon his misfortune, when a funeral, with the greatest magnificence, passed along the street where he was. He was so buried in thought that not minding what he was doing, he had not the least curiosity to enquire who it was for whom the inhabitants of Zab shed so many tears; and when the hearse came by, he did not rise up like the rest of the spectators. Everybody was so offended at this neglect, which they imputed to contempt, that they loaded the prince with a thousand abuses. He did not think fit to make any answer, considering with himself what injuries we are exposed to by poverty. But his silence being likewise interpreted ill, one of the officers of the funeral struck him rudely on the face with a wand which he carried in his hand.

Utzim-Ochanti was so transported with rage at this blow that drawing his sword he parted the head of that insolent officer from his shoulders. This bold action amazed all the spectators: they ran upon the prince, but he, defending himself like a furious lion, despatched thirty of them before they could seize him. But, opprest with numbers, he was at last taken: they tied his hands, and were just carrying him to a shameful prison, when his six companions come luckily to the place where this bloody scene had been enacted. They all in a moment drew their sabres, and falling suddenly upon those who had made themselves masters of Utzim-Ochanti, soon delivered him out of their hands. The prince then again took up his sabre, and joining his defenders, they spread such terror throughout the city that the attendants quitted the funeral, and all fled away with the utmost speed.

Ahmadi, upon inquiring of Utzim-Ochanti what was the occasion of all this disturbance, was very much surprised to find that he did not know himself; but having learnt of him that drove the hearse that it arose from his not having paid the respect due to the corpse of the king of Zab, named Mazuan, who died without any heir; he resolved to take advantage of the general fear, and advising the prince and his comrades to sheathe their sabres, he led them towards the place whither the people had betaken themselves in their flight. They arrived at an open part of the town, where the inhabitants were assembled, and walking with a grave pace, he accosted some of the prime men, who beheld them with a sort of respect mixed with terror. Ahmadi then made a sign that he had something of importance to communicate to them. There was presently an universal silence, and that wise Chinese spoke to them in their own language with so much eloquence that all the people who were about him did not at all grow weary of hearing him, and seemed to look upon him as a man inspired. He soon improved this credulity, and pretended to have been forewarned by our great Prophet of all that was to happen after Mazuan's death, and that to put an end to the differences that might arise among the chief men of the province about the election of a new king, he had received orders to bring them from the furthermost parts of the earth a young prince of unheard-of bravery: he then commanded them in so absolute a manner to receive Utzim-Ochanti for their king that nobody durst contradict him. He afterwards gave them a ravishing description of his wisdom, and particularly of the valour he had shewn such prodigious tokens of, and concluded by promising them all manner of prosperity under his government.

This discourse, pronounced with the air of a prophet, and heightened with all the charms of eloquence and of graceful action, surprised even the least credulous minds. The people gave a thousand shouts of joy. Let this young hero, sent us by Mohammed, reign over us and over our posterity, cried they; and let the man who opposes his elevation be looked upon as an enemy to the great Prophet.—Though the pretenders to the kingdom themselves had undertaken to cabal against the prince of China, they could not have convinced the people, nor removed the prejudice they were in; but, on the contrary, they themselves giving credit to the mandarin's words, with one voice proclaimed Utzim-Ochanti king of Zab: and he was immediately carried about the city, which owned him for its sovereign. That prince was in a surprise not to be expressed. He took this adventure for one of those agreeable dreams which a man is unwilling to come out of; but finding it real, he received with gravity the honours that were done him, ordered Mazuan's funeral to be continued, assisted at it himself with his companions, and having taken out of the public treasury a hundred thousand dinars of gold, he distributed them among the people. That there might be nobody discontented in the whole city of Zab, the new king, after having caused the bodies of those whom he and his followers had deprived of life to be buried, commanded a magnificent tomb to be raised to their honour, and made Ahmadi affirm that they all should enjoy the reward set apart for good Mohammedans; and, to comfort their families by something more substantial than words, he gave their widows and each of their children ten thousand dinars of gold.

Ahmadi and Bakmas hardly ever quitted the prince, who regulated his conduct entirely by their prudent counsels; he liberally rewarded the other companions of his travels; and was nearly five years upon the throne, adored by all his subjects. But the love of his own country working upon him, and incessantly calling to mind the grief his absence must cause to the king his father, he resolved to return to China. For this purpose he assembled the prime men of the kingdom, and having made them acquainted with his intentions he begged them to choose two from among themselves to govern the state with Ahmadi and Bakmas, until they heard from him; and desired them, in case they should receive no news from him for three years, to proceed immediately to elect a new king.

I shall pass over in silence, my lord, continued Ibn Aridun, the arguments that were used to dissuade the prince from going, and the regret his subjects shewed at parting from him. Whatever sorrow he perceived in their countenances, and whatever uneasiness he himself felt at leaving them, he remained firm in the same sentiments, embraced his six companions, who would fain have gone with him, took a large quantity of gold and jewels, and departed alone and *incognito* from his capital. Ahmadi, who had raised him to the throne, was the most concerned at the absence of the prince. My dear lord, said he to him, receiving his farewell, since you are inflexible, and I must lose you perhaps for ever, accept I beseech you this carbuncle, presenting Utzim-Ochanti with a precious stone of the bigness of a nut and full of talismanic characters. The light of the sun, said he to him, is not more radiant than that which this carbuncle emits in the dark. It was given me by a sage cabalist; and I put it into your hands, my lord, as the most precious thing that I have. You will perhaps have occasion for it in the tedious journey you have undertaken. The prince accepted Ahmadi's present and, after having tenderly embraced him, he set forward for the dominions of the king his father.

There happened nothing extraordinary to the prince of China in the several courts through which he passed. He generally remained some time at each, where he made a very noble figure. But he was quite cured of the extravagance which had before made him so miserable. At length after a year's travelling by sea and land, he came to the dominions of a prince named Kusah. At the entrance into his capital was a great open square, made spacious by the destruction of an old temple, which idolaters had formerly dedicated to a deity called Pudorina. It was upon the foundations of that temple Kusah had built a magnificent palace, in front of which stood a great obelisk of black marble, upon which on one side were carved in letters of gold the fundamental laws of the kingdom, and on the other several maxims of gallantry.

The young prince of China was amusing himself with examining this whimsical pyramid, when he perceived at the windows of the palace two women of uncommon beauty. He was at once struck with their charms, and enquiring who they were, he learnt that they were the king's two daughters, the eldest of whom was named Modir, and the younger Gulpanhi. He admired the former extremely, but some strangers gave him so horrid a

character of her, that it speedily effaced from his heart the
impression she had made there. That princess, said they,
is never the same; one day she is fair, and the next day
black; she abhors one week what she loved to distraction the last. Her caprice is an indispensable law, it extends its power even to the language; and she keeps the
subjects of the king her father in so servile a dependance,
that nobody, without running the risk of being thought
ridiculous, can do or say anything that is not approved
by this fantastical princess.

As for Gulpanhi, said a sensible old man to him,
though less handsome, she is much more to be feared
than her sister; it is almost impossible to resist her
charms. She keeps an old black woman-slave named
Kurum, who changes her figure and clothes every moment,
to surprise young strangers who arrive in this city. This
dangerous princess has built a sumptuous palace adjoining
to the king's. The gardens are delightful; there are in
them several labyrinths ingeniously contrived, where she
generally wanders with her lovers; but they have no sooner
entered into a little walk embroidered with roses, than
they come immediately into a vast open country, called
the Meadow of Satiety. In this place no roses are to be
seen; they are all stript from their leaves, and in their
room there grows an ugly fruit, long and reddish; and all
taste of pleasure is so lost there, that every body wishes
for nothing but to escape from thence for ever. In vain
Gulpanhi has placed a large dyke at the end of the rose
walk; there is hardly anybody, especially the men, but
who easily leap it.

After having left this wise old man, the prince was
reflecting upon what he had heard, when he was accosted
by a woman, covered with a very thick veil. My son,
said that woman to the prince, taking him by the hand,
and drawing him aside, you are but newly arrived in this
country. I perceive it by your indifference, and by your

carelessness in not going in quest of some lucky adventure, which is not uncommon here for such men as you. I bring you tidings which you ought to esteem the chief happiness of your life: only follow me and be discreet. Curiosity hurried away Utzim-Ochanti, he followed the woman without asking any questions, and after a pretty long walk he came to a very narrow street at the end of which his guide, having opened a little door, led him up a staircase, and through a dark entry into a hall, illuminated by more than a thousand tapers, and enriched with the most brilliant ornaments that art and nature could afford. It was perfumed with such delightful odours as enchanted the senses; and the woman having left him to give her mistress notice of his arrival, the prince contemplated all the beauties of the place he was in. He was soon diverted from that employment, by the entrance of a young lady into the hall. He was struck with her charms the moment he saw her, and casting himself hastily at her feet: How much to be envied is my fortune, madam, said he, which brought me hither to swear to you an eternal love! No, madam, all that is most beautiful upon the face of all the earth does not come up to——The prince was going on, when she suddenly raised him up: Sir, said she, with some emotion, and her face all over-spread with that lovely blush which modesty alone produces, have a care what you do, I am not she that ought to cause these violent transports. I am but an unfortunate slave; but let my present condition be never so mean, I would not change it for that of the lady you are going to see. If her rank is noble, her conduct is so far from it that I am ashamed of her every moment. You are now to think of nothing but how to make a proper return for the tenderness she is so indiscreetly lavish of to all mankind.

The prince of China was listening with surprise to this beautiful person, when the old slave, who had conducted him thither, entered with the princess Gulpanhi, who rested upon her arm.   Imagine, my lord, continued Ibn Aridun, what was the surprise and uneasiness of the prince: he had been so prejudiced against her by the old man he had met in the square before the palace, and by that lovely person, that he remained speechless; and the princess might easily have perceived his indifference, if she had not been so accustomed to flatter herself that she interpreted his silence in her own favour. Though she was dressed in the most gallant manner in the world, and the prince beheld in her a thousand charms capable of moving the most insensible of mankind, he received her caresses with an insensibility that exceeded all imagination. His mind was wholly taken up with the young beauty to whom he had at first addressed his vows; and he thought her behaviour so noble and so different from that of Gulpanhi, that he had much ado to refrain, even in her presence, from giving that charming creature new marks of his love; but reflecting that such an imprudence might perhaps deprive him of her for ever, he put a constraint upon himself, and pretended, for some moments, to answer the favours Gulpanhi shewed him. The prince was ashamed of her advances; but, in spite of his repugnance, they were so engaging, that he might perhaps have been overcome by them if one of the princess's slaves had not come in to tell her that the king her father would speak with her that moment. Gulpanhi seemed vexed at this interruption. I will soon return, said she to the prince, and I dare say you will not be impatient in the company wherein I leave you. She then ordered the young person whom Utzim-Ochanti already adored, to converse with him until her return; and went out immediately with Kurum, the old woman who had accosted the prince.

He was not at all sorry for Gulpanhi's departure, and making the best of her absence, he threw himself a second time at the feet of that incomparable woman. How much have I suffered, madam, said he, in the little time I was with the princess! In vain she is so liberal to me of her charms; she shall never be mistress of a heart over which you alone have a sovereign empire.—Sir, replied the young lady proudly, I am not so easy as Gulpanhi. Though I am reduced to an ignominious slavery, my soul is more free than is her's; and the idleness and luxury which reign in this court have not yet been able to corrupt my heart. It is decreed my hand shall be his who shall have the courage to put me in possession of my dominions, after having revenged the death of the king my father. The tears that upon these words streamed in abundance from the princess's eyes pierced the very soul of the young prince. Nothing, charming princess, will seem impossible to me, said he, to re-establish you in all your rights. Name but to me your enemies, and I will convince you that the sole heir of the king of China is not utterly unworthy of your affection.—The princess earnestly viewed the prince: Ah! my lord, said she, my pride in vain opposed the inclination I found in myself towards you: I am now fully assured that you are destined to be my husband. Yes, prince, I accept you for my defender, and I do it so much the more joyfully because I may now depend upon being shortly revenged on a traitor who has occasioned all the misfortunes of my life. Gulpanhi's absence, continued she, will give me time to inform you of the particulars of my adventures. I know the reason of the king her father's sending for her. A young prince, named Atabak, arrived yesterday in this court to treat of some affairs with king Kusah; this monarch, very uneasy at having his pleasures interrupted, and unfit to carry on a war which Atabak comes to declare against him from a very potent king if he does not obtain the satisfaction he demands: this unworthy monarch, I say, has agreed with his daughter that she shall use all her arts to seduce the heart of that young prince. She will certainly succeed in this design, and while she employs herself to her satisfaction in this new conquest, I shall, perhaps, have leisure enough to tell you my misfortunes. Utzim-Ochanti a thousand times embraced the princess's knees, who was not displeased with these transports, and having made him sit down by her upon a sofa, she began her story thus :

HISTORY OF GULGULI-CHAMAMI, PRINCESS OF TIFLIS

I owe my birth, my lord, to the wise Gomar-Yusuf, king of Tiflis, and to the princess Aynah, the daughter of the Enchanter Zal-raka, king of Palabad ; but though my birth was illustrious, I have never been the more happy for it ; on the contrary, scarce did I begin to see the light when heaven, resolved to persecute me, shed upon me its blackest influences. The enchanter Zal-raka, my grandfather, after having endowed me at my birth with all the qualities necessary in a princess, gave me also an extraordinary patience, foreseeing, without doubt, that it would be one of the most necessary virtues he could bestow upon me, and named me Gulguli-Chamami.

The wise Gomar-Yusuf, my father, made it his whole business to instruct me in all the most sublime parts of nature and religion. At fifteen years old, I possessed almost all the sciences besides the talents I had cultivated in the other occupations of my sex. One day as I was walking with the king, my father, in the gardens of the palace, he stopped of a sudden to listen to the chirping of several birds. I observed that he harkened to them with great attention, and I was amazed to see him laugh

without any cause. This surprised me in a man of his
wisdom; I was so importunate with him to know the
reason of his doing so, that he told me he understood the
language of all animals, and that two wrens had just
brought a piece of good news to the other little birds. —
And what is this news? cried I, laughing, imagining my
father did but jest.—It is, said he, that a miller's mule
having fallen down near the fountain of Jasmins, the sack
she has upon her back is broken, and there is a great deal
of corn spilt upon the ground.—I begged Gomar-Yusuf,
continued the lovely Georgian, to carry me to the
fountain. He did so, and indeed I beheld so great a number of birds busied in picking up the corn which the miller
had left upon the ground, that I was in the utmost amazement. I persecuted my father to teach me that language;
and almost neglecting all the other sciences to apply myself wholly to that, I became in less than a year's time as
skilful in it as was Gomar-Yusuf himself. It is impossible,
my lord, continued Gulguli-Chamami, to conceive the
pleasure it affords one to understand the different jargons of
animals; it is much more full of wisdom and nature than
that of men; and I may perhaps relate to you hereafter
things of it, which will give you no small delight; but at
present let us return to my story.

I had now attained my sixteenth year, and we were
very far from expecting the misfortune that hung over us,
when a traitorous Enchanter, named Bisah al-Kasak, acting from an old aversion he had to our family, surprised us
one night with a numerous army. He strangled the wise
Gomar-Yusuf and the queen my mother, and was going to
deprive me too of life, when touched by my cries, or perhaps
by some little beauty he perceived in me, he contented
himself with carrying me with him to an island in the
middle of the Caspian Sea, where he shut me up in a
strong tower. This island was guarded by phantoms,
that were incessantly upon the watch; horrible tempests

continually dashed its coasts, and no mortal could
approach it with impunity, except only on one day in the
year, on which all the enchanters, fairies, jinnis, and other
spirits of that nature were indispensably obliged to
assemble in a grotto of Cochin China, in order to give an
account of their actions to him who had been chosen
their king the year before, and to proceed to a new election
of one from among themselves.

The perfidious Kasak had no sooner brought me to this
melancholy prison, than he tried to assuage my grief by the
most respectful manners. My despair was so violent that
I loaded him with the bitterest reproaches, and I testified
so much horror for his person that he was twenty times
upon the point of destroying me; but hoping perhaps
that time would bend the stubbornness of my temper, he
only laughed at all I could say; and leaving me a prey to
the sharpest affliction, he did not come to me again until
eight days afterwards. I tremble yet, my lord, when I
call to mind that dreadful moment. The traitor endeavoured in vain to persuade me; but finding that my
sorrow, instead of diminishing, increased every day, he
flew into the most violent fury, and told me in plain terms
that I must consent immediately to his infamous designs,
or he would cause me to be burnt alive. This choice did
not all frighten me; I beheld with great tranquility the
preparations for my death, and ran to it with joy; when
the Enchanter, who had no designs upon my life, carried
me back to the tower. I am now going to Cochin China,
said he, whence I shall return in four-and-twenty
hours. I allow you that further time to come to a resolution; and if I do not find you obedient to my absolute
will, I shall use the utmost violence towards you. I did
not condescend to answer these insolent menaces, and
being resolved to destroy myself, rather than endure that
barbarian's brutalities, I saw him depart without the
least fear of his return.

Zal-raka, my grandfather, was not ignorant of the place of my confinement, nor of the author of my misery. That Enchanter impatiently waited for Kasak's absence. He no sooner saw him depart for Cochin China, than by the power of his art he dispersed the black clouds which concealed me from the eyes of all the world; he freed me from the dismal tower I was in; and after having set me upon terra firma, he caused the island which was the habitation of the perfidious Enchanter to be swallowed up in a moment in my presence: and conveying me through the air with incredible rapidity, he placed me in a vast open country, whence one might behold the city of Palimban.

It is impossible to give you an idea of the excess of my joy; I embraced my grandfather with all the tenderness imaginable. My daughter, said he to me, I must go without delay to Cochin China, where we are obliged to be before sunrise. I will there put up all my complaints against your persecutor. You are no longer in his power; do you now go in quest of the prince. At these words, my lord, continued Gulguli-Chamami shedding a flood of tears, Zal-raka stopped short. A cold sweat rose upon his face: he lost the use of his speech for some moments, and then returning to himself: Ah! my dear daughter, said he to me in a weak voice, my hour is come. I see the sword of the angel of death ready to cut the thread of life; all my art cannot save me from going to give an account of my actions before the tribunal of our Almighty Allah; but I have the consolation at my death to know that a young prince, after having slain your tyrant, shall marry you and restore you to the possession of the dominions the traitor has usurped from you. Then my grandfather having struck the earth with his foot, there arose out of it a dun mule, richly caparisoned. There is something, said he in a dying voice and embracing me for the last time, to carry you where your destiny calls you; only remember, my dear Gulguli-Chamami, added he, that you were born a princess; that memorandum includes all your duty.

Zal-raka had scarce said these words when he expired in my arms. Judge, my lord, of the excess of my grief and fear; I had lost the only support I had in the world, at the time when he was most necessary to me. My despair was somewhat heightened by the impossibility of my paying him the last duties, and I could not resolve to leave his body to the wild beasts. Suddenly there arose out of the earth a magnificent tomb of porphyry and jasper; I put Zal-raka into it, in a coffin of cedar, and shutting the door of the tomb, which I washed with my tears, I saw rise up over against me a group of brass, representing the cruel Kasak, whose head was severed from his body, and a young man with a sabre in his hand. As the statues were very high, I could not distinguish the features of my tyrant's conqueror; I only observed that he wanted a finger of the left hand; and as, before I began to make you this relation of my misfortunes, I took notice that you want the little finger of the left hand, I at once judged it was you, my lord, whom the great Prophet has chosen to avenge me. I then gave myself up, without reserve, to all the tenderness that is due to him who is one day to be my husband.

The prince of China, my lord, continued Ibn Aridun, threw himself that moment at the feet of the princess of Tiflis. He could not find words strong enough to let her know the excess of his joy, when she raised him up with extreme goodness. Let me make use of Gulpanhi's absence, said she to him tenderly, to finish my story; I shall afterwards find time enough to make a return to these protestations of love, which are the only happiness of my life. The princess then, resuming the thread of her discourse, went on thus:

I mounted upon my mule, and had travelled almost

three hundred leagues without meeting with any accident, when one morning, stopping to make her drink at a spring, the water of which was extremely clear, she would not come near it; for my part, being very thirsty, and ignorant of the consequences that attended the drinking of the water, I got off my mule and took some in the hollow of my hand. I had no sooner brought it to my lips than I fell backwards: I know not, my lord, what became of me in that moment, I only remember that when I recovered from the trance I had been in I found myself in the arms of a huge black man, whose under lip was so thick that it hid nearly all his chin. I gave a terrible shriek at the sight of this monster; he only laughed at it, and throwing me into a great leathern sack, which he afterwards closed up, he put the strings of it under his left arm: and I cannot tell, my lord, whither he was going to carry me, when a man, so little that he might easily have walked between the black monster's legs, rode up at full speed upon a horse, whose height was proportioned to his own. Stop, cruel Kusayb! cried he to him at a distance: it is time to put an end to your tyranny.

Kusayb, which was the name of the frightful black, gave but little heed at first to the little man's threats; yet when he was at a certain distance from him I thought I could perceive, by the motion of his arm, that he trembled all over his body. He presently hung the sack in which I was upon the branch of a tree, and put himself into a posture of defence, with an iron club all full of spikes. For my part, my lord, I had my thoughts about me; with a dagger that I had at my girdle I made a hole in the sack large enough to see through it the combat, which I imagined must conclude entirely to the black's advantage; but judge of my surprise when, after an obstinate resistance on both sides, I saw that little hero, with one back stroke of his sabre, cut off both his enemy's legs, and afterwards sever his head from his body. I cannot express to you the joy I felt at so incredible a victory. I ripped the sack enough to put my head out, and, addressing myself to my deliverer, I let him know in a few words the infinite obligation I had to him. The little man was surprised to see me in that posture; he seemed extremely troubled that he could not reach to help me down; but I, being more fruitful of invention than he, cut the sack in such a manner, that having made two large strong straps of it, I slid down to the ground without hurting myself in the least. Madam, said the little dwarf to me, whatever pleasure it gives me to have come in time enough to hinder you from being the last object of Kusayb's cruelty, I should not perhaps have had that happiness unless I had been spurred on by a desire to revenge a sister, who has too long felt the tyranny of the villain I have just now slain.—I am very much beholden to chance then, replied I. But, sir, forgive my curiosity; how is it possible that, with the disproportion there is between Kusayb and you, you could yet overcome him?—It is no hard matter, replied the little man, to satisfy you. If you will come with me to Akim, where the king my father reigns, I will on the way inform you of the motives of my revenge, and by what supernatural assistance I was able to conquer the traitorous Kusayb. I mounted again upon my mule, continued Gulguli-Chamami, and this is what my deliverer related to me:

HISTORY OF BULAMAN-SANG-HIR, PRINCE OF AKIM

Who would think, madam, to look upon my stature, that I am the son of a giantess? Yet nothing is more true than that I owe my birth to Fag-Huri, princess of Sarandib, who is almost eight feet high ; but then you should know that to make amends for that, my father, named Kutar-Aasmai, king of Akim, is yet smaller than myself. Love makes everything equal : my father, who in his travels became passionately enamoured of Fag-Huri, did not think she was too big for him ; and the princess, my mother, touched with his solemn protestations that he would love her all his life, never minded the great inequality there was in their stature ; as she was mistress of herself, because the king her brother who reigned in Sarandib was but seven years old, she consented that my father should carry her to Akim, where he espoused her.

My mother was brought to bed of me four months and a half after their marriage, according to the manner of the pygmies, from whom my father was in a great way off descended, and I was named Bulaman-Sang-Hir ; but as she had conceived two children at the same time. after four months and a half more, she likewise brought forth a daughter, who, taking after her, and being born according to the common order of nature, was called Agazir the Tall ; thus though my sister and I were born at different times, and were of different statures, that did not hinder us from being twins. When Agazir was grown marriageable, her beauty made so much noise that she was sought in marriage by all our neighbouring princes ; but one of ourrelations, who was called Badim, and who reigned at Padir, prevailing above all the rest, was just upon the point of seeing his passion crowned with success, when unhappily the cruel Kusayb fell in love with Agazir. The refusal he met with from the king my father enraged him. He warned anybody from pretending to marry the princess upon pain of his wrath ; but his threats were despised, and my father was resolved upon Badim's marriage with my sister. Part of the ceremony was over, when all the spectators were strangely amazed to find the prince without motion, and to see that he was nothing but a statue of marble. This dreadful metamorphosis struck my father and all the court with horror. My sister, who tenderly loved Badim, almost died with grief; and the most valiant men of Akim, seeing how much my father laid this accident to heart, resolved to seek out Kusayb, to deprive him of life; but of all those who have been upon this design, I am the only one who has ever come back. You are to understand, madam, continued Bulaman-Sang-Hir, that it is impossible to come by land into our dominions, but through that place where my combat with Kusayb was fought. That perfidious wretch, as I was afterwards informed, very well knew he must expect to be punished for his crime. He formed the enchantment which you certainly felt the effects of. You have no sooner come hither, than a burning thirst obliges you to refresh yourself at that pernicious spring, whose water immediately takes away the senses; and several brave men of Akim have in all likelihood perished by that surprise, which has put them into the power of the cruel Kusayb. At length my sister was almost reduced to be his victim, when walking the day before yesterday very uneasy upon the banks of the canal, which is at the bottom of the gardens of the palace, I saw a boy, about nine or ten years old, trying all manner of ways to get a tortoise out of its shell; and not being able to do it, he threw it several times with all his force against a great stone. The shell of this tortoise was so brilliant, that it seemed studded with diamonds. I took it out of the boy's hands and was viewing it narrowly, when I thought I heard some complaints proceed from it; I put it to my ear, and indeed heard it begging me to throw it again into the canal. I was at first somewhat frightened at so extraordinary a thing; but though I was very desirous to have kept it, I immediately obeyed, being very little accustomed to such requests. I had scarce put the tortoise into the water,

when it appeared again, and thanked me for the service I
had done her. Ask whatever you will, said that little
creature to me, and you shall see how grateful the fairy
Mulladin will be, for so essential a piece of service as
you have done her. I remained for some time motionless
with terror, continued Bulaman-Sang-Hir, but animated
by revenge: Succourable Fairy, replied I, since you put
so great a value upon so small a kindness, furnish me, I
beseech you, with the means to deliver my sister and
prince Badim from Kusayb's persecutions.—Stay for me
here a moment, answered the tortoise, I will fetch you the
assistance you want. Then re-plunging for some time
into the water, she came again to the top, holding in her
little claws the sabre I made use of; and having informed
me of the enchanted spring, she ordered me to go and
fight Kusayb; and without waiting for my answer, dived
into the canal. I did not a moment delay the execution
of Mulladin's command, added the little prince of Akim; I
flew to my revenge, notwithstanding all the arguments of
the king and queen, who looked upon my death as
certain; and I arrived very luckily to deliver you, madam,
from that monster's brutality.

CONTINUATION OF THE HISTORY OF GULGULI-CHAMAMI, PRINCESS OF TIFLIS

JUST as the prince had ended his story, continued
the fair Georgian, we arrived at the palace of Kutar-
Aasmai, king of Akim. They had looked upon the ap-
parition of the fairy Mulladin to the prince as a vision,
and were so doubtful of the success of the combat that
they were bewailing his death, when they perceived that
the king of Padir had resumed his former shape. That

monarch, who ceased to be a statue at the very moment when the monster expired, came to meet us with the king, the queen, and the princess Agazir. As soon as the prince of Akim had told the particulars of his victory, which I confirmed, nothing was to be heard or seen but rejoicings; everyone ran to see the black giant, who, dead as he was, had still in his countenance something so menacing, that he frightened the most intrepid. The king commanded a great fire to be kindled, into which the traitor's body was thrown; and having given orders for building in that place an eternal monument of the prince of Akim's victory, he caused that happy day to be celebrated by a thousand joyful diversions. Badim and his illustrious spouse overwhelmed me with marks of friendship; and I could willingly have passed a considerable time with them, if a desire of revenge had not carried me away to find out my deliverer.

It was not without great violence to himself that Bulaman-Sang-Hir could resolve to let me go. He had become passionately enamoured of me. But though his little person was very agreeable, and he had an infinite deal of wit, and I was indebted to him for my life, yet as I very well knew that he was not decreed to revenge me me of my tyrant, I begged him earnestly not to think of loving me any longer. The little prince was ready to die with sorrow at my feet. However, he did all he could to obey me; and contenting himself with my esteem, he saw me embark with a great deal of tranquility in appearance.

I was born, my lord, to fall out of one misfortune into another. We had scarce sailed a hundred and fifty leagues, when our vessel was attacked by a famous corsair; as we were much weaker than he, we were forced to submit. It was not without tears that I saw myself again deprived of my liberty; but a moment afterwards I had not so much reason to complain, when Faruk,

which was the name of the corsair, accosted me with a
certain timorousness very unusual in men of his profession. It is not just, madam, said he to me very civilly,
that such beauteous hands as your's should be loaded
with chains; you are from this minute free. How happy
should I be if your heart were as much so as your person,
and if my respect and complaisance could one day deserve it! Whatever my surprise was at so speedy and
passionate a declaration, I thought it would be my best
way to dissemble with Faruk. I gave him some glimpses
of hope that I might in time be sensible of his love, and
upon this I enjoyed a perfect freedom. I began to exercise the power I had over his mind by delivering from
chains not only all those that he took in our ship, but
even some slaves whom he had taken upon other occasions. He did more; he restored them one half of what
they had lost, put them on board a little brigantine, gave
them arms and provisions, suffered them to take what
course they pleased, and reserved out of all his prizes
but one young Hindu woman, whom he designed to keep
me company.

This woman, continued the princess of Tiflis, was
of a ravishing beauty. A majestic port, a noble air,
sparkling eyes, a mouth and teeth extremely lovely,
black hair that set off a skin as white as snow, and a
charming neck, formed one of the most bewitching
women that my eyes ever beheld: and all these perfections were heightened by a graceful way of speaking,
which stole away the hearts of her hearers. However
violently I was afflicted, the young Hindu was still more
so; her bright eyes were continually drowned in tears,
and though I gave her a thousand caresses to stop their
course, it was all in vain at first. I represented to her
that I was perhaps yet more unhappy than herself; but
that, humouring the times, I put a constraint upon myself to conceal my grief from Faruk.—Ah! madam, said

she, I have not as much strength of reason as you, and cannot so easily assuage my sorrow: the condition I am in reduces me to despair.   I pressed that amiable creature to tell me the occasion of this sharp affliction. Spare me such a relation, madam, answered she ; my ill fortune is not worthy to give you a moment's concern.   But in short, continued Gulguli-Chamami, I so often embraced the young Hindu, mixing my tears with her's, that at length I engaged her to speak to me thus :

STORY OF SATCHI-CARA, PRINCESS OF BORNEO

BRUNINGHAR, king of Borneo, having wedded Gulbias, princess of Sumatra, had by her two daughters, of whom I am the younger.   The king and queen, who loved one another tenderly, died after twelve years' marriage, and consequently left us very young.   Though my sister was then but nine years old, and I a year less than she, we felt all the grief imaginable at this loss ; but if anything could diminish it, it was that my sister and I were not parted from one another's company.   Ghionluk, king of Java, who had espoused my mother's sister, and whom at her death she begged to take care of us, came himself to Borneo.   He left a viceroy there, and taking us with him to Java, committed us to the management of the queen his wife.   That prince had but one son, who was a little older than my eldest sister.   He was continually with her, and saw with pleasure that Sirma, which was my sister's name, made a suitable return to his affection. It was indeed almost impossible she should refuse her heart to a prince who had so many good qualities.   He was of a charming person, and his countenance had something in in it so engaging that it was impossible to see him without loving him. But what made him most agreeable to my sister was the sweetness of his temper and the sharpness of his wit.

The king of Java cherished the memory of our mother in her children: he had formerly paid his addresses to her himself; but falling into a long and dangerous sickness, during which his life was often despaired of, he was very much surprised at his recovery to hear that he was forestalled by the king of Borneo, our father, the king of Sumatra having disposed of Gulbias in his favour. This gave him a great deal of uneasiness; but the princess Gulnad-hari, my mother's youngest sister, being a lively image of the elder, Ghionluk could think of no way to mitigate his sorrow for the loss of the other, than by demanding her in marriage. He easily obtained her, and had by her at the end of ten months Samir-Agib, the model of all perfection.

That prince was now above twenty years old, and the king his father, beginning to think of a wife for him, threw his eyes upon the princess Bisnagar, the only heiress of the kingdom of that name. This was indeed so advantageous a match for the prince of Java that Ghionluk imagined his son's ambition would be very well satisfied with the alliance. He informed him of the resolution he had taken to send ambassadors to the king of Bisnagar, in order to obtain the princess; but he observed the prince to be so uneasy at the proposal that he was persuaded it was not agreeable to him. Perhaps the weight of the engagement frightens you, my lord, said he to him mildly; but if you knew the princess of Bisnagar, who is called Donai-Karin, because there is nothing in nature more charming, you would quickly change your mind. I give you a month's time to come to a resolution; let me have an answer by that time, such as may suit with the obedience I am to expect from you. The prince made a profound obeisance, without returning any answer; then he retired into his own apartment, and being a little recovered from the trouble he was in, he came into that in which my sister and I were together. He looked upon us in sadness for some time without speaking a word, and his tears beginning to fall notwithstanding all he could do to restrain them, Sirma in abundance of emotion asked him kindly the cause of his affliction. Ah madam, said Samir-Agib to her, redoubling his tears. what a barbarous command I have just now received! The king my father designs me for the princess of Bisnagar, and I have but one month to resolve on a union, which would be the most insufferable misfortune of my life, if I had not courage enough to resist my father's will. My sister, continued Satchi-Cara, seemed thunderstruck at this news; she looked steadfastly upon the prince, and seeing him extremely dejected: Ah! Samir-Agib, said she, how miserable shall I be made! You will obey your father's command; and I love you too well not to advise you to do so. What is Borneo, in comparison to Bisnagar, or a rough pearl to a perfect one?—Hold, madam, cried the prince of Java, comparisons are odious. Donai-Karin, let her be ever so deserving, shall never possess either my hand or my heart: they are both reserved for Sirma alone; and I will sooner die than break the oaths I have so often made to be none but your's.

How tender and generous was this conversation, and how pleased was my sister with these fresh protestations of the prince her cousin! He came every moment to assure her of his love; and above three weeks had passed of the time Ghionluk had given him to consider, when that monarch, walking one evening in the gardens of his palace, perceived the prince his son entering by himself into a little grove. He had observed that he had grown of late melancholy and thoughtful, and that he had always loved solitude ever since he had spoken to him of the fair Danai-Karin. He was desirous to know the cause of this alteration; and therefore, commanding his followers to wait there for him, he slipped behind a close row of trees, whence he could easily see and hear Samir-Agib. That prince, who thought himself alone and at liberty to complain, at first gave himself up to a profound thoughtfulness; afterwards he seemed to listen with attention to some little birds which filled the air with their accents. Happy birds! cried he, who are not constrained in your loves; and who submit to no other laws than those which your inclination prompt you to; continue your agreeable songs. My soul, which is plunged in the sharpest grief, cannot behold your felicity without envy; it renews my own torments. The time approaches, he went on sadly, when I must return an answer to the king my father. O heaven, how shall I acquaint him with a passion so contrary to the interests of his greatness! The princess of Bisnagar will undoubtedly weigh down in his heart that goodness which he would shew me on other occasions; but what woman, besides the princess of Borneo, can touch a soul so insensible as mine? What rose can boast a colour so beauteous as that which shines on the cheeks of the lovely Sirma? Or who can shew such divine charms as appear in her face, from which the heavens themselves seem to borrow their serenity? Hope not, feeble mortals, to come into competition with my adorable princess; she deserves to give laws to the whole universe.—But whither does my passion hurry me? said Samir-Agib, mournfully interrupting his own extravagances. Alas! the more charms that princess is mistress of, the more tears the privation of her must cost me. But why should I shed tears? Can I burn with a more glorious flame? Ah! charming princess of Borneo, you have not yet power enough over my heart; a love so violent as mine ought to serve as an example to all the world. Let us break a timorous silence, and endeavour to obtain you of the king my father; and if neither my prayers, submissiveness, nor tears can move him, let us teach mankind that it is dangerous to irritate a heart that looks upon death as the end of misery.

Samir-Agib went out of the grove in this resolution, and left Ghionluk as much surprised as afflicted at what he had learnt. The prince his son was very dear to him; he had a great kindness for my sister and for me, continued Satchi-Cara, but the kingdom of Bisnagar inclined him in favour of Donai-Karin. He retired, nevertheless, very uncertain what to fix upon; and after having rejoined his train he locked himself up in his apartments, and would be seen by nobody. His mind was in great agitation all the rest of that day and the following night; but his son's satisfaction being dearer to him than that which he expected from seeing him united with Donai-Karin, he no longer hesitated what to do, but sent for Samir-Agib. My son, said he to him, I know what passes in the bottom of your heart; you are in love with Sirma, and whatever reasons I may have to oppose this passion, I yet approve it, because it is, I find, the chief happiness of your life. But as the authority I have over the princesses of Borneo might induce the world to believe that I made use of that power to unite you together, we must think of some means to bring it about without endangering my honour. Samir-Agib at these words was as much amazed as it is possible to imagine. He blushed, bent his eyes to the ground, and was some time without answering the king his father, fearing that monarch might make use of this artifice only to discover his passion for Sirma; but having come a little to himself, he thought he saw so much ingenuousness in Ghionluk's actions that, throwing himself at his feet: Ah! my lord, said he, embracing them, how can I express the sense I have of your goodness? You restore me to life in the very moment when perhaps I was going to give myself up to the most fatal despair. Yes, my lord, I adore the lovely Sirma. The blood that joins our families has so bound our hearts to each other that nothing but death can dissolve so lovely an union ; and since your Majesty is willing to consent to it, there is a sure way to avoid wounding your delicacy in this point. The princess is of age to fill a throne. Give me leave, my lord, to place her upon that of her ancestors. Borneo is the fittest place for me to win her in ; and there I am in hopes love alone will prevail with her in my favour.—How ingenious is your passion, replied Ghionluk, embracing the prince his son. Go then, said he, inform your princess yourself of this news, and make all the necessary preparations for conducting her to Borneo.

I was with my sister, continued the young Hindu princess, when Samir-Agib entered her apartment. Joy sparkled in his eyes, and he was so transported with the conversation he had had with the king his father that it was some time before he could speak. He embraced Sirma's knees in a rapture. Charming princess, said he, at length everything conspires to my good fortune ; Donai-Karin is now no longer mentioned; you are from this day queen of Borneo : I have just received orders to prepare everything for placing you on the throne of that kingdom; there you will be absolutely mistress of your own will; and there I will live and die your slave. My sister felt an infinite deal of joy at this news ; she raised up Samir-Agib. My dear cousin, said she to him, my will shall always be submissive to your's, since from this day I accept you for my lord and husband, and I shall never think myself happy any longer than while I enjoy your tenderness. I was present at this conversation, which gave me inconceivable satisfaction, continued Satchi-Cara ; it ended in new assurances of love, and the prince then retired to give orders for our departure, which was fixed for the fifteenth day following. During that time, my sister received the compliments of the principal lords of Java ; every one of them, in order to ingratiate himself with the young prince, whose passion nobody was unacquainted with, made magnificent presents to the new queen of Borneo, and our apartment, which was generally accessible to none but Samir-Agib, was open to every body during the time we were to stay at Java.

This, madam, continued the young Hindu princess, was the beginning of my misfortunes. A Jew named Isaac Miyah, as I learnt afterwards, made a wrong use of this liberty. He saw me ; I had the misfortune to please him, and he had the insolence to raise his wishes even to possessing me. As he knew not what way to bring about his desires, he had recourse to a famous Enchantress, named Dubana, and promised her a considerable sum if by her art she should make me inclinable to return his passion. Dubana, under the most modest appearance in the world, insinuated herself into the palace, got acquainted with some of my women-slaves, and engaged them, with my permission, to go and make merry at a little house which she had in a delicious place called the Fountain of Roses ; because indeed, there is a spring there that takes its source from the foot of a rose bush, which bears flowers all the year round; it was not two leagues from Java to that house. My women on their return gave me so delightful an account of it, that I was curious to be a judge of it myself. I would have persuaded my sister to have gone with me; but she was too much taken up with preparing for her voyage; so I let Dubana know that I would come the next day to see her country house, accompanied only by eight of my women, and by twelve black eunuchs.

I was received by the perfidious woman with all the appearances of the sincerest respect. After having seen the house, which was very neat, I went down into the gardens. As it was yet pretty hot, Dubana presented me with a veil of a rose-colour, which I put upon my head; but I was hardly covered with it, when I found an unknown fire running from vein to vein. I was ignorant what it was that I felt; a languishing tenderness had seized all my senses, and I was ashamed to think of the reflections on which my mind was then employed. In short, madam, I walked off alone from my train, musing upon the extraordinary circumstances I was in. Modesty induced me to be desirous of solitude. I turned into a little wood, and had several times walked over all the alleys, when Isaac Miyah, whom I did not yet know for what he was, accosted me with an air very full of perplexity. I then grew sensible of my imprudence, and would have avoided the sight of that man by hiding myself in my veil, when I saw him at my knees, declaring his love in terms I was hitherto unacquainted with. I at first repulsed him without making myself known; but as he followed me wheresoever I went, I was resolved to inform him of my quality; by this means I thought to have put an end to his importunity; but what was my wonder when the insolent spoke to me thus! I am not ignorant, madam, that I address myself to the princess Satchi-Cara, nor how much distance there is between her and me; but my love is stronger than all the reflections I can make to extinguish it. Consent with a good grace, madam, continued he impudently, to unite your destiny with mine; as all the powers upon earth cannot save you from being forced to do so. I trembled with indignation at these insolent threats; but whatever venom lay hid in Dubana's veil, it had not all the effect that was probably expected from it. I could no longer endure the boldness of the Jew. Wretch! said I, in a tone full of anger, whoever thou art, fly from my presence this moment, if thou wouldst avoid the punishment thou deservest!

Isaac Miyah was surprised at the firmness with which

I spoke to him; he flew away trembling, and went to give the Enchantress an account of the little success he had met with. I remained quite lost in my reflections, and could not recover from my surprise, when Sidhim, one of my maids, came running to me: Ah! madam, cried she in a terrible fright, what place have we come to? The famous Enchantress who is mistress of it has grossly deceived us by her virtuous appearance, which would have blinded anybody. That base woman conspires against your honour. I was behind a thick row of rose bushes, when I saw a man in great disorder accost her, and whisper something which I could not hear. Dubana studied for some moments, and then directing her speech to him: Let not the princess's resistance disturb you, said she to him; I will soon deliver her to your desires. Only take care of one thing; it is but a short half-quarter of a league from hence to the habitation of Firnaz, who is called the jinni of wisdom; hinder the princess from turning her steps towards her palace. All my powers are useless if once she sets her foot there; and we may both repent the undertaking we have embarked in as long as we live. Go back, therefore, immediately to Satchi-Cara, and do not leave her until I come to you; I will in the meantime give such orders as are necessary for breaking this stubborn virtue of her's. —Ah! let us fly this moment, my dear Sidhim, cried I; I tremble all over. Let us save ourselves, if possible, from this pernicious abode, and fly to seek the protection of Firnaz.

Two young hinds frightened by the noise of the huntsman could not have run more swiftly than we then did. We fortunately met with a little door that opened out of the garden into an avenue full of thorns and brambles, and which in some places was so narrow that we tore our faces and hands. Slighting this obstruction, we made our way through a thousand bushes that dyed us all in blood, and we soon perceived a little palace of an antique structure, which I judged to be Firnaz's by the difficulty there was in getting to it. We were now but a few steps from it when the perfidious Enchantress of a sudden rendered it invisible, and stopped our passage by a wide river which appeared before our eyes. This at first frightened me; but choosing rather to die than to fall into Dubana's power, I took Sidhim by the hand and precipitated myself with her into the stream, when I found myself pulled back by my clothes. You fly in vain, said the deceitful Enchantress to me: I shall now make you obey my pleasure. I tried to no purpose, madam, to move her by my tears and entreaties; the villanous Jew that accompanied her gave me to understand that nothing could dissuade him from his resolution. And they were carrying back Sidhim and me towards the fountain of roses, when a nightingale flying to me with all its speed, perched upon my shoulder, and dropped in my bosom a ring of gold. I looked upon this ring as a present from heaven: I at once put it upon my finger, and had no sooner implored Firnaz's assistance, than Dubana and the Jew fell backwards, the river that had stopped me from entering the jinni's palace disappeared from before my eyes, and I no longer saw upon my head the Enchantress's pernicious veil.

In that situation, madam, continued the princess of Borneo, I left this vile sorceress and the execrable Jew, and entering into the palace of Firnaz, I found my dispositions entirely changed from what they were before. The jinni received Sidhim and myself with extreme tenderness. My dear children, said she, addressing herself to me, few persons of your age and sex are disposed to visit me. My name alone has become so detested that mankind seldom approach my palace till they are worn out with age, or debauched with sensuality. But since you have sought my protection, it was but just that I should

counteract the infamous Dubana, by sending you the
ring of reflection. This ring is of mighty efficacy, it
rectifies in youth the violence of our passions, and teaches
us to follow with pleasure the strict rules of untainted
purity. And though you have less need of such a ring
than another, preserve it, I conjure you, as an eternal
pledge of my friendship, for it will shortly direct you in
the choice of a spouse worthy of yourself.—Mighty Firnaz,
propitious jinni, answered I, prostrating myself at her feet,
how obliged I am to you for this seasonable assistance !
The remembrance of it will be gratefully impressed upon
my mind even to my dying hour; but to this unmerited
goodness, add one instance more. Tell me I beseech you,
who is this odious creature with whom the sorceress
would have united me ?

The jinni, madam, as I have the honour to inform
you, soon acquainted me that the audacious villain was
the son of a Jew, and called himself Isaac Miyah. She
then drew his character in such hideous colours that I
trembled to recall the danger I had undergone. But,
madam, said I to the jinni, must this perfidious magician
still continue to seduce with impunity the young and inex-
perienced, and must the infamous Isaac receive no punishment for his crime ?—My dear daughter, replied the jinni,
this truly laudable resentment highly delights me. I have
already anticipated your severest wishes. Dubana shall
be punished in that way which most sensibly affects a
woman. She is driven with shame and confusion from the
Fountain of Roses; her figure has become so frightful as to
inspire mankind with horror. As for the Jew, he is from
this hour confined in a large iron cage, where four monsters
shall continually drain off his purest blood, if anything pure
can flow from a body so contaminated as his; and in this
condition he is doomed to end his days, overwhelmed
with the stings of a guilty conscience.—This method of
executing justice pleased me wonderfully, and having

again thanked the jinni, I desired her to permit me to return to the palace of Ghionluk. She transported me thither in an instant; where, after re-assembling my women and eunuchs, who had attended me to the Fountain of Roses, all Java was informed of this surprising adventure. As Firnaz had charged herself with the punishment of those wretches, we thought no more of them, but parting from Java, we happily arrived some days after at Borneo. My sister was then proclaimed queen, and immediately published her nuptials with the prince her cousin. The uucommon good qualities of Samir-Agib were so well known at Borneo that the folk were delighted with his accession to the throne. Nothing was to be seen but joy and festivity for upwards of a month, and the principal lords of Borneo every day invented diversions to entertain the new king.

I confess, madam, I could not behold my sister's good fortune without some degree of regret; and I conceived such a high opinion of her happiness that I incessantly wished to be as grand as the queen of Borneo. One evening, as I was walking in the gardens of the palace with Sidhim, I saw something glitter at my feet on the gravel; I picked it up hastily, and found it to be a picture in miniature, enriched with diamonds of an extraordinary size. I gazed, not without some emotion, on this lovely picture, which represented a young man of exquisite beauty. Upon consulting the ring of reflection, I perceived my heart violently attached to the original; but distrusting the surprise I was in: Where are you, powerful Firnaz? cried I. Surely you will never approve that I should so suddenly abandon myself to so flattering an inclination which draws me to such a charming object.— You may resign yourself without reserve to the secret motion with which love has inspired you, replied a voice, which I knew to be that of the jinni without seeing her. The prince whom that picture represents shall be thy spouse. I was transported with joy to hear the jinni of reason authorise me to love a prince so completely perfect: I flattered myself that I should one day be advanced with him to enjoy supreme felicity.

Judge, madam, if I flattered myself without a cause. Saying this, she put it into my hand a little gold box which contained the picture of her lover. I had no sooner opened it than I cried: O heaven, what do I see! What! Is this the picture of your intended spouse?—Satchi-Cara was astonished at the exclamations I made. Do you know then, said she very earnestly, this prince? Ah, madam, if you do, answer me directly, I conjure you.—I hesitated a few moments but the princess growing impatient, I was obliged to tell her that I owed my life to the little Bulaman-Sang-Hir, who, it seems, was all this time her lover. This prince, said I, is very accomplished, and extremely well made; I say nothing of his other charms, as that picture resembles him to the life. It is true, his great soul is enclosed in a little body, which is the only defect, if it may be called one, that belongs to him. I then recited the particulars of the combat between the prince of Akim and Kusayb, and acknowledged in a few words the obligation I was under to the prince. The young Hindu being put to a nonplus, consulted her ring with great attention, and after a considerable pause, replied thus: What! though the size of this prince is but little, as you assure me, that defect is of no consequence, provided the goodness of his heart compensates for the shortness of his stature. The jinni, who is my protectress, is too wise to suffer me to be matched with an unsuitable person. However, let us submit without complaining of our destiny, and patiently resign ourselves to the disposal of the god Vishnu.

She then resumed the thread of her history in the following terms. The lively impression this picture made on my mind kept it always before my eyes, and whenever

I attended the king and queen to the chase, I withdrew purely to indulge the dear delight of gazing on it alone, and without interruption. One day as I was thus occupied, a violent storm of rain overtook me, darkness succeeded the storm, and when I would fain have gained the middle of the chase, my horse, being startled at the thunder and lightning ran with me through unknown paths. Night was at hand, and being greatly perplexed I alighted, and leading my horse by the bridle, perceived a light at a great distance, glimmering through some trees. Turning my steps that way, the further I walked the further it appeared. I followed it nearly an hour, without being aware of the danger to which I was exposed. At last, being heartily tired, I tied my horse to a tree, and lay down and slept very comfortably. But when I awoke, judge, madam, if you can, the terror I was in, to see myself on the verge of a tremendous precipice; for if I had proceeded a few steps further, I should infallibly have been dashed to pieces. I recollected, as soon as my fright would permit, that I was conducted to this place by one of those elementary spirits who sport themselves with the lives of persons travelling in the dark. Altering my course, I proceeded very slowly for about an hour, when I found myself on the sea-shore. I was now dreadfully alarmed, for not a soul appeared to put me in the right road. In the midst of this cruel perplexity out started four negroes from behind some rocks, and seizing the bridle of my horse, they took me in their arms, and in spite of my cries, bore me to a shallop close by. Two of these wretches rowed with all their might, while the other two prevented me from plunging into the sea, till they reached a ship which rode about half a league from the place where I was so unhappy as to lose my liberty. They presented me to the master of the vessel, who was a very tall lusty man, and whose thick hanging eye-brows, lowering aspect, and short wry neck, were frightful enough.   He carried me into his cabin, and accosted me with an insolent air.   Dry up your tears, said the brute, and thank the great Prophet that he has destined you to the honours of my bed.   Far from complying with his orders I redoubled my tears.   The hardened villain, without regarding my anguish, approached to embrace me, which so provoked me that I snatched a dagger from his side and plunged it directly into his heart.

The noise of his fall alarmed and brought several of the crew into the cabin, which rang with their cries.   I still held the dagger in my hand, and was just going to turn the point of it to my own breast, when one of them held my arms.   It was the cruel Nakur, the unworthy son of him whom I had just killed.   Perfidious ! said he, foaming with rage, the death you are about to inflict upon yourself is too mild and too glorious.   No, you shall expire under the most excruciating torments ingenuity itself can invent.   My hands and feet were presently chained, and when I was turned down into the hold, the principal officers were summoned to determine the manner of my execution.   But while they were thus consulting about my death, a sail appeared, steering directly towards them. A thirst for prey suspended all thoughts of vengeance. Nakur addressed himself to the attack ; but when he saw the enemy hoist his flag, he trembled for the event, as he well knew it to belong to the celebrated Faruk.   This latter had never been vanquished.   Fortune and the sea, which are so inconstant to others, had hitherto been subject to him.   Our ship being boarded, an obstinate engagement ensued ; at last Nakur, and the stoutest part of his crew being killed, the rest were obliged to surrender their arms. The conqueror entered and visited every part of the ship, and being informed of the cause of my chains, he highly applauded the resolution I had taken ; and having ordered me to be unbound, I was, with the rest of the prisoners,

conducted to his ship, and that of Nakur was immediately sunk.

Behold, madam, continued Satchi-Cara, behold the
source of all my woes! You see how the stars persecute
me, they set me for a mark for the wicked Jew, and if I
had not owed my escape to a miracle, I should infallibly
have fallen a victim to his horrid designs. Afterwards I
fell into the hands of a brutal corsair, and now I have
become the captive of another. And though I have nothing to apprehend from Faruk, yet it must be allowed that
a chain of misfortunes has always attended me; and notwithstanding the predictions of Firnaz, I see no likelihood
of a period being put to my affliction.

CONTINUATION OF THE HISTORY OF GULGULI-CHAMAMI, PRINCESS OF TIFLIS

I USED, my lord, continued the lovely Georgian,
every effort I was mistress of to dispel the melancholy of
this captive princess. And indeed her grief began visibly
to abate, when we were encountered by a ship, whose
poop and masts were gilt, and whose sails were of a flame-
coloured satin. This singularity inspired Faruk to attack
this vessel, though by her appearance she could not be a
corsair; however, upon giving the signal, they engaged
with prodigious ardour and intrepidity.

The commander of this ship was a black about six
feet high; he exposed his person to every danger, and by
his presence and example so animated his soldiers that
they all fought like a company of heroes. This warrior,
who seemed to recover new strength, leaped into our
ship, and as soon as he beheld Satchi-Cara and myself
he hewed down all that stood in his way.

Faruk began now to be greatly alarmed at the un-exampled courage of this mighty hero, and believing that himself alone was able to oppose him, closed with him. Never, my lord, were champions seen to exert more skill and courage; the soldiers on each side suspended their blows, that they might behold those of their respective commanders. At last fortune decided the victory, or to speak more properly, the arms of the black captain were better tempered than those of Faruk, who received two large wounds, which he sunk under. In this condition the corsair thought it no disgrace to surrender. I am vanquished for the first time, said Faruk; but, sir, if you will spare my life I shall be eternally indebted to your generosity. Rise, then, said the conqueror, reaching him his hand; others, perhaps, might have loaded you with chains, instead of which I admit you amongst the number of my friends; and as a proof of my esteem, I restore you your ship, with all her company, except these two princesses, whom I demand as the reward of my victory.

How great soever the passion might be with which I had inspired Faruk, continued Gulguli-Chamami, he strove to suppress his affliction when the conqueror claimed Satchi-Cara and myself. The life, sir, said he to the black captain, which you offer me is less dear to me than is one of these princesses; however, I yield her up, and though penetrated with a lively sense of her loss, I do not repine at your good fortune. The young princess and myself were more dead than alive; and having tenderly embraced each other, we were on the point of jumping into the sea rather than become a prey to the black captain, when this illustrious warrior, taking off his turband, discovered a face which before was concealed under a very fine black crape. We were all struck with amazement, but nothing could equal the astonishment of Satchi-Cara and myself; she perceived in the conqueror the original of her picture, and I beheld all the features of the little prince of Akim. We stood fixed like a couple of statues, when the hero, smiling at our surprise, directed his speech to me. You are not deceived, most amiable Gulguli-Chamami. The prince who is now in your presence is not unknown to you, though he must never appear again under his former character. The fairy Mulladin, who protected me from the tyranny of Kusayb, extends her favours even beyond my most sanguine expectations; the history of which I am going to relate to you. Saying this, he conducted Satchi-Cara, Faruk, and myself to his own ship, where we reposed on cushions of embroidered gold, and after Faruk's wounds, which were not dangerous, were dressed, he thus began :

CONCLUSION OF THE HISTORY OF BULAMAN-SANG-HIR, PRINCE OF AKIM

IT is impossible, madam, for me to express the extreme anguish I endured when I saw you ascend your ship, and after you were embarked. As I had not the happiness to obtain a place in your affections, despair seized my mind, and my next resolution centred in death. Full of this design, I went back to the palace and directed my steps to the edge of that canal where I was once so happy as to oblige the fairy Mulladin. Here being agitated by some unknown impulse, I took a resolution to put a period to my days : this thought was no sooner conceived than executed. I threw myself headlong into the water, and after some struggling, sank to the bottom. But how amazingly was the scene changed when I found myself in a palace of crystal, reposing on a sofa of yellow amber! Astonished at this miracle, I thought it was but a dream, when the fairy appeared to me again. My lord, said she, your distress grieves me much, and I am sorry, as you love Gulguli-Chamami, that I cannot with all my art assist your passion; a stranger, it seems, is destined to possess her hand and her heart. However, be comforted, I will assist you to choose another mistress from among a number of the most charming princesses in the universe. Saying this, she uttered to herself certain mysterious words, and from that moment, madam, I confess I perceived in my heart that the extreme passion which I had entertained for you gave place to esteem only for you. And now the fairy, having entirely changed my sentiments, led me into a private cabinet, where upon looking into an enchanted glass, I saw some of the most beautiful princesses in the universe. A great number of them escaped me without the least attention; but not so when I beheld the lovely Satchi-Cara; her appearance renewed those delightful transports in a more lively manner than I had ever felt before.

At these last words, continued Gulguli-Chamami, the princess of Borneo blushed extremely, and was about to interrupt the prince, who perceiving her confusion, prevented her reply. Permit me, said he, madam, first to finish a history so particularly rare and uncommon as mine. Then resuming his discourse, he thus proceeded. As soon as the fairy observed the risings of a fresh passion for this amiable personage, she rallied me very agreeably. You see, my lord, said she, how effectually the charms of the brown lady can obliterate those of Gulguli-Chamami! But that nothing may be wanting to complete your good fortune, I will repair in an instant the injustice you have received from nature. Drink this liquor without fear, and you shall soon perceive its happy effects. No sooner had I obeyed the fairy, than I felt a strange kind of tremor run all over my body, and my limbs seemed as if they were disjointed, till my whole frame, without altering my features, became proportioned just as you now behold me. But this is not all, added Mulladin, which I intend to do for you. I will send your picture to the princess, who will crown your utmost wishes, and you shall receive her's in return. She then presented me with a box enriched with diamonds, in the bottom of which was pourtrayed the adorable Satchi-Cara, adorned with all those graces with which she is now possessed, and having enclosed my resemblance in another such box, she further informed me that in a short time it should have the like effect on her heart as her picture had already had on mine. I was so transported with a sense of the fairy's goodness that I prostrated myself at her feet without being able to utter one word. She raised and tenderly embraced me. Go, my lord, said she, go and deliver the dear object of your affections from a miserable captivity, and at the same time set Gulguli-Chamami at liberty. The fairy, having disguised me with her veil, in order to surprise you the more agreeably, transported me in this gilded vessel, and the winds have wafted me where my presence was most necessary. I have obeyed the commands of Mulladin, and am so happy as to have executed in a short time all that can contribute to my future happiness, if the charming Satchi-Cara is disposed to follow, without reluctance, the wise counsels of the fairy my protectress.

The prince of Akim, having finished his narration, continued Gulguli-Chamami, the princess of Borneo refused her consent, while her heart was struggling between a tenderness for the prince and the great modesty with which she was inspired by the fairy Mulladin and her ring of reflection. But after I had strongly pressed her, she no longer scrupled to confess that she loved this charming prince from the moment she found his picture. Bulaman-Sang-Hir was overwhelmed with joy when the princess apprised him with her own mouth of his

good fortune.   He expressed a tender and lively sense of
the many and great obligations he was under to Mulladin, when that fairy suddenly appeared in a ship, far
more splendid and magnificent than that of the prince of
Akim.   She had all this time been concealed in a
cloud which had rendered her invisible.   The fairy was
accompanied by the king and queen of Java, and by prince
Samir-Agib and the princess his spouse.   I come, said
Mulladin, to crown my work.   Behold, my lord, said she
to Bulaman-Sang-Hir, these are the only persons who
could oppose your good fortune, and they are now so
favourably disposed that they consent heartily to your
union with the beautiful Satchi-Cara.   They all embraced
each other with great tenderness ; and the fairy, who was
unwilling to defer their bliss any longer, transported them
in an instant to Borneo, where, after Faruk was cured of
his wounds, the nuptials of this illustrious pair were celebrated with feastings, triumphs, and a thousand other
demonstrations of joy.

CONTINUATION OF THE HISTORY OF GULGULI-CHAMAMI, PRINCESS OF TIFLIS

For my own part, continued the beautiful Georgian,
however solicitous I might be to find the prince whom my
destiny had allotted for me, I was far from being tired
with this illustrious company.   Faruk was resolved not
to forsake me, and following the example of the prince of
Akim he converted the violence of his passion into a
high esteem for my person.   Madam, said he one day,
since I have not the happiness to be chosen by the great
Prophet to reinstate you in your kingdom, I cannot contribute less to your good fortune than to assist you in
your search after the prince whom the stars have or-
dained for that purpose.   As I was fully satisfied of this

good man's sincerity, a virtue seldom found in persons of his profession, I made no difficulty in closing with his offers, and without the least hesitation put myself again under his protection.

At length, my lord, after a considerable stay in Borneo, I embarked with Faruk. The winds were very favourable for the first three or four days, but on the fifth there was such a surprising calm that we could neither advance nor put back. Though Faruk's uneasiness at this delay was different from mine, he neglected nothing which might serve to divert my chagrin during a calm of nine days. To dispel which he strove to amuse me with several entertaining histories; and as he was very polite, and possessed a large share of good sense, he acquitted himself so well that I heard him with prodigious delight. But, sir, said I to him, amongst all these singular adventures am I to be left ignorant of your own ? Your conduct to me hitherto makes me suspect that you are different from what you appear to be ; and, therefore, I am more curious to know your history than any I have hitherto heard. My suspicions were presently confirmed, for Faruk, by an involuntary sigh, discovered that my curiosity had brought something painful to his remembrance. You have, madam, too much power over my mind, replied Faruk, for me to conceal any longer from you who I am. Prepare, then, to hear the history of an unfortunate prince, whose life has almost always been marked with some sorrowful catastrophe :

CONTINUATION OF THE TALE OF UTZIM-OCHANTI, PRINCE OF CHINA

JUST as the princess of Tiflis, continued Ibn Aridun, was about to relate to Utzim-Ochanti the history of Faruk, Gulpanhi entered the hall. She presented her hand to the young prince of China, and led him to a cabinet, in which was a carpet of gold and silk, strewed over with flowers of an odoriferous smell. He was then presented with rose-water to wash his hands, and his beard was perfumed with a fragrant composition enclosed in a vessel of gold; after this a magnificent collation was served up, which being ended, Gulpanhi ordered all her women to withdraw. The prince trembled at this order, and Gulguli-Chamami who was not excepted, gave him such a sorrowful look at parting that he was once inclined to rise from the sofa and leave Gulpanhi to herself; but considering such a step would be highly imprudent, he was constrained to stay, and though the princess used every artifice to engage his affections, he received all her caresses with coldness and indifference.

A behaviour like this would have highly disgusted any other but Gulphani; but that princess either feigned herself ignorant of this indifference, or else attributed it to some other cause than that of contempt. She appeared, however, highly delighted with his conversation till the hour of parting arrived, when she consigned him to the care of Kurum, who was an old and faithful confidante of her pleasures. The prince followed her, but in passing through a kind of dark gallery, somebody ingeniously slipt into his hand a billet, the substance of which was couched in the following terms :

"It is difficult enough to resist the dangerous blandishments of the person whom you have just now quitted. But, my lord, I am of opinion that you may elude her artifices. Dissemble awhile, till you can deliver me from this miserable captivity. I hope to see you to-morrow at the combat of tigers, with which king Kusah intends to entertain prince Atabak. If there is no speaking to you then, I will contrive towards evening to convey you into my apartment, where I have a thousand things to say.

"The Princess of Tiflis."

Utzim-Ochanti kissed this letter a thousand times, and now his fidelity being strongly confirmed, he lay down with a heart full of excessive joy. The next morning Gulpanhi, pursuing her design, sent to the prince before he was well awake a basket embroidered with gold, in which was a magnificent rich scarf; intimating at the same time that it would be very agreeable to the princess if he was disposed to rise. As the apartments of the princess were exposed to all comers, he flattered himself that Gulguli-Chamami would be there. He was not mistaken, for this latter was appointed to receive the prince, if he arrived before the princess was awake; but as Gulpanhi had this meeting too much at heart to sleep long, the young prince could do no more than just assure his mistress that he would love her for ever.

The indifference with which the prince had received Gulpanhi's passion had affected her so much that this princess had enjoyed but little sleep. She was not willing that this conquest should escape her, and she no sooner knew of his being with the princess of Tiflis, than she sent for him. When she left her bed, clad in a seductive deshabille, she appeared so charming that the prince would have certainly been ensnared if he had been less fortified. The princess without taking the least notice of his indifference, received him with a great deal of joy. She caused him to be seated on a sofa, and bending her ear towards him, asked him very obligingly, why he had neglected to put on the scarf she had sent him? telling him at the same time that he was surely ignorant of its great value.—Madam, replied the prince, I dared not appear in this court with such a glorious, unmerited mark of your kindness; but since you are pleased to permit me, I will do myself the honour to wear this illustrious proof of your goodness.

Their conversation had held near an hour, when

prince Atabak, who knew that the princess was always easy of access, entered suddenly. She had but just time to tell the prince of China that after dinner he would find her at the combat of tigers, and that he should place himself at as little distance from her as possible, because she desired to have some further discourse when the diversion was ended. The prince obeyed her orders, and fixed upon a place beneath her balcony; and as Gulguli-Chamami was on the same side with Gulpanhi, his eyes were always turned towards the former without giving the least umbrage to the latter.

During the combats of some lesser animals, Atabak entertained the princess Gulpanhi with great politeness and vivacity. These being ended, a monstrous tiger and a prodigiously large lion were let into the arena, and after they had fought nearly an hour and a half with equal success, and with inconceivable rage and fierceness, they rolled over each other directly under the balcony where Gulpanhi was placed. The ladies, that they might take a better view of the engagement, all bent forwards; but while they were in this attitude, the princess of Tiflis dropt from her finger a ring, on which was an eagle was engraved in a jewel. O heavens! she cried, perceiving it near those outrageous animals, must I to-day be so carelessly unhappy as to lose the only real good I possess! Gulpanhi was so touched with the extreme anguish of her favourite, that she called out, but in vain, to the keepers to pick up the ring; no one was hardy enough to execute her orders, though she offered a considerable reward. When behold! the prince of China leaped into the arena, and picked up the ring the princess had dropped from her finger. Luckily for him, the lion and tiger had spent the greatest part of their strength in the long fight they had sustained; but as soon as they saw the prince, they quitted each other, as it were by consent, and turned all their rage against him.

The prince was only armed with a sabre, which was however well tempered, and he wielded it with such success that leaving them both dead, he returned unhurt with the ring to the princess of Tiflis.

If the intrepidity of the prince astonished the king and all the spectators, Gulpanhi was surprised to the last degree: she began now to open her eyes, and rightly judged that the coldness with which she was treated proceeded from the charms he had discovered in her favourite. She could not indeed publicly disapprove an action so truly heroic; on the contrary, she bestowed high encomiums on the prince but conceived at the same time a lively resent-ment against the preference he had given to the princess of Tiflis. With respect to king Kusah, he was so little accustomed to achievements of this sort, and was so charmed with the behaviour of the young prince, that he perfectly loaded him with caresses. An action so super-latively great as this deserves, said the monarch, the highest praises and the largest rewards; and I would, young stranger, find how to recompense so much valour, if there be anything in my kingdom that is worthy of your acceptance. If there be, demand it boldly, if it be even one of my daughters, I can refuse you nothing. Utzim-Ochanti replied with great modesty to these encomiums of the king. My lord, said the prince, a private gentleman, as I am, ought not to aspire to the honour of your alliance. I am not so ambitious; but since your Majesty has assured me of your esteem and goodness, permit me to make one small request in favour of Gulguli-Chamami, which is, that she may be set at liberty.

The king, my lord, was still more astonished to see this young man set such a narrow bound to his wishes, which he esteemed as nothing in comparison to those immense treasures with which he was ready to honour him. Gulguli-Chamami is from this moment her own mistress, replied the monarch embracing the prince, and I heartily wish she may make you a suitable acknowledgment ; and I believe the princess my daughter will not oppose my will. Gulpanhi was almost choked with rage : the visible contempt the prince entertained for her charms threw her into despair. But being a perfect dissembler, she embraced the princess of Tiflis with all the marks of tenderness and of sincerity, and taking from her hair a cluster of jewels of a prodigious worth, she joined this as a present to the liberty she had just obtained. The beautiful Georgian was in the utmost confusion ; joy and terror had successively made such impressions on her mind that she had fallen into a swoon. She could scarcely believe when she recovered, that her dear prince was alive, even when he informed her that he had obtained her liberty.

They returned to the palace and the king ordered an apartment for the prince ; and being invited by prince Atabak to a repast, that he might give Utzim-Ochanti the greater pleasure he caused Gulguli-Chamami to grace the table with her presence. But this princess was more attentive to the behaviour of Gulpanhi, than to the honours which were paid to the prince her lover. She remarked in spite of all her artifice, something stiff and reserved in her looks and behaviour ; and even her very jests had a tincture of that rancour which predominated in her heart. In short she was very uneasy, as she was too well acquainted with the genius of this malevolent princess. Supper being ended, and having passed into a magnificent hall, they were entertained with a fine concert of vocal and instrumental music. Gulguli-Chamami took an opportunity to tell the prince not to come to the place appointed in her letter, but gave him the key of a wardrobe, which communicated with her apartment.

The concert being finished, the prince retired to

the chamber which they had prepared for him, and dismissing all his attendants, he hastened to the wardrobe of the Princess of Tiflis. As he was greatly fatigued, and not choosing to be seen, he concealed himself under a table which was covered with a large carpet, and fell into such a profound sleep that the princess, after she had put Gulpanhi to bed, entered the wardrobe without giving him the least disturbance. As she did not perceive her lover had come, she fancied he could not execute his promise; but not despairing of his appearance, she lighted two wax candles, and placing them on the table, she lay down on a sofa, and fell into a calm sleep; but, my lord, how great was the surprise of these two lovers when they were awakened by the violent noise of a person falling with all her weight on the floor, and whom they soon perceived to be the princess Gulpanhi, in the very agonies of death. O heavens! cried the prince, dreadfully frightened, and creeping from under the table, what fatal object is this! Am I asleep or not?—Alas! replied Gulguli-Chamami, would to God it were a dream, it would quickly be dispelled! but, unfortunately for us, this is a sorrowful truth. The princess, animated by revenge, has entered my apartment with a design to deprive me of my life; but heaven, who always preserves the innocent, has given this event another turn. Judge you by these fragments of this glass tube, and by the convulsions of the unfortunate Gulpanhi. Watching for you, my lord, I grew sleepy, without knowing you were so near; and I slept quietly, whilst the princess with the help of another key, stole hither, without doubt to put an end to my life. She had filled this tube with a powder which was poisoned, and had then applied it to my nose, when suddenly awaking, I sneezed with such violence that instead of receiving it in my nose, it went into her mouth. According to all appearance, this poison is of so subtle a nature that she fell backwards on the spot, and as you see is just ready to expire.

The prince, being shocked with the blackness of this deed, resolved to abandon the wretch Gulpanhi to her fate. Let us fly from an object so full of horror, said he to the princess, that we may elude the wrath of the king; for though we are entirely innocent, these appearances will certainly condemn us.—Ah! my lord, replied the princess, how shall we fly? The gates of the palace are all guarded; but, continued she, casting her eyes on the prince's scarf; yes, my lord, I perceive our remedy must spring from the source of this evil. This scarf is enchanted, and will deliver us from perils wherever we are; for it renders those who wear it invisible till it is turned, and it was to secure you from being slandered as you passed to and fro in the palace, that the princess made you this extraordinary present; which virtue she had undoubtedly not yet explained to you. The princess then put on the scarf, and became invisible immediately, nor did she become visible to the prince till she had turned it again.

While the two lovers were waiting for day, that they might escape the king's resentment, the convulsions of Gulpanhi redoubled. Her eyes emitted only a feeble kind of lustre, which, upon fetching her last sigh, was for ever extinguished; she died in their arms, and a moment after, looked so horrible, that notwithstanding her former ill intention, these two lovers could not refrain from tears. The gates of the palace being at length opened, these lovers made their escape by means of their scarf, and without being perceived, walked to the next village, where they refreshed themselves; and then pursuing their journey, they made no stop till they were clear of the dominions of king Kusah. They had now time to rest, and the prince recollecting the adventure of the ring, desired the princess to explain the reasons which rendered it so precious to her. It is a present, said she, which my grandfather Zal-raka made me, and put it on my finger when he was dying, which was a circumstance in the history of my life I had forgotten to inform you of ; he assured me that when my misfortunes were drawing to an end, I should perceive in this ring as in a glass in what manner I should regulate my conduct ; but I was to take care that it did not touch a drop of blood, for from that moment it would lose all its virtue. I know not what possessed me to wear it at the combat of tigers but you now may judge of my distress when I dropped it from my finger. I shall be for ever obliged to you for the unparalleled proofs you then gave me of your love and intrepidity.—Permit me, madam, replied Utzim-Ochanti, to examine this invaluable ring ; besides, it is high time that we should even consult it.

The princess then pulled out a little perfumed purse, in which the ring was preserved ; she presented it to the prince, pronouncing at the same time some mysterious words taught her by her grandfather, when on a sudden it darted such rays of light that they were both of them dazzled with it for some time. After the light had abated, the prince examined the ring with great attention ; he beheld in minature, and in order, all the adventures of this princess. Here, king Kusah was seen in all the agonies of despair for the death of Gulpanhi; a stately monument was erected to her memory ; and as these two lovers seemed to be the sole authors of her death, a considerable reward was set upon their heads. This new discovery which they had made of the virtue of the ring rejoiced them exceedingly. They read in it every day, if I may so speak, how they should conduct themselves ; and regulating themselves by its instructions, they pursued the road to Georgia.

They had now travelled more than two months, when forgetting one morning to consult their ring, they had scarcely proceeded a league, before there arose a great fog, which quite obscured the day, and involved them in thick darkness. This prodigy astonished our adventurers; but the prince having taken out the carbuncle which he had received as a present from Ahmadi, it emitted such a bright light for twenty paces round them, that they could easily consult their oracle. If the carbuncle was useful to them on the present occasion, how great was their grief to find by their ring that they must shortly be separated, and would meet no more till they had each of them surmounted several dangerous adventures! The idea of their separation drew tears from their eyes, when in the midst of their grief, the horse on which the prince was mounted suddenly took fright, and in spite of all his efforts carried him out of sight. The Princess followed him for some time by the light of the carbuncle, but that light ceasing, and it being very dark, she was obliged to stay till it grew light, when in about an hour after, the day began to appear again. The princess was almost in despair for the loss of her lover; to complete her misfortunes the prince had carried away her ring, so that she was at a loss what course to steer; and after having searched in vain for him, she resolved to direct her way to the kingdom of China, where after a tedious journey she arrived, not doubting his appearance there sooner or later.

CONTINUATION OF THE HISTORY OF GULGULI-CHAMAMI, PRINCESS OF TIFLIS

Utzim-Ochanti, my lord, continued Ibn Aridun, had been absent from his father above six years. The good king Fanfur, believing him to be dead, was at length resolved to give his kingdom a new heir. It was not more than three months after the king had raised to his throne a very beautiful slave, when Gulguli-Chamami entered Nankin, the residence of the king, and the capital of China. As she did not desire to be known, she concealed her sex under the habit of a man; but in spite of this disguise, that graceful ease and charming air diffused all over her person rendered her none the less observed by the inhabitants of Nankin. Fanfur, with his new spouse, was standing at a window in the palace the very instant the princess passed by, and being desirous to know who this stranger was, sent word that he should be glad to speak with him. Guguli-Chamami appeared before the monarch, and with a truly charming air informed him that she was a son of a prince of Georgia, and that she only travelled for pleasure, and that she was called Suffal, and should make no long stay at Nankin.

The queen Kamsim (for that was the name of the slave the king had exalted to his throne), was present when the princess paid her court to Fanfur: she represented how much beneath his grandeur it would be to suffer a stranger of Suffal's rank to have apartments out of his palace. The good king, following the example of persons at a certain age who marry young women, was entirely governed by his wife, and highly approved of this advice, which was given rather from a principle of love, than of generosity, to Suffal. She could not but perceive a visible disparity between the latter and her husband, and as she had never had any inclination for the king, he appeared odious to her from this moment, and her heart conceived a violent passion for the young Suffal.

The favourable reception which the queen gave Suffal did not give the least alarm to Fanfur, who, thoroughly satisfied with the prudence of the queen, soon prepared apartments for Suffal; and the queen was not long before she disclosed what passed in her own heart.

Gulguli-Chamami, who had attributed the kindness of this princess to quite a different motive, was astonished at such a sudden and pressing declaration. She stood fixed like a statue; but the queen, putting a too favourable construction on this silence, pursued thus: I love you, my lord, said she, and I hate the king; and I am so powerful in Nankin, that if you are a man of spirit and of resolution, it is easy for me to give you the throne of China. I will myself poison the king; and I only wait your approbation of the project. The princess, trembling at this discourse, started back with horror. O heavens! madam, cried she, that such a base design should ever enter your heart! And can you believe me capable of such an execrable attempt? Judge better of Prince Suffal, madam, and know that I would not accept of a throne on a less condition than to punish you for a crime, the bare mention of which has filled me with horror.

The queen of Nankin being convinced of her imprudence, from that moment her love was extinguished, and rage and vengeance took possession of her heart. Dissembling her resentment, My lord, replied she, we easily forget our duty when we are captivated by love, and you cannot but own that the excess of my passion has put me upon forming this strange project; I thought the enjoyment of my person alone was too little to offer you, and that a throne would tempt you. It is a glorious thing to reign, and I cannot put the crown on your head without the death of my spouse; but since you disapprove of my proposal, you may at least be grateful for the goodness which a woman of my rank has for you, and consider that a refusal can only be paid for by death. The princess of Tiflis, besides the impudence of Kamsim, remarked a great indignation in her countenance, when the king entered the apartment of the queen. His unexpected arrival greatly disconserted Kamsim. She was so confounded, and the princess in such a disorder, that the king was not able to comprehend the cause of their confusion. What is this, madam, said he to the queen, which I perceive in your countenance, and in that of prince Suffal? Does my presence disturb you?—No, my lord, interrupted the queen very briskly, taking her resolution on the spot. If you see me in a surprise, it proceeds from this young hero's proposal. He has come, continued she, to throw himself at my feet in order to obtain your permission to fight with the blue centaur, which will appear to-morrow before the city gates; and he declares he will lose his head if he does not conduct him alive to one of your prisons. Though the princess of Tiflis trembled at the beginning of this discourse, she immediately took the hint, though she was an utter stranger to the blue centaur. My lord, said she to Fanfur, I do not retract my word to the queen, and I earnestly beg that you will not oppose the design I have conceived to rid you of this monster. The king was astonished at this resolution of Suffal, and at first opposed his design. I admire your intrepidity, said he, but I greatly doubt the success of your undertaking. But since the queen has desired my consent, go, my lord, and be well assured that an ample reward attends the execution of so dangerous an enterprise.

STORY OF THE BLUE CENTAUR

You are to understand, my lord, pursued Ibn Aridun, that not far from the city of Nankin there stood a little mountain, at the foot whereof was a cavern, from which, for five years past, on a certain day, issued forth a blue centaur, who, approaching the gates of the city, carried away with him both cows and oxen: several

arrows had been discharged against him, but to no purpose, for his skin was harder than iron. The king had
several snares set, all of which he eluded with great
address, and though that monarch offered considerable
rewards for him either dead or alive, nobody was able to
seize him; and all who had endeavoured, perished in the
attempt. But to return to Gulguli-Chamami. This
princess, after she had saluted king Fanfur very respectfully, retired to her chamber, and having informed herself of the history of the blue centaur, rightly conceived
that it would be much easier to circumvent him by some
artifice, than to seize him by force. With this view
she resolved to avail herself of Gulpanhi's enchanted
scarf, which luckily remained with her in the moment of
her separation from the prince of China; and at length
hit upon the following expedient which I am going to
rehearse to your Majesty. She demanded of the king of
China a chariot to be drawn by two strong horses, some
large iron chains, four great copper vessels, a tun of the
best wine, and some cakes made of the finest meal.
Fanfur having complied with these demands, the princess
ordered them to be laid in the chariot, and being directed
to the place where the centaur made his retreat, on the
eve of the preceding day she went thither in her chariot;
and having placed the vessels on the ground, filled them
with the wine she had brought, and having scattered the
cakes about piece-meal, she retired to a little neighbouring wood, where having turned her scarf, she passed
the night in great tranquility.

As soon as the morning began to dawn, the princess
awoke, and from the place where she was concealed,
distinctly saw the blue centaur coming out of his cavern.
He was amazed to see the four copper vessels, and the
odour of the wine drew him near; but first he tasted
some of the pieces of the cake, and finding them to be
exquisitely good, he greedily devoured the rest; and

after that, swallowed all the wine. He had taken in such a large quantity of the wine, that being thoroughly intoxicated, he could stand no longer, but was soon obliged to lay himself down on the earth, and fell into a profound sleep. The princess of Georgia perceiving this, ran quickly to secure the blue centaur; with the chains she bound him so fast, as to render it impossible for him to break them, should he exert all his might; and having with some difficulty fastened him to her chariot, she mounted it herself, and then moved towards the city, whose gates were opened to receive her. The rumbling of the chariot dissipating by degrees the fumes of the wine the centaur had swallowed, he appeared in the utmost astonishment on perceiving himself bound; and when he found that all his efforts to obtain his liberty availed him nothing, he lay down to be conducted like another beast.

All the inhabitants of Nankin were struck with terror and admiration: Gulguli-Chamami alone appeared upon the chariot with the blue centaur, modest and serene. They had advanced a good way into the city, when their march was interrupted by the funeral of a young Chinese, whose father wept bitterly for his death, while one of the bonzes, who conducted the funeral pomp, chanted merrily a kind of hymn in praise of Rama and of Vishnu. The blue centaur raised his head at that instant, and having for some time attentively surveyed the ceremony, he burst into such a violent fit of laughter as almost deprived him of his breath, and at the same time, threw the princess into the utmost consternation.

The princess, as we observed, beheld with surprise this sudden sally of mirth. But she had not proceeded far before it was considerably increased, for in passing through a great place, the centaur broke out again into louder fits of laughter at the people, who looked with

pleasure on a young thief fastened to a gibbet, and who
was just going to be turned off. The more the centaur
laughed, the more the princess was astonished. They
continued their course amidst a prodigious throng of
people; but when they arrived before the palace of the
king, nothing was to be heard for some time but the
shouts of the people, crying: Long live! long live the
brave courageous Suffal! at all which the centaur
laughed more loudly than he had done before. The king
upon these acclamations descended into the court of his
palace, leading the queen by the hand. The centaur
fixed his eye steadily upon the queen, and then upon the
ladies of her train, and having successively surveyed
them all, he set up such peals of laughter afresh, that
the king, with his whole court, were beyond measure
astonished.

Fanfur asked the princess why the centaur laughed so
heartily; she replied, she could not tell, and then related
to him all that had passed since he was taken. Upon
this, the king asked the centaur himself, but received no
answer. The centaur was then put into a double iron
cage, secured with two keys, one of which the king kept
himself, and gave the other to Gulguli-Chamami; both
of them failed not to visit the centaur twice a day, and
treated him with all the kindness he could possibly
receive.

Kamsim, who reckoned herself sure of Suffal's
overthrow, was strangely surprised to see her designs
defeated. The sight of this accomplished princess re-
kindled her passion, and being resolved to attempt the
conquest of her heart once more, she sent for her, under
pretence of congratulating her upon her late victory.
Gulguli-Chamami was forced to obey; she attended the
queen, who was alone, and in her cabinet. You see, my
lord, said this vile woman, that in seeking your life, I
have covered it with glory: but let this experiment

suffice. I love you in spite of your rigour, and must freely own that, if you had fallen a prey to that monster, I should have died with grief. But if your heart is not softened, I have other means to effect your ruin. Leave then your stubbornness, my lord——No, madam, interrupted Suffal, the ascendency you have over the king, joined to all your threatenings and entreaties, shall never force me to forfeit my honour. Abandon all hopes of ever seducing me, and tremble and fear lest in the end I should advertise the king of your ungovernable passion. These remonstrances rendered the queen quite outrageous. Perfidious! said she, thou shalt insult my beauty no longer; at the same time she scratched her face, and cried out with all her might; then commanded the eunuchs whom her cries had brought thither to seize Suffal, while she ran all in tears to the king, to demand justice upon the prince of Georgia, for endeavouring to violate her honour.

Fanfur, being prepossessed with the seeming modesty of his wife, never doubted the truth of her complaints. He was in a violent passion with Suffal, and without further enquiry, loaded her with chains, and conducted her to the prison where the blue centaur was confined. He reproached her with her attempt upon the honour of his queen, assuring her that she should shortly be put to a most shameful death. As soon as the centaur heard these threatenings, he laughed so violently, that the vaults of his prison perfectly echoed. The king was now more surprised than ever. This extraordinary laughter redoubled his curiosity, and he desired him to explain the reason upon the spot, and declared that if he did not deceive him, he should be set at liberty; otherwise, he should be put to death before the day expired. The blue centaur, flattered with the hopes of liberty, and frightened with the thoughts of death, approached to the bars of his cage. King of Nankin, said he, will you keep your word?— I swear by my head that I will, replied the king, astonished to hear the centaur speak for the first time.— Assemble then in this place, rejoined the centaur, the grandees of your court, the queen and all her slaves without exception, and I promise in their presence to give you all the satisfaction you can desire.

The king, who had a great desire to know the cause of his laughter, instantly summoned his whole court before the blue centaur. The assembly being completed, the king called upon the centaur to keep his word, but he refused to open his lips until Suffal was unbound. This desire being executed, he thus addressed himself to Fan-fur. King of Nankin, if I laughed heartily at the funeral of the little child, it was to see his reputed father weep so bitterly, while one of the priests, who, it seems, was the real father, maintains a criminal correspondence with the good man's wife. He sang with all his might at the solemnity, nor could he forbear laughing to himself at his mistress's husband's sorrow for the loss of a son he him-self had begot. Again, who could forbear laughing on seeing a thousand thieves, who every day rob, over and over again, the public of immense sums; who, I say, could help laughing at hearing them extol your justice in executing a young man whom necessity had forced to steal ten dinars, for the support of himself, his wife, and children; whilst they for their extortions, ought to have been in his place?

Here the centaur stopped; and seemed as if he would proceed no further; but on the king's urging him afresh, he replied: King of Nankin, do not compel me to come to a further explanation; I had rather be silent than discover things which will infallibly torment you. The king, who was now more curious than ever, replied, However disagreeable what you have to say to me may be, I conjure you to discover all you know.—Well then, replied the centaur, how could I keep from laughing

with all my heart, to hear the people shout : Long live
the brave Suffal, the heroic conqueror of the blue centaur ! when, at the same time, I knew that habit concealed a beautiful young virgin, for whom your son, who
is not dead, entertains a strong passion ?

If Gulguli-Chamami, my lord, blushed at this discovery, a livid paleness covered no less the face of the
queen, whom the king beheld with indignation. As she
stood near the iron cage, the centaur seized her arm.
Cruel and lascivious woman, cried he, your deceit is but
in part discovered to that monarch. When I renewed
my laughter, it was to see you attended by a train, who
are all privy to your debaucheries ; and when the
innocent Suffal was unjustly accused and imprisoned,
had I not sufficient cause? Since it is impossible a
woman could have her honour attempted, who takes so
little care of it ; for there are two men concealed among
your slaves, who daily disburden you of the little tenderness you have for the king. As these were truths easy
to be discovered, Kamsim was ready to die with fear.
The king caused her to be taken from his presence, and
in spite of Gulguli-Chamami's intercession, condemned
her, with her two gallants, to be burnt alive, and then
ordered all her slaves to be strangled. But, madam, said
the king to the princess, how shall I repair the injustice
which a blind passion for Kamsim hurried me to commit
against you ? Happy should I be if my son, my dear
son, whom I have so long lost, to whom I understand
you are so dear, would by his unhoped for return acquit
me to you, by sharing with so charming a princess that
crown whose weight, since his absence, has weighed me
down ! The remembrance of the prince of China drew
tears from Gulguli-Chamami's eyes, when the centaur,
who was now set at liberty, thus spoke. King of Nankin, said he, cease to afflict yourself; and do you, fair
princess, dry up your tears, your sorrows shall soon ter-

minate in the return of a dutiful son and a faithful lover. Go, meet the prince, who, while I am now speaking, is entering Nankin. Saying this, the centaur arose like a cloud, and vanished from all their eyes.

The king and the princess could scarcely contain themselves with joy. The centaur had performed such wonders, as left no room to doubt the truth of this agreeable news; they went directly to meet the prince, and found him surrounded with the people, who testified by a thousand cheerful shouts the joy they conceived for his return. Utzim-Ochanti would have thrown himself at his father's feet, but that monarch prevented him, and tenderly embracing the prince: O my son, said he, what showers of tears has your absence caused me to shed! But I forget all that is past, and think only of what has befallen me to-day.—I am not ignorant, my lord, of all your sorrows, replied the prince, and in what manner they are terminated by the princess of Tiflis. A celebrated enchanter, who assisted me to punish the persecutor of this adorable princess, has informed me of all that has passed in your court. He was so firmly attached to my interest that he concealed nothing from me within the compass of his art, and then he transported me hither with inconceivable rapidity, after he had apprised me of the just revenge you had taken on the perfidious Kamsim's infidelity.

It is impossible to express the pleasure the princess felt from the return of her lover. She was no longer afraid of losing him again, since she received him now as the vanquisher of the perfidious Bizag al-Kasak. She then expressed an ardent desire to be acquainted with the particulars of this glorious victory; when, after he had entered the palace, and had recited to his father all his adventures from the moment of their separation, he continued his history in the following manner:

CONTINUATION OF THE TALE OF UTZIM-OCHANTI, PRINCE OF CHINA

You very well remember, madam, I could not govern my horse; for in spite of all my endeavours, he carried me out of your reach. It is true, the light of my carbuncle dispelled the darkness which covered the earth, but my horse ran at such a rate, that I could scarcely distinguish the objects that surrounded me ; yet, as far as I can remember, the road on each side was full of dangerous precipices, so that I could not proceed without running the hazard of falling with my horse to the bottom. After all, I am not sure whether the ground failed under his feet or not ; but falling from his back, I rolled nearly a quarter of an hour without stopping, and after remaining senseless for some time, I found myself on a green turf, near the mouth of a frightful cave. It was doubtless a good while before I recovered from the swoon my fall had occasioned, and when I came to myself, I saw nothing near me but these pits. I entered the cave by the light of my carbuncle ; I walked nearly an hour, and met with nothing but reptiles of all kinds, which fled before me ; at last I came to a rock, which shone so bright that it looked as if it was set with diamonds; on the top thereof sat an ape of a fiery colour. As soon as this animal saw me, he descended from the rock, and prostrating himself at my feet, bestowed on me a thousand caresses.

As I was afraid of being surprised, I had drawn my sabre at the entrance of the cave. The ape made signs to me to strike the rock in that part which shone brightest ; I did so, and it immediately split in two, and discovered a black marble staircase, with steps of solid gold. I did not hesitate, continued the prince, to follow the ape, who had now become my guide; and having descended nearly five hundred steps, we arrived at a large hall, illuminated with twelve crystal lamps, in the midst of which was raised a tomb of white marble, whereon were represented several apes in different attitudes. This sight surprised me not a little, when I beheld the living ape sprinkle some water on them, which he drew from a fountain in one corner of the hall; they started up and bore him in triumph to the basin, and all plunged together into the fountain. This fantastic ceremony surprised me greatly; but while I was impatiently waiting for the event, there arose out of the tomb a man of gigantic size in a coat of mail. He advanced towards me with his sabre drawn; I prepared to defend myself, and after a very obstinate fight, I threw him to the ground, and on going to unlace the straps of his armour, how great was my astonishment to find I had all this time been only engaged with an empty piece of armour, artfully disposed, without a body to occupy it!

An enchantment of this kind very much surprised me. I then collected all the straps which laced this armour together, and throwing them into the fountain, my ears were immediately saluted with soft symphonies of music, after which I beheld several men and women, who had been changed from those apes and monkeys who had before plunged into the fountain. At the head of this company there appeared a man of a very majestic stature, clothed in a long robe of the colour of fire, embroidered with gold, and adorned with pearls and diamonds. He accosted me with a noble air. My lord, said he, I have waited impatiently a long time for you, to put an end to an adventure on which the future happiness of both our lives must depend; since in delivering my spouse from the cruel Kazak, and by destroying that monster, you will effectually re-establish the princess of Tiflis in her dominions, and become possessed of that charming person. You stand amazed, my lord, to hear that I am acquainted with your passion, but this wonder will cease when you know who I am ; and seating me on a sofa near himself, he thus began :

STORY OF BIZAG AL-ASNAH

My name is well known among the enchanters, they call me Bizag al-Asnah ; not that I am more beautiful than another, but to distinguish me from my brother, Bizag al-Kasak, whose surname was given him to denote the depravity of his manners. His power has been always superior to mine, by means of evil jinnis with whom he holds a close correspondence, and who have inspired him with an extreme malice, that I was always unwilling to attain.

There dwelt near us a beautiful virgin, called Sahik. I had often visited this damsel, and finding a mutual sympathy of inclinations, we soon discovered it by a mutual esteem for each other. As you know, my lord, the close connection between love and esteem, the latter was soon swallowed up in the former. I proposed to bind our hearts with the most sacred ties, she consented, and a day was set for the conclusion of that ceremony. Though there was but little correspondence between my brother and me, I thought it would be civil to acquaint him with our intentions. He not only approved of the match, but must needs settle our nuptials himself. Though I well knew he was capable of the blackest designs, I imagined that he would at least regard the ties of blood, little dreaming of the bloody treasons he has of late executed against me.

We enchanters are in general partly on a footing in point of science ; we can neither destroy nor hurt the designs of each other, except it be on our wedding day, and then, during that time only, we are deprived of our power, unless we espouse a fairy or an elementary spirit, which does not make us degenerate; for this cause we seldom match with simple mortals, and when we do, it is with as little noise as possible. My perfidious brother took this advantage; either he was enamoured of my wife, or his own evil inclination disposed him to act so by me; he had the assurance to accost Sahik in a very unbecoming manner. This I at first attributed to his folly; but perceiving my presence set no restraint to his insolence, I resented it. He then rallied me for a jealous fool, and in short extended his impudence so far that losing all patience I was going to fell him to the ground with my sabre, to prevent which he touched me with his wand. Be not so rash, he cried; though I am not disposed to stain my hands with your blood, I will punish you in a way which shall more sensibly affect you. Be transformed into an ape of the colour of fire, and become a witness to the happiness I intend to enjoy with your spouse. No sooner had this perfidious brother uttered these words than I took the figure of the ape which conducted you hither. The traitor received no other treatment from the amiable Sahik but what testified her horror and aversion. He then caused this marble tomb to rise out of the earth, in which he enclosed that armed enchanted figure you defeated, and after he had changed all my retinue into apes and monkeys, he caused the palace in which our nuptials were celebrated to sink deep into the earth, and conducted me to the top of this shining rock, where I have been confined upwards of a year. Judge, my lord, what anguish I have sustained in that cruel situation. Your valour has already indeed terminated my misfortunes in part, and there remains no more than to break the enchantment of the tomb, to effect which you must seize on the golden chain; but before you proceed, you must refresh yourself after the combat you have been engaged in.

CONCLUSION OF THE ADVENTURES OF UTZIM-OCHANTI, PRINCE OF CHINA

I FOLLOWED the enchanter, continued the prince, into a cabinet, where I soon recruited the strength and spirits I had lost, with a magnificent collation; afterwards we returned into the hall, and as soon as I had seized on the golden chain, there fell from the ceiling two fiery globes; each of these opening in the middle, discovered a monster in human form from the waist upwards. These two monsters ranging themselves on each side of the tomb of white marble, endeavoured to hinder my approach; when, behold! there arose out of the middle of the tomb a pillar, on which was engraved in letters of gold, "𝕾trike, 𝕯efeat, 𝕯escend." This incident greatly encouraged me, though I had resolved to engage with the two monsters; and, being aided by the enchanter, whose blows were all well timed, we vanquished every obstacle; for the fiery globes and the two monsters were swallowed up; and on my approaching the pillar, both that and the tomb, from the bare touch of my sabre, were reduced to a powder.

We went down a kind of trap-door, and descending a staircase hewn out of the rock, were conducted to the banks of a river, whose waters were very black. Here we found a little boat, furnished for a long voyage with all sorts of provisions. The enchanter and myself entering the boat, put off, and falling down the stream, arrived about a month after at the mouth of a cave into which these waters were discharged. Though the current which brought us thither was very rapid, we were five days in crossing it by the light of my carbuncle; and we did not recover the light till about that time. We then moved but slowly, and coasting along the banks, beheld at a distance two women bathed in tears running towards us; we beckoned to them, and making directly for the shore leaped out upon dry land and joined them immediately. Ah! my lord, cried one of them, if you have any pity for the beautiful Sahik make haste and rescue her from the perfidious Kazak. He has persecuted her a whole year, and she is resolved to suffer immediately the most cruel death rather than espouse the barbarian.—As the charming Sahik has defended herself so well, it is time, my lord, cried I, addressing myself to Bizag al-Asnah, to revenge the treason of your perfidious brother; let us fly to the rescue of your beautiful spouse, and not spare a monster.—I am infinitely obliged to you, interrupted the enchanter; but there is another method, more sure and less dangerous, for my revenge. Kazak is so blinded with his brutal passion that he thinks no more of me. I intend he shall proceed so far as even to marry my dear princess; then, as soon as he has divested himself of his power, I shall punish him for his wickedness to me. This resolution the enchanter committed to writing, and instructed Sahik at the same time so to behave that Kazak might be effectually ensnared; and gave what he had written into the slave's hands who had come to implore his succour. Carry this, said he, to your beautiful mistress, and tell her here is a remedy enclosed for all her misfortunes. The slave was out of sight in an instant, and acquitted herself forthwith of her commission; and upon Sahik's opening the letter she was ready to die with joy to find her dear spouse had recovered his primitive shape. Kazak entering her apartments, she dissembled her sentiments admirably. Well, my lord, said she, with an air that appeared serene, since I must resolve, I consent to marry you this day, provided you abstain for three days from consummating the marriage rites ; my hand is yours on that condition only.—Ah! madam, replied Kazak, transported with joy, I swear by all the tenderness I feel for you, your will shall be obeyed, and may I be for ever deprived of my power if I once violate my oath ! Upon this assurance Sahik espoused him, and he adorned his nuptials with every pleasure his art could furnish or his fancy devise.

During this interval Kazak omitted nothing which might divert the princess, who grew very uneasy till the return of her real spouse. At last, to the dreadful astonishment of Kazak, we entered her apartment. He would fain have fled, but his brother prevented that, and touching him with his wand: Stay, traitor, cried he, and make a suitable acknowledgment of thy crime. As soon as Kazak found his feet fixed to the floor so that he could neither advance nor retreat, he grew so outrageous that without discovering the least remorse, he uttered against his brother everything rage and despair could possibly suggest. Transported beyond all bounds, I cried: This is too much, my lord, to be any longer endured, this wretch has lived too long : and so, without regarding the interposition of his brother, I struck off his head. The enchanter had no sooner expired than all the people of his retinue, who groaned under his tyranny, threw themselves at his brother's feet to implore his clemency. He received them very graciously, and having transported us in an instant to his palace, he banished by his presence sorrow, which had long reigned there. After he had indulged in a few moments' tenderness with his spouse, he conducted me in an instant to Tiflis, where having assembled the states of your kingdom, I declared to them the death of the usurper, and at the same time renewed in your behalf those oaths of allegiance they owed to you. He then informed me of the cruel trial that the infidelity of Kamsim

had put you to for having slighted her love. He instructed me in the victory you obtained over the centaur,
who, it seems, is an enchanter, and was condemned for
some fault to waste nine years under that form, unless
he should happen to be overcome by the address of a
virgin, by whose means he might obtain his liberty.
After this, Bizag al-Asnah bore me with inconceivable
swiftness through the air, and landed me at the gates of
Nankin just in the instant when the flames were putting a
period to the life of the perfidious Kamsim.

This narration wonderfully delighted the king and
the young princess. My dear son, said the good father,
I can defer your happiness no longer : I am too much
obliged to this amiable princess not to admit her with
joy for my daughter. But this is not all ; I will forthwith surrender into your hands the kingdom of China,
and I will——No, no, my lord, replied the prince, embracing his knees, you shall by no means quit your
throne. If ambition had been my ruling passion I need
not have wanted for a kingdom, where, I can truly say,
I might have enjoyed the affections of the people : but I
parted from thence without regret, purely for the sake of
re-visiting you. The kingdom of Tiflis is sufficient to
bound my utmost views ; but if my advice has sufficient
weight with the princess, I had much rather, my lord, be
the first subject in your court than reign in Georgia.
Gulguli-Chamami was so charmed with this truly noble
behaviour, that her will seemed to be entirely resolved
into that of the prince ; and Fanfur was forced to give
way to their united instances, but on this condition,
however, that the prince should share the diadem with
his father ; and as this latter would be obeyed, Utzim-
Ochanti was proclaimed king. He then espoused the
princess of Tiflis, and enjoyed complete felicity with that
charming lady, uninterrupted by those accidents to which
the lives of princes are so subject.

*   *   *   *   *

Here the new wazir stopped, and Shams al-Din declared himself highly satisfied with his discourse. Thy conversation enchants me, said the monarch, embracing him; but, my dear Ibn Aridun, how is it possible that all these adventures occur to your memory? I am surprised to hear with what ease you have related the history of the prince of China, together with all those which are comprised in this narration.—Ah! my lord, replied the son of Abu Bakr very modestly, I rather apprehend from your Majesty's observation, that I ought to have been less prolix in my narrations, and that I should have passed on to the histories of the prince of Akim and of the young princess of Borneo; this I perceive myself. But to this is owing the suspension of those adventures which could not be so well related till those of Utzim-Ochanti were all unravelled.—Never mind that, replied the king of Astrakhan, I shall not lose the thread of your narrations. I well remember how ingeniously you brought Gulpanhi back to the hall just as the princess of Tiflis was going to rehearse the history of Faruk the corsair, and I observed at the same time you did not explain by what means this princess lost the protection of that brave man, so as to become Gulpanhi's slave.—This, my lord, replied Ibn Aridun, was a circumstance I purposely omitted, in order to shorten the history of that corsair. But as your Majesty desires to be instructed, I will tell you how the beautiful Georgian became the slave of Gulpanhi.

*   *   *

The calm which had lasted so long ceased at length, and one night when the ship was under full sail the princess was attacked with a great sickness at her stomach; she walked out upon the deck to take the air, and bending over to discharge what offended her stomach, a sudden squall of wind throwing the ship on that side, she fell into the sea.   It was very dark and they did not perceive the loss of the princess, but hearing something fall into the water the pilot imagined it was one of the seamen; several planks were directly thrown overboard, one of which the princess happily gained, and she floated about between life and death till break of day, when a little vessel, hastening to her succour, took her up.   The master of this vessel was a dealer in slaves, and though, the lady was half dead he perceived, as she was very beautiful, she would bear a considerable price ; with this view he took great care of her, and the capital of the kingdom of Kusah being the first port he landed at, he sold her to the princess Gulpanhi for eight hundred dinars of gold.

Thus, my lord, you have heard all the adventures of this beautiful princess, continued the son of Abu Bakr ; and as for those of Faruk, if you please, they shall be postponed a few days longer.   Meanwhile, I shall begin such an entertaining story as I dare say will highly amuse and divert your Majesty.—Proceed, then, my dear Ibn Aridun, replied the king, and you will oblige me infinitely.   The new wazir being permitted, resumed his discourse in the following terms :

STORY OF AL-KUZ, TAHAR, AND THE MILLER

There lived at Baghdad two young merchants, who had contracted from their infancy such an esteem and friendship for each other that they were never asunder. Everybody talked of the friendship of Al-Kuz and Tahar and as they had neither of them a father, and were their own masters, being resolved to be more closely connected, they entered into partnership, and in less than three years they made a very great gain. Tahar as he was talking one evening with Al-Kuz, observed that he was thoughtful. What, said he, is wanting to your happiness? Our stock is increased fourfold, and our warehouses are stored with the best commodities; yet I have observed for some days past that you are very melancholy, and that you seem to delight in nothing but solitude. Am I not worthy, then, to be entrusted with your secrets?--Ah, my dear Tahar, replied Al-Kuz, I am ashamed to confess my weakness to you, which, if it were possible, I would even conceal from myself; but I feel it has an absolute power over my heart. Do you know Bahul the Barber, who lives not far from Baghdad bridge? Yes, replied Tahar; he is better known by his daughter's being reputed the handsomest girl in all Baghdad, than by the lively repartees which have gained him the name he is called by; and I begin to think by your sighing that you are not insensible to the charms of that adorable girl.—You have guessed right, returned Al-Kuz, blushing, I love the beautiful Lira, and I shall go distracted if I do not enjoy her; and I believe from the conversation which has passed between us, i am not wholly indifferent to her. I wavered, you see, whether I should acquaint you with my passion, fearing it might make some alteration in our friendship.—I know, replied Taher, that matrimony will deprive me at least of one half of your friendship. But my dear Al-Kuz, I prefer your satisfaction to my own, and I will go and endeavour to promote your happiness. As you know, my mother had the honour to give suck to Ja'afar, first wazir to the illustrious Harun al-Rashid the sovereign Commander of the Faithful, during the sickness of that Barmaki's mother, which hindered her from suckling him. I intend to use his authority with Bahul, and then I am sure to obtain the consent of the beautiful Lira. Al-Kuz tenderly embracing his friend, conjured him to lose no time, and the wazir engaging in the affair, Bahul soon consented to the marriage of Lira to Al-Kuz.

This couple loved each other beyond example; fruition rather renewed than extinguished the ardour of their passion; and they shewed such frequent and strong marks of perfect love in the presence of Tahar, that he could not forbear envying the good fortune of his friend. The innocent caresses the wife of his friend bestowed on him, inflamed him to such a degree, that to avoid being unfaithful to Al-Kuz, he resolved to take his leave of this tender pair. Accordingly he departed, under some pretence, for a few days, but in spite of the resolution he had taken, he was unable to preserve it long : he sank under the restraint he laid upon his passion and in trying to extingnish it, he fell a prey to a dangerous distemper. Al-Kuz and Lira never quitted the bolster of Tahar's bed; but they were so far from contributing to his recovery, that their presence increased rather than abated his disorder, which grew so violent, that the most eminent physicians in Baghdad despaired of his life. Tahar being on the point of death, both Al-Kuz and Lira wept bitterly at the imminent danger of their friend. His youth however and the strength of a good constitution overcame the distemper, but left him in a very weak condition.

The partnership which subsisted between these dear friends obliged one of them to go and settle some affairs in Cairo. As Tahar was too weak to undertake this voyage, Al-Kuz was obliged to go himself; and after he had made the necessary preparations, he took leave of Tahar, and recommended his dear Lira to his care, whom he tenderly embraced, with his eyes all bathed in tears; then parting for Bassorah, he embarked in a vessel which was going to Cairo. Tahar, far from complying with the intentions of his friend, no sooner saw him depart from Baghdad than he took as much care as possible never to be alone with his wife; but at last this beautiful creature, observing his behaviour, which appeared rude to her, said to him one evening: You always avoid me, and she took him at the same time tenderly by the hand. Since Al-Kuz's absence I have been considering if I have done anything to displease you; but I cannot comprehend the meaning of the coldness which appears in your behaviour. Such a conduct is really injurious as well as unkind; and I desire you will either treat me with less reserve, or else tell me wherein I have offended. Tahar was in the utmost confusion at this remonstrance; the tears which he shed without daring to look upon Lira, touched her in a most lively manner. She pressed him to come to an explanation; but Tahar throwing himself at her feet conjured her not to put this violence on his inclinations. Urge me no more, madam, said he, to open my heart; you will regard me as the vilest of men, if I discover all that passes in it, since neither the sacred ties of friendship, nor the near approaches of death, can triumph over a criminal passion; and I feel that——Stop, Tahar, cried Lira in the utmost confusion, I begin to understand you now. How is it possible that you could forget your obligations to my spouse, so as to conceive a passion so prejudicial to my honour? Ah! if this be true, let me be for ever ignorant of it.—No, madam, replied Tahar, it is no longer time to dissemble; I confess I am a traitor, a villain; but I am so in spite of myself, for I have used every effort I was master of, to extinguish these lawless flames. I would have died the most cruel death, and I condemned myself to an eternal silence, but you forced me to speak; however I shall soon punish myself for having invaded the rites of the strictest union. Here glancing his eyes by accident on Lira, and perceiving she was thoroughly incensed, such was the violence of his grief, that he sank at her feet in a swoon. To this at first she seemed insensible; but pity at length getting the better of her just resentment, she did all she was able to restore him to his senses, and the unhappy lover, feebly opening his eyes, saw how anxious she was for his recovery. Let me die, madam, said he tenderly, your assistance is cruelty: and my life after having offended you has become odious to me, and I quit it without regret. He then fell into another swoon, and Lira verily thought he had but a few moments to live.

Hitherto, my lord, pursued Ibn Aridun, I have drawn you a beautiful picture of this lady's conduct; but as there sometimes occur moments when the virtue of certain women is reduced to a dangerous crisis, Lira notably proved this truth. Terrified at the resolution of her lover, and softened by the excess of his passion, she made a sudden transition from the violence of her resentment to the most lively transports of tenderness. What has Al-Kuz done for me equal to this? she cried that moment to herself. He never loved me half so much as Tahar does, or he would not for the sake of a little paltry gain, which he could easily have slighted, have undertaken a voyage from which he is not likely to return for a twelvemonth. It is done then, my dear Tahar; I will both live and die for you; and since you died for me, I sacrifice to you without further scruple, all the tenderness I entertained for Al-Kuz, and which he so little merited. Live then, my dear lover, and live for Lira. These protestations of this beautiful person, my lord, were accompanied with caresses so touching that Tahar soon recovered from his fit; and the extreme surprise he was in, to find himself enclosed in the arms of his mistress, who perfectly overwhelmed him with the most lively marks of her passion, quickly restored him to his senses. He thought he ought not to neglect an opportunity so favourable to his love, and forgetting his obligations to his friend, and taking advantage of the weakness of his beautiful spouse, be became at length the complete conqueror of her affections. The sacrifice which Lira made of her virtue was attended, however, with some degree of shame and remorse; but as this was not a time to refuse anything to her lover, those impressions were easily effaced; his tender and respectful behaviour was such, that she thought no more of Al-Kuz, than if he had never been her husband.

Entirely given up to their passion, they dallied away nearly a year in the enjoyment of those pleasures, which appeared to them to be always new; and not content with seeing each other every moment, they must needs express their love by the most passionate letters they could devise. Thus losing their memory, the one of his friend, the other of her spouse, neither of them ever dreamed of his return from Cairo. Al-Kuz however, little as they expected him, returned to Baghdad, after he had terminated his affairs at Cairo. Though his presence was not very desirable, they received him with open arms and deceived him with their caresses. His long absence made him fancy that his wife looked more charming than when he parted from her; not a moment escaped without his bestowing on her some marks of his tender affection, and so far was he from suspecting her fidelity, that he furnished her with frequent opportunities of being alone with Tahar.

One evening as Lira lay reclining on her sofa, she was seized with a violent headache. To assuage this she wanted to apply a kind of distilled water, which was reckoned an excellent remedy for such disorders; but being distracted with pain, she gave her husband without a thought, the key of a little cabinet, where the bottle was which held this water. Al-Kuz, who tenderly loved his wife, ran to the cabinet, but he had no sooner gone than Tahar was surprised to see his mistress tearing her hair. Ah! said she, my life, my dear love, we are are utterly ruined! My imprudence will be the future source of our misfortunes. I have been so thoughtless as to give my husband the key of my cabinet wherein all the letters lie in which you have expressed the liveliness of your passion. Al-Kuz in his rage will doubtless spare neither his wife nor his friend. Tahar was vexed to the last degree, but being a man of great presence of mind, he ran after Al-Kuz, and the closet door being open, he saw him reading one of these letters; then shutting it softly upon him, he double-locked it and stole away with the key, while Al-Kuz's surprise at the infidelity of his wife and friend was too great to suffer him to attend to the motions of the latter. Tahar went directly where the cash was kept, and taking all the gold he could find, fled away with Lira to the first village which offered, where being mounted on two horses, they pursued their journey all night, till they were gotten more than twenty leagues from Baghdad.

In the meantime Al-Kuz, having read all Tahar's letters, which left him no room to doubt of his misfortune, took a dagger, and would have descended directly to pierce the heart of his wife, but to his great surprise found the door locked upon him. He called to his slaves to come and open the door; the key was not to be found. Al-Kuz, enraged at this, ordered it to be broken open, which being done, he ran directly to the hall where he had left his wife, but neither she nor her lover was to be found; he was informed that they had both gone together in great disorder. He went to the place where the cash was kept, and finding his coffers empty he threw himself on the ground, and his cries terrified the boldest of his attendants. None of his slaves durst demand the cause of this fury, but being recovered from his first emotions, he sent them about their business. Whatever may be my unhappiness, said he, let me act with prudence on this delicate occasion, and not expose myself to ridicule. I am, it is true, said he, betrayed by my friend, and my wife is unfaithful; and this is a sore affliction I must own. But ought I to bear myself the punishment of their guilt? No. Let them groan and die under a sense of their perfidy; the loss I have felt to-day is not so considerable as wholly to obstruct my future happiness. Then banishing Tahar and Lira suddenly from his mind, he despised them so much that he never once thought it worth while to pursue them; but leaving them to their destiny, he applied his mind as usual to his business; and sought to repair in the embraces of other women the loss he had sustained.

Six months had now elapsed since the departure of Tahar and Lira, when Al-Kuz was advised of the death of one of his correspondents in the East Indies. As that man was considerably in his debt, and had never settled with him, he was resolved to go thither and settle his accounts with the heirs of the deceased. With a view to this he left his effects in the hands of his nephew, in whom he entirely confided, and embarked at Bassorah, in a vessel which he had loaded with sundry kinds of merchandise. They touched at several isles, where

Al-Kuz bartered his goods at an advantageous rate, but especially for diamonds, which he always preserved in a leather purse in his girdle. A sudden storm overtook them at length, and after the ship had for some time borne up against the winds and waves, she unfortunately foundered. During the tempest Al-Kuz happily laid hold of a plank, and in spite of the winds floated two days and two nights; at last he was thrown on an island, which appeared to him to be wholly uninhabited. Being almost dead with hunger, he ate some fruits that grew wild and which were of a delicious taste; and marching afterwards nine days without meeting with any habitation, he arrived towards the close of the tenth on the banks of a little river, which he crossed by swimming, and descended a charming fine meadow, which led to a noble city called Brava.

As Al-Kuz made but an indifferent figure in point of dress, and fearing to be insulted, he declined entering the city till night. After he had refreshed himself with the remainder of those fruits he had brought with him, the coolness of his situation invited him to rest; and as it was a good while since he had enjoyed a comfortable repose, he fell into a profound sleep, out of which he did not wake before the night was far advanced, when he was suddenly awakened. A dreadful fire, which reflected its blaze from a fine house that stood detached from the city, quickly opened the eyes of Al-Kuz. He immediately ran to afford his assistance, and hearing several frightful shrieks from within, took up a great piece of timber which lay before the street door, and having broken it open, and also two others which communicated with the apartments of the women, they were happily rescued from the flames, and saved themselves without staying to thank their deliverer. After this he penetrated into a little closet, whose door he drove inward; here he perceived an old woman half burnt, and a young lady of exquisite beauty, almost naked, but more beautiful than any he had ever seen, fainting away by herself; and taking her in his arms he carried her in the condition in which she was to the place where he had slept.

This young woman, whom he imagined the smoke had suffocated, was no sooner restored to the fresh air than she opened her eyes. The day appeared, and she was surprised to find herself in the country; but being informed by her deliverer how she came there, she beheld him with less reluctance, and began to consider him as the only person to whom she owed her life. She told him her name was Salle; that her father, who had been dead three years before, was a rich jeweller, and that she lived with her mother and some slaves in that house which was now burnt. She then expressed great uneasiness about the fate of her mother, and having learned from Al-Kuz that he had seen the body of an elderly woman half consumed in the closet from which he had saved her, she no longer doubted her loss, and abandoned herself to the most lively sorrow. Al-Kuz did everything he was able to console this beautiful person; he returned with her to her mother's house, which was now entirely reduced to ashes. This mournful spectacle drew a fresh torrent from her eyes, and reduced her to the utmost misery. Al-Kuz, who began to conceive a violent passion for her, conveyed her from this fatal place, and conducting her into the city of Brava, at once provided new habits both for her and for himself, by the sale of one of his diamonds, and having hired a house ready furnished, he carried her thither; and in a few days after repaired her losses by buying in her name the house in which she lodged, and presenting her with a young slave.

The person of Al-Kuz, my lord, was very well made: he had saved the life of Salle, and his conduct to her was such as excited her gratitude. He passed several months with this beautiful creature in the softest and most endearing delights, and learned with excessive joy from her own lips how deeply her heart was impressed with his tenderness.   Never was Al-Kuz in such a happy situation before.   The caresses of a mistress are of quite a different nature from those of a wife, and Salle continually bestowed on him such lively marks of her love that he had reason to think he was the most beloved of all men.   But though the passion he entertained for this lady was very great, yet as the conduct of Lira had inspired him with a general distrust of the whole sex, he watched the actions of his mistress so narrowly that he thought he beheld her not altogether indifferent to a young man of Brava who passed frequently through her street, and whom she often seemed to regard with more than ordinary attention.   Whatever regret he felt, he discovered nothing of his suspicions to his mistress ; but one evening this youth, more indiscreet than usual, had placed himself opposite to the door of Salle's house, who, as she was at her window, appeared highly delighted with his gestures and manner of expressing his passion. Al-Kuz could not govern his passion ; he descended hastily into the street, and running abruptly to this giddy-headed youth, gave him such a violent blow that he fell to the ground.   The youth, astonished at this treatment, got up directly, drew his sabre, and made furiously at Al-Kuz.   But he having more strength and address than his antagonist, with two strokes of his sabre put an end to the combat, and left his rival all bathed in his blood.

The cries which Salle made when she saw the bloody condition of her new lover alarmed all the neighbourhood. As there was now no safety for Al-Kuz in Brava he fled directly, and having gained several bye-streets, which conducted him to one of the city gates, he stopped a little, not knowing what course he should take ; but being informed that the young man whom he had wounded, and perhaps killed, was a person of consequence, he judged it would be very improper to return to the city. He had about him, besides the greater part of his jewels, a purse full of gold. Travelling with these all night and several days afterwards, he arrived at length at Barboa. Here he embarked on the river Quilmanca, which empties itself into the Oriental ocean, and pursued his voyage to the Indies. There he arrived without any accident, and having settled his accounts with the heirs of his correspondent, he made a purchase of pepper, cinnamon, and amber, by which he gained cent. per cent. Afterwards being re-embarked, he returned without any accident to Bassorah, whence he sent by land his merchandise to Baghdad; but stayed at Bassorah for some time to recover from the fatigues of his voyage.

One evening as he was walking out of the gates of the city he drew near to a mill, and observing the miller's wife to be very pretty he became passionately in love with her. He accosted her without ceremony, and then made her a declaration of his love, accompanied with a very handsome ring, which he put on her finger. He found she was not averse to his wishes. Come here, said she to him, in the evening; my husband will be absent three or four days, so that we shall pass away the time together very agreeably. In the meantime I will go and prepare something for supper. Al-Kuz returned to his lodgings; he bathed himself and changed his habit, and returned towards sunset to find the miller's handsome wife; the neatness of her dress was sufficient to inspire him with delight and she received him with the most passionate caresses. In short, my lord, they had dallied away a part of the night, when on a sudden the door of the mill was opened, and they saw a man habited like a merchant enter the chamber. The miller's wife, looked at Al-Kuz with great surprise, and turned pale at this sight. She arose to excuse herself to this new comer, but he answered her with a blow, and followed it with several other insults. Al-Kuz, highly provoked with this brutal behaviour, seized the man by the collar. As neither of them was armed, they could only scuffle with their fists. But the miller's wife interposing between them, how great was their surprise when they, on surveying each other with a little more attention, found that one was Tahar and the other Al-Kuz! This latter, was in a rage at seeing the former, and calling his treason to mind in that instant, was just going to throw a joint-stool at his head, when Tahar perceiving it, prostrated himself at the feet of Al-Kuz. My brother, said he to him with great submission, I confess myself guilty of the blackest perfidy. I have merited death for robbing you of the affections of Lira; but, if you were to know what I have suffered during my absence, and with what remorse I have been agitated, you would undoubtedly pardon me a crime which I committed in spite of myself.

This submission of Tahar, being attended with a flood of tears, wrought greatly with Al-Kuz. As he believed he had entirely forsaken Lira, he threw himself on the neck of his friend. I pardon thee, Tahar, said he, and whatever reason I had to hate thee, it shall never more be said that a woman dissolved so amiable and so long a friendship as ours. But, prithee, now tell me, what has become of Lira?—Ah! replied Tahar, embracing his friend, I conjure you to enquire no more about a person, whose memory perhaps is still dear to you.—No, no, returned Al-Kuz, Lira does not in the least trouble me; her infidelity has entirely effaced her from my heart, and to convince you of the little regard I have for her memory, let us return with this miller's wife to the table, and, since she is disposed to divide her favours between us, let us both love her without jealousy, and drink to the good

health of her husband. The miller's wife soon poured
out some drink, and peace being restored, all three returned to the table, and Al-Kuz and Tahar, with glass
in hand, swore to maintain an eternal friendship with
each other.

After the wine had a little enlivened their spirits, the
miller's wife renewed the conversation. Though Al-Kuz,
said she to Tahar, is incurious to know what has become
of his wife, or to be informed of what passed between you
two, I conjure you to tell me without further delay. As
for him, I am persuaded he will hear you without pain ;
and I shall consider this recital as an ample satisfaction
for the violence you have committed. Tahar, however,
hesitated to gratify her request ; but when his friend
assured him that Lira had become so indifferent to him
that his passion for her was not only absolutely extinguished, but that he would see that the history of her
infidelity would not so much as make a change in his
countenance, he proceeded to inform him in the following
terms :

I shall, my dear friend, pass lightly over the passion
I felt for Lira. The beginning of it had well nigh been
fatal, since it brought me to death's door. I was not
master of my destiny; the beautiful Lira triumphed over
my resolutions. I would rather have died than have betrayed my friend; and her imprudence in trusting you with
the key of the coffer where all my letters were, obliged me
to fly with her, to avoid your just vengeance. Although
my mind was often tormented for my perfidious treatment
of you, I expected to be very happy with Lira. But, alas!
I had never sufficiently studied the character of this
woman. How great soever that passion was which she
testified for me, I soon perceived a coquettish air to run
through all her actions, and wherever we went, this
foible seemed entirely to possess her whole behaviour.
I spoke to her about it several times, whenever she vouch-

safed to hear me on the subject. At last: Tahar, said she to me smiling, it is extremely unkind to become jealous. Canst thou doubt of my tenderness, after I have done so much for thee? Go, my dear, set your heart at ease, for I love you only, and do not tease me with your unjust suspicions. These words were so far from being satisfactory, that they stung me to the quick; and yet I bore them with patience. After we had passed through several cities, we arrived at length at Visapur. I took a resolution to settle there, and hired a house, handsomely furnished, from a Jew, which stood in a very agreeable quarter, but I did not observe what a dangerous neighbour I had. An amorous handsome young Hindu lived it seems in the next house to mine. I watched both Lira and him for some time, without. seeing anything suspicious in their behaviour: but unexpectedly, one evening, entering the hall where Lira used to pass the whole day, I was in the utmost surprise to see a man slip behind the hangings of the wall, and endeavour to pass through an opening that communicated with the next house. I ran after the man, and seizing him by the foot, brought him back into the hall; and soon discovered him to be the young Hindu who had given me so much uneasiness. I then seized Lira with my other hand, and after having reproached her for her infidelity in the sharpest terms rage and fury could dictate, I was preparing to punish the affront the young man had offered me, when Lira threw herself betwixt us. Hold, Tahar, said she, in a very haughty tone, restrain yourself a while, and remember that you deserve at least the same chastisement. Learn to respect the man I love. What right have you to control my actions? Am I your wife? Am I your slave? And ought you to hope, in our situation, that I must be more faithful to you than I have been to my husband? If you think I love you better than another, you are under a mistake; my inclinations are

13—2

not to be forced, and my heart is just now fixed upon this new lover, till I shall think proper to dispose of it in favour of another.

This assurance of Lira struck me with such astonishment, that I remained some time motionless; and the young Hindu taking advantage of this, escaped through the hole in the wall, and before I could speak a word, closed the breach with some planks. Recovering my speech at last: Lira, said I to her, very calmly, I did not suspect your bosom enclosed a heart so black; but since you have thought proper to take off the mask, let us break off all further correspondence. Let us divide the rest of the money, and separate for ever. Lira received this proposal with joy. I had still nearly seven thousand dinars left. I gave her one half, and quitted her without regret. I departed from Visapur fully convinced of the infidelity of all women, and with a resolution to despise them. I then embarked at the first seaport, pursued a voyage to Arabia, and arrived at Brava, where, as soon as I landed I went to a tailor's shop to be provided with some new clothes. I bargained with him for a complete suit, and after I had paid him, I was going from thence, but on my way I observed on the other side of the street, two women in veils, sitting on a stone bench; one of them appeared to be in a swoon, and the other endeavouring to recover her. I at once offered my services, which were accepted. Taking the sick lady under my arm, I conducted her, with the help of her slave, to her own home. We entered a little house very well furnished, which by its appearance, seemed to belong to some private person. We laid the lady on a sofa, and her slave lifting up her veil for the sake of air, how was I ravished, my dear Al-Kuz, at seeing one of the most beautiful persons in the universe! Dazzled by this charming object, all my resolutions vanished in a moment. I fell deeply in love with this young beauty, and heartily sympathizing with her

offered her everything in my power. Sir, replied the
charming creature, with her eyes bathed in tears, I
have just lost the man who was going to complete my
happiness by a union with me, if a brute in my presence
had not put an end to his life. We were to have been
married to-morrow; and my lover, according to custom, was
coming to visit me about the time of evening prayer, when
a perfidious Mohammedan, who waited for him at the
corner of a neighbouring street, gave him two blows with
his sabre, which laid him dead at his feet. At my cries the
villain fled. I descended hastily into the street, and saw
as they were carrying him home bathed in his blood, that
the angel of death had seized his soul. Behold, sir, the
real cause of my grief! The young lady then renewing her
tears, discovered a despair so violent, that I began to
apprehend her life was in danger. I never left her ; and
when she was put to bed, stayed by her with her slave all
night to comfort her. The next day she appeared more
composed ; and having thanked me for the care I had
taken, she fixed her eyes steadfastly on me, and burst forth
into a fresh torrent of tears. I was surprised at this new
affliction, and upon demanding the cause very respectfully:
Ah ! sir, said she, sobbing as she spoke, the more I look
upon you, the more I see my sorrows augmented. The
features of your face bear such a lively resemblance to
those of my lover that I cannot behold you without being
softened for the irreparable loss I have sustained. From
this similitude of features, continued Tahar, I took care to
insinuate myself so far into her affections that she began
to forget the death of her former lover.

Whatever prudence the example of Lira had inspired
me with, I believed I should now be the happiest of men
if I could espouse a lady whose heart appeared so well
formed. This resemblance of features, which I mentioned,
did my business effectually ; and in fine, I was so favourably attended to, that I became the spouse of this

beautiful creature, without having sighed for her more than eight days. Never did I taste such perfect pleasure as I enjoyed with my new spouse; and to add, if possible, to my happiness, she told me some days after our marriage that she was with child. This news redoubled the ardour of my passion, and she appeared so superior in wit and beauty to all other women, that I was for ever bestowing on her fresh marks of tenderness. But though my wife made very affectionate returns, I found that all my caresses could not entirely dissipate a melancholy which hung on her spirits. As I imputed this to the loss of her former lover, I took no notice of it ; but it was not long before I discovered the true cause.

Returning home one evening, about three months and a half after we were married, my wife who had some days before been slightly indisposed on account of her pregnancy, complained of a violent colic. I did not perceive that my presence embarrassed her ; on the contrary such was my tenderness, that when she desired me to retire into another chamber, I would not quit her for a moment. But, my dear brother, how was I surprised, when in the midst of her pains, I perceived she was delivered of a girl! I became more cold than marble. O heavens! I cried, after I had recovered a little from my astonishment, am I then to be betrayed by every woman I love ! Perfidious Salle, continued I, addressing myself to her—How! interrupted Al-Kuz, was your wife named Salle ?—Yes, my dear friend, returned Tahar.—And did she not live in the Banker's street, opposite a lemon-merchant, in a little low house ?—Right, replied Tahar, and this house her lover, she said, who was killed the very evening I arrived at Brava, had given her ready furnished. At this, my lord, continued Ibn Aridun, Al-Kuz laughed so heartily that he fell backwards, and remained so long in that posture that Tahar and the miller's wife were surprised to the last degree. What is there in all this to be

laughed at? replied Tahar; I do not say, indeed, you
ought to be afflicted.—What, my dear brother, interrupted
Al-Kuz, laughing more heartily than before, was this
woman, who mourned the loss of her lover so tenderly,
and whom you afterwards married, and who in three
months and a half was so happily delivered in your arms,
the very Salle that lived in the Banker's street? Oh! my
dear friend, a history so singular as this deserves to be
transmitted down to posterity. You must understand, my
poor Tahar, that this little girl, which thy wife would have
fathered upon thee, was of my begetting. Salle, without being my wife, gratified my warmest wishes, after I
had rescued her from a fire which had consumed her own
house; and it was I who furnished her with that she
occupied at Brava. A new lover having engaged her, I
was so transported with jealousy, that with two blows of
my sabre, I mortally wounded him. This obliged me to
provide for my own safety, and to leave Salle, who had
been pregnant above four months and a half.

An adventure so singularly rare surprised Tahar. He
then recalled to his mind that of Lira. Now we are even
with each other, cried he, laughing with all his might.—
Yes, my dear friend, replied Al-Kuz, embracing him, there
is no room left for reproach, since our revenge has become
mutual.—It is beyond comparison, said the miller's wife,
and you see, instead of being offended, this accident alone
has amply revenged you of your rival. I assure you, returned Al-Kuz, the characters of these women are so extraordinary, that they have almost destroyed our tenderness
for them; and this double trial of them may make us wise
for the future. Let us henceforth fly all such engagements
with the sex. Let us put upon a footing with ourselves
those sots, who securely repose on the deceitful caresses
of their wives; and among that number, let us begin to
place the husband of this charming creature. The two
friends, after they had embraced this new proposal, swore

never to quit each other. Tahar then continued his history, and informed them that such was his vexation at having been so cruelly deceived by his wife, that he left her immediately, without taking his leave; and being resolved to forsake Brava, he embarked for Bassorah, and arrived there about a month ago, during which time he had carried on a tender engagement with the miller's wife, without being aware that it would end in his being reconciled to Al-Kuz.

Al-Kuz and Tahar, after making themselves very merry with their adventures, upon all which the miller's wife heartily rallied them, had disposed themselves to pass the rest of the night very agreeably, when the miller who had finished his affairs sooner than he expected arrived very abruptly at the mill. Great was the astonishment of all parties; and the miller, who saw how well the table was spread, little expected to find his wife in such good company. But she informed him that these two gentle-men, being overtaken with a shower of rain, had desired shelter in the mill, which she thought it would be uncivil to refuse; and that, the rain continuing ever since, she had given them a collation. He seemed satisfied with this excuse, though he was inconceivably enraged. He had before now suspected the fidelity of his wife, but as the proofs were not very strong, he had dissembled his resent-ment. Having sent for fresh wine, he sat down at the table with his guests, who made him drink as long as he was able to.

It being now too late for Tahar and Al-Kuz to return to Bassorah, when they got up from table the miller con-ducted them to a chamber, in which was a pretty good bed, where they reposed themselves waiting for the re-turn of day. The miller then went to his own bed, and was just going to lie down by the side of his wife, when he observed she was buried in a profound sleep. As a thirst for vengeance entirely occupied his mind, he went down into the stable, took the halter off his mule, and slipping it round his wife's neck, was on the point of strangling her, when happily for her she awakened in the very moment he was beginning to execute his cruel design, and artfully slipping her hand between the halter and her neck, without making the least noise, she affecting to be as stiff as a person deprived of breath, and made the miller, who was all this while in the dark, believe she was quite dead; he being afraid of being punished, stayed no longer in the mill, but mounting his mule forthwith, fled as fast as possible from Bassorah. The miller's wife no sooner perceived her husband had left the mill, than she arose in a very trembling condition, and locked the doors after him; she lighted her lamp, and went to awaken her two guests, who had fallen into a sweet sleep. She acquainted them with the danger she had undergone, and then shewed them her neck, on which were impressed the marks of her husband's cruelty.

Tahar and Al-Kuz were surprised at this resolution of the miller's. If every loose woman were to be punished thus, said Al-Kuz, whispering to his friend, we should never find halters enough. But my dear friend, continued he, raising his voice, let us leave the mill directly; the miller will undoubtedly accuse us of the murder of his wife, and though she can readily confute him, it is best for us not to be involved in such an affair.—That is right, replied Tahar; but must we leave behind the miller's beautiful wife?—No, no, said she, I will follow you wherever you go, provided you can accomodate me with the habit of a man. This may easily be done, continued Tahar, and as we are pretty near of a size, if you will come to my lodgings in Bassorah, we shall find a complete suit. This resolution being taken, the miller's wife stript the mill of everything they could conveniently carry away, and set out with her lovers as soon as it was light, to

Tahar's lodgings, where the lady being disguised, they passed several days with great pleasure.

Al-Kuz and Tahar shared together, without jealousy. their good fortune. But Al-Kuz, who had sent his merchandise to Baghdad, fearing a further delay would retard the sale, and diminish the price of his wares, proposed to Tahar to take their route to that city. The miller's wife followed them thither, and as they travelled but slowly, it was nearly ten days before they arrived at the end of their journey, which happened to be in the evening, just as the gates of the city were going to be locked. This obliged them to take up their lodging in the suburbs; but as they were going to the first caravanserai that offered, they were overtaken by a violent shower of rain, and leaving their horses to the care of a slave they had bought at Bassorah, they ran to seek a retreat, and leaned back against a little door, over which there was a kind of pent-house. The rain, being no more than a sudden shower, was soon over; but as our three adventurers, who waited till it was fair, that they might go and seek a lodging, were thus supporting themselves against the door, which probably was not well hung, the weight of their bodies forced it off the hinges, and all three tumbled backwards on the ground. The noise occasioned by the falling in of the door with our three travellers, together with their loud laughing at this accident, alarmed three persons who lay on one bed in a lower apartment, and who demanded in very high tones why they disturbed their repose. The two friends and the miller's wife approached the bed to see who spoke to them. They perceived by the light of the moon, which now shone full upon the bed, a porter lying between two handsome women, who, as well as the porter, immediately hid their faces under the covering. Al-Kuz and Tahar renewed their laughter at an adventure so uncommon as this. Their curiosity being excited, they forced off the covering; but how unutterable was their

astonishment, when these two women were known to be
Salle and Lira! Perfidious, infamous wretches! cried the
two friends at once, do you carry your debaucheries to
such a length, as to take up with a rascally porter? Then,
drawing their sabres, they were going to sacrifice their
wives and the porter to their just revenge, when the miller's
wife, hastily rushing between them, cried out: Ah!
gentlemen, suspend your rage a little, and look well at the
features of that man, whom a double amazement has
thrown into a swoon. I will then give you no further
interruption, if you think well to follow the first emotions
of your blind resentment.

Al-Kuz and Tahar had so much complaisance for their
mistress as to govern their rage, till they had examined the
porter; and having discovered who he was, in spite of the
paleness of his face, they were now both ready to die with
laughter. They threw down their sabres, and redoubled
their laughter to such a degree, that their wives were convinced their lives were out of present danger. And taking
advantage of this sudden change of humour in their husbands, of which they knew not the cause, they threw
themselves from off the bottom of the bed, and prostrating
themselves at their feet, implored, in a trembling manner,
a pardon for all their crimes. But the porter had no sooner
opened his eyes, and turned them towards his disguised
wife, than he closed them again, believing without all
doubt that the devil had come to carry him away. Sirs,
said she, laughing with all her might at the porter's
imagination, I no longer hinder you from following your
first resolutions: I leave you to consider whether in
justice you ought not be revenged on this man.—No, no,
replied Al-Kuz, talk no more of revenge; on the contrary,
this is a pleasant adventure. Behold! we are all three
upon a level, and since the miller (for it was no other
than himself) has lain between our wives, we have no
more grounds of complaint against him, than he can have

against us; it is but just to admit him into our friendship, and we will share our fortunes together, as we have
done our wives. The presence of Lira, unfaithful as she
has been, has revived the remainder of a love, not wholly
extinguished in the heart of her husband. I go, said he
to Tahar and to the miller, who by this time had come to
himself, I go to set the first example of perfect reconciliation. Then raising his wife, whose confusion had
made her speechless, he embraced her tenderly. Lira,
said he, I forget all that is past, and will not even be informed of your conduct since your infidelity, lest it
should renew that wound, of which I would not have the
least mark remain. I desire my two companions to do the
same; and I do not doubt but that they, from my example,
will sincerely pardon their wives. Tahar and the miller,
without opposing Al-Kuz, tenderly embraced their wives,
and were perfectly reconciled to them. After several
mutual and lively caresses, these three extraordinary
couples could not look upon themselves without recalling
everything that had passed between them; a thousand
circumstances of their adventures, each more pleasant
than the other, which passed through their minds,
afforded them excessive matter of mirth.

The Caliph Hárún al-Rashíd, pursued Ibn Aridun,
whom I had the honour to mention to your Majesty,
frequently used to walk out in the night disguised, with
his first wazir Ja'afar, and Masrur the chief of the
eunuchs. He passed by just at the time that this
singular adventure was transacted; and the loud laughing exciting his curiosity, he entered the house (which
was wide open) without ceremony, and civilly saluted the
four men, for the miller's wife by her dress still
appeared to be one. Gentlemen, said he, as your mirth
seems to be grounded on something extraordinary, pardon
my rudeness if in entering without your permission, I
desire to share a part of your pleasure. I love dearly to

laugh, and you cannot oblige me more than by acquainting me with the object of your mirth. Al-Kuz and Tahar turned their eyes directly to their wives, and perceiving that both blushed, and that the request was not agreeable to them, they desired the Caliph in handsome terms, to excuse them the recital of an adventure which it was their interest to conceal. The Caliph, my lord, pressed them no further ; but as this place was very incommodious to pass the night in, he offered them one more agreeable, which stood at a little distance. They accepted his kind invitation, and following him to the walls of the city, he led them through a subterranean passage into it, and conducted them to a little house, very decently furnished. A handsome collation was instantly served up, with some excellent Greek wine, of which he made them drink heartily ; and when the Caliph perceived it began to operate, he again desired them to acquaint him with the cause of their extraordinary laughter. Al-Kuz and Tahar would fain have concealed their adventures from this generous man ; but as the miller threatened to publish his in spite of their opposition, Al-Kuz informed the Caliph of everything I had the honour to relate of these six married persons. Harun al-Rashid, who had never heard a history so singularly interesting as this, thanked his guests for their complaisance ; and in order to further his pleasure at their expense, he caused them to replenish their glasses, into each of which he commanded Ja'afar to infuse a certain kind of powder, which had the virtue of laying them asleep for twelve hours, not sparing even the wazir himself, nor Masrur ; and, having ingeniously given each his dose, they presently fell asleep. The Caliph then called up two mutes, and ordered them to lay these eight persons on a chariot which had been brought there by his orders, and then conducted them two leagues from Baghdad, to a very fine house on the banks of the Tigris, which belonged to the surveyor-general of his buildings. Here he caused the three men and their wives to be stript naked in his presence, and, having put on them fresh linen and fine drawers, he commanded them to be put, two and two, into three beds, which were fitted up under one alcove. After this, he painted the grand wazir all black with his own hands, and causing him to be clothed like a slave, and Masrur like a woman, he placed them on a Persian carpet, near the men and their wives; the Caliph then hid himself behind a curtain, and waited impatiently for the time when they should all awake. These eight persons recovered from their stupefaction almost at the same time, but especially Al-Kuz, Tahar, the miller, and their three wives. They were amazed to find themselves in bed, in a place to which they were utter strangers, and to see likewise the rich embroidered robes which seemed to be designed for their use. They considered all this as a dream, with silence and astonishment, when the wazir, seeing the chief of the eunuchs in a woman's dress, burst out laughing. Goodmorrow, my pretty brunette, cried he, how have you slept to-night ? The eunuch having observed his garb, was for some moments perfectly confounded, but as soon as he had taken a strict survey of the wazir he laughed as loudly on seeing how black he was painted. Good-morrow, handsome black, replied he merrily, one may see by the freshness of your countenance that you have had a sound sleep.

This answer surprised the wazir, who examining his hands and his slave's dress, mused some time upon this pleasant adventure, and not being able to recollect anything of the room he was in, was at a loss to comprehend the meaning of his own and of the eunuch's disguise ; but, remembering the three men and their wives to be present, he immediately determined how to act. This is doubtless, said he to himself, some new frolic which the Commander of the Faithful has contrived to please his fancy : we will humour the jest, and endeavour to make him merry with the scene we are to act.   Then embracing Masrur in a jocose manner : my lovely companion and light of my eyes, said he, let us follow the example of these happy married folk ; I promise to restore you my affection, if you will be more faithful hereafter ; but if ever I surprise you with the handsome Zamtud, who was with you yesterday, I swear I will either stab or poison you in revenge of your perfidy.   The chief of the eunuchs, amazed at this behaviour of the wazir, and looking steadily at him : Are you mad, Ja'afar ? said he.   Have you forgotten who you are ?—No, my dear Zulicah, replied Ja'afar, I remember perfectly that I am Chapur, your faithful spouse ; why do you pretend not to know me ? Have you forgotten since yesterday the goodness of our master Sa'ad, who reconciled us together ?   And did you not promise him never to see your spark Zamtud again ? And do not you remember to have heard the history of these gentle husbands, whom he engaged to come and live with him, and from whose example I am induced sincerely to pardon your past behaviour, on condition that you are more faithful for the time to come ?

The more seriously the wazir talked, the more Masrur believed him to be out of his wits, and yet neither could account for this strange metamorphosis.   What senseless discourse is this, my dear friend ? replied the eunuch.   Compose yourself, and remember that I am Masrur, the chief of the eunuchs of the sovereign Commander of the Faithful, to whom you are the grand wazir ; cease then this pleasantry, and suppress——You mistake, interrupted Ja'afar ; you are mad to think so ridiculously ; I wish you would come to yourself ; but the wine you drank yesterday has confounded your ideas. Remember that we are no more than the poor slaves of Sa'ad, who is certainly the best master in all Baghdad. Ja'afar, on pronouncing these last words, was going to embrace Masrur a second time; but this last, rudely repulsing him, cried out : You are mad yourself; and I appeal to these good people whether we had not yesterday the honour to accompany the Caliph in his nocturnal ramble? Did not we go with him into a house in the suburbs of this city, being led by the extraordinary laughter of this company? Did not we engage them to pass the night in a house close to the palace, where we had an excellent collation, and where they entertained us with their adventures, which were very extraordinary? Did not we infuse into their wine a powder, which laid them instantly asleep? What! am I now dreaming? And are you not distracted, or is not your mind at least disturbed with the fumes of the wine, of which you yesterday drank too plentifully? Al-Kuz, Tahar, the miller, and their wives, my lord, who listened in profound silence, were in the utmost astonishment to hear this dispute between the wazir and the eunuch. They were not unacquainted with the frequent and comical adventures of the Caliph: but Ja'afar and Masrur were so perfectly disguised, that they imagined them to be the two slaves who had attended him, whom Masrur said was the Caliph.

In the mean time, Harun al-Rashid, who was concealed behind the curtain, beheld with infinite pleasure all that passed between these eight persons. He could scarcely forbear laughing to see the chief of the eunuchs torment himself on account of the obstinacy with which Ja'afar insisted that he was his wife. I am not, said the eunuch again, your dear Zulicah, neither is Zamtud my spark, nor do I believe there are in all Baghdad any such persons. You are certainly still drunk. If you are not, I cannot tell what pleasure you can take in wearying my patience; and though I cannot devise how we came by these clothes, yet I am sure my name is Masrur, and that I am the chief eunuch to the Commander of the

Faithful; and in spite of that sooty complexion, the features of your face declare you to be no other than Ja'afar, the grand wazir. It is true, I am not able to comprehend how we and these three couples were transported to this strange place, yet in spite of these delusions, which can never alter our state, I shall always be Masrur, and you will never cease to be Ja'afar.

Though Al-Kuz, Tahar, and the rest, bore no part in this conversation, yet they were thoroughly provoked at the obstinacy of the eunuch, who could not be brought to acknowledge Ja'afar for his husband. This last, who played his part to perfection, at length pretended to fall into a furious passion with Masrur. He had already cuffed him with his fists, which the other bore very gravely, when the Caliph, who was clothed like a merchant, and had hitherto restrained his laughter, entered the chamber where this merry scene was exhibited. Zulicah, said he to the chief eunuch very gravely, why does your husband still retain these marks of resentment? Did not you both promise me yesterday to live in perfect union? Are all your promises come to this? Some fresh subject of jealousy occasioned, I suppose, by the handsome Zamtud, has authorized Chapur to treat you in this sharp manner.

The sudden appearance of the Caliph, the discourse he held with Masrur, and the name Zulicah which he had given him, so disconcerted the eunuch, that he was was at first struck dumb; but on recovering from his surprise, he quickly perceived the Caliph had diverted himself at his expense, and that Ja'afar had acted the wisest part. He then burst out laughing : My Lord, said he to the Commander of the Faithful, prostrating himself at his feet, I am clearly convinced Ja'afar has a hundred times more wit than I have; but I esteem myself happy, if through my foolishness your Majesty has for a few moments been agreeably entertained.—I should have been very sorry, my dear Masrur, replied the Caliph, if you had discovered the same presence of mind as Ja'afar has done, as it would have deprived me of an infinite pleasure. But now as we have taken off the mask, I should be glad to know how Al-Kuz, Tahar, the miller, and their wives, relished your dispute.— Sovereign Commander of the Faithful, replied Al-Kuz, for decency would not permit him to prostrate himself with the rest before the Caliph, as he was in bed: the magnificence of this apartment, and the splendour of the robes lying on these sofas, induced us to regard the dispute between Ja'afar and Masrur only as a dream arising from the intoxicating fumes of the wine. Nay, I am not yet sure, while I have the honour of speaking to your Majesty, whether we are awake, so wonderful and so supernatural does the whole transaction appear. The Caliph laughed at this thought of Al-Kuz. No, no, said he, you are all wide awake; but rise and let each of you put on those robes which I designed you as a reward for reciting your pleasant adventures, and when you are disposed to depart, you will find a chariot ready to carry you home.

Harun al-Rashid, my lord, then retired with Ja'afar and Masrur into another chamber, where the wazir cleaned himself, and all three changed their habits. In the meanwhile the six married people dressed themselves with those magnificent robes the Caliph had appointed for them, and after having demanded and easily obtained leave, they thanked the Caliph for his generosity, and were conveyed to their habitations. But I am ignorant, my lord, whether Lira, Salle, and the miller's wife, were afterwards as faithful to their husbands as they had promised.

*   *   *   *   *   *

A history so singular as this, which Ibn-Aridun had rehearsed to Shams al-Din, wonderfully delighted him: and afflicted as this unhappy prince was, he could not forbear laughing several times at the comical adventures it contained. My dear wazir, said he to the son of Abu Bakr, if the loss I have sustained in my dear Zabd al-Katon could be erased from my mind, you doubtless would be able to banish it from my memory; but as I well know this cannot be effected by human art, I submit myself to the supreme disposal of the Almighty. The only request I daily make is, that you at least may survive to entertain me till the great Prophet shall be pleased to present me before the throne of his divine Majesty.—Ah! my lord, replied Ibn Aridun, tenderly embracing his feet, why is this goodness extended to such a slave as I am? And why am I not permitted to lay down my life, that I may render my sovereign perfectly happy? Yes, I swear, by the six drops of sweat of Mohammed, which produced the rose and rice, that I am ready to sacrifice my heart for your Majesty. But, my lord, we should not despair, for if we ought to give any credit to a dream, that which I had last night would incline me to think your misfortunes may be relieved.—And what hast thou dreamt last night? returned the king, very eagerly.—I dreamed my lord, replied he, that I was in a deep sleep, when a great wind opened my chamber window, at the noise of which I was suddenly awakened, and to my astonishment, beheld at my bolster the Al-Borak[1] of our great Prophet who bestowed on me a thousand caresses. Inspired without doubt in that moment, I arose and purified myself, and having offered my devotions, I mounted this divine animal, who transported me through the air with incredible swiftness, till at length I arrived at Sarandib, where the first person I saw was my father. I hastily

---

1 The Al-Borak is an animal less than a mule, and bigger than an ass; it partakes of the nature of both those animals, and the Mohammedans believe it was sent by Allah to carry their great Prophet into Heaven.

got off the beast, which I fastened to a tree. Abu Bakr took me by the arm and conducted me to a Mosque, whose door spontaneously closed upon us. Adore, said he, the messenger of Allah, and he prostrated himself. I immediately threw myself with my face to the earth. There is no God but God, I cried, and Mohammed is his Prophet. Scarcely, my lord, had I finished a prayer so usual with us, when Mohammed appeared from a shining cloud; he led a lady in his hand, who appeared to me far superior in beauty to all the women I had ever seen. Happy Shams al-Din! said he, for thy destiny is worthy of envy; thou shalt recover a wife whose merits are equal to one of my huris. Were I to return to the earth, my utmost desires would be bounded by the possession of a beauty like her's; then putting her into the hands of Abu Bakr, darkness instantly concealed the Prophet from mine eyes; and finding myself insensibly remounted on the Al-Borak I flew with the same velocity as before, and re-entered my chamber. I went to bed again, and slept till morning, when the hour of prayer awakened me; but I was so fatigued that if I had really undergone the journey to Sarandib in so short a time, I believe I should not have been more weary. This, my lord, was my dream, and I wish it may portend a happy issue to your misfortunes. —Ah! my dear Ibn Aridun, replied the king in a sorrowful tone, even should the return of thy father restore me to my sight, I must yet be miserable, since my dear Zabd al-Katon is irrevocably lost; but as I promised Abu Bakr, in the moment of our separation, to subscribe without reluctance to the decrees of my destiny, I will banish from my breast an idea so frightfully afflicting as this; though I cannot but observe, that if Mohammed had pleased, he might long ago have ended my distress by depriving me of a miserable life; but then my sorrows would not have been so agreeably beguiled with thy entertaining histories. Pursue, my dear friend, pursue thy career, and remove the melancholy remembrance that overwhelms me, with some fresh narration.—Yes, my Lord, replied Ibn Aridun, who had much ado to restrain shedding tears for the misfortune of his sovereign; is your Majesty then disposed to hear the adventures of Faruk, the corsair?—Very willingly, returned the monarch; I am interested in the destiny of that unfortunate prince, and if I rightly remember, he assumed that title himself.—It is true, my lord, replied the young wazir, and you will perceive his life to be a complication of evils; and I shall not only rehearse his history from the time when he was separated from the princess Gulguli-Chamami, but also everything recorded of him by an ancient Arabian author, who wrote a history of the princes who reigned in the Isles of Divanduru.

STORY OF FARUK

On Mount Caucasus there formerly stood a little city called Gur, from the multitude of wild asses which inhabited a neighbouring forest. The king of this country had four sons, by as many different sultanas, all born in one day. The first was called Suffrak, the second Kobad, the third Bzarmahar, and the fourth Faruk. As this monarch treated his four sons with equal indulgence, it was impossible for them to judge who should be his successor; but if anyone deserved to fill the throne preferably to the rest, it was undoubtedly Faruk; in him were united all the eminent qualities necessary to form the character of a great prince. He had scarcely attained his twelfth year, when by rivalling his brothers in every manly and military exercise, he attracted the daily applauses of the people of Gur, and your Majesty may well suppose these encomiums penetrated like poisoned arrows into the hearts of Faruk's three brothers.

Faruk frequently talked with his brothers of the difficulty that would arise about the succession to the kingdom. As there can but one of us ascend the throne, said Faruk, what will become of the other three? I perceive, if either of them cherish the least spark of ambition, his situation will be pitiable indeed. Let us then, replied Suffrak, prevent this disappointment in good time; there is the illustrious Zayfadin; by his sage counsels it seems as if the sun and stars were taught to regulate their course; his admirable skill in astrology is so extensive that his mouth is the treasury of the sublime sciences. Let us go and consult him on our duty, but under such a disguise as his art only can detect; and since we firmly believe his predictions to be ratified by Heaven, we will each of us take a solemn oath to abide by his decision; then without murmuring, let those who are excluded the throne depart hence, and by their valour procure other kingdoms. This resolution being unanimously adopted, the four brothers disguised themselves, and set out on their journey without any retinue, and in a few days arrived on the summit of Mount Caucasus, where Zayfadin made his abode.

This admirable person was at his devotions when they knocked at his door; as he did not interrupt himself to let them in, they knocked again. Princes, cried he, without stirring, wait a little; he whose hand turns the celestial spheres ought to be preferred to all mortals: I will attend to you in an instant. The princes of Gur were struck with admiration to hear that Zayfadin, before he had seen their faces, was apprised of their dignity. They waited very respectfully till he had finished his devotions, and then the door was opened; but how was their astonishment increased, when he called each of them by his name, and recounted the object of their journey! It is easy, my lords, said he, to gratify your curiosity, but it is almost always dangerous to pry too narrowly into future events, and you will not be contented with my answer; forasmuch as I foresee that he who is to succeed the king, his father, shall not only risk his life in returning home to Gur, but his own brothers will one day become his most inveterate enemies. This reply, one would have thought, was sufficient to terrify the young princes, and indeed Faruk advised them not to carry their curiosity further; but his brothers, who contemned his wise counsel, pressed the astrologer to gratify them about what they so passionately wished to know.

Since you are not to be deterred from your designs, said the sublime Zayfadin, descend the mountain by that narrow path and towards the close of the day you will find a woman, who shall inform you which of you four is destined to wear the diadem of Gur. The princes obeyed, and following the astrologer's directions, arrived in the evening at a little plain, surrounded with mountains from the midst of which arose a thick smoke out of a pit, not much broader than the mouth of a well. The woman was sitting on a great stone on one side of the pit. This is she, said the brothers, from whom we are to learn our destiny. They approached the sorceress, and having acquainted her with the object of their visit, she ordered them to take off their sandals, and throw them, one after another, into the pit. Suffrak had no sooner obeyed, than their ears were assaulted with a dreadful noise, and his sandals being thrown up with impetuosity, they fell at his feet all blackened with smoke, and half burnt. Kobad and Bzarmahar were repulsed in like manner; but Faruk's treatment was quite different; the noise ceased, the smoke vanished for a little, and his sandals were cast up without being in the least injured. It is you then, my lord, said the old woman, who are destined to be one day king of Gur; since here are the certain marks by which Zayfadin, who foresaw your arrival, assured me I should know you. Take, then, your sandals, my lord, and continue your way.—If the heart of Faruk was secretly elated with this prediction, his brothers were no less swelled with rage and jealousy. However they discovered nothing of their minds, but resolving to deprive Faruk of his throne, they secretly contrived amongst themselves to make away with him.

As they were obliged to return home by the same road they arrived, their way necessarily led them between two mountains. This place was dangerous to stay all night in, on account of its being infested with monstrous serpents, who then came out to take food and air. Here it was that the three envious brothers intended to destroy Faruk, who was ignorant of this dangerous circumstance. They proposed to him to pass the night in this place; Faruk agreed, and, after a slight repast, they lay down on the grass; but as soon as Faruk had fallen into a profound sleep, his three perfidious brothers suddenly started up, and left him in this dangerous place. The serpents according to custom, assembled in the middle of the night; their frightful hissings might be heard more than half a league, and approaching the place where Faruk lay, they surrounded him, and were just on the point of throwing themselves on him, when, by the greatest good fortune, a friendly jinni, who traversed the air, took pity on this unfortunate prince; some words he pronounced fixed the serpents to the earth, and rendered them so stiff, that they seemed as if they were all petrified.

At length Faruk awoke, but how great was his fright to see himself, as it were, surrounded with death! He imagined his brothers were destroyed by the serpents; but observing that they were all immoveable he had the boldness to venture through them, and, without their being able to offer him the least injury, he continued the road to Gur. He wept bitterly for the supposed death of his brothers, but he was informed, about six hours after his arrival, that they had safely returned. They were astonished to see him, and pretended that they were so dreadfully affrighted with the hissings of the serpents that each fled for his life, without being able to reflect on the almost certain death to which he was exposed. Faruk, rather than suspect his brothers to be guilty of so black a treason, admitted their excuse; he discovered not the least discontent, but lived with them as usual, without even pressing them to observe the oath they had taken to depart from Gur as soon as the astrologer should have decided in favour of one of them.

It was not more than eight months after the princes had consulted Zayfadin, when the king, their father, whilst hunting, fell backwards from his horse and was unfortunately killed on the spot. As he had nominated no successor, the three brothers refused to abide by their former agreement; but endeavouring to exclude Faruk, each gained over a party to elect himself in his place. This last proceeding discovered to Faruk all the ill faith of his brothers; he directly convened an assembly of the states of Gur, and acquainted them with their journey to the astrologer; and, whether they thought, or loved, him better than his brothers, they did not hesitate about declaring for him.

There were in Gur at this time four parties who were ready to tear one another to pieces with a civil war, when behold! all the people, as if inspired, laid down their arms, and unanimously proposed to the princes to abide by the decision of the first person who should enter the city the following day; and at the same time declared that if they refused to accept this condition all four should be excluded from the throne. The three brothers consented with great reluctance, but Faruk shewed not the least opposition. The grandees, having confined them in separate apartments, posted sentinels to prevent their designs being eluded, and then locked the gates of the city, which were also very strictly guarded. All the people passed the night on the walls, impatiently waiting the appearance of one who was to give peace to Gur. The day broke without discovering anybody, when at last there was seen coming at a great distance an old kalandar almost naked. The air was rent with the joyful shouts of the people ; they directly opened the gates on that side on which the kalandar was seen ; they ran to meet him, and bore him in triumph to the palace, where the corpse of the deceased king was deposited. The kalandar was greatly surprised, and knew not what to make of these proceedings ; but he was soon informed that he was appointed to give them a king, and that he was to choose one from among these four princes, who were to acquiesce in his judgment. As the kalandar was a man of age and experience, he was not ignorant that in nominating one of these princes he should create to himself enemies of the rest ; and therefore to avoid determining himself, he proposed the expedient I am about to relate to your Majesty. He caused the corpse of the deceased king to be bound to a tree, and having measured from it a considerable distance, he declared whichever of the four brothers had skill to discharge an arrow into the heart of his father should be his successor.

That there might be no grounds for complaint among them, the princes drew lots who should begin, and Kobad being the first, he discharged his arrow, and pierced the throat of his father. Bzarmahar, a little more ingenious, struck him in the breast, without touching his heart ; and Suffrak wounded him in the lower part of his belly. There was now only Faruk left to try his skill, and the people knowing his ability were in no doubt as to his gaining the prize; when this prince broke his bow and arrow to pieces. What barbarity is this? cried Faruk. My lords, said he addressing himself to the grandees of the realm, I renounce the throne, if it must be acquired by an action so unworthy and so inhuman. Let my brothers reign if they please, I shall behold their good fortune without envy; as for me, I will never pollute my hands with an action so impious as that which they have been induced to commit. The principal lords and all the people were to the last degree astonished, and were so touched with this greatness of soul in Faruk, that they pressed the kalandar with one voice to determine in his favour. That was my own intention, replied this wise old man; I proposed this expedient with no other view, than to leave yourselves to discern perfectly which of these princes is worthy to fill the throne. Humanity and piety ought to be the prime virtues of a monarch, and as Faruk has given you natural proofs of them, I believe the great Prophet would be offended if I did not agree with you that he alone is worthy to reign. This decision of the kalandar was immediately received with a thousand joyful acclamations, and the three princes retired from the city, overwhelmed with shame and confusion; they conceived a violent despair, not only at being excluded from the the throne by the voice of the people, but also at seeing that their ambitious thirst after power had betrayed them into the commission of an impiety which they themselves regarded with horror; and resolving to work their brother's destruction, they departed from Gur with a full purpose to put their design into execution.

Meanwhile the oath of fidelity was taken to the new king. He celebrated the obsequies of his father with great magnificence, and would fain have retained the kalandar near his person. But this good old man desired to be excused. It will be thought, my lord, said he, that your goodness is only the effect of a base complaisance which caused me to decide in your favour. But I would have it known that I followed the dictates of conscience, without the least view to my own interest. May heaven grant you a happy reign! and when you approach the end of your life may the angels who are to register all your words present those only which are most agreeable to the Divine Being! Saying this, he departed from Gur, without receiving the least mark of generosity from this prince.

Three months had now passed, my lord, continued Ibn Aridun, during which Faruk possessed his throne in peace, and his subjects were rendered happy under his mild and gentle administration, when his brothers surprised the city one dark night at the head of six thousand men, of whom the greatest part were Arabian robbers. These villains, taking advantage of the general fright which prevailed, massacred all that opposed their fury; but while they were busied in plundering the inhabitants, Faruk having rallied all the officers and soldiers he could collect, fell like a lion upon his enemies. He performed everything that could be expected from the bravest of men; but perceiving his attendants were almost all slain, and that it would be rashness to expose his person to further hazard, he changed clothes with an Arabian, whom he had killed with his own hand, and having disguised his face, he retired alone from Gur, and sought his safety by flight. The horrors of the day succeeded those of the night; nothing was to be seen in all parts of the city but torrents of blood ; and the Arabians not only found amongst the slain him whom they mistook for Faruk by the richness of his dress, but also Suffrak, Kobad, and Bzarmahar, who all perished by the divine justice. The Arabians, having finished the plunder, and having massacred all the inhabitants, without sparing either age or sex, set fire to the four corners of the city, and to the middle of it, which in three days' time reduced it to ashes.

The unfortunate Faruk, not only deprived of his throne, but also reduced to extreme misery, could not depart from Gur without shedding a flood of tears. The flames which now appeared at a great distance, took from him all hopes of ever re-ascending the throne of his ancestors. He hastened, therefore, as fast as he was able from this frightful place, but with a resolution to conceal his misfortunes from all the world. The prince had travelled three days through several bye-roads, when he encountered two kalandars sitting by a fountain at a slight repast. He approached them, and as they conjectured from his looks he wanted something to eat, they invited him to sit down with them. Faruk, who was almost famished with hunger, and needed no entreaties, devoured in a short time all the provisions they had. As soon as the prince had appeased the rage of hunger, he crossed his hands on his stomach, and fixing his eyes on the earth, became so deeply absorbed in his sorrowful reflections, that he continued nearly an hour in that melancholy posture.

The kalandars, who beheld him with astonishment, were touched with a lively sense of his affliction ; and the eldest having broken silence : My brother, said he to the prince, we are so deeply concerned for the profound anguish under which your mind seems to labour, that though we have known you but a few moments, both this young kalandar and myself will omit nothing in our power to assuage your grief, and to dispel that gloom which overcasts your mind. Speak, sir, and do not relinquish the assistance we offer ; weak as it is, it may do you more service than you are aware of at present. The prince of Gur, who had hitherto kept silence, was roused from his meditation by the obliging offers of this good old man. Generous kalandar, said he, excuse my rudeness ;

the cruel situation I am in is ready to overwhelm me;
seek not to be acquainted with my distress I conjure you.
If I have appeared insensible to your kindness, I heartily
thank you for your generous sentiments: and all the
favour I require is to be received into your company,
and to be permitted to conform to your rules, and to wear
the habit of your order. How, sir! returned the old man
a little astonished; are you really desirous to become a
kalandar?—Yes, replied Faruk, with a sigh, I was determined from the moment I came hither, since at present
I know of no better course; here is a ring, it is all I have
left out of a considerable fortune I once possessed; I will
sell it the first opportunity, and while the money lasts we
will live as brothers.—You know us badly, replied the
younger of the two kalandars; the sale of your ring is
useless; it should be kept for the last extremity. We are
of a profession that suffers us to want nothing, provided
we do not want assurance; therefore keep that precious
toy till another season, and in the mean time never be
perplexed how to live.—This young kalandar, replied the
old man, has spoken rightly; our first institution teaches
us to forsake a little, that we may gain much; this doctrine may perhaps be difficult to comprehend. Here it is
explained; we possess nothing in this life but the bare
enjoyment thereof, because death obliges us to quit all
the riches upon earth; why then do we suffer our minds
to be distracted and cruelly harassed, to preserve those
riches which oppose such enemies to us? Let us only
practise those maxims of philosophy which are peculiar
to our profession. We commonly begin by spending all
we possess, at least this is the practice of the wisest
amongst us; and when we once get this habit on our back,
we look upon the patrimony of others as an inexhaustible
resource on every occasion. In short, who of any spirit
will refuse to entertain a kalandar, let him be in what
part of the earth soever? Who is there, from the king

to the meanest artisan, that does not think it an honour
to admit us to their tables, and to help us to the most
delicious morsels?　It is true, we are obliged to wear a
mask, and to appear different from what we really are ; it
is that which lays jealous husbands asleep, and renders
us agreeable to the generality of their wives, who are
scarcely visible to any but ourselves, through the blind
confidence they place in our habit.　In fine, my dear
brother, there is not a life more delicious, nor more
sensual, than that of an able kalandar ; and when once
you possess the true relish thereof, you will never desire
to change.

Faruk listened very attentively to the old man's discourse, notwithstanding his grief, and observed that it
abounded with good sense.　Your way of life appears, said
he, so agreeable that from this picture alone which you
have drawn of it, I long to become a kalandar, and to take
the habit.—Four snips of a pair of scissors will initiate
you into our Society, answered the younger kalandar,
and you have nothing to do but to strip off your habit
for a moment.　Faruk obeyed in an instant, and
taking his garment, he cut it to pieces, and sewing it
neatly together again was forthwith recognized by the
other two kalandars.—They had now sat long enough
by the fountain, and all three starting up, steered their
course to the first city which presented itself to their
view.　The prince who could not so soon forget his misfortunes, sighed now and then, which the old kalandar
observing, reproached him with it, as unworthy of the
profession he had embraced.　Come my dear brother, said
he, remember that in putting off your garment, you have
divested yourself of all human weakness ; drive therefore
from your mind those gloomy reflections which continue to
disturb you. Any person of less experience than ourselves,
would desire to be acquainted with the history of your adventures, and would probably say that the recital of them

would assuage your grief, but nothing is more false than such reasoning; for it would renew the remembrance of those misfortunes which you ought to forget. We shall not press you upon this head, till we may jndge by your behaviour that you have become altogether insensible of your past misfortunes. No more grief, my dear brother; let us banish it from our company, it is a mortal poison to the human mind. Let us for the future breathe nothing but joy! And to inspire you with it, I will acquaint you with the history of my life, from which you will learn my reason for wearing this habit; listen to me, and the journey we have to go will appear the shorter:

ADVENTURES OF THE OLD
KALANDAR

I was born at Baku, and my father was a rice-merchant, who lived near a convent of darwayshes. He lived an irregular life, and was scarcely ever to be found in his shop; and as besides he had but little business, he was soon reduced to extreme poverty. A darwaysh, who used frequently to come to our house, conceived a friendship for me, and taking compassion on me took me into his convent, when I was about five years old; so that I was no further expense to my father, who having passed through a wearisome life, died when I was twelve years old. I went to see my disconsolate mother, and wept tenderly for the loss of my father, when my mother spoke to me in in this manner: Do not afflict yourself for my husband, forbear shedding tears for one who deserves them so little; weep no more as for a father, for one who had no share in your birth. This discourse surprised me, and I looked steadfastly at my mother. You are astonished, said she. —I have reason to be so, I replied; for if the deceased was not my father, which he was always taken for, whom am I indebted to for my being ?—To the old darwaysh who has brought you up, answered my mother; you are his son and mine; without his assistance we should have lived this long time past in the most shocking indigence, for my husband's idleness and excesses had reduced me to a state of beggary, even a long time before you came into the world. This darwaysh has been our entire support, by supplying us abundantly with the necessaries of life. On my side I was not ungrateful; the darwayshes do nothing for nothing, and I do not repent the return I have made this one. My mother was still in tears, when the darwaysh entered; she told him that she had just informed me of his being my father, and this man embracing me in the most tender manner: Child, said he, behave yourself well, and honour your mother and you shall want for nothing. I made a suitable return to these expressions of parental affection from my new father, and growing tired of the life I had hitherto led among the darwayshes, I begged of him to leave me with my mother. He granted my request, and gave us money to buy rice; and as my mother lived in a very frugal manner, and almost entirely at the convent's expense, she saved in seven or eight years about four thousand dinars.

I often heard my mother speak of a very handsome girl in our neighbourhood, and I became so enamoured of her from the bare report of her beauty, without ever seeing her, that I sought every opportunity of making myself known to her. At last one offered; the girl's father came to our house to buy a quantity of rice-meal, and agreed with my mother for a large sack of it that contained about twelve bushels. My want of experience made me look upon this as a favourable opportunity for seeing my mistress; and listening only to my foolish passion, with the assistance of a young man of my own age I put myself into the sack, which was then filled with meal as high as my chin, and was in this situation carried in the dusk of the evening to Kalim's house (this was the name of the girl's father), where they set me down in the corner of a room in which the family generally ate. I had made a hole in the top of the sack, through which I could easily see everything that passed. I was scarce set down when a darwaysh appeared, but I could not see his face, as he sat in a dark part of the room; there came in with him Kalim, his wife, and the beautiful Djanjhari-Nar, my mistress, with a little dog under her arm. A slave having laid the cloth, they immediately sat down to supper. Djanjhari-Nar happened to sit just facing me, and I was so transported at the first sight of her, that forgetting the company I was in, I foolishly cried out : Ah! what a fine creature! This indiscreet exclamation, which the company heard without knowing whence it came, terrified them greatly; they got up in a great hurry and confusion, looked everywhere except at the sack in which I lay hid, and finding nothing, sat down again to supper, where the voice they had heard formed the chief subject of their conversation.

Djanjhari-Nar happened not to take the same seat, and not being able to see her face, I was still indiscreet enough to attempt turning myself about in the sack, to have the pleasure of enjoying a full prospect of her charms; but I went about it so unskilfully, that the sack unfortunately overturned. Kalim with all his family and the darwaysh were greatly surprised at the sack's fall; but the darwaysh seeing that my mistress's little dog barked furiously at it, began immediately to suspect what might really be the matter; he therefore raised up the sack, and untied the top of it, when I appeared; but my face was so covered with meal, that it was impossible to know me. Upon this, Kalim flew into a great fury, ran to a dagger that hung up against the wall, and was upon the point of running me through the body, when I threw a handful of meal into his eyes which, by blinding him for a moment or two gave me an opportunity of leaping out of the sack in my slippers: and laying hold of a sabre that happened to lie in my way, I might easily have killed Kalim and the darwaysh and have then made my escape; and as it was the only way left of saving myself, I had my sabre ready to strike the blow, when upon looking on the darwaysh, whose face I had not seen before, I found it was the person to whom I was indebted for my being. Ah, darwaysh, said I, dropping the point of my sabre, see I am Hanif, whom your constant friendship has always made you consider as your own child! I am upon this occasion more indiscreet than criminal. I loved the charming Djanjhari-Nar on the bare report of her beauty, and not meeting with any other means than the present of satisfying my earnest desire to see her, I buried myself in this sack, inconsiderately indeed, since I did not know how I should be able to get out of it.

The darwaysh was greatly surprised to see me in this condition, and Kalim having at the same time recovered his sight by rubbing his eyes, perceived that I was son to the woman from whom he had bought his rice meal; and seeing by the posture in which I had put myself, that I was resolved to sell my life at a dear rate, he was the more easily appeased by the darwaysh, so they soon found it impossible not to laugh at the comical figure I made. Since this young man loves Djanjhari-Nar, said the darwaysh, let him have her, I beseech you, my dear Kalim. He is an only son, and I will take upon me to make his mother give up her shop, with at least four thousand dinars. I do not believe you can find in all Baku a son-in-law who has been better educated, is an honester man, and who will behave towards you, as a father-in-law, with more respect.—Ah! said I, it is not enough that Kalim consents to make me happy; I renounce his good will, if the charming Djanjhari-Nar does not approve of me. This delicate way of thinking made so great an impression on Kalim, that he took me in his arms, telling me that his daughter was her own mistress, and that she might that very moment decide my fate. She must first then, said the darwaysh, see her new lover such as he is. And upon this, he immediately conducted me to another room, where I cleaned myself; and Kalim, who was pretty much of my own size, having put one of his own gowns on me, I made my appearance before the beautiful Djanjhari-Nar, who liked me so well that she immediately accepted me as her husband. The darwaysh, impatient to see my happiness completed immediately sent for my mother, who was greatly surprised at my adventure, and who consented to all I wished for. The marriage-contract was drawn up and signed, and that very evening the Imam joined our hands. I slept at my father-in-law's, and my wife was so well satisfied with her choice, that the next morning she ordered for my breakfast a large dish of sheeps-feet with vinegar-sauce.

I was now, my dear brother, married to the charming Djanjhari-Nar, and was the happiest man living, if my want of sense had not made me the most miserable. Everything seemed to conspire to make me happy, my bride in a manner adoring me ; yet, without any just cause, I took it into my head to be jealous of her, to a degree that is scarcely credible. Everything alarmed me; did she speak to my mother I fancied that my mother had conspired with her to betray me ; even her innocent marks of affection for the darwaysh, to whom we were so much obliged, alarmed me so much that I used to forget his being my father, and my evil genius made me consider their behaviour as criminal. In fine, continued the old kalandar, I did nothing but exclaim against Djanjhari-Nar, and scarcely ever permitted her to see the light of day ; yet, though I gave her no rest, she never made the least complaint of my ill usage. My mother and the darwaysh made me many representations on my foolish jealousy. It is neither bolts nor locks, said they, that can secure your honour; an honest woman is her own guardian, and your groundless suspicions tend more to make her forget her duty than to persevere in it. But I was deaf to their advice, and at last my madness increased to such a degree, that they resolved to try every method of getting the better of it.

One day, the darwaysh was conversing with my mother, whilst I was employed in making some entries in my books. There has arrived here, said he, within these three days, a young darwaysh from Circassia, whose beauty surpasses anything that has yet appeared at Baku. I imagine that the pages, who are to serve us with fruit in the paradise of our great Prophet, can scarcely compare with him, since so much modesty has never been seen united with so many other perfections. His chamber is next to mine and in consequence of this neighbourhood, we have contracted a great friendship for one another. I am to give him a breakfast to-morrow, and therefore beg of you to send me a pullet and rice of your own dressing, and a dish of pillaw.[1] My mother promised to comply, and accordingly got everything in readiness for these ex- cellent ragouts, which she sent my father next morning at the appointed hour. I had heard all their discourse, without seeming to take notice of it, but my curiosity prompting me to see so handsome a man, I resolved to make one at breakfast with my father. I kept my mind to myself; when the dishes where sent off, I went into my wife's apartment. She was still a-bed, on account of some slight indisposition, and was in a profound sleep. I did not think proper to awaken her, but only looked at her attentively for some time, when I shut the door, and

----

1 This dish consists of rice stewed with butter, or suet, and is a very common favourite food all over the East.

having given the key a double turn, according to custom, I ran and knocked at the door of the convent of the day-wayshes. I asked for the darwaysh, who was my father, and on being told he was in his chamber, I immediately ran to it; but I had scarcely entered it when I grew pale and cold at the sight of his friend.

I had no sooner perceived in him all the features of my wife, than falling down with mere weakness on a sofa of rushes, and wiping my face, I cried out: where am I, and what prodigy is this? My father interrupted me here, getting up in great confusion, and taking me into his arms in the tenderest manner, asked me what was the matter, and what dark cloud had overspread my imagination? I answered that I found myself disordered the moment I entered his chambers, and that I chose to return home immediately. Upon which he led me back to the door of the convent; and as I had only the street to cross to get home, the moment I left him I flew to my wife's apartment. I began to respire, my dear brother, when I found her in the same condition in which I had left her the minute before, and my joy on the occasion was so great that I caught her in my arms, and embraced her with the warmest expressions of affection, which she returned in the most endearing manner. However I made no great stay with her, but hastened back to the convent, and ran directly to my father's cell, telling him I had got the better of my indisposition, and had come to breakfast with him. You are welcome, said he; this handsome Circassian and I have already made a beginning. Sit down to table, and first satisfy yourself with a glass of wine. I rinsed a glass, and my father was going to pour me out some wine, when the Circassian prevented him. Brother, said he, let me have the pleasure of helping him; I intend this day to do the honours of your table. The sound of these words made me tremble; my hands in an instant became so weak,

and my eyes so fastened on this young man, whose voice
perfectly resembled my wife's, that I spilled all the wine
upon my clothes and on the table-cloth. I made in a single
instant a thousand afflicting reflections; and quitting the
darwayshes in an abrupt manner, I made but one leap from
the convent to my house, where my wife was still a-bed.
I was so thunderstruck that I could not speak to her.
What is the matter with you, dear light of my life? said
she, starting up in her bed in the greatest confusion; has
any accident happened? Do not permit me, I beseech
you, to remain any longer in so cruel an uncertainty.

I returned a little to myself. Ah! Djanjhari-Nar,
said I, may I believe what I hear?—Why, replied she,
what do you see and what do you hear? Satisfy my
curiosity instantly.—No, said I, I am certainly deceived;
I must again try if my eyes are faithful witnesses of what
has happened in the convent of the darwayshes. I then
left her, and shutting the door as I had already done, I
returned to my father's cell much easier in my mind than
when I had left it. I beg your pardon, said I at my first
appearance, for the ill manners I have been guilty of. My
reason for leaving you in so great a hurry was that I had
forgotten to leave money with my mother to answer a
demand she expects in about a quarter of an hour. I have
now no more business to take me away, and nothing can
be more agreeable to me than to remain with you and to
enjoy the pleasure of your company.—Let it be so, said
my father, we may spend all the morning here very
agreeably. Taste this dish of pillaw, which has not as
yet been touched; as to the fowl and rice we despatched them during your absence. I now began to
think of eating some pillaw, but happening to give a look
at the young Circassian, just as I had taken some into
my mouth, I found it impossible to get it down, my astonishment increased to such a degree. The young darwaysh was the very counterpart of Djanjhari-Nar, both

in voice and in gesture; everything, in fine, conspired to make me believe that no two persons had ever been so like each other. What is the matter with you, son, said the old darwaysh. You betray in all your actions so much uneasiness and distraction that I am at a loss what to think of you to-day.—Have I not, said I, the justest reason in the world to do so? Who the devil would not take this young Circassian for my wife? I must own to you that I ran home to be sure I had her. I found her both times in bed, and this circumstance should have dissipated my apprehensions, notwithstanding which I find myself unable to master those jealous suspicions which tear my mind to pieces.

The two darwayshes laughed heartily at this my candid confession. As for my part, I was at a loss how to behave on the occasion, when the young darwaysh took me up. What, sir, said he, can a slight resemblance then between your wife and me disorder your brain in this manner? And shall jealousy tyrannize over you so far as to make you commit the extravagances with which we have for this hour past been entertained? How much I pity your spouse! Certainly she must have a great fund of virtue not to take vengeance for your unjust suspicions. I can easily forgive a delicate jealousy; but by carrying it the length you do, according to the report of this honest darwaysh, believe me, sir, you take the readiest way of making your wife punish you as you deserve. I listened with great confusion to this lecture by the young darwaysh, and began to be ashamed of my past conduct, at the same time resolving, in a manner, to trust Djanjhari-Nar entirely to her own virtue; when the young preacher, in moving himself a little, discovered to me near one of his ears a mark in every respect like one that my wife had in the same place. This strange sight wound up my madness again to the highest pitch. I gave a great shout, which surprised the darwayshes. Ah! said

I, I am certainly betrayed, and all my suspicions were too well founded.—What sudden fury has seized you? said my father. Have you lost your wits, or——I did not give him time to make an end of his discourse; I slipped out of his hands, and ran home in the greatest hurry and confusion, where I found my wife employed in making the abdest. I drew near her in the greatest perturbation, and having examined the mark near her ear, I clapped my hands together, with my eyes lifted up to heaven, and was ready to faint away with surprise. My mother, who was in the shop, which was contiguous to my wife's apartment, came in on hearing my cries. She and my wife inquired earnestly what might be the cause of my disorder, and of my so often going out and in : but I did not as yet think proper to give them any satisfaction. I only begged of my mother to prepare a dinner for ourselves and for the handsome darwaysh of Circassia and his companion, whom I told her I intended to invite ; telling her, withal, that I should give before them a full account of everything that had happened to me that morning, which she must agree was very strange and uncommon.

I then left them, and at my return to the convent, found my father and the young darwaysh still at table. I must, said I, acquaint you with the full extent of my weakness. The mark which this handsome darwaysh has near his ear gave my jealousy a new alarm; for my wife has one in the same spot so very like it that I again took it into my head that it was her very self that I saw in this disguise. I ran back to the house to clear up the matter to myself, but, thanks to heaven! I found her at her usual purification ; so that all my suspicions are at an end, and I have returned, easy and satisfied in my mind, to spend with you the interval between this and dinner, to which I invite you. I have a mind to convince this young darwaysh that, as he cannot be a twin of my dear Djanjhari-Nar, since she is an only child, nature has formed so great a resemblance between them that it is impossible not to be deceived by it.—I accept your invitation, replied the young Circassian, with great pleasure ; nothing can be more agreeable to me. I am curious to see this extraordinary likeness you speak of, about which, however, the darwaysh, my companion, is not altogether agreed ; but then it is only on this express condition, that no fit of jealousy shall be permitted to interrupt our joy, for I am disposed to be merry, and perhaps at your expense.—Ah ! said I, interrupting him, I promise that you shall do at my house as you like. I have suffered so much this morning in the many struggles I have had to sustain that I am resolved for the future to make myself easy.—It is the best thing you can do, replied the young man ; were I a woman, and disposed to play my husband a trick, he would find it to no purpose to watch me ; I could easily triumph over all his precautions, and I shall convince you of it presently at your own house.—You will oblige me greatly, said I, in so doing. I will endeavour to entertain you well ; and you cannot do me a greater favour than that of curing me radically of my troublesome passion.

I spent a couple of hours very agreeably with the two darwayshes till dinner-time drawing nigh, I left them to prepare for their reception. I thought proper before my guests arrived, to see my wife, to make a merit to her of my conversion, and to assure her that for the future she should enjoy all the liberty decency might allow. But, my dear brother, how great was my surprise on opening the door of my room, the key of which I had never let go out of my possession, when I found her missing ! Great, however, as my surprise was at not finding my wife, it was much increased by finding instead of her the two darwayshes whom I had but just now left at the convent. So unexpected a sight struck me motionless, and I should no doubt have fallen to the ground if my mother, who had followed close after me, had not supported me in her arms. I remained a long time without being able to utter a single syllable: but having at length come to myself: O heaven! said I, do I dream, or is it the devil who has persecuted me all the morning, that still takes pleasure in imposing upon me?—No, no, my dear Hanif, replied the old darwaysh whom I told you was my father, you are not asleep; there is no more than a little contrivance in all this illusion. Your jealousy had become so ridiculous that we undertook to rid you of it. I contrived, with your mother and your wife, everything that passed in my apartment this morning; your behaviour fully answered our intentions, and the beautiful darwaysh is no other than the incomparable Djanjhari-Nar. No doubt you will find it a difficult matter to comprehend what I tell you, and I know you will scarcely even credit it, but it is easy to convince you. —Ah then! said I with the greatest eagerness, lose no time in doing it; let me know how it was possible that my wife should at one and the same time be in her bed and in your cell, in her night-clothes and in the dress of a darwaysh.—I shall immediately, replied my father, satisfy your curiosity in this respect.

Djanjhari-Nar is no longer ignorant how I am related to you. I found myself under the necessity of revealing to her the secret of your birth, in order to obtain her concurrence to the measures we wanted to take. You must know that your mother's deceased husband used to be sometimes jealous of her, and his sudden starts often disconcerted the schemes we had laid to see each other, which gave us no small concern. But as, in quality of treasurer to the convent, I had money at will, I seized on the opportunity of the brute's going to the country for a fortnight, and employed workmen whom I could confide in to make a passage between my room and this apartment under the street, which is very narrow; two trap-doors, with proper counterpoises, do the rest. It is an easy matter to go from this to my cell in less than two minutes by the trap-door you now look at, whereas, in the common way, a person must traverse our court, which is pretty long, and open and shut doors; so that you may easily judge if it was impossible for your wife to put on the habit of a darwaysh, to throw it off, and to get into bed again, in the interval of time requisite for you to make so great a circuit to get into our convent, or out of it, and to arrive at this apartment. Here is then, my dear child, a plain discovery of the whole mystery. But I must add that it was with the greatest difficulty imaginable I prevailed on Djanjhari-Nar to act her part in it. She was willing to put up with all your extravagances rather than expose herself to your displeasure, till I obtained her concurrence by assuring her that if so rude a trial did not bring you to a better way of thinking you should never know anything of the trick that had been played on you, and that I should soon make the handsome Circassian set out for his own country.

We have, I believe, succeeded, my son, continued the old man, since you have given me your word that you will be no more guilty of the same folly; and, indeed, no man ever had less reason to be jealous. Your wife is a most virtuous woman, she has stretched her complaisance for your weakness more than could be expected; but, though she were ever so much the reverse, judge, my dear Hanif, by your own experience, what love is capable of. There is nothing that it does not invent and compass to get the better of a jealous person's vigilance, and the surest course a man can take is to trust entirely to the virtue and fidelity of his wife. I know very well that this is looked upon as a very foolish maxim in these eastern countries; but there is a difference to be made between living in the common way, which requires that women should appear but seldom in public, and treating them with that injurious diffidence which you have done with the charming Djanjhari-Nar. You have carried your jealousy to such an excess as to take umbrage at me, who am your father. Even your mother's affection for her daughter-in-law has given you uneasiness. Who can you think, my son, should have your honour more at heart than your mother and myself? And yet you have been weak enough to suspect us of a design upon it.

My surprise and confusion were so great, continued the old kalandar, that I was at a loss what answer to make to the darwaysh's wise discourse. My dear father, said I, how much am I obliged to you for having undertaken my cure, and having succeeding so well in it! I now see all the force of your arguments, and I am ready to sink with shame for my past conduct; but I am resolved to make amends for my folly by so contrary a behaviour that the beautiful Djanjhari-Nar shall have no less reason to commend me for the future than she has had just cause to complain of me for the time past. Upon this I threw myself at my wife's feet, who still continued in the darwaysh's dress, and asked her pardon for my ridiculous jealousies with such expressions of love and of tenderness as drew tears from my father and mother. Djanjhari-Nar, unable likewise to contain her's, immediately raised me up. My dear lord, said she, if I have always loved you in spite of the hard manner in which you have sometimes treated me, guess to what a pitch my love must be increased now, when you assure me of an alteration which makes me completely happy! She seasoned her discourse with so many endearments that I kissed her a thousand times, and cried out in the transport of my pleasure: No, my dear Djanjhari-Nar, there is no difference between the zephyr of spring and the mild breath of your mouth, which refreshes my heart and my soul. I am a new man, and the most agreeable moments of my life will be those which I shall spend in seeking the means of pleasing you. This sudden change in me gave my father and mother the most sensible satisfaction. Nothing could equal the pleasure they enjoyed in having been instrumental in reclaiming me; as for Djanjhari-Nar's joy, it was great beyond expression. We now sat down to dinner, at which everything passed in the most agreeable manner, and I ever afterwards punctually fulfilled the promise I had given.

I lived thus with my wife about thirteen years, during which time I buried the darwaysh and my mother. The children I had by my wife lived but a short time. In fine, I lost her, my dear brother, after a sickness of four months, and you may judge how sensibly afflicted I was at the loss of a woman of so great merit. All my friends came to condole with me on the occasion, and endeavoured to dissipate my grief; but what they could not do time effected. As time brings about everything, so it insensibly wore out the memory of my deceased wife. I at last began to think of nothing but how to divert myself, and giving myself up entirely to my pleasures I fell little by little into a state of the greatest debauchery and excess. By neglecting my business, my affairs soon fell into disorder, and at the end of two years I was so loaded with debt that, unable to satisfy my creditors, I had no other choice left than flight to avoid a prison. I therefore sold my effects privately for half their value, and escaped out of Baku in the disguise of a kalandar. From the very first day of my taking the habit I liked it so well that I resolved never to leave it off; and I have now persisted in this resolution upwards of thirty years. I have made in it the tour of Persia and of Tartary, during which I have met with a great number of adventures too long to relate. I intend, besides, to take a journey to the Indies and to China, and for this purpose I joined company two months ago with this young man, who has turned kalandar after my example, and whose adventures are at least as uncommon as my own.

When the old kalandar had made an end of his discourse, Faruk, my lord, who had listened to him with infinite pleasure, thanked him for his kindness. Nothing, said he, can be more original than your history; and whatever assurance you have given me, I can scarcely believe that of your companion can compare with it.—You shall soon have an opportunity of judging for yourself, replied the young kalandar.

ADVENTURES OF THE YOUNG KALANDAR

My mother, for I must tell you I never had the the pleasure of knowing my father, being so young when he died ; my mother, I say, lived at Shiraz, and carried on a pretty considerable trade in milk, butter, and cheese, the produce of flocks that belonged to her, and which she used to send me to town to dispose of ; but I soon grew tired of this way of life. There happened to arrive from the Indies about two years before, a company of comedians, who commonly exhibited their performances in the market-place, where they afterwards used to sell remedies to which they attributed a surprising efficacy in all manner of disorders. As they knew but little of the Persian tongue they at first played nothing but pantomimes, and employed an interpreter to dispose of their drugs ; but as they began by degrees to make themselves understood, they acquired so much reputation that everybody saw them act with pleasure. I never went to Shiraz without going to see their entertainments, and I took so great a liking to them that I offered to make one of their company. I had naturally a genius that way ; I begged they might give me some under part ; they pitched upon a very diverting one in the first play they acted, and I behaved so much to the liking of all the spectators, that I soon looked upon myself as qualified to appear to advantage in the most difficult characters. Particularly, I excelled in acting the drunkard, and played so well the parts of the fool and of the blockhead, that I might have been mistaken for a real inhabitant of Siwrihissar. At length, my dear brothers, the drollest scenes had no merit but what I gave them. But not satisfied with the character of an excellent actor, I had likewise a mind to shine as an author. Till then we had played nothing but scraps of comedies, and almost always without any preparation. On my part, I resolved to connect scenes, and thus form a contrived piece; and I succeeded so well that my first essay proved a masterpiece. I gave a little farce, called " The Kadi Outwitted." I shall inform you of the subject in a few words.

A kadi of Kandahar, who is a great miser, has a very pretty daughter, with whom a young Persian falls passionately in love. This kadi has promised the girl to a very rich old Mohammedan ; the Persian is ready to go distracted for fear of losing his mistress, and after having thought of many different ways of preventing a marriage which must make him unhappy for the remainder of his life, finds none so likely to succeed as the following. He waits on the kadi, who does not know him, to consult him about carrying away a young woman. The judge at first looks upon it as a very criminal undertaking, and falls into a great passion, but is soon softened by a purse of gold ; and thereupon gives his advice in writing that the girl may be carried off on account of the disproportion in point of age between her and the man her parents would marry her to, and especially as the person who intends to carry her off does it with a view of making her his wife; and in consequence of another purse of gold he forbids the girl's father to give her lover any uneasiness, on pain of receiving one hundred blows on the soles of his feet. The young Persian literally follows the advice, or rather the commands, of the kadi, and carries off the daughter; and the outwitted father finds himself under the necessity of bestowing her as a wife upon her ingenious lover.

Such was the plan of my piece; but I painted in it the kadi's avarice in such lively colours, at least as far as I may judge of the matter, especially in a scene where I played the blockhead to admiration, that I could heartily wish you had seen my comedy acted. What! said Faruk, should not a comic writer have his performances by heart from one end to another? What can hinder you from giving us this diverting scene?—Ah! brother, answered the young man, it is impossible it should appear in this place to the same advantage as it did on the stage.—That is no matter, replied the other two kalandars, we shall make allowance for the want of actors. We know that it is no easy matter for one man to play different parts.—Since you are so earnest then, said the comedian, I shall endeavour to satisfy you.

You must first represent to yourself the kadi alone at his house, complaining of the too good behaviour of the inhabitants of Kandahar, and that business was very slack this year, especially in a criminal way. I enter his room with one of my companions dressed like country-men; we appeared to be both of us quite out of breath, and make him almost mad by a very comical dumb scene. In fine, impatient at seeing us speak only by signs, and curious to know the matter, he begins as follows:

Kadi. These two scoundrels must certainly be drunk or dumb with all their signs, of which I can make nothing.

First Clown. [This was my part, my dear brother]. Oh!——with your worship's leave, we have hastened with so much diligence——to——Ah!——how I am out of breath!——gossip, tell his worship yourself what we have seen, you can best clear up the matter to him.

Kadi. Plague on the brutes!

Second Clown. [*crying.*] Tell it yourself if you can; I am so beside myself, and so troubled.

Kadi. I believe these animals are come to make me mad. Will you speak or not, scape-gallows? Let me know what you have seen.

First Clown. Softly, softly, please your worship; you are going into a passion; for as Lokman[1] says very justly, in his book of animals——

Kadi. Ah! you scoundrel, you, let Lokman and his animals alone; what have his fables to do with what you have to say?

First Clown. Your worship is in the right. But your worship knows that people who have wit, are fond of shewing it; and if your worship had not interrupted me, I should have compared your worship to an ass.

Kadi. Would you, rascal? But there is no taking notice of what the stupid dog says. Friend, I beg you will make an end, and let me know what has brought you here.

First Clown. By all means, sir, with a great deal of pleasure.—Ah! why do not you satisfy his worship? Now, sir, we came to tell you, that as my gossip and myself were jogging along, without thinking anything of what was to happen, we saw [*cries*]—Ah! my heart is ready to break when I think of it; it makes such an impression on me, that I cannot go on.

---

1 There is a collection of fables under the name of the wise Lokman; and the accounts given of this Lokman by the people of the East resemble very much those the Greeks have left us of Æsop.

Kadi. Go on, villain, or I shall punish your insolence. Is there no one there ?

First Clown. Well, well, please your worship, since you will not give me leave to recover myself, to cut short, I shall tell you without any perambulation, that——But hold, I'll lay you a wager, that with all your penetration you cannot guess what we have seen.

Kadi. [*Seizing him by the throat.*] Hangman that you are, have you a mind then to make one go mad in good earnest ?

First Clown. He ! he ! Well, please your worship, let me go, and I shall immediately tell you how we are come to let you know that we have seen a man murdered.

Kadi. Now I am myself again. So much the better, it is good news ; here is a job to buy me a good supper.

Second Clown. Ah ! please your worship, the worst of it is, that the man that is killed was my son-in-law as he has married my daughter, and nothing worse could happen to me.

Kadi. So much the better, I tell you; it is a very good affair.

Enter one of the Deputy Justice's Thief-takers.

Thief-taker. Please your worship, we have just this moment apprehended a murderer a little way from Kandahar.

Kadi. Haste, haste, my gown and my turband. Have you any witnesses ? [*To the country-fellow.*]

First Clown. Ay, that we have——let us alone—— there will be some to spare.

Kadi. As that is the case, I shall set out this instant for the spot where the crime has been committed. But I must first know the circumstances of the criminal.

Thief-taker. He is——

Kadi. What is he ?

Thief-taker. He is a clown belonging to the next village.

16—2

Kadi. A clown belonging to the next village! I am in a fine hole truly. What right have such scoundrels to commit murder? Ah! I am ready to go mad. This job would not buy me a cup of water if I wanted it. [*To his servants.*] Hold, here is my gown and turband.

First Clown. Let us be gone, for the criminal may escape, while we are here chattering in this manner.

Kadi. So much the better. Nothing is more natural; and, 'faith, it is an affair that won't pay for shoe leather.

Second Clown. But then——

Kadi. Turn these fellows out, who split my head with their importunate discourse.

Enter the Kadi's Deputy.

Deputy. I wish your worship joy——A murder has been committed.

Kadi. I know it.

Deputy. And if you do, why do not you run to the spot?

Kadi. There is no time lost.—We shall have daylight enough to-morrow.

Deputy. But then——

Kadi. Say no more of it.

Deputy. Your worship's indifference surprises me! The beast is well shod.

Kadi. What do you mean?

Deputy. You do not know then, that the murderer was driving sheep to market,

Kadi. Sheep, say you?

Deputy. I say sheep.

Kadi. And well, what have you done with the sheep.

Deputy. A fine question, truly. I immediately sent them to prison. [*In a low voice.*] A novice in the trade would have taken care of the criminal, but I have studied your example too well. I gave the murderer an opportunity of making his escape, and have kept the sheep.

Kadi. Quick, quick, my gown and my turband. Let my mule be bridled. [*To the deputy.*] You will one day

make a figure in my station.—[*To the clowns.*] You asses
you, why did you not inform me at first that the murderer
had sheep?

First Clown. Truly, please your worship, we did not
think he was the more guilty for having sheep.

Kadi. You are mistaken. A man murdered, and
sheep! It is enough. Nothing shall pacify me, I will
make an example this moment——of the sheep.

First Clown. Your worship is in the right. He
deserves to be hanged; but the poor sheep, sir, have done
nothing, and [*crying*] we ask your worship's pardon for
them.

Kadi. No, no! no quarter; justice must be done. I
shall just step into this closet with my deputy, and be
with you in a minute or two.

Second Clown. Faith, this is comical work. So then,
when a man has got sheep, the trial is over——he may
think of the gallows in good earnest.

First Clown. Ah! Gossip, while fortune smiles on
us, and the kadi is in the murdering humour, let us take
vengeance on our neighbour Khalib, who is constantly
playing us some trick or another.

Second Clown. The fellow has better than a hundred
and fifty sheep. This is a fine opportunity of getting rid
of him, or at least of procuring him a bastinado.

First Clown. You are in the right, and 'faith, we will
do for him. He will have good luck if he escapes with
blows, and we may afterwards divert ourselves well at
his expense.

This is, my dear brothers, continued the young
kalandar, a sample of my performance. I afterwards
introduced the young Persian drawing, by force of money
from the covetous kadi, an advice so contrary to his
design of marrying his daughter to the old Mohammedan;
but I shall not entertain you with that scene, though
pretty original, I think, in its kind. It is enough that I

have lately made you sensible of my genius. I now
return to my history.—Permit me first to assure you, said
Faruk, that the scenes with which you have entertained
us, are the prettiest that I ever saw.—Your commenda-
tion, replied the young kalandar, is very moderate; my
play, from beginning to end, is a most excellent and
charming performance, and none of our comic writers
has produced anything more perfect and natural; all
Shiraz did me justice; but the kadi of the town, of
whom I never thought in composing my comedy, judged
otherwise of it. He took it into his head that he saw
himself represented in it in the most natural colours,
and entering into a furious passion against both the
author and the players, he drove us all out of Shiraz,
and forbade us, on pain of death ever to appear there
again in that quality. I shall not enlarge upon a little
bastinado that I received by the kadi's order, in the name
of our company; it was by the way of acknowledgment
for my being a satirical author; all the other profits were
equally divided amongst us. After this I proposed to
them that we should go and settle in some other town,
where the kadis might be of a better way of thinking;
but they treated me with great harshness, in spite of all
the apologies I could make for what had happened; so
that I resolved to renounce the profession and to return to
the business I carried on before I took to the stage.

Upon this then I went back to my mother, who
received me with open arms. I had saved some money
during the two years I had spent among the players. Part
of this money I laid out in the purchase of a stock of
cattle, and being resolved to indulge myself, could not
think of travelling on foot to sell my butter and cheese;
I therefore bought a little mule, which cost me thirty
dinars. As I was going home very quietly on my new
purchase, driving before me a purblind horse which I
generally made use of to carry our butter to market, I

met at about a quarter of a league from the town, a man who asked me if I had come from Shiraz.—You may see, said I, that I have but just left it.—No doubt, replied he; have you been making some purchase at the fair there?   I have bought this mule there, answered I.—What mule?—Why the mule I ride on.—Are you in earnest?—Certainly, it cost me thirty dinars.—Upon this the man began to laugh ready to split his sides. the plot was well laid, continued he; whoever sold you the beast was no fool, to palm an ass on you for a mule. He then continued his journey towards Shiraz, laughing all the way as long as he continued within hearing.

I really pitied the fellow, as I took him for a fool; when behold! about half a league further, another asked me pretty nearly the same question. I answered him as I had done the first; but when I came to tell him that I had bought a mule: What! said he, do you take me for a fool to think of making me believe an ass is a mule? I had a mind to prove that he was mistaken; but he fell into a passion, abused me severely and went on, leaving me in the greatest astonishment imaginable. I now began to think in good earnest, that I might really have been imposed upon; so I got off my purchase and examined it from head to foot, without finding anything to make me alter my opinion of its being a mule. However, unwilling to rely entirely on my own judgment, or to trust entirely to my eyes on the occasion, I made myself a promise to lay the affair before the next man I met; and swore that, if he judged in favour of the ass, I would at once make him a present of it.

I had scarcely gone three hundred paces when I met with a kind of country fellow. Brother, said I, let me know, I beg you, what kind of a beast I have got under me?— A comical question, this, replied he; don't you yourself know better than I can tell you?—Let me know it or not, said I, you will oblige me in telling.—Well then,

said the countryman, it is no hard matter to know that
it is an ass. This answer thunderstruck me. I got off
the beast which I had taken for a mule, and begged the
man to accept it as a free gift. I had no occasion to
press it upon him; he thanked me for my present, and
leaping on the beast, gave her a kick or two with his
heels, and flew off like lightning. I got home on foot,
not a little vexed at the trick that had been played me;
my mother, who soon perceived the trouble I was in,
asked me the cause of it. I gave her an account of what
had happened; she could not forbear laughing at it.
Poor unthinking creature, said she, have you not sense
enough to see that they were three sharpers, who spread
themselves on the road to Shiraz, and who laid a scheme
to get your mule from you? You must be very simple
indeed, to be caught by so glaring a piece of knavery.
My mother's raillery stung me to the quick; I saw now
that I had suffered myself to be imposed on, and forming
a resolution to be revenged on my sharpers the very first
opportunity, I returned to the market the next day but
one. I knew them again, though they had changed their
dress; and as I saw, by two or three of their tricks, of
which I happened to be a witness, that they were not the
cunningest of their trade, I thought I might safely defer
my vengeance to another opportunity.

After having taken my measures very well, and informed my mother of what I was about, I put a pair of
empty baskets on a mottled goat that I had bought from
one of my neighbours, and went with her to the market
of Shiraz. I had scarcely arrived, when my three sharpers
perceived me, and surrounded me, thinking they would
soon be able to make a prey of me as they had done
before. I pretended not to know them; bought a leg of
mutton, a turkey-cock, and three chickens; and putting
them into my goat's baskets: Pretty creature, said I, loud
enough for them to overhear me, make haste home; tell

my cook to dress this leg of mutton with rice, to make a stew of the turkey-cock, and a fricassee of the chickens; but above all things let her not forget to make an excellent tart for the dessert; let her likewise set eight bottles of wine to cool. I then gave the goat a little lash, and off she capered. The three sharpers were greatly surprised at this odd scene. What then, brother, said one of them, do you imagine that this creature will obey your orders?—No doubt, answered I, she will; this is not a common goat, she knows my intentions, and I am certain she will to a tittle fulfil them. Upon this they fell a-laughing. It is no joke, said I very seriously; if you doubt of it, come home and dine with me, and judge for yourselves. The sharpers took me at my word, and curious to know the truth of what I had told them, stuck close to me, while I took some turns in the market to make a few purchases; which done, we all set out together on foot. I had no sooner got home, but, in order to deceive them the better, I began to question my mother, as if she had been the cook. Well, said I, has the goat come home?—She arrived, answered she, a long time ago, you will find her browsing on the cabbages in the garden, and your dinner would have been ready by this, but that the guests you invited sent word that some unexpected business deprived them of the pleasure of waiting on you this day; however, the leg of mutton is almost done; another half hour will complete the turkey; the fricassee is quite ready; the tart is in the oven, and the bottles are in snow, as you directed.—It is all very well, said I : here are three gentleman, whose company will make me amends for the absence of those I invited. You may send up dinner as soon as you please.—Nothing could come up to the astonishment of my guests at the answers given me by my mother. They went into the garden, and knowing the goat again by the marks she had, which they had narrowly examined, they resolved to have her at any price.

Dinner was soon served up, and I made my sharpers, who suspected nothing, drink very copiously. At length, when we had almost done, one of them asked me if I would not part with my goat? I pretended to be willing enough, provided I got the worth of her. They first offered twenty dinars of gold, but I refused them with contempt ; in fine, my dear brothers, I played my part so well that I got out of them all the money they had, which in the whole made sixty and some odd dinars. We fell to our liquor again to confirm the bargain, and my guests left me towards evening, half drunk, and thoroughly satisfied with their purchase. The day following, they thought proper to make a trial of their goat, in order to know if she would obey their commands with the same obedience they imagined she had done mine the day before. For this purpose they loaded her as I had done, gave her her directions, and then sent her off; but they waited in vain for her return, she never came back.

I must here, my dear brothers, explain this mystery to you. One of my neighbours had two white goats spotted with black, but so like one another, that it was impossible to find any difference between them. These goats I bought, in order to be revenged on my sharpers. I made my mother acquainted with my design, gave her, if I may say so, orders for dinner ; and after having tied up one of my goats in the garden, led the other to market, where I bought the same provisions which I had desired my mother to get ready. I then put them on my goat, and after having given her directions to carry them home, turned her adrift, for anyone that pleased to lay hands on her. nor did I ever learn to whose lot she fell. My orders were so punctually complied with, my mother acted her part so naturally, and the other goat, which my sharpers found in the garden, was so very like that which they had seen with me at Shiraz, that they really imagined that there was something above nature in the creature, and so bought her at the dear price I have been telling you. But she met, no doubt, with the same fate that her sister had done before her: some stranger laid hold of her, and made a property of her, and of the provisions with which she had been loaded.

I made no doubt but that, when they found themselves deceived, they would call upon me for their money, but I waited for them undauntedly. They knocked at my door, threatening what an example they would make of me. I let them in myself, asking them quietly what could be the cause of their being in so great a passion; they then told me it was owing to the loss of their goat. Have you not curried it this morning, said I, with the left hand, as I desired my cook to tell you yesterday you ought to do? She ran after you to acquaint you with that important circumstance, which the wine I had drunk made me forget, when we had concluded the bargain.— What cook? replied the sharpers. Since we left your house, it never came into our heads to curry the goat with the left hand, as you never acquainted us with that ceremony. Upon this, I immediately called to my mother, who came in trembling, on account of the great passion I pretended to be in. How comes it, wretch, said I, in a great fury, that you did not tell these gentlemen, as I had so expressly commanded you, not to omit currying the goat with the left hand, as I used to do myself every morning?—My dear master, said she, throwing herself at my feet, it was my intention so to do, but I could not; I ran after them a great way, without being able to overtake them.—Ah! you careless slut, said I, this is one of your common tricks; no doubt you stopped to chatter away with some gossip, and it is thus you undo me by your neglect: but, I swear by Mohammed, it shall not go far with you. With these words I took her by the hair, and drawing a dagger from my girdle-belt, gave her so home a stroke with it in the belly, as immediately laid her flat on the floor. In a minute she was all covered with blood, and my three sharpers were so stunned at it, that they immediately began to think of making their escape. Gentlemen, said I, she had only what she deserved; nor need you be in any pain about her. I can in an instant, if I please, restore her to life, but she is not worth taking any trouble with; only help me, I beg of you, to bury her in my garden.

The three sharpers did nothing but stare at each other for some time, till one of them breaking the profound silence that this murder had cast them in: What! said he, and is it really in your power to bring the poor creature back to life again?—No doubt it is, I replied.—Ah! then work, we beseech you, this miracle in our presence, and we will renounce all claims we may have on you on the score of the goat. I made some difficulty about giving them the satisfaction they required; they pressed me the more eagerly. At last: It is impossible, said I, to refuse such worthy gentlemen; upon which, I opened a box, and taking out of it a hunting-horn, played two or three very brisk tunes in the ears of the deceased. As I played, my mother seemed to recover life by degrees; in fine, she was well enough in a quarter of an hour to sit up, without expressing the least inconvenience from the wound I had given her. This strange sight threw my sharpers into the greatest amazement, and gave them so great a longing for the horn, that they already began to think how they might strip me of it. They asked me from whom I had this so miraculous an instrument. I answered them, that I had bought it from a stranger for one hundred and four dinars, and that he told me it would lose its virtue should anyone take it forcibly from me; but that it would retain all its power in the hands of anyone I made it over to, provided I got for it eight dinars more than it cost me; because it was absolutely necessary that in thus passing from hand to hand the price should rise eight dinars, which was all it cost at first, so that I was the thirteenth person who had enjoyed it.

My guests speedily swallowed the bait, and nothing could equal their longing for the horn, but they did not choose to pay so dear for it ; however, they at last came to the resolution of letting me have for it the price, under which I told them it could not be sold, and pressed me so hard, that I at length, after making a great many difficulties, suffered myself to be persuaded, and took their one hundred and twelve dinars. They immediately went home, and as they all lived under the same roof, they sent for their wives, sat down to table, and there spent the rest of the day. Night coming on, when they had almost finished their meal, and had sufficiently heated themselves with wine, they thought proper to try their horn, and for this purpose endeavoured to pick a quarrel with their wives, who being provoked by some smart blows, reproached their husbands with every crime of theirs they could think of, and even threatened to inform the kadi of the life they led. This was exactly what the rogues wished for. At these menaces they pretended to fall into the greatest fury, and with their knives at once cut the throats of the three women, who at bottom were as bad as their husbands. The unhappy creatures were no sooner stretched out upon the floor, than the murderers fell to their horn, but the wretches were deaf to their music, and no sign of life appeared. Upon this they fell to it again, but finding that all their skill was to no purpose, they too late perceived, that they had met with one cunninger than themselves ; and that I had, instead of stabbing my cook, only ran, as was really the case, my dagger into a bladder of blood. You may now imagine them not only in the greatest agonies at my having outwitted them, but in the greatest despair for having killed their wives, without knowing how to dispose of their dead bodies. Whilst they were deliberating on the means of being revenged on me, and of getting rid of the unhappy victims of their stupidity, who should pass by but the kadi's deputy with some asses! Hearing the sound of the horn, he knocked at the door to know the reason of so unseasonable a noise, that broke the rest of all the neighbourhood.

The three sharpers began now to consider themselves as lost men, and were so terrified that instead of opening the door they thought of making their escape. But the kadi ordered the door to be burst open, and on seeing the three bodies weltering in their blood, he commanded his attendants to seize the murderers, and to conduct them to prison. His attendants, no doubt, were earnest enough in obeying his orders, notwithstanding which, one of the murderers somehow or other made his escape. The two others represented in vain to the kadi that they had been imposed upon, and that they never imagined their wives would be killed outright. He listened to the story of the hunting-horn as to a fable, and the next day I had the pleasure of seeing my two sharpers hung up in front of their own door. Much as I was pleased at my vengeance, the escape of one of the criminals gave me no small uneasiness. I began to be greatly afraid that he would one day or other play me some unlucky trick. I therefore kept myself on my guard for a considerable time, but at length, in spite of all my vigilance, I fell into his power.

One evening as I was returning home pretty late from Shiraz, I unfortunately met this arch-villain. He was so much disguised that I did not know him; but he knew me very well, for he had no sooner perceived me than he seized me by the throat, and with the assistance of three other wretches like himself, crammed me into a sack that one of them had under his arm, and after tying the mouth of it with a strong rope, loaded me on their shoulders, with the intention, as I could plainly discover, of throwing me into the river of Badamir. I now, my dear brother, gave myself up for lost, and began to be heartily sorry for having sought any vengeance for the loss of my mule, when my assassins, alarmed by the approach of some horsemen, threw me into a hole that lay at a small distance from the road, threatening to be revenged on me if I made the least complaint ; which done, they ran off, with the intention of soon returning to take me away with them. In this terrible situation I recommended myself earnestly to our great Prophet ; but I did not place so much confidence in him alone, as not to invoke, in spite of the orders I had received from my assassins, the assistance of those who might at that time happen to pass that way.

Accordingly, a butcher, who was driving before him a flock of thirty sheep, hearing my cries, came up to the place where I was, and asked me what I was doing in the sack, and what was the cause of my lamentation. Alas! said I in a very sorrowful tone, I believe they are going to drown me, because I will not consent to marry the kadi's daughter.—Not marry the kadi's daughter! and why so, you blockhead ? said he. What reason can you have for not accepting her for a wife? She passes for one of the handsomest girls in Shiraz.—A little piece of nicety hinders me, answered I ; she is with child ; it is none of my doing ; and the kadi who has a mind to screen his daughter's honour, wants me to repair a fault committed by another ; but I would rather die a thousand times than submit to such an affront.—Plague on your stupidity! replied the butcher. I wish I was in your place, they should not have occasion so much as to pull me by the ear to make me comply, I would marry her directly.—There is no difficulty in the thing, said I, you only need put yourself into this sack.—With all my heart, my good master blockhead, replied the butcher, and you shall have my sheep into the bargain. But now I think of it, how will the kadi like the exchange?—He wants nothing but a son-in-law, answered I. He had given full directions to his slaves to stop the first passenger they should meet, and enquire of him if he was married, because his daughter's lover having died a few days ago, he was at a loss how to repair her honour. The lot fell upon me, but his daughter's big belly disgusted me at first sight. Upon this he fell into such a passion that he scarcely condescended to look at me, but ordered I should be thrown into the river if I did not alter my mind.—Since it is so, brother, I will readily change my situation for your's, said the butcher. And accordingly he untied the sack, and fixed himself in it in my place. I tied it in my turn, and driving his sheep before me, made the best of my way towards the village I belonged to.

In about half an hour, my sharper returned with his companions to take up the sack. It was in vain that the butcher within it cried out: Gentlemen, gentlemen, take me back to the kadi; I have altered my mind, and will marry his daughter, let her be ever so big-bellied. The rogues imagined that despair had turned my brain, and so without answering his remonstrances they went and threw him into the river of Badamir, where the poor fellow ended his days. It grieves me when I think of it; but in fine, I am better pleased he should be there than myself. The robbers, after this exploit, turned towards the village I lived in, to complete their revenge by burning my house. They happened to arrive at the very moment I began to knock at my door; and the unexpected sight of me caused them so much terror, that they were ready to die with fear. Oh Heavens! said they, what a prodigy is here! how have you escaped drowning? Whence come you? Where have you got all these sheep?

To be plain with you, I little expected to see these assassins so soon again. At first I was struck dumb by

their presence and their questions, but my usual readiness
of thought coming to my assistance: Go to, said I, you
are a pack of asses; if you had thrown me but four
fathoms farther into the river, instead of thirty sheep I
should have brought home three hundred.—What is the
meaning of all this? asked they.—Why answered I, no
other than this; there is in that part of the river a good
jinni, who received me very graciously, made me a
present of these sheep, brought me back with them to my
house, and assured me that had I dropt into the water a
little further, I should have carried away with me eight
times as many. This piece of news greatly surprised the
robbers; and after they had conferred together for some
time in a low voice, one of them raising his voice: No
doubt, said he to his companions, there is something very
mysterious in this affair; for nothing is more certain than
that we threw this young man into the river; he had no
sheep, we have had but time to come here, yet he is here
before us with thirty sheep, and there is not on his clothes
the least sign of their having been even wetted; as for
my part, I think it very well worth our whiles to make a
trial, and to judge of the matter for ourselves. Upon this,
he turned about to me, and asked me if I had any sacks.
I have, I believe, said I, half a dozen.—It is two too
many, replied he; put up your sheep, take four sacks,
and come with us. I cheerfully obeyed them; they
brought me to that part of the river where they thought
they had just now thrown me in. They even went to
get a little boat that I might throw them further into the
water, and then went each of them into a sack, whose
mouth I bound up very fast; which done, they suffered
themselves to be tumbled headlong into the Badamir to
fish for sheep. But I have not since, my dear brothers,
heard a word of news from them.

I now returned quietly home, well satisfied with the
vengeance I had taken on my enemies. I lived well on

their money, and on the sheep I had from the poor butcher: but my good fortune was very short lived. One night my mother unluckily set fire to our stable; the blaze soon spread itself, and not only mine but seven houses more were burnt down to the ground. My poor mother, who saw herself reduced by this accident to the greatest poverty, soon died of grief. As for my part, as I had a profession and a genius for it, I resolved to make the most of them. I left Shiraz, with an intention of joining some of the company of comedians that stroll from one town of Persia to another. I met with this old kalandar; we travelled some days together, his conversation and way of life pleased me greatly. I have now become a kalandar likewise, and we have undertaken a journey to the Indies, where I do not despair of being again able to shine as a comedian, in case I should chance to grow tired of this habit.

*   *   *   *

Faruk, my lord, continued Ibn Aridun, had listened with infinite pleasure to the young kalandar's story——I can well believe he did, said the king of Astrakhan, interrupting him, nothing can be more agreeable than the adventures of the two kalandars, and I make no doubt of their having been able to suspend that prince's grief for the loss of his kingdom; since I who have more reason to be afflicted than he, have not so much as thought of my misfortunes during the entertaining recital of them. But return, I beg of you, to Faruk's history; this unfortunate prince has so much interested me in his favour that I burn with impatience to know the rest of his adventures. —I shall go on with them with pleasure, my lord, replied the son of Abu Bukr, it is an easy matter for me to satisfy your curiosity.

CONTINUATION OF THE STORY OF FARUK

FARUK and the two kalandars had now traversed almost all Persia, without meeting with anything worth your Majesty's attention; when one day to avoid the insupportable heat of the sun they quitted the high road, and retired into a little wood to take their usual refreshment. They had not been there long, when hearing the cries of somebody that had fallen into bad hands, they immediately ran to the place whence the noise came; but they came too late to assist an unhappy traveller, whom four assassins had just killed with their daggers. As these wretches were well armed, far from flying at the sight of the kalandars, they stripped the unhappy victim of their fury, and one of them proposed that they should cut him into small pieces. Faruk shuddered at this piece of barbarity: Ah! gentlemen, said he, with great humility, surely you may be satisfied with having robbed this poor man of his life, without treating his dead body with a cruelty beyond example; for heaven's sake do not carry your fury to greater lengths. One of the murderers looked at Faruk with a stern countenance. Wretch, said he, why do you trouble your self about what in no way concerns you? Keep your remonstrances for others. As you regard your life, take yourself away, you and your companions. Stop but another moment, and I shall send you to bear him company, for whom you interest yourself so unseasonably. The prince of Gur did not suffer himself to be disheartened by this speech. But, sir, continued he, how great soever your fury may be against this dead body, if I were to offer you two thousand dinars for its ransom, would you not be better pleased to take them, than to treat it in so outrageous a manner?—No doubt, replied the robber.—Swear then that you will let me have the dead body, said Faruk, and you shall have the money this instant.—I swear then, said the wretch; may the scorpion of Kachan sting us all four in the hand, if we do not keep to our word! deliver us the two thousand dinars, and the body is your's, to dispose of it as you please. Upon this, my lord, Faruk, taking out of his bosom the only ring he had left, and which was worth a great deal more than he had promised them, gave it up without shewing the least concern, and the wretches left him in possession of the body of the poor man they had murdered.

The two kalandars were extremely surprised at Faruk's behaviour, and could not but admire his generosity or his folly; and indeed they considered it as folly more than anything else. What then, said they, can be your intention in doing what you have done? This ring was all that remained of your riches; it was a sure resource for you in any extremity, and you parted with it to redeem a dead body; can anything in the world equal your extravagance? For, in fine, what can you pretend to do with this body?— I intend, answered Faruk, to bury it in this spot; good works are never lost; and you have told me yourselves, that in that kind of life I have embraced, this ring was altogether useless to me; why then would you have me for the sake of a stone, which men are pleased to call precious, and which only serves for a superfluous ornament, lose the opportunity of performing so holy a duty as that of laying in the ground a Mohammedan who may one day or other perhaps intercede for me in heaven?— Your thought is very good, replied the kalandars, but do not take it amiss that we leave you alone to go through the pious ceremony; it is somewhat dangerous to bury a person who has been murdered in this place; and so good an action is capable of receiving a very bad interpretation; we shall, therefore, go and wait for you outside the wood,

and if you make any delay, we will meet you before nightfall at the gates of Ormuz, which is not above a league off.
The kalandars upon this came out of the wood, in which
Faruk went to work with a stake, labouring with all his
strength to make a grave for the dead body; but while he
was thus employed, the kadi of Ormuz happened to be going
by. As in this life people generally judge according to appearances, the magistrate seized upon Faruk, on the presumption that it was he who had killed the man he was
going to bury. It was to no purpose that he appealed to
heaven for his innocence; they tied him to a horse's tail,
and dragged him to Ormuz, where they threw him into
a dungeon. The two kalandars saw him go by in this
deplorable condition. We foretold what would happen to
him, said they to themselves, and he may thank his
obstinacy for his misfortune. However, they followed
him at a distance, though for fear of being made parties
in so delicate an affair, they thought proper not to appear
on his behalf.

The prince of Gur remained all night in the dungeon,
and next morning they brought him before the kadi; the
magistrate examined him, but nothing he could say to
justify himself met with any regard, so that he
was condemned to death, and conducted directly to
the market-place, to be hung according to his sentence.
This monarch behaved at the foot of the gallows with
surprising intrepidity. Heavens, cried he, you are just!
Must I then be punished for an action, which in the
sight of God, deserves to be rewarded? I now perceive,
O wise kalandars! that you were in the right in
striving to dissuade me from giving burial to this
dead body. Just as the prince was finishing this exclamation, he happened to throw his eyes upon the kadi's
hand, who thought proper to assist at the execution, and
seeing on his finger the ring which he had given the
murderers: Ah! said he, my lord, our great Prophet, who

no doubt interests himself in my favour, thinks it improper that an innocent person should suffer; you have actually got on your finger the ring which I gave to those who, after having killed the Mohammedan, wanted to exercise on his body an unheard-of piece of cruelty; it will now be an easy matter to find out the criminals; and the two kalandars, my fellow-travellers, who must now be in Ormuz, cannot but know the murderers again as well as myself. The kadi turned paler than death at this news, put off the execution, and ordered the prince of Gur back to his house.

No wonder the kadi should be greatly surprised, when Faruk assured him he had his ring, whereas he had bought it from his only son for two thousand three hundred dinars; and his son was looked upon as a person of a very loose way of life, and was suspected of keeping company with robbers, assassins, and other wretches. The first thing the judge did when he reached home, was to send for his son. A slave told him that he was at a party of pleasure, with ten or a dozen friends, at a garden a little way out of the town. The kadi followed him there instantly, and having seized the whole company, had them brought before Faruk, to see if he could discover the murderers amongst them. The prince narrowly examined every face, and fixing upon two, in spite of their disguise: It is to one of these men, said he to the kadi, at the same time pointing out his son, that I gave my ring, to hinder him from cutting the dead body into pieces. It is he, and one of these disorderly young fellows, that committed the murder, of which two kalandars and myself were witnesses. As to the two other murderers, I do not see them here; and if you doubt what I say, cause enquiry to be made after the two kalandars, my fellow-travellers, who must now be in Ormuz, and if they do not confirm my testimony, I am satisfied to lose my life by the most cruel torments.

It was no hard matter to find the kalandars, who were brought to the garden before the kadi. Here they examined the twelve prisoners, and having confirmed Faruk's testimony, they were surprised to see the kadi tear his gown and his turband, and throw himself flat upon the ground. Unhappy father! cried out the magistrate, must you then deliver up your only son to an infamous death! No, wretch, said he, I will save myself that dishonour; but you shall die notwithstanding, and I will be your executioner. Upon this, he seized upon the sabre of one of his attendants, and struck his son's head off at once with it; and having put the other eleven prisoners to the most cruel torments, and made them confess a thousand horrid crimes, he directed they should be cast from a high tower upon iron hooks, giving all Ormuz in this manner a most dreadful example of his justice.

This upright and honest magistrate shuddered at the thoughts of the sentence he had pronounced against Faruk. Heavens! said he, had it not been for this ring I should have robbed an innocent person of his life! How confined is our knowledge! How easy is it for those in my station to be led astray by prejudice! I need no more proof of it. I renounce my profession, and will spend the remainder of my life in seeking God's pardon for the faults I have committed as a judge, through ignorance, prejudice, or want of application. Upon this, turning to Faruk, who when he pointed out to the kadi the person to whom he had given the ring, knew nothing of the criminal being so dear to him: Pious kalandar, said he, throw off this habit, and be to me what the wretch was whom I have just now punished for his many crimes. I give you up all that I am worth, seeing you know how to make so good a use of riches. I beg you may accept them, and let me not go to the grave, into which I find myself ready to sink, with the disagreeable thoughts of your having refused me. Faruk, my lord, touched to the heart with the words of this unfortunate father, cast himself at his feet. My presence, said he, generous kadi, would only serve to fix your thoughts on the unhappy death of your son. Permit me, therefore, to remove far from your sight an object——On the contrary, replied the judge, it will wear out of my mind a remembrance, which that retirement to which I have devoted the rest of my life would otherwise render perpetual. Do not abandon me, I again beeseech you, if you have any compassion for an unfortunate father. In the meantime, the kadi embraced Faruk in the tenderest manner, who, unable to resist his tears, granted him his request.

The king of Gur was now adopted by the kadi of Ormuz, and was under the necessity of remaining at Ormuz. As for the two other kalandars, they continued their journey, in spite of the handsomest proposals which the prince made them. They continued fixed in their design of visiting the Indies and China, and all the favour Faruk could obtain of them was for each of them to accept a present of two thousand dinars of gold. The prince of Gur, my lord, lived very quietly and happily with the kadi, who had resigned his commission much against the will of the king of Ormuz. Faruk behaved towards this venerable magistrate with all the tenderness of a son, and the good old man had every day reason to bless the Almighty for having permitted him to make so worthy a choice; but he enjoyed but a short time the fruits of his prudent adoption. At the end of eight months he fell dangerously ill, and, in fine, resigned his just soul into the hands of the Angel of Death. Faruk was deeply afflicted at so great a loss; and finding that the effects left him were considerable, he made two shares of them. One share he took to himself, and laid out the other in building a Mosque and a caravanserai at the gates of Ormuz; near which he caused his benefactor to be buried, with a marble column at the foot of the grave, on which was engraved an epitaph of his own composition, worthy of the deceased.

The prince of Gur, having fulfilled all the pious duties of a good son, began to grow tired of Ormuz, for want of employment. The remembrance of what he had been was constantly animating him to the performance of some actions that might restore him to his primitive grandeur. To accomplish this, he came to the resolution of equipping a ship, with which he might acquire an illustrious name; and he soon put this design into execution. For this purpose he engaged the bravest men in Ormuz, and in a short time the fame of his conduct and valour was so well spread over the Arabian sea, and the Indian ocean, that his successes and victories made the subject of every conversation. It was at this time, my lord, that the princesses of Tiflis and of Borneo fell into his hands. You know the remainder of his history to the time when Gulguli-Chamami fell into the sea. I shall now give you the continuation of it, extracted from the annals of the Islands of Divanduru.

Faruk, when he awakened, was in the utmost surprise not to find the princess on board his ship, and when he learned the accident that had befallen her, he was so much afflicted at it, that he several times made an attempt on his own life; the attendants hindered him from committing so desperate an action, and by dint of reason, brought him at length to a soberer way of thinking. The prince was now beginning to enjoy some peace of mind, when he discovered at a distance two ships which had the wind of him. He did not hesitate a moment to wait for them, and having attacked them he in his despair achieved such prodigies of valour that he soon obliged them to strike. He then went on board these vessels, and having sent on board his own ship such of the prisoners as appeared of any consequence, he ordered the rest to be ironed, but only for his own safety and till he arrived at some port, where he intended to set them at liberty again.

Among the prisoners that Faruk ordered on board his own ship, were two well-looking young men, very well dressed, whose features the prince thought he had some knowledge of. He examined his memory for a long time, in order to recollect where he might have seen them, but all to no purpose. Upon this, he asked the prisoners if they had not met him some where or another; but one of them answered that he did not believe he had ever had that honour, and that they had been three years travelling through China and the Indies. Faruk, thinking himself mistaken, put up with this answer, and after having spent the rest of the day in quietness (all the quietness he could enjoy after the loss of the princess of Tiflis) he withdrew to his cabin, where, oppressed with fatigue, he fell into a sound sleep.

He had scarcely slept two hours, when he started up, awakened by a dream, to which he thought himself obliged to give some attention. The traveller, whom he had buried some years before at Ormuz, appeared to him: You were in the right, my lord, said the ghost to him, in representing to the two kalandars who wanted to hinder you from bestowing the last rites upon me, that a good action never goes unrewarded. The time is now come, that I may acknowledge your pious earnestness on that occasion. The two men that you could not yesterday recollect, are my murderers; I mean those who fled to avoid punishment. On their part they know you very well again, in spite of the alterations in your con-dition, and fearing your just vengeance, have already dispatched the sentinel that was placed at your door, and are now ready to come into your cabin to stab you.—The prince, who, as I have already told you, my lord, awoke at the close of this dream, thought he could not, in prudence, neglect so salutary an admonition;

he got up, and hearing a noise at the door of his cabin, which was dimly illuminated by a lamp, he took up his sabre, placed himself in a posture not to be surprised, and thus waited the event of so uncommon a dream. He had not been long in this situation, when his door opening very softly, two wretches came in, each with a dagger in his hand. He did not hesitate a moment to put it out of their power to hurt him, and having struck off the arm of one of them with his sabre, and stunned the other by a back blow of the pommel in his face, he called his attendants, ordered them to seize on the assassins, and after reproaching them with the murder they had committed near Ormuz, he caused them to be hung up at once to one of the masts.

Faruk, having given his ship's company an account of his dream, retired to his cabin. He there threw himself on his face, to thank the great Prophet for the salutary informatian he had received, and being again laid down to rest, he had scarcely fallen asleep, when the same ghost appeared again to him. It is not enough, said the phantom, that I have preserved you from the hands of those who had a design upon your life; it was the least I could do for you; but then I must let you know to whom you are indebted for so seasonable an admonition. My name was Almaz; I was the only heir of Zalabdin, king of the islands of Divanduru. About six years ago, I obtained leave of my father to travel, and I set out, with three attendants only, to visit Persia and Tartary. My three attendants died during the journey, and I was returning alone and incognito to Ormuz, to take ship to Divanduru, when I was cruelly murdered by the son of the kadi of Ormuz. My father, who has had no news of me since I left him, and who impatiently expects my return, has been this month past confined to his bed by a disorder, of which it is written on the table of life that he will not recover; and our great Prophet has obtained of

God in my favour, that the sword of the angel of death should be withheld by rust in the scabbard till you have reached the islands of Divanduru, where you are to marry the princess Garun, my sister. Proceed there then without fear ; I will give them notice of your coming, and that they may not commit any mistake on this occasion, I will seal you with the seal of the elect. The ghost upon this having pressed, pretty violently, a fiery seal on the prince of Gur's arm, he at that instant felt so great a pain from it, that he gave a roar which awakened all the people on board the ship. They immediately gathered about him, and he gave them an account of his second dream ; and as the impression made on his arm in which were distinctly to be seen the name of God and that of his great Prophet, left him no room to doubt of the reality of the vision, he without the least hesitation directed his course for the isles of Divanduru, where he arrived in about five weeks.

The favourable winds he had during his passage had brought him into port exactly at the time mentioned by the ghost. The king of these islands was now very far spent, and the princess, his daughter, who never stirred from him, was in the greatest affliction for his melancholy situation ; the approach of her father's death rendered her condition very deplorable in every respect. The king of Cananor, whose ancestors had formerly some pretensions to the islands of Divanduru, only waited the death of Zalabdin to invade his territories, and to take advantage of his son's absence. But Faruk, my lord, soon gave another face to Zalabdin's affairs.

Almaz, having appeared to the king his father the night before the arrival of the prince of Gur, gave him an account of his violent death, of Faruk's compassion, and of the orders he had received from Heaven to mark him with its seal, and to send him to Divanduru, there to marry the princess, his sister. He, moreover, directed his

father, in the name of the great Prophet, to prepare himself for a holy death. Zalabdin, surprised at this dream,
considered it however as the effect of a burning fever;
but how great was his surprise when Garun, who slept
at but a little distance from his bed, got up in a hurry,
and just throwing a gown over her shoulders, came running to his bed-side. Ah! said she, my lord, the tears
gushing from her eyes, my brother no doubt is no longer
among the living. He has just appeared to me covered
all over with blood, and has informed me that he had been
murdered by a son of the kadi of Ormuz; that a young
prince, disguised in the habit of a kalandar, had bestowed
the last rites upon him; that this very prince, whom we
should know by the name of God, which my brother had
imprinted on his arm, is just on the point of arriving here
to oppose the unjust undertaking of the king of Cananor;
and that it was written in heaven that I should marry our
deliverer.—Alas! my dear Garun, replied the afflicted
Zalabdin, your dream is but too true. Almaz, who has
but this instant appeared to myself, has told me the very
same things, with one more, which perhaps your tenderness conceals for fear of terrifying me. Azrail is now at
the side of my bed; he there waits for my soul, whose
union with my body is to last so short a time that I shall
scarcely enjoy the pleasure of seeing you united with the
prince of Gur.—Ah! my lord, it is true enough that I
intended to hide this circumstance from you, replied the
princess of Divanduru; must I then lose you, my lord?
—Yes, my dear, answered Zalabdin undauntedly; let us
prepare ourselves for this bitter separation by an edify-
ing submission, which the agreement between our dreams
requires of us; and read for me, I beseech you, those
verses of the Koran which serve to take off the terror
that naturally attends this unavoidable transition.

Garun, all in tears, took the Koran out of its case
of green cloth, and read to her father till it was day-light,

a great many chapters of this divine book. She was thus piously employed when a messenger entered with the account of a ship having just come into port, that brought some news from his son, Prince Almaz. Upon this, the good king's grief broke out with new vigour. He gave a great shout : Ah! my dear Garun, said he to the princess, our dreams then, you see, are now accomplished. Go, prepare yourself to appear before the prince of Gur, and give orders that he should be immediately introduced into my apartment. Garun obeyed ; she went to dress herself, while messengers were carrying to Faruk the orders of Zalabdin. The young prince being conducted into the chambers of the dying monarch, saw so much grief painted on his countenance, that he had not resolution enough to inform him of his son's death. Zalabdin discovered the perplexity Faruk was in. Sir, said he, with a weak voice, as I am not unacquainted with your name or your errand, do not be afraid of increasing my grief, by giving me an account of the death of my beloved son Almaz; he has himself taken care to give me notice of so afflicting a catastrophe. Faruk, my lord, hesitated answering the questions of Zalabdin, when the beautiful Garun made her appearance. At the first sight of her, the prince of Gur almost fainted away, and even fell on the bed of the sick monarch ; this accident threw the king and his daughter into a great amazement.

Nature, my lord, had taken pleasure in preparing the ways of love between Faruk and Garun. This princess so perfectly resembled Gulguli-Chamami, that the prince of Gur could not look at her without an extraordinary emotion. He got the better of his weakness by degrees, and finding by the difference of their heights that he was mistaken, he however judged it would be improper to let Garun know the cause of his sudden fit. Turning to Zalabdin: Ah! my lord, said he, pardon this involuntary breach of respect; the fine eyes of the charming Garun sent such irresistible arrows to my heart that I had not strength enough to bear up against them; but in endeavouring to excuse one fault I see that I commit another. It ill becomes me to speak of love in places full of grief and horror, and though I may think myself authorized to behave in this manner by the words of the prince your son, and by the divine characters he imprinted on my arm, I am thoroughly sensible of my indiscretion. You cannot, sir, give any offence, replied the afflicted Zalabdin, since heaven has chosen you for the husband of the beautiful Garun; it would look very ill of me to find fault with a passion that is to constitute all the happiness of her life; on the contrary I am extremely glad that her charms have made so quick and so lively an impression on the senses of so accomplished a prince. But be so kind, sir, as to acquaint me with the fate of my son, since you are the only person who can give me any certain account of him. Faruk could no longer defer satisfying Zalabdin's reasonable curiosity; he related to him all the circumstances of Almaz's death, but as briefly as possible; likewise the punishment of the murderers, the unhappy prince's appearance to him, and his positive orders to come to Divanduru, where he assured him he should have the good fortune of winning the heart of the accomplished Garun.

The prince of Gur, my lord, had scarcely finished his relation when word was brought to the king in a great hurry that the king of Cananor in person had just landed in the island and was laying waste every place with fire and sword. Ah! my lord, said Faruk, it is my business to revenge you of the oppression of this unjust monarch: I will perish with all my people, or bring you back his head in a very short time. The prince after this, making a low reverence to his Majesty, turned to the princess. And you, charming Garun, said he, may

I flatter myself with the hopes of being dear enough to you to deserve your vows to Heaven for a prince who will spill the last drop of his blood rather than suffer the king of Cananor to succeed in his wicked and cowardly pretensions? These words deprived Garun of the power of answering him; she was at a loss how to return the compliment; but as her love seemed to be authorized by the great Prophet, and by her father: Go, my lord she replied, where honour calls you, our cause is too just for ·Heaven to give the day to the king who would oppress us; but do not yield to your courage enough to give me fresh affliction. The princess could not finish these words without a blush; and Faruk, transported at seeing he had an interest in the princess's heart, ran to put himself in a condition to execute what he had promised. He immediately assembled his followers, and being reinforced by Zalabdin's troops, went in search of the enemy with so much resolution, that the marks of victory were already visible in his countenance.

The king of Cananor had at first spread so universal a terror, that all the inhabitants fled before him; but Faruk's presence inspired them with new courage, and he attacked the invader with so much resolution and vigour, that he obliged him to retreat in his turn. The king of Cananor, enraged at seeing himself defeated by a single man, (for it was Faruk alone, in a manner, that brought victory to the party he sided with) made his way through a thousand swords to attack personally the young hero; who no less desirous of measuring his courage with the king's, flew more than half way to meet him, bearing down everything that opposed his progress; so that a terrible battle soon ensued between the two chiefs, in which, however, Faruk at length proved victorious. The king of Cananor lost his life in it, and his death having disheartened his troops, they immediately endeavoured to get back to their ships; but the

prince of Gur pursued them so closely that they were all
cut to pieces, and their ships given up to be plundered
by the victorious soldiers. After so complete a victory
the prince returned to the palace amidst the acclamations
of all the people. The king and the matchless Garun
especially received him with unspeakable joy. Sympathy
which generally penetrates a great way in a very short
time had so perfectly gained him the heart of this
princess that she could scarcely keep within bounds
the transports she felt at the thoughts of being matched
with so accomplished a prince.

Faruk, my lord, was perfectly well made; his
features full of life, his air noble, his soul answerable to
his make, very skilful, and courageous beyond imagination. So many shining qualities were more than sufficient
to inflame a young princess, whose happy resemblance
to Gulguli-Chamami rendered her extremely precious in
the eyes of the young hero. In a word Zalabdin thought
it improper to keep these happy lovers to sigh for an
union any longer. He joined them together that very
day; and after declaring Faruk his successor, went in a
few days more to give an account of his actions before
the throne of Almighty Allah.

You have now heard, my lord, the adventures of
Faruk. This prince, cherished by the beautiful Garun,
after having sincerely lamented the death of Zalabdin,
spent his days with his illustrious consort in a manner
worthy of envy, and left children whose descendants
reign to this day in the islands of Divanduru.

RETURN OF THE PHYSICIAN
ABU BAKR

JUST as Ibn Aridun was finishing the history of Faruk, Astrakhan rang with a thousand acclamations of joy, which reached the palace of Shams al-Din. The monarch, surprised at so uncommon a noise, immediately ordered the wazir Mutamhid to enquire what was the cause of it. Mutamhid accordingly went out of the palace to get intelligence, but immediately came back. Ah! my lord, said he in a transport of joy, I have just had a sight of Abu Bakr, conducting towards the palace a lady covered with a veil. No doubt your misfortunes will soon have an end, and it is the presence of those two persons which gives your subjects a pleasure they cannot contain. Mutamhid had not finished this agreeable account, when the father of Ibn Aridun entered the hall where Shams al-Din was seated, followed by a crowd of people who had forced their way after him. The old man threw himself prostrate at the king's feet, and said: Here is, my lord, your faithful slave returned sooner than I promised your Majesty, and I bring back with me a treasure, which I could not find anywhere but at Sarandib. It is the woman who is to restore you your sight.—Come near me that I may embrace you, my dear Abu Bakr, answered the king of Astrakhan; such subjects as you and your son deserve all the love and confidence of their prince. Let this so rare a woman make a trial of her skill; but I assure you beforehand, that though she should not succeed, I shall not think my obligation to you the less.

On the king's giving this order, the veiled lady drew near his Majesty's throne, all the spectators waiting impatiently for the event; but few of them, the physicians especially, thought any good of this remedy, when the woman, taking out a golden bottle which she opened, washed the king's eyes with the water she had gathered on the wonderful tree of Sarandib. This divine liquor had scarcely touched the king's eyes, than he perceived in them a salutary coolness, which he felt even at his heart; two kinds of films, which obstructed the passage of the rays of light, fell from his eyes; and the prince recovering his sight as perfectly as he had ever enjoyed it, before Ibn-Bukr had so barbarously deprived him of it, cried out in a transport of joy: Heavens! is it possible that the darkness, in which I have lived so long a time, should be so soon dispersed? Yes, I again know you, my dear Mutamhid, and you my other faithful subjects, whose features have not beee worn out of my memory by so long a blindness. At last then I can enjoy the light.

The surprise of all the spectators was so extraordinary, and the joy was so great, that nothing was to be heard in the hall but clapping of hands. But the king, having ordered silence, turned himself to the lady, who had remained standing with modest silence. Whoever you are, said he, illustrious heroine of your sex, you may expect everything for a service too great to have a price set upon it. The loss of my dear Zabd al-Katon does not leave me at liberty to divide my throne with you. No woman, let her be ever so handsome, shall hereafter have dominion over my heart; but you may depend on a gratitude without bounds, and which will be every day as new and as lively as the first. Do not then, madam, hide any longer from me and from my subjects, a person to whom I am so much obliged; throw off this veil, I beseech you, and let us see those eyes whose vivacity dazzles me, though their fires are blunted by the gauze that covers them. The lady in the veil thought herself obliged to comply with this request and accordingly unveiled herself. But what became of Shams al-Din at this sight, which he was not able to bear! He fell back on his

throne speechless, and it was some time before he came
to himself enough to express his surprise. Ah! Zabd
al-Katon, my dear Zabd al-Katon, cried he, is it yourself,
then, that I have now the pleasure of beholding ? or may
not my heart, upon which your image is so deeply engraved, mistake for you everything that my eyes now
discover?—No, my lord, answered the lady with tears of
joy, I am that Zabd al-Katon whom you had given up
for dead. I am still alive, and happy to be instrumental
in putting an end to your misfortunes.—Ah! no doubt,
replied the king, at the same time tenderly embracing
his beloved spouse, all my misfortunes are at an end
indeed, since I behold you. I appeal to Heaven, if I
have been a single day since our cruel separation without shedding a flood of tears for your loss; but the source
from whence they sprung is now dried up.

This discourse, and the mutual and tender caresses
of this illustrious pair, sensibly affected all the spectators.
So strange and miraculous an adventure filled them all
with astonishment, even Abu Bakr himself, who had
conducted the lady from Sarandib to Astrakhan without
knowing that she was Zabd al-Katon. Soon after this
happy discovery joy and pleasure took the place of silence
and affliction. The king loaded with favours Abu Bakr
and his son, whom he ever afterwards retained about his
person. He distributed immense sums among the con-
vents of darwayshes and the Mosques, to thank the
Sovereign Prophet for his protection : but as he was
impatient to know by what supernatural power his consort had been restored to life, and by what accident Abu
Bakr had met with her, he had no sooner returned to
his palace with his wazirs and his physician, than he requested Zabd al-Katon to satisfy his curiosity in their
presence. The queen loved the tender Shams al-Din
too well to defer his satisfaction a single moment, and
began as follows :

STORY OF ZABD AL-KATON

It would be to no purpose, my lord, to put you in mind of the last words I said to you at our separation. They were dictated to me by our great Prophet ; and as Azrail was at that time so near my pillow, I did not imagine we should ever meet again. However, life did not totally forsake me, a lethargic vapour deprived me of my senses, enough, no doubt, to make everyone believe that I was really dead. Even you yourself were deceived on the occasion, and ordered, as I have since been told by Abu Bakr, who, without knowing who I was, related all your misfortunes to the king of Sarandib in my presence ; you ordered, I say, that I should be shut up in a coffin adorned with precious stones, but forbade at the same time that my face should be covered ; a precaution which proved the happy means of saving my life. The jewels and gold with which my coffin was covered made the Arabian robbers decide to remove me to a place of safety ; and accordingly they did not divide their plunder till they had got about ten leagues from the place where they attacked you. After they had broken my coffin to pieces they began to strip me, in order to throw me into a pretty deep river that ran hard by ; when one of them, in endeavouring to rip the sleeve of my gown, to which an emerald was fastened, was unskilful enough to prick me in the arm, and this accident, my lord, secured me from a real death. My blood flowed so freely that the robber was surprised at it ; and this circumstance, with some remains of heat and a feeble palpitation, made him conclude that I was not dead but in a deep lethargy. However, he thought proper not to acquaint the other robbers with what he had observed,

but throwing me on his shoulders he carried me towards
the river, in order to make them believe that he really
intended to throw me into it. In the meantime the
robbers moved to a greater distance, without suspecting
that he understood something of surgery. He let my
blood run as much as he thought my condition required,
bound up my arm with the muslin of his turband, and
throwing water on my face brought me back to myself
by degrees.

At length, my lord, I opened my eyes, and when I
grew strong enough to look attentively at the objects
about me I was not a little surprised to find myself
alone in the company of a man I had never seen before.
As he soon perceived my grief and surprise by my eyes
and actions: Take courage, madam, said he, your life
is in safety in my hands, and your honour runs no risk
since it is out of my power to attack it, though I were
were ever so ill-disposed. These words quieted me a
little, and having enquired of him in what manner I had
fallen into his hands, I was told, my lord, that your little
caravan had been attacked by the wild Arabs at some
days' distance from Cairo; that you had made the
boldest resistance; but that at last, overpowered by
numbers, you had fallen, with all your attendants, surrounded by more than thirty of your enemies, whom you
had killed with your own hands. You may guess, my
dear prince, the greatness of my despair at hearing this
cruel news. I no longer reckoned you among the living,
and being desirous of paying your remains the same
honours you had bestowed on me, I requested the Arab
to conduct me to the spot where the engagement had
happened. He was so good as to comply, but I was so
weak that I could not reach the place in fewer than four
days. We examined together all the dead bodies; but
as they were no longer distinguishable on account of the
wounds which they had received on the face, and the

blood that covered them, and by lying so long exposed
to the air, it was impossible for me to tell exactly which
was you. However, finding one that appeared to me
of your size, I concluded it was you, and washed its
face with my tears. I even thought I could discern some
of your august features, which so increased my grief that
I fainted on the body, which I held clasped in my arms.
The Arab separated me; I remained above an hour in
this condition, but at last I came to myself. With some
broken sabres that we found on the spot we then dug a
hole large enough to contain this body, which we accordingly put into it; and having covered it with earth,
we left the place, full of horror and affliction.

I was so amazed, notwithstanding my affliction, at
the civilities and politeness of the Arab, that I could
scarcely refrain a moment from expressing my gratitude.
My lord, said I, how is it possible that having embraced
the life of a robber, you should preserve so noble a way
of thinking and of acting? Certainly, you were not born to
so base and cruel a condition; your living amongst them
must be owing to some very pressing necessity.—Ah!
madam, replied the Arab, though I am but of a middling
condition, I never imagined I should be obliged to take
up with the company of such wicked wretches. It was
the desire of being revenged for the greatest injury
which can be done a man that alone induced me to unite
with the Arabian robbers; but the death of my enemy
has not restored me what his unjust fury had deprived
me of. These last words drew from him a flood of tears,
which having awakened my compassion and strengthened
my curiosity, I requested him to give me some account
of his misfortunes. His relation was to the following
purpose:

ADVENTURES OF THE ARAB
ABAN-AZAR

I am the son, madam, of a pretty considerable jeweller of Aden. My father had an intimate friend in the same business, whose name was Saman; and Saman had a daughter four years younger than I was, whose rare beauty eclipsed that of every other girl in Aden. My father and his friend, to strengthen their friendship, had agreed that their children when grown up should become man and wife; so that I had scarcely attained the use of reason when Abdarmon was taught to consider me as her spouse, and my father gave me to understand that I should only please him in proportion to the progress I made in the esteem and affection of my little mistress. It seldom happens that the hearts of children given away at so tender an age follow exactly the wills of their parents; one would even imagine that this kind of tyranny inspires them with quite contrary sentiments. However, madam, it was quite the reverse in our case; the more we grew up the more we answered the intentions of our fathers; I used to spend whole days with my little mistress, without desiring any other enjoyment; and on her side, she did not appear to have any satisfaction greater than that of seeing me in her company; so that if I stayed away but a single moment beyond the time at which I generally used to wait on her in her apartment, she reproached me in the tenderest manner, and thereby added new strength to my passion. You do not love me so much as you ought, my dear Aban-azar, said she to me one day, and I find that I am not handsome enough to make you entirely mine; you often appear distracted in my company, at the same time that you take up all my attention.

What is there, then, wanting to complete your happiness? Alas! did I know what it was, I would with joy sacrifice my life to the satisfaction of my lover.—You are very unjust, answered I, and at the same time, very ingenious in making yourself uneasy. Why load me with reproaches that I so little deserve? I languish in every place in which I do not find you. I love nothing but you; on your love alone depends all my happiness; and if anything can give me pain, it is only the thoughts of being obliged to wait four years before becoming the spouse of my dear Abdarmon.

My young mistress, continued Aban-azar, was scarcely ten years old, and I scarcely fourteen, when we entertained each other in this tender manner. Judge then, madam, how passionate our conversation must have been, the nearer we drew to the term of our happiness. In fine, madam, I do not think it was possible for two young persons to love each other with greater delicacy; and we were now on the point of seeing so pure and so faithful love crowned by the happy union with which our parents had flattered our hopes, when suddenly we were made the most unfortunate lovers that ever existed. Our fathers fell out through a jealousy, created by their being of the same profession. A mortal enemy of mine made it his business to foment the quarrel by a thousand false reports, and the wretch succeeded so well that their enmity grew to an inveterate hatred. The first thing they did was to break the engagement which Abdarmon and I had entered into by their orders. We were forbidden to see each other, or to entertain the least hopes of ever being united. What a sensible stroke was this! I thought I should have died of grief; and I must do Abdarmon the justice of saying that her grief was so great that it brought upon her a violent fit of sickness, which at length reduced her to the last extremity. The news of the danger she was in threw me into perfect despair. I ran to Saman's house, fell prostrate at his feet, and made use of the most submissive expressions to engage his pity : but I found him inflexible to my entreaties. I then made use of the danger my dear Abdarmon was in to endeavour to soften him, but all to no purpose. Though I love my daughter, said he, as much as any father can love a child, I should be better pleased to see her in the grave than in the arms of the son of my most cruel enemy. You must therefore think no longer of prevailing over me, but withdraw yourself quickly, lest I forget the kindness I still have for you. I had a mind to reply, but his cruelty afflicted me so much that I fainted away at his feet. My grief made no impression on him ; so far from it, that he ordered two slaves to take me in the condition I was in and throw me out of doors. My father, on his way home from some business that he had been transacting, unfortunately for me happened to pass at that very moment through the street where Saman lived, and having heard of this cruel behaviour he was exasperated at it to the last degree ; he ordered me to be carried home, where in some time I came round to myself.

The affront I had received was so public that my father ordered me, on pain of his indignation, never to commit the same fault again. But I had little inclination to obey him. The beautiful Abdarmon had made too deep an impression on my heart to be so readily forgotten ; on the contrary, I carefully sought every opportunity of assuring her personally of an eternal tenderness, though all to no purpose ; she was too narrowly watched, and it was impossible for me to approach her. Upon this I fell sick with grief, and had scarcely recovered when to complete my misery I heard she had just been married to Ilikhan, the son of our enemy. What an impression the fatal news made on me ! I uttered against Saman everything that rage and despair could inspire. Ah ! I cried, is it possible then, charming Abdarmon, that you should

become the prey of the vilest and most brutal of all
mankind ?   And indeed, madam, Ilikhan had so mean a
look, so savage a countenance, and so much rusticity in
his behaviour, that he was universally hated.   But his
father had prevailed on Saman, by the most artful flattery,
especially by representing to him that he could not revenge himself on my father better than by giving Abdarmon
to his son ; so that Saman did not hesitate a moment to
sacrifice his daughter to his vengeance ; and thus the
beautiful Abdarmon fell a sacrifice to the animosity of
our families.

It was not without the greatest reluctance imaginable
that Abdarmon delivered herself up into the hands of
Ilikhan, nor till she had tried every method she could
think of to avoid it ; but her father was inexorable.   It
was not, however, possible to extort from her a formal
consent to an union, to which she would have preferred
death itself had she been left to her choice; but
Saman forgot on this occasion his quality of father, to
become her executioner.   He put her into Ilikhan's
hands, who brought her home without troubling his
head about the aversion she expressed against him ;
and thinking that Saman's consent was sufficient to
entitle him to exact from Abdarmon what no wife
ought to refuse a husband, he met with such opposition
from this virtuous girl that neither prayers nor threats
made any impression upon her.   His impatient temper
made him hasten away to Saman with a complaint
of his daughter's behaviour, and Saman reproached
her most severely on the occasion ; but the generous
Abdarmon, without failing in the respect she owed
her father, courageously protested that she never would
be Ilikhan's wife.   No, my lord, said she, it is in vain
that you try every method of making me unfaithful;
my heart has contracted a long and pleasing habit of
loving Aban-azar ; in this I have only obeyed your orders,

and the most cruel death cannot make me alter my sentiments. Saman was amazed at such a resolution, but flattered himself that time might get the better of it. He therefore advised Ilikhan to treat Abdarmon with great mildness, giving him hopes that he might in that manner overcome the courage of the young heroine. It was with great difficulty that Ilikhan could moderate himself so far as to follow his father-in-law's advice. He determined, however, to wait for some days to see if a respectful behaviour would not make some favourable impression on Abdarmon, resolved to make use of his authority if he did not succeed by fair means.

It was with unspeakable joy that I heard of Abdarmon's noble resistance and of the resolution which Ilikhan had formed; I thence conceived some favourable expectations, and making use of every stratagem to defeat the designs of my base rival, I found means of gaining over one of his slaves, whom I prevailed upon to introduce me by night into his mistress's apartments. For this purpose I had put on a woman's dress, to give the less cause of suspicion to those who might see me go into the house; and in this condition I was introduced into Abdarmon's apartment. I found her negligently stretched on her bed, with her arm under her head, in the posture of a person that laboured under some great uneasiness of mind. I threw myself at her feet, and kissed one of her beautiful hands with so much transport that she could not fail to know that no one but a lover, sensible of his mistress's love, could take so great a liberty. If the sight of me gave her exceeding joy, my being in a house of which Ilikhan was master gave her no less uneasiness. Ah! my lord, said she, embracing me in the tenderest manner, fly, I conjure you, from a place where I have much reason to fear your life is in danger. Put yourself, if you can, in a condition that may enable you to snatch me out of the hands of my tyrant, and be persuaded that I am ready to suffer the most cruel torments, nay, death itself, rather than break the vows I have so often made of being yours only.—If it is so, madam, answered I, come away with me this very instant, and I will deliver you out of the hands of a man whose behaviour ought to be held in aversion by all the world. The slave, whom I had at first bought over, opposed himself to my resolution, but a diamond staggered him. I promised to take him away with us, and to requite his services so well that I at last made him consent to everything. I then embraced my Abdarmon with an extraordinary transport ; and we were on the point of quitting her apartment and of making our retreat, when Ilikhan appeared with a sabre in his hand, and followed by eight slaves armed in the same manner. This unexpected sight stunned me to such a degree that I gave the wretches time to secure me.

Abdarmon knew by the rage that appeared in the eyes of our enemy that we had no mercy to expect. She did not condescend to ask for any, but looking at him with indignation : I never concealed from you, tyrant, said she, the violent passion I have always had for Aban-azar. He is lovely ; he pleased me ; I have appeared in his eyes preferable to all the giris of Aden. He has loved me with all possible delicacy ; and I belonged to him before an unjust animosity, which has divided our families, made my father take the resolution of giving me into your possession. This, savage, is all the crime you have to punish ; but it is too glorious a fault to be sorry for having committed it. She then reached me her hand, saying : I see, my dear lover, that we must die. The un-worthy Ilikhan is not generous enough to restore us to ourselves. Let us therefore courageously prepare to pass over to a more easy and delightful life, where our enjoy-ments shall not be interrupted by the hatred of our parents. We shall have no jealousy or tyranny to fear there ; and as we shall bring there hearts inflamed with love, we may promise ourselves a reception amongst those happy lovers whose sole occupation will be to give themselves up entirely to the pleasure of loving and of being beloved. This discourse, which had so much sweetness in it for me, and so much bitterness for my rival, served only to increase his anger. Yes, false woman, said he to Abdarmon, who had thrown herself into my arms; yes, you shall die, and you shall die by my own hands. I should not fully satisfy my vengeance were I to trust anyone else with the execution of it. Upon this he plunged his sabre into the breast of my dear mistress, who had just time to turn her eyes towards me and to give me the last farewell.

Ah! madam, continued the Arab, drowned in a flood of tears, which the remembrance of so moving a scene had drawn from him, you cannot conceive the condition I was in at the sight of so bloody an action. I had till now, in a manner, continued motionless with surprise, but the death of Abdarmon soon brought me to myself again. I gave a shout that terrified those who held me, and my fury was so great that I forced myself from them and fell upon the barbarous Ilikhan. I soon got him under my feet, and snatching a dagger from his belt, I made such use of it that in spite of all his slaves could do I gave him a great many wounds with it; but I was so beside myself that they were all very slight ones. I was at length beaten to the ground in my turn, and the fury of my rival being wound up to the greatest pitch by seeing his blood: Traitor, said he, do not imagine that my vengeance has nothing worse than death in store for you. No, no, you must not think of going to meet your Abdarmon. I intend to punish you in a manner more terrible than any punishment in itself can be. Having upon this ordered his slaves to bind me hand and feet ——Ah! madam, continued Aban-azar, with an unusual flood of tears, shame and despair will not let me speak;

what shall I say to you? The barbarous Ilikhan made me cease to be a man, without depriving me of life, and afterwards ordered me to be carried, weltering in my blood and in a state of insensibility, to my father's house, where through compassion, or to give him sooner the mortification of seeing me in so cruel a condition, the slaves knocked with all their strength.

My father at this noise immediately got out of bed, lighted his lamp, and came down into the street. What a sad spectacle had he then before him! His cries raised all our neighbours. I was immediately carried to my bed, and an able surgeon sent for, who with some specific herbs soon staunched my blood, and having then applied an excellent balm, I began to open my eyes, and gave some signs of life. But I had no sooner entirely recovered the use of my senses, than on considering the sad condition I was in, and the loss of Abdarmon, I resolved to follow her. I therefore tore the dressing from my wound, and gave such signs of despair that the assistants were obliged to tie me, and to cure me in spite of myself. My father was perfectly mad when he heard that it was Ilikhan who had treated me so barbarously. He would have gone directly to his house to revenge the indignity done me by his death, but I hindered him. Leave to myself, my lord, said I, that care; and if you have any regard still left for me, do not make my shame public in Aden. I shall soon find out the means of punishing my enemy for his cruelty. My father yielded to my request. In fine, madam, in about four years' time, I found myself in a condition to execute what I had proposed. But I must acquaint you with what happened at Ilikhan's house, after the barbarous usage I had received from him, and after the punishment of the slave who had given me admittance to Abdarmon.

The wretch immediately sent for Saman, though the night was pretty far advanced. As the messenger assured him it was on business of importance, he made no stay but came immediately with him.   My lord, said Ilikhan to him, if you were in my place, and after the strictest charges given to your daughter to have no correspondence with Aban-azar, you should find them together conspiring your ruin, and in such a manner as to leave no room to doubt of their having already destroyed your honour, what measures would you take on finding your love so cruelly despised ?—The quickest and most violent, answered Saman; in my just anger I should bury my dagger in their hearts.—I am very glad, replied Ilikhan, that we think alike; come and see if I know how to revenge an insult.   Upon this he conducted him to Abdarmon's apartment, and after shewing her to him weltering in her blood, he acquainted him in a few words in what manner he had punished my love for her.   Saman could not but shudder at the sight of his murdered daughter: for what he had said had proceeded rather from the hatred that prevailed between our families, than from his real opinion.   However as he had himself con-demned us, he could not recall his sentence. so that this tragical event served only to confirm him in his aversion; and with a view of doing us all the mischief in his power, when any opportunity should offer, he united himself more firmly than ever with Ilikhan and his father, in order to accomplish his wicked designs.

As the cowardly Saman made no noise about Abdar-mon's death, I began to imagine that he had formed some evil designs.   I therefore left Aden, and meeting with a company of wild Arabs that infested the neighbourhood, I begged of them to admit me among them.   I was well acquainted by means of a faithful slave with all the proceedings of my enemies, and being one day informed that they were all three out of town, in order to spend some days at a country house of Saman's, as I knew the place perfectly well, and in what manner it

could be surprised, I proposed to the chief of the
Badawin to make him master in one night of more than
one hundred thousand dinars, provided he gave me a
sufficient detachment, and also leave to be fully revenged
on three of the cruellest enemies I had in the world. The
Arab received my proposal with joy. I picked out twenty
resolute fellows; I informed them of my intentions, and
conducted them all that night to Saman's country house,
and even led them to the hall, where he was at table with
Ilikhan and his father; after having secured some slaves,
whose cries might have made our project miscarry. I
was so well disguised that it was impossible to know me.
We immediately secured my enemies, and with our
daggers to their throats, threatened instantly to take
away their lives if they did not give, each of them, a
note by which we might receive the cases in which they
kept their diamonds. This they consented to, thinking
thereby to save their lives; but they had no sooner
complied than I immediately laid hold of them, and
ordered their hands and feet to be tied, their mouths
gagged, and they and their slaves to be driven by blows
into a little wood, which the company I belonged to had
that night chosen for a retreat. I then delivered their notes
to our chief, who thought proper to be himself the bearer
of them, and having disguised himself for that purpose,
with three other Arabs, he went at day-break to Aden,
where the clerks of Saman, Ilikhan and his father, (for
the two last dealt likewise in jewels) seeing their masters'
orders so precise, made no difficulty in giving up their
diamonds. I afterwards related all my adventures to
our chief, the cruelty of Saman, and the barbarous usage
of Ilikhan. Take vengeance, said he, on the traitors; I
give them up to your discretion, but it must not be to
pardon them; if you did so, I should myself be their
executioner and your's. Upon this I set the slaves at
liberty, so that they should not know me again, and having

thrown off the clothes that hindered my enemies from knowing me, I soon appeared to them for what I was. They shuddered at the sight of me, and the tears with which they implored forgiveness, began to move me to compassion, when calling to mind their barbarity I reproached them with it in the most furious terms. I immediately dispatched Saman and the father of Ilikhan with my dagger. As for Ilikhan himself, there was no torment I could think of, that I did not inflict on my base and cruel rival before I put him to death; I myself cannot think, without horror, upon what I made him suffer. But will not a man do, when injured in so cruel a manner? After having thus completed my vengeance, I wished immediately to leave the Badawin; but it is dangerous to associate one's self with such kind of people, as one cannot withdraw from them when one pleases. The affair of the diamonds had acquired great reputation for me among them; it was conducted so prudently that our chief confided entirely in me. He was therefore so far from letting me go, that he would undertake nothing for the future without taking my advice; and thus I have been obliged to remain with him these two months past till yesterday your spouse killed him with his own hands. As we bought this victory very dearly, by the loss of eight hundred Arabs, and as our strength was thereby greatly weakened, it was not thought proper, for fear of a surprise, to divide the plunder on the field of battle; we therefore removed it all, and as your coffin was adorned with jewels, I had the charge of it. We did not begin to divide it till we reached the place at which, on the pretence of throwing you into a little river which is pretty deep in some places, I parted company with the Badawin. The confusion and disorder that then reigned amongst them did not permit them to take notice of my absence, which I am now resolved to take advantage of, and by endeavouring to do all the good I can, to obtain pardon for my crimes. And indeed, madam, I shall never have done reproaching myself with my unheard-of cruelty towards my enemies.

You have now, madam, had a short but sad relation of all my misfortunes. Judge therefore if you need scruple to repose an entire confidence in me, when I offer to conduct you wherever you may think proper to go.

CONTINUATION OF THE STORY OF ZABD-AL-KATON

I LISTENED, continued the beautiful queen of Astrakhan, with great attention to Aban-azar's relation, and as I thought I could not fall into safer hands, I agreed to his proposal, and we both set out by bye-roads for Aden. He was under some apprehension of being suspected of having had a hand in the murder of his enemies, for which reason we did not enter the town till after nightfall, and went directly to his father's house, to whom he gave an account of the horrible vengeance he had taken of them, and in what manner he had met me. The old man was ready to die with joy at the return of his son, of whom he had heard nothing for a long time, and he received me likewise with great kindness ; and as it was to his interest to assign some good cause for his son's absence, he gave out that he had been at Saaquam, where he had married me. Few persons were thoroughly acquainted with Aban-azar's disgrace, except the surgeon who took care of him during his illness ; and he was now dead, and Ilikhan had never made a boast of his vengeance. As I ran no risk in countenancing so well invented a story, I passed at Aden for this young man's wife, and remained there as such for about three years.

19—2

I desired he should not inform his father who I really was but give the old man to understand that I was the widow of a Tartar, who had been killed by the Badawin on his return from Meccah. He complied with my request, but his doing so had like to have been very prejudicial to me.

Aban-azar's father, though advanced in years, was still a well-looking man. I behaved towards him with the greatest complaisance and respect, which he probably imagined he could not better acknowledge than by making love to me. I believed he struggled with his passion for a long time before he made any declaration of it ; but at length he confirmed himself so well in his resolution, that he thought proper to open his heart to me. Though of an imperious temper, he made use of some precautions in acquainting me with his intentions, which he informed me of in a pretty odd manner. You pass in Aden, said he, for my son's wife ; but at the same time that people extol his choice of your person, they pity him, madam, on account of your barrenness. These discourses give me great uneasiness, and I am afraid that a discovery of our imposition would furnish sufficient proofs of his having murdered Ilikhan, and our other two enemies ; the memory of our quarrel begins to revive, and people speak of the cruel vengeance taken by my son : I have even heard some reports sufficient to make some ill-natured people believe that my son is guilty. I cannot be easy in so critical a conjuncture, and there is no one but yourself, madam, who can put an end to such disagreeable and dangerous reports.—I, sir ! said I, in the greatest surprise ; I am too sensible of everything that concerns you, to refuse you anything. Only speak, my lord : let me know how I can make you easy, and you shall immediately see me do everything in my power, and with the greatest joy, to give you satisfaction.—Well, then, madam, replied the amorous old man, you can only do it in this manner.   As my son is not capable of stopping the tongues of ill-natured people, I thought it my duty to make up his insufficiency, as I do not as yet think myself too old to put an end to a barrenness that is the common subject of discourse in Aden; consent to become a mother, madam, and let it be by my means. By so doing, you will disconcert my enemies, who will take my own children for my grandchildren, and by ceasing to reason on a subject which causes me the greatest uneasiness, the life of my son will be secured.

I was surprised to the last degree, continued Zabd al-Katon, at the old man's proposal.   I was often on the point of letting him know who I was; but as I apprehended he would look upon my declaration as a mere pretence for refusing his request, I thought proper to turn his love into a joke.   This gave him offence, and we at last quarrelled.   Some time after, he came and asked pardon for his rudeness, but, notwithstanding, renewed his arguments so often and so eagerly, as to give me the greatest reason to be in pain for the consequences of his extravagant passion.   I therefore thought proper to inform the son of it.   He asked me a thousand pardons, and taking a resolution worthy of an honest man, made me a proposal to embark on board a ship that was to sail next day for Ormuz, and I complied with the greatest pleasure.   Upon this he supplied himself with jewels; we both went on board, and were at a good distance from Aden before the ridiculous lover had any suspicion of our flight.

You must now, my lord, represent me to yourself at sea with Aban-azar, with the intention of setting out for Astrakhan as soon as we should arrive at Ormuz.   The winds proved very favourable, and we were in hourly expectation of reaching our port, when a terrible storm surprised us, which after beating our vessel for sixteen days successively, at last dashed it to pieces against a rock that seemed to lie at no great distance from the mainland. Few of us perished by this shipwreck, as we floated ashore on the remains of the vessel. But judge what was our surprise, when our pilot informed us that we were on a desert island, to which the king of Sarandib generally banished such of his subjects as deserved death; that there came no ship to it but once a year, and that sometimes even, for want of criminals, there did not come any ship for many years. This was very disagreeable news. We surveyed the island however, but found only a few slight houses in ruins, and no inhabitants. For a whole month together we subsisted, by dint of economy, on some provisions which the waves brought us from the wreck, and we were afterwards obliged to have recourse to some fruits of a very disagreeable taste. In fine, my lord, the greatest part of the ship's company were dead, through want and hardship, when we perceived, at some distance, a ship, that seemed to be bound for the island; nor were we deceived in our conjectures. It proved to be a ship with criminals from Sarandib, by whom we learned that no ship had been there for three years before; and had this ship arrived but a few days later, we should all have infallibly perished. The criminals, who amounted to five only, were put ashore with some few eatables, and then, the captain having taken us on board, we set sail for Ormuz.

There now remained but nine of us alive. Abanazar was of this number, and I arrived safe with him at Sarandib. I shall not enlarge, my lord, on the riches and magnificence of its young monarch, but must just tell you, that he is one of the wisest and most powerful kings in the whole world, and that he received us with the greatest distinction. My sufferings on the desert island, and the fatigues of the voyage, had made such an impression on me, that I was no longer the same person. His Majesty, however, thought he could distinguish some

remains of beauty in my features, and having ordered
that I should be treated with the greatest tenderness and
respect, rest and good fare soon made such an alteration
in me for the better, that it engaged his Majesty's particular
attention.   I lodged with Aban-azar, who always passed
for my husband, in a house near the palace, and received
every moment fresh marks of the desire his Majesty had
of contributing to my satisfaction ; but his assiduities
were too respectful to alarm my modesty.   His passion,
however, increased daily, and in a short time became so
violent that he resolved to do everything that in justice
could be done, to break an union, whose closeness created
in him so much jealousy.   He sent for Aban-azar, and
after having made use of the greatest precautions to discover his love to him, he offered him immense riches, and
his choice besides of twenty of the finest women in his
seraglio, if he would but surrender me to him, and would
engage me to make his passion a suitable return.

Aban-azar, my lord, who was well acquainted with
the secrets of my heart, and knew that I would pay but
little regard to the king's interested sentiments, was
thunderstruck at this proposal.   My lord, said he to the
king, if it depended on me alone to satisfy your Majesty's
desires, I assure you I would readily sacrifice my own
interests and inclination ; but when I married the beautiful Fatmi, (this was the name I gave myself at Aden
and at Sarandib) I bound myself, by the most dreadful
imprecations, never to divorce her against her consent.
If therefore you can prevail on her to consent to my parting with her, I swear not to oppose her inclinations, notwithstanding the grief I must feel at the loss of a wife of
so much merit, but shall surrender her to you directly.
But you must prepare her for the proposal by every kind
and engaging means your ingenious love can devise ;
otherwise, she would certainly take fright at the bare
thoughts of a separation, which she has a thousand times

assured me, would make her the unhappiest woman in the whole world. It was impossible to answer the king of Sarandib in a more prudent and discreet manner. The amorous monarch embraced Aban-azar a thousand times, and loaded him with favours.

I was soon made acquainted with the king's pretensions. Whatever reluctance I felt in flattering a passion to which I was resolved to make no concessions contrary to those tender sentiments which my heart ever cherished for your august Majesty, Aban-azar recommended the imposition with such solid arguments, that I was obliged to feign, and to express some regard for this prince. He no sooner began to perceive, as he imagined, the progress he had made in my affections, than he gave me the most open marks of his satisfaction, by a thousand public rejoicings, where profusion and magnificence vied with each other. Aban-azar even, my lord, who, as well as myself, imagined you were dead, advised me with great earnestness to make the king's tenderness a suitable return, and to accept of the crown of Sarandib. But I can easily assure you, my lord, and the rest of my adventures prove it, that I never seriously listened to the proposal, however glorious it might have been. In fine, the monarch, who had abstained for three months from any precise declaration, began to flatter himself so much with the hopes of being loved, and of obtaining my consent for a separation from Aban-azar, that he was on the point of offering me his hand and his throne, when Abu Bakr's arrival at Sarandib put an end to all his designs.

I shall now leave, my lord, to this faithful subject the care of acquainting your Majesty with the rest of my adventures, and shall only tell you, that I was transported with joy when I learned from him that you were still alive; the knowledge of which made me think it proper to inform the king of Sarandib of my rank, and of the imposition of Aban-azar. However amorous this

monarch was, as soon as he got the better of the amazement caused in him by the relation of my own and of your
Majesty's adventures, he generously renounced his pre-
tentions to a heart which could not consent to be his, and
offered me every assistance within the reach of his
greatness for my return to Astrakhan. I only accepted of
a ship to carry me to Ormuz. Our voyage has been
happy. After this I crossed Persia, with no other company than that of the faithful Aban-azar, whom I now
present to your Majesty, and Abu Bakr, who did not
know who I was; and I have had the comfort, my lord,
of restoring you your sight, and along with it a spouse,
who has always accounted it hitherto, and will ever
account it, her chief happiness to please your Majesty,
and to be tenderly loved by you.

The king of Astrakhan could not restrain his tears at
these new assurances of tenderness given him by his
beloved Zabd al-Katon. On his side, he vowed her a
thousand times an eternal love; and afterwards turning
to Abu Bakr, desired him to speak in his turn. Whatever impatience I may have, my dear friend, to hear the
conclusion of the adventures of my beautiful queen, I must
desire that you will not omit any circumstances of those
you must yourself have met with in so long a voyage. I
make no doubt but that some of them have been singular
enough; but be that as it may, I am ready to hear you
with the greatest pleasure. Abu Bakr replied only by a
profound inclination to signify his obedience, and then
returning to his seat, gave his Majesty an account of
what had happened to him since his departure from
Astrakhan, in the following manner.

ADVENTURES OF THE PHYSICIAN
ABU BAKR

You know, my lord, that the jokes of the physicians of Astrakhan proved a powerful motive to spur me on to undertake this voyage; but I must candidly own that I soon began to repent having given credit to the Arabian manuscript. I was very young when I had read it, so that I retained but a very imperfect and confused notion of its contents, and was in noways certain that the bird in question was to be found in Sarandib. I resolved therefore, before I took the road for that island, to go and consult some of those famous philosophers who live on a small mountain in the heart of India. I therefore left Astrakhan with this intention, and, after crossing the Caspian sea, arrived at Darbant, where I sought in vain for the woman I wanted, to restore your Majesty's sight ; she was not to be found there, nor in any other part of Persia. I then went to Tauris, from Tauris to Ispahan, and from Ispahan to Shiraz, where I made some stay. But may I take the liberty of acquainting you, sir, with my adventures in that city? I think I may, as your Majesty has so peremptorily commanded me not to hide any part of them, and this part may afford you some diversion.

I had heard some people speak of the Kadi of Shiraz's daughter, as of a complete beauty. I had often seen her pass by the door of the house where I lodged, and though her face and her shape were hid by a large and very thick veil, I had formed to myself so ravishing an idea of her perfections that I entirely lost my appetite. But a sudden blast of wind having one day raised the veil that hid so many perfections, the sight of them dazzled me so much that I resolved to try every means of gaining the

heart of so accomplished a lady.   I did not recollect that
I was almost fifty, and consequently no longer at an age
proper to excite tender desires in the heart of a young
person; my foolish passion made me forget everything.
I acquainted an old woman, who lived in the Kadi's neighbourhood, and who had access to his house, with my love
for Shahryar (this was my charmer's name), and promised
her a considerable sum if she could make any impression
on the young lady's heart in my favour.   The old woman
pretended to go about the affair with great earnestness,
and after representing my mistress to me as sometimes
cruel, and sometimes compassionate, at last assured me
that she was ready to make me happy.   I paid dearly
for this information, and prepared myself for the rendez-
vous I had received.   I dressed myself in the most
elegant manner I could, and failed not to attend at the
hour appointed.   The old woman introduced me into the
Kadi's house, and a young female slave having conducted
me by the back stairs to the top of the house, shut me up in
a closet, where the object of my wishes soon after made her
appearance.   I was so ravished with the sight of her
that I immediately threw myself at her feet, which I was
embracing in spite of all the resistance she could make,
without being able to speak a single word, when the kadi,
her father, entered the room.   I was thunderstruck at
the sight of him; Shahryar fainted away on seeing the
fury that appeared in his eyes.   He ordered her to be
removed to her apartment, and I remained the sole object
of his vengeance.   At first he appeared determined to
have me immediately put to death, but changing his
resolution, he ordered me to be bound hand and foot, and
left me in the charge of two slaves till the day following,
when he intended to punish my insolence in a public and
exemplary manner.

It is impossible for me, my lord, continued Abu Bakr,
to make you sensible of my grief and confusion in this

sad situation. I saw I was to die, but I was only sorry for it on your Majesty's account. I did nothing but reproach myself with being the cause of rendering your sufferings perpetual. I thought I could discover in the slaves that watched me, some signs of compassion for my concern. I offered them everything in my power if they could let me escape. At first they rejected my proposal; but one of them, feigning himself more affected at my distress than the other, at length argued his companion into compliance. Nothing therefore remained but to determine in what manner I should make my escape. The closet where I was had a little window looking on to the street, and they proposed letting me down through it with the ropes that served to bind me. I accepted the proposal with joy ; and after being untied, prepared myself to put it into execution, but unluckily the window was so small that it was with much ado I could get through it, even naked. I made no difficulty of stripping myself for that purpose all to my shirt, my keepers promising to throw me my clothes as soon as I had got down. I then, with some difficulty, worked my way through the window, and slipped down the rope, which unfortunately proved too short for my purpose, and the darkness of the night hindered me from seeing how much it wanted of reaching the ground. However, as there was no other way left of escaping the Kadi's anger, I resolved to let myself fall to the ground at all events. Accordingly I let go my hold ; but I leave your Majesty to judge of my surprise, when I found myself surrounded with a net, that had been placed on purpose to receive me, and heard my guards ready to burst with laughing at the condition I was in. Ah ! my lord, you cannot conceive the greatness of my grief and rage, in finding that I had been thus tricked by Shahryar, and that she took so cruel a vengeance on my passion for her. I made a thousand sad reflections on my misfortunes, and as many attempts to force the meshes of my net, but all

in vain, the scheme was too well concerted. I passed the
night, which was very cold, in this cruel situation, and
the next day had the mortification of seeing all Shiraz
flock about me to see so diverting a spectacle. In fine,
the Kadi put an end to the entertainment in the evening;
the net was let down, I was taken out of it, and then
received by his directions fifty strokes of a stick, well
laid on, on the soles of my feet; they then gave me back
my clothes, and set me loose, to return to my lodging by
favour of the night. I got home with some difficulty,
without letting my landlord know the real cause of my
absence. He had been one of the first spectators of my
disgrace, but happily without knowing who I was. However, I had the mortification of hearing my adventure
related from beginning to end, and even of being obliged
to laugh heartily at the scene, for fear of leaving him any
room to suspect me of having acted the principal part in
it.

You may well imagine, my lord, that I soon got the
better of my passion, and that I made no great stay at
Shiraz, where I had been played such a trick. The day
following, I set out for Ormuz, where going on board the
first ship bound for India, we landed at Diu; but I had
no better success here than elsewhere; what I wanted
was not to be found. I then traversed part of India, and
at length arrived at the habitation of the sages, or gym-
nosophists, of India. These philosophers live on a very
high mountain, almost in the midst of a plain, surrounded
with a rock, as likewise with a strong wall. This place
is generally covered with a very thick fog, which
serves to render its inhabitants visible or invisible, as they
think proper; but it is probable they were not averse to
my undertaking, since I easily reached their mountain,
where I saw these uncommon rarities, the well of sin, the
basin of pardon, the tuns so serviceable to India, and the
sacred fire, which they boast to have kindled directly by the

rays of the sun. Ah! my lord, you may conceive better than I can express what reason I had to be satisfied with my journey to this place, when the sages informed me that I should not only find at Sarandib the bird mentioned in the Arabian manuscript, but likewise the only person destined to restore you your sight.

I set out then for Sarandib, full of confidence in the promises of the Indian sages. I passed through a great many towns without meeting with any accident; but as I was making my way through a pretty thick wood I was stopped by eight robbers, who after having taken from me my horse and everything I carried with me, held a consulation about cutting my throat. Some of them were for doing so, but the rest being of a more cruel disposition, were of another opinion. One of these last, who had a very bad horse, took mine instead of it, and ripping open the belly of his own with a sabre, emptied it; and having stripped me quite naked, and bound me hand and foot, crammed me into it, fastening it together in such a manner that it looked as if it had never been opened. They then left me to perish by a kind of death never before thought of. I was in a very short time almost suffocated, and no doubt on the point of breathing my last, when my lamentations reached the ears of some travellers who happened to be going the same road. They looked out for me a long time, without being able to find me; but one of them at last drawing near the horse, imagined that the noise they heard proceeded from its belly, but then he immediately withdrew in a great fright. His fellow-travellers, however, had courage enough to turn the horse, and having ripped it open, drew me out of its belly with the greatest surprise imaginable. On my part, I was half dead, but I had scarcely breathed the fresh air, when I began to shew signs of life, and in a little time I was able to give my deliverers an account of my misfortune. They shuddered at the thoughts of it. I then washed myself in a rivulet, and put on a ragged old coat that one of them gave me. As they were going to the same place I was bound to, they permitted me to travel in their company. We arrived at Jingi, and putting up at a caravanserai, I was there extremely surprised to meet my horse and my robbers. I let my friends know the fortunate discovery I had made, upon which some of them went to the governor of the town, who immediately came back with them and seized the wretches. They not only confessed this last crime, but also several others, and were the next day, after the governor had returned me everything I had lost, punished in the manner their cruelty deserved. As, in giving my deliverers an account of my adventures, I had informed them of my being a physician, and that I was bound for Sarandib to procure a remedy for your Majesty's blindness, they cried up my capacity to the governor of Jingi, and I found an opportunity of practising it in a very odd, but diverting manner, upon one of his sons. But I do not know, my lord, if I can relate this passage with a delicacy becoming your Majesty's presence.

Saramah (this was the governor's name) expressed great pleasure at seeing me : I am told, said he, that you an able and experienced physician, and I cannot doubt it since the king of Astrakhan has sent you to look for the remedy he wants at so great a distance. A son of mine has been afflicted with a severe hypochondria these eight days past, and not one of our physicians has been able to cure him of his folly. I must own indeed that it is quite new and singular. He has taken it into his head that he shall one day lay under water the kingdom of Bisnagar ; nothing can free him from this odd conceit. And accordingly, he retains his urine so obstinately that he must speedily fall a victim to his madness, unless means can be found of restoring him to his right senses.—That, said I, my lord, is a very difficult task ; the disorders of the mind are harder to be cured than those of the body; nevertheless I can assure you that in fewer than four hours I shall give him relief. Saramah upon this looked upon me with admiration ; he ordered me to be conducted immediately to his palace, where I had the patient put into a warm bath. When I found the young man of the temperament I desired, so that nothing was wanting for his cure but a real desire of it in himself, I went into another room, and ordered Saramah's slaves to cry out : Fire ! Fire ! with all their might, and with resin and brimstone to form the appearance of a conflagration at the door and windows of the patient. I then returned to him in a great fright : Ah ! my lord, said I, all our hopes now centre in you alone. Behold the ravages which an irresistible fire makes at Jingi ! Half the town is already in ashes ; the flames begin to reach the palace, and everything is lost if you do not speedily interpose your assistance. The patient upon this got out of the bath in great confusion. And what then, said he, must I do to extinguish it ?—Ah ! my lord, said I, give your water a free passage ; this alone, powerful as the cataracts of the Nile, can stop the furious conflagration.—You are in the right, replied the young man, with all the seriousness imaginable ; I did not in the least think of it. It never entered my thoughts that an inundation which I feared might prove so fatal to my country, for whose sake I was ready to sacrifice my life, should turn out so much to its advantage. Upon this he yielded to my advice, and delivered his water, that had been so long pent up, with the greatest freedom. I ordered that the flames should be removed, in the proportion the young man might have reason to think he extinguished them, and my orders were punctually obeyed. I had likewise posted people to come and thank the patient for his seasonable interposition, and thus ended this diverting comedy, which was re-acted as often as the governor's son relapsed.

Saramah, my lord, thanked me in the most grateful manner, and very generously rewarded my success in relieving his son, who is now, as I have heard since my return, radically cured. I then set out for Nagapatan, where I thought to take ship for Sarandib; but the nearer I approached the port, the nearer, too, I in appearance drew to destruction. I had but a few leagues to make to reach Nagapatan, when I met with two Hindus a-foot, whom I took to be very honest men. We travelled the same road together for some time, discoursing on different matters; but as I was on horseback, and the town was at no great distance, I thought it would be unmannerly not to make the rest of the journey a-foot. I therefore alighted, and was walking in the greatest security with these two men when one of them throwing a rope about my neck drew me, with the help of the other, out of the high road to the skirts of a wood. Here they robbed me, and stripping me naked, threw me into a ditch that was twelve feet deep. After this, the two wretches, of whom I had not entertained the least suspicion, tied my horse to a tree, and, sitting on the brink of the ditch, began to joke about my simplicity and to divide their plunder. Oh! gentlemen, said I, have some compassion on me, and as you did not think proper to take away my life, do not leave me a defenceless prey to wild beasts! I only beseech you to return me my bow and arrows, to keep them at a distance as long as life remains. The robbers did not think they ought to refuse me so small a request; they threw me my bow and arrows; but I soon paid them for their folly, for before they could get out of their place, I pierced each of them with an arrow so fortunately, that they immediately tumbled down dead, with all their spoil, into the ditch. Having taken from them everything that belonged to me, I placed one a-top of the other, and raised myself by this means enough to get out of the place in which I was.

I then got on horseback again and reached Nagatapan, whence, after a few days' stay, I took ship for Sarandib, and at last fortunately arrived there.

My first care, my lord, as soon as I landed on the island, was to enquire where I could find the bird I was in search of. I heard with great pleasure that it was in the king's gardens. I then thought of nothing else but discovering the woman that was likewise requisite for the occasion, and for this purpose, I assembled by proclamation the wives of all the blind men in the island. There appeared an infinite number of them. I let them know my business, and promised them great rewards, but not one of them would venture to climb the dangerous tree, or flatter herself with the hopes of being able to restore your Majesty's sight. I was prodigiously cast down at this disappointment, and began to doubt of the truth of the Indian sages, when the king of the island sent one of his wazirs to me. My adventures had made too much noise in the island not to have reached his Majesty's ears. He was curious enough to desire to hear them from my own mouth, and I had the honour of relating, my lord, all your history from its beginning to my departure from Astrakhan, in the presence of a well-looking young man and a lady in a veil, who seemed to be mightily affected with everything I said.

This monarch expressed great concern at your misfortunes, but he could not refrain from laughing at my uneasiness at not finding a woman, who thought her virtue and conjugal affection pure enough to climb the tree of Sarandib. There is a tradition, said he, that the wonderful bird in one of my gardens is a jinni, who has lived in that form these two hundred years past on account of some offence given by him to one of the sages who live on the mountain of the sacred fire. I know likewise that he is to continue in bondage till a woman shall have climbed up to the top of the tree where he resides, and after gathering some of the divine liquor that distils from his bill, shall get down again, without experiencing the fatal effects of the tree; but then she must have so many and such rare qualifications, that I really believe the enchanter must always remain a bird, and that the king of Astrakhan will never recover his sight by this means.

The lady in the veil expressed some resentment at the king's raillery. But what, my lord, said she, because such a woman is scarce, do you think it impossible to find her?—If you will permit me, madam, to speak ingenuously, replied the king, I believe Abu Bakr looks for what he will never meet, and that a woman of so singular a character can only be considered as an imaginary being.—Well then, my lord, said the lady, raising her veil, I am resolved to convince you of your mistake, and to vindicate the honour of my sex, which you so much despise. I myself will make a trial of the dangerous tree, and will shew more resolution than a great number of women, who have, as well as myself, the conditions requisite to climb it, and only want the courage to attempt it.—You, madam! cried out the king of Sarandib, in great consternation; you try the dangerous tree! Do you consider well what you say? And though I should permit you to undertake it, you ought to reflect a little that you have not all the necessary qualifications; that to succeed you must be the wife of a blind man and that your husband has a good pair of eyes.—Let that not make your Majesty uneasy, replied the lady, with great coolness; I shall in due time clear up that mystery to you; but I cannot consistently with my duty, defer any longer the steps necessary for the king of Astrakhan's recovery.

The frightened monarch, my lord, in vain opposed the lady's resolution; she was not to be diverted from it, and all the satisfaction he could obtain was to make her defer the execution of her design to the next day. I lodged this night at the palace by the king's orders ; and the report being spread all over the island that a woman was found bold enough to venture up the dangerous tree, the palace was by daybreak surrounded by an infinite number of people who petitioned that they might be permitted to behold so strange a sight. The king granted their request, ordered the gates of the garden to be thrown open to them, and then conducted by his hand the lady, who had no doubt informed his Majesty of her name, to the foot of the tree, as he had no longer any reason to be in pain about her safety. She then threw off a long gown that might encumber her, and climbing with great ease from branch to branch, at length reached the top of the tree, gathered the precious liquor that distilled from the bird's bill in a flagon of gold tied to her girdle, and came down with the same ease that she went up. Upon this the air resounded with a thousand acclamations of admiration and of joy ; and the surprise of the spectators was still further increased on seeing the bird, who had been so long confined, soar freely into the skies, and the tree wither away to such a degree that there did not remain a single leaf on it.

The king of Sarandib thought he could never sufficiently commend and admire a lady who had given so shining an example of virtue and of conjugal affection. How happy is Shams al-Din, said he, to possess such a woman ! Ah ! my dear Abu Bakr, let him know, I beg of you, how rejoiced I am at his good fortune. It is so extraordinary, that I cannot see anything to equal it. The lady in the veil listened to these praises with a modesty which added new charms to her beauty. What more shall I say to you, my lord ? continued the physician. After having stayed at Sarandib as long as it was necessary to prepare for our return, we left it, loaded with favours by the wise and powerful monarch who reigns there with so much justice and moderation, and we arrived at Ormuz without experiencing any of those disasters which voyages by sea of such a length are generally attended with.   We then crossed Persia, and are now at last happily arrived at Astrakhan, where I have now learned for the first time, from the mouth of the incomparable Zabd al-Katon, that Aban-azar, whom I always considered as her husband, is not so; and I have the happiness of finding, that at the same time I have contributed to restore you your sight, I have likewise the pleasure of bringing you back an illustrious consort, whom you had so long bewailed as lost for ever, and without whom your joy would have been imperfect.   May heaven, my lord, propitious to my vows, grant your Majesty, and this incomparable princess, a long series of happiness, un-interrupted by sickness or by old age, and may the huris of paradise, on Allah's assigning one day their portions to your love, place all their happiness in being beloved by you as much as the divine Zabd al-Katon has now the happiness of being loved !

The wishes of Abu Bakr, which put an end to his story, were fully accomplished.   Shams al-Din, the happy Shams al-Din, loaded him, Aban-azar, and Ibn Aridun, with favours, and lived in a most exemplary union with his wife who bore him many children, worthy heirs of their royal parents' virtues.   And this illustrious pair felt for each other in their old days those tender sentiments which one would imagine youth alone could experience.

END OF THE THOUSAND AND ONE

QUARTERS OF AN HOUR

Printed and Published by H. S. Nichols & Co., 3, Soho Square, London, W.